The Shadow of Memory

Also available by Connie Berry

A Kate Hamilton Mystery
The Art of Betrayal
A Legacy of Murder
A Dream of Death

The Shadow of Memory

A Kate Hamilton Mystery

CONNIE BERRY

CROOKED
LANE

NEW YORK

Published in the United States by Crooked Lane Books, an imprint of The Quick Brown Fox & Company LLC.

Crooked Lane Books and its logo are trademarks of The Quick Brown Fox & Company LLC.

Library of Congress Catalog-in-Publication data available upon request.

ISBN (hardcover): 978-1-64385-908-8
ISBN (ebook): 978-1-64385-909-5

Cover design by Alan Ayers

Printed in the United States.

www.crookedlanebooks.com

Crooked Lane Books
34 West 27th St., 10th Floor
New York, NY 10001

First Edition: May 2022

10 9 8 7 6 5 4 3 2 1

For Kristine, my almost-sister

"Memory was a slippery thing—slick moss on an unstable slope—and it was ever so easy to lose one's footing and fall."

—Kelly Barnhill, *The Girl Who Drank the Moon*

Chapter One

Friday, August 21
Long Barston, Suffolk, England

The last place one expects to find a dead body is a graveyard. *Above ground*, I mean.

It started with Angela Vine's hen party, what we in the States would call a bachelorette. There were twelve of us. Besides me, the only American, Angela had invited seven girlfriends from her days at university and veterinary college plus her very pregnant sister from Sudbury—the designated driver and the reason the party was being held three weeks before the wedding.

The festivities began with a champagne brunch at the Henny Swan, a lovely pub on the River Stour, followed by Angela's final dress fitting in Bury St. Edmunds. That evening we were joined by Lady Barbara Finchley-fforde, Long Barston's local peeress, and Vivian Bunn, the bossy, opinionated, and lovable seventy-something with whom I was currently living.

After a smashing dinner at Finchley Hall, courtesy of Lady Barbara, we headed to the Finchley Arms for drinks and all-girl dancing. At nine thirty we were on our way to the Rectory, where Hattie Nuthall, the rector's loyal housekeeper, had promised us quantities of strong black tea and something sweet.

As far as hen parties go, Angela Vine's was pretty tame. Of course, when you're marrying a clergyman in the Church of

England, a certain decorum is expected. Anyway, Angela wasn't the type to hire male strippers or swill massive quantities of booze.

Good thing. I have a graduate degree in British history and literature. More than two glasses of wine and I'm liable to start telling *Beowulf* jokes.

We marched arm in arm up Long Barston's High Street, singing an off-key version of "Going to the Chapel."

"I'm glad you came, Kate." Angela threaded her arm around my waist. "We haven't known each other long, but now you're engaged to that handsome detective inspector, we have so much in common."

"We do," I lied. Actually, I had no idea what we might have in common. Gift registries? Baby plans? Not likely. I was a forty-six-year-old widow, the mother of two grown children. Angela was not quite thirty, just starting out in life.

In three weeks, she and Edmund Foxe, rector of St. Æthelric's (I'd finally stopped calling him *the dishy vicar*), would be jetting off for a two-week honeymoon in Majorca. Then Angela would move into the Rectory, where she would make the perfect clergyman's wife—caring, approachable, diplomatic, down to earth, and far too busy to pry into other people's lives. She had her own veterinary practice, keeping Long Barston's dogs, cats, budgies, hamsters, and occasional horses and farm animals in the peak of health. As much as I liked her—and I really did—Angela's future was falling along pleasant but predictable lines.

Then there was *my* future—adrift, like my wedding plans, in a Never-Neverland of uncertainty. Tom and I, both widowed, both in our mid-forties, had been engaged for nearly three months. We still hadn't decided when we would tie the knot, much less where we would settle down as a married couple or how we would solve the thorny problem of two careers on two very separate continents. I owned a thriving antiques business in Jackson Falls, Ohio. Detective Inspector Tom Mallory—soon to be detective chief inspector when the odious DCI Dennis Eacles departed for his new position at Constabulary Headquarters—was busy catching criminals and generally keeping the peace in the English county of Suffolk.

Tom had hinted at a ring, rather mysteriously I thought, but had yet to produce one. Not that a ring mattered to me in the slightest. What did matter was the question of our future domestic arrangements. Tom owned a lovely period farmhouse in the nearby village of Saxby St. Clare. It came complete with a thatched roof, an inglenook fireplace, an Aga cooker, a beautiful garden, and a mother-in-law—Tom's mother, Liz, who, I suspected, was still plotting my overthrow.

Buckingham Palace wouldn't be big enough for the two of us.

"Come on, Angie," one of the younger women called over her shoulder.

Angela jogged up to join them, her short tulle veil bouncing behind her. By the time we reached the Rectory, we'd segued into "Girls Just Wanna Have Fun." Even Vivian, not famous for frivolity, joined in.

We tumbled, laughing, through the door to find a table spread with homemade French macarons, individual raspberry cheesecakes, and tiny heart-shaped petit fours decorated with pink frosting roses and a toothpick flag saying *I Do*.

Later, after the tea and sugar kicked in, the mood turned nostalgic as the young women told stories about Angela's days at university and peppered her sister with questions about pregnancy and childbirth. Angela was showing her ring around for the third time when Poppy, her best friend and former roommate at Leeds, took the empty chair next to me.

"Your turn soon, I hear," she said, giving me a lopsided smile. Poppy was a tall girl with an angular face and a long-standing boyfriend who, according to Angela, had so far shown no sign of moving the relationship forward.

"I don't know about soon," I said honestly. "Tom and I are still making plans."

"Angela told us how you and Inspector Mallory caught that killer last Christmas. But she never explained what you were doing in Long Barston."

"No mystery. My daughter reads history at Oxford. She was one of the interns at Finchley Hall over the holidays. She invited me to stay with her for a couple of weeks."

"Is that when you and Tom met?"

"Actually, we met a month before that in Scotland."

"In *Scotland*?" Poppy sighed. "How romantic."

"I was married to a Scot. He died four years ago. I went to the Isle of Glenroth to visit his sister. She owned a country house hotel there. Tom happened to be staying."

"The *Highlands*." Poppy sighed again. "Was it love at first sight?"

"Something like that." I decided not to tell her about the brutal murders, my own brush with death, and how, for a time, I had suspected Tom was the killer.

Poppy's eyes looked slightly glazed, and I wondered how much she was taking in.

She covered a yawn. "Has anyone ever said you look like Charlize Theron? When her hair was dark, I mean. And, of course, your eyes are blue instead of green."

"Kate, dear." Lady Barbara approached us. "It's rather late for the senior set. Time Vivian and I were tucked up in our beds."

"Of course. Let me say goodbye to Angela and Hattie."

"No, no—you stay and enjoy the fun. Vivian will see me home."

"Actually, I'm ready for a good night's sleep myself." That wasn't quite true, but with Lady Barbara's failing eyesight and the slight unsteadiness I'd noticed in Vivian recently, no way would I allow them to trek through Finchley Park alone in the dark.

We gathered our belongings, thanked Hattie for the boxes of goodies she'd packed up for us, and said our goodbyes.

We followed the gravel path through St. Æthelric's graveyard. Above us, the sky was a deep inky blue. The nearly full moon glowed like a giant baroque pearl, lighting our path.

I let the older women walk ahead of me so I could keep my eye on them. They were giggling like schoolgirls, which made me wonder how many Pimms they'd downed at the Arms.

Something purple caught my eye.

It was a sock. In a shoe. Attached to a leg.

A man sagged against a headstone. His chin rested against his chest.

"Stop," I called out. "Someone's ill."

Crouching, I placed my finger on his neck.

I was wrong. Someone was dead.

Laying just beyond the man's outstretched fingers, partially hidden by a tuft of grass, was a piece of folded paper.

I picked it up and read *Vivian Bunn, Rose Cottage, Long Barston.*

*   *   *

"Who is he?" I asked Vivian as we waited for the police to arrive.

"I've never seen him before in my life."

"Nor I," said Lady Barbara.

"What was he doing with my name and address?" Vivian was clearly upset.

"We don't know the paper was his," Lady Barbara said. "Someone else probably lost it."

As none of us believed this, we let the comment drop.

The night was chilly. Normally, I'd have immediately escorted the two older women home, but when I called Tom, he'd asked us not to leave the body until the police arrived. I found a place for Vivian and Lady Barbara to sit—one of the newer gravestones, a modern design with a flat rectangular top and an inscription that read *To the Memory of Letitia Hubbard, Loving Wife and Mother.*

Vivian screeched. "We can't sit on Letitia."

"She won't mind." Lady Barbara settled herself on the granite slab. "Letitia was always a very welcoming person."

Vivian lowered her ample bottom. "*Oo*—like perching on a slab of ice."

"Poor man. Should we cover him?" Lady Barbara began to unwind her soft woolen shawl.

"He doesn't need it," I said. "On the other hand, you do. Scoot together and both of you get under the shawl."

Taking Vivian's pocket torch, I went back to view the body.

The man had been somewhere in his seventies, I judged. I couldn't see his face properly, but his white hair was short, still fairly dense, and neatly clipped. He was tall and well dressed, with wool trousers and a tweed sports jacket under a khaki raincoat—conservative except for the bright purple socks, which gave the corpse an almost jaunty appearance.

I saw no blood, no obvious signs of trauma, but a stain on the front of his crisp white shirt and a whiff of vomit told me he'd been sick. I was tempted to check his pockets for identification but curbed my curiosity. Tom would be there soon.

And then he was.

The emergency vehicle arrived first, lights flashing. Then Tom's new black Range Rover, followed by a Vauxhall, one of the police cars. The Rover pulled up to the lych-gate.

As the EMTs converged on the body, Tom and his sergeant, DS Ryan Cliffe, strode toward us along the gravel path. Tom was in full-on policeman mode. He gave me a quick nod and a pat on the arm. "Thank you, Kate. Cliffe will drive Vivian and Lady Barbara home. We can interview them in the morning. Would you mind going along? If you're up to it, come back. I'd like to take your statement tonight while everything is fresh in your mind."

"Of course. But the man is a complete stranger. He was dead when we got here." I handed Tom the note. "I found this."

Tom took a look at the note. He gave Vivian a curious look but said nothing.

"This way, ladies," said Sergeant Cliffe.

We dropped Vivian off first at Rose Cottage, her thatched-roof bungalow—one of the tied cottages on the Finchley Estate and my current home. Fergus, her elderly pug, was overjoyed. Time for his evening walkies. Then Cliffe drove around to Finchley Hall, the seat of the Finchleys since the sixteenth century. We left Lady Barbara in the capable hands of Francie Jewell, her cook, cleaner, and now—I'd recently learned—her live-in companion.

On the way back to St. Æthelric's, I thought about the dead man. If he wasn't local—and Vivian knew every living soul within a fifty-mile radius—what had he been doing in the graveyard after dark? Visiting a grave? Not likely. He'd probably been taking a shortcut as we had done, which meant he'd been on his way somewhere—to see Vivian seemed the likeliest answer, given the note. On the way, he'd experienced some kind of episode—a stroke, perhaps, or a heart attack. In any case, death had been unexpected. Presumably he'd parked his car nearby. The police would identify him and notify his relatives, whoever they were. Hopefully they'd be able to explain why an elderly stranger had come to Long Barston in search of Vivian.

Back at the church, Cliffe parked behind the emergency van. Reporters had begun to gather. A flash went off. Cliffe whisked me away before they could descend.

Tom was speaking with the head of the crime scene team. Seeing me, he broke off. "I know it's late, but could we find a place to talk?"

"The Finchley Arms is still open."

Ten minutes later we were seated in a corner of Long Barston's oldest drinking establishment. The jukebox was silent. Most of the tables were empty. Only a few die-hards remained, determined to get in a last pint before closing time.

We ordered two mineral waters and chose a quiet table away from the bar.

"Who was he?" I asked Tom. "Vivian swears she doesn't know him."

"Good question." He traced his finger along the condensation on the glass. "We found no wallet, no ID, no car keys, and so far, no car."

"Someone robbed him?"

"Maybe, but apart from a slight redness on his neck, he had no visible injuries. He'd been sick several times. The coroner will do tests, but at the moment I'm inclined to believe he died of natural causes. He was a pensioner—that age, anyway."

"And you have no idea what he was doing in Long Barston or why he had written down Vivian's name and address?"

"Not a clue. Could you go through exactly what you saw?"

"I don't think it will help. We left the Rectory a little before ten and cut through the graveyard. I stopped because I caught a glimpse of a purple sock. I felt for a pulse. He was already cold."

"No rigor, though, which means death occurred fairly recently. Two to six hours is the best guess."

"Wouldn't someone have noticed him lying there?"

"It's possible no one passed that way all evening. Did you see anyone? Hear anything? Notice anything unusual?"

"Just the note. If it hadn't been for the purple sock, I wouldn't have noticed him at all."

"Where was the note?"

"Near him in the tall grass. I assume he dropped it when he had his attack."

"Are Vivian and Lady Barbara sure they don't know him?"

"They said they'd never seen him before in their lives."

"Well, if you think of something—"

"I'll be sure and let you know." I threaded my arm through his. "Poor man. Someone will be missing him."

"Time, lads." Stephen Peacock, aging hippie and proprietor of the Finchley Arms, announced closing time. His wife, Briony, was already washing up behind the bar, her sleeves pushed up over her elbows. Arthur Gedge, the old gardener at Finchley Hall, slapped his flat cap on his head, nodded vaguely in our direction, and lurched toward the door.

Life as usual in Long Barston. But for one family, somewhere, this night would mean pain and grief.

The memory blindsided me—watching helplessly as my husband, Bill, lay on that pier in Scotland, cold as ice, his life ebbing away.

"Kiss me," I told Tom, moving closer to him.

He did, a kiss so sweet I actually felt my heart warm.

"Are you all right?" He looked at me with concern.

"Sometimes a girl needs a kiss."

"Happy to oblige, miss—any time." He touched my cheek. "I'd better get back. Long night ahead. Tomorrow we should have some answers." He stood and took a long, last drink of his mineral water. "What are you doing tomorrow? Can we meet for dinner somewhere?"

"Oh yes, please. Better make it late, though. Ivor and I are driving to the coast to do some appraisals. I'm not sure when we'll be back."

Ivor Tweedy, a dealer in fine antiques and antiquities, owned a shop in Long Barston—The Cabinet of Curiosities. We'd become friends last December when he'd helped me defend my daughter against a murder charge. And so, last May, when he'd needed someone to keep his shop open during his recovery from hip replacement surgery, I'd gladly stepped in.

"You mean the Suffolk coast?" Tom asked.

"A place called Miracle-on-Sea."

"Old resort town. There was a holiday camp there—long gone now, I suppose. Ivor has a client?"

"We hope so. Some London developer is turning an old Victorian mental institution into deluxe flats and townhouses—Cliff House, they're calling it. They're selling off some of the old artwork—including what they describe as an exceptionally fine Dutch medieval painting. They've asked Ivor to do preliminary appraisals. If they like the results, he'll handle the auction."

"Sounds like a great opportunity."

"Yes." I couldn't help feeling skeptical. "So did the sale of that ancient Chinese húnpíng jar last May, and we all know how that turned out."

"That's not likely to happen again, is it?"

"No—you're right." I really had to stop being so pessimistic. We stood and pulled on our jackets.

"Come on—I'll drive you home," Tom said. "Text me when you get back from the coast tomorrow. I'll pick you up at Rose Cottage. We have decisions to make."

Chapter Two

∽

Saturday, August 22
Miracle-on-Sea, Suffolk

I pulled my leased Mini Cooper up to the scrolled iron gates of Cliff House. A placard instructed visitors to wait, then follow signs for the visitors' parking area. I'd given my plate number in advance, and it must have been recognized by some computer somewhere because the gates swept open, allowing us entrance into the luxury housing estate built in and around the old Victorian hospital.

I stifled a yawn. I'd lain awake most of the night, thinking about the body in the graveyard. If I'd gotten there a little sooner . . .

Ivor, having heard the news (I suspected Vivian had made a few late-night phone calls), phoned at seven, asking if I wanted to postpone the appointment. I assured him I was fine. Sad as it was, elderly people died all the time.

Except this one had died alone in a graveyard in a strange village. And I'd found him.

Cliff House rose before us, its public face angled toward the North Sea and the Deben estuary. The former Netherfield Sanatorium, a private lunatic asylum—yes, that's what it was called in the nineteenth century—stood on a low rise. The impressive High Gothic structure had been constructed of red brick, with stone dressings and stepped gables over perpendicular traceried windows. Solid, institutional, slightly foreboding.

Would people actually choose to live there?

Ivor sat beside me in the passenger's seat. Only three months ago he'd undergone bilateral hip replacement surgery, and almost lost his life in the process. But he was healing well—so well he'd given up using a cane, a decision I hoped he wouldn't regret.

"Shall I drop you at the entrance?" I asked him.

"Certainly not."

Leaving the gates behind us, we drove between lines of young oak trees, recently planted. Vast green lawns spread away from the main structure. We followed signs for visitor parking, claimed the first spot, and walked the quarter mile or so to the main entrance. The day was bright, with a thin scattering of clouds. A stiff breeze carried the tang of salt. Gulls shrieked and wheeled above us.

Since his surgery, Ivor's old rolling gait, a product of the years he'd spent in Her Majesty's Merchant Navy, had become more of a shuffle. I watched him out of the corner of my eye, ready to steady him if necessary. Overprotective? Probably. But I'd never forget the fall he'd taken—or the days I'd spent at his hospital bedside, not knowing if he'd recover.

Ivor's period of recuperation had been difficult for him. Now he was back in top form, his near-encyclopedic knowledge of the antiques trade in the UK intact—who sold what and to whom, the price they got for it, and what it was really worth.

Cliff House was Ivor's first important commission since spring. Several weeks earlier he'd received a letter from the board of directors, explaining that they wished to sell certain pieces of art that no longer represented "the fresh, contemporary ambiance" they were seeking to create. Among these items was a painting attributed to the fifteenth-century Netherlandish artist Jan van Eyck. That made our eyes pop.

We were instructed to arrive at one PM, join the board members for a light luncheon (not the usual procedure), and then take a preliminary look at the objects. Tony Currie, chairman of the board, was our contact.

"How did they come up with your name?" I asked Ivor, knowing he wouldn't take offense. A painting as important as a Van Eyck would normally be handled by Sotheby's or Christie's. Still, not everyone wanted that publicity, as I'd recently learned.

"Interesting question." He raised his eyebrows. "I assume they contacted one of the auction houses in London first. Perhaps my fractionally lower commission rate attracted them."

Ivor was keeping up a good pace, but I could tell it was a chore.

"Why lunch?" I slowed down, but not so he'd notice. "Buttering us up?"

"Sizing us up, more like. Not that I blame them. If the Van Eyck's genuine, it should fetch an enormous price at auction and"—his lips curled in a smile—"an enormous commission."

We climbed the steps toward the entrance, tucked beneath a vaulted stone archway.

In the reception area, dark, linen-fold paneling created a rich backdrop for furniture and fabrics in contemporary designs and neutral colors. Over the carved oak fireplace hung a splashy, colorful landscape—not a Hockney but that style.

We were greeted by a pleasant young woman, immaculately turned out in a dark tailored suit. "Welcome to Cliff House." She smiled. "You must be Mr. Tweedy and Mrs. Hamilton. I'm Cordelia Armstrong. Please make yourselves comfortable. There's iced lemon water in the urn. Mr. Currie will be with you shortly."

Shortly was an understatement. We'd barely settled ourselves into a pair of comfortable armchairs when a man in his late forties or early fifties strode through the double doors at the far end of the room. His dark hair was on the long side, beautifully cut and styled. He wore a light gray suit with a patterned blue silk tie and handkerchief.

"Mr. Tweedy." He stepped forward to grasp Ivor's hand. "Thank you for coming. I'm Tony Currie, chairman of the Cliff House board of directors and managing director of Pyramid Development, the construction company in charge of the project.

The other board members will join us shortly in the private dining room."

He turned his gray eyes on me. "You must be Ms. Hamilton. I understand you had a bit of a shock last night. We heard on the news this morning. Nasty. Have they learned anything more?"

"Not yet." Hmm. Some resourceful reporter had pried my name out of someone.

Currie led us through the doors by which he had come, along an oak-paneled hallway and into a charming room with a table set for six. A drinks tray stood near one of the traceried windows.

"May I offer you a sherry—or perhaps a whiskey?"

We opted for two dry sherries, which he poured from a cut-glass decanter into small glasses engraved with a capital N—for Netherfield, I assumed.

The door opened to admit two men and a woman.

"We're all here, then." Currie whipped out an index card with handwritten notes. "Today we welcome Mr. Ivor Tweedy, a dealer in antiquities; a longtime member of the British Antiques Dealers' Association, the Antiquities Dealers' Association, the Oriental Ceramic Society, the English Ceramic Circle, the French Porcelain Society, and a founding member of SOFAA, the Society of Fine Art Auctioneers and Valuers."

The directors clapped with the heels of their hands.

Really? I hadn't known that. I gave Ivor a surreptitious nudge. He smiled smugly.

Currie turned to me. "And, of course, his colleague, Ms. Kate Hamilton, from O-hi-o." He separated the syllables as if sounding out an unknown language. "Ms. Hamilton is a member of . . ." He looked at me for help. "What is it, now?"

"The Art Dealers Association of America and the American Society of Appraisers." I felt like inventing a few more organizations to impress them.

"Of course." Currie bowed his head in apology. "Shall we sit down?" Currie took the chair at the head of the table. "As soon as we're settled, I'll introduce the members of the Cliff House board."

Chairs scraped on the polished wood floor. Linen napkins were shaken out.

"Hello, Kate. I'm Nicola." The woman seated next to me was handsome, somewhere in her early fifties, with a carefully made-up face, just beginning to lose its battle with gravity. She wore a beautifully tailored suit in a shade of caramel that highlighted her blonde hair and green-gray eyes.

"Mr. Tweedy and I are delighted to be here." Always put your best foot forward. Just don't trip anyone.

"Tony told us about the body in the graveyard," she said. "I'm surprised you can be so calm."

"Unfortunately, there was nothing we could do. The police are trying to identify him."

"You're American," she said. "How did Mr. Tweedy persuade you to move to England?"

"He hasn't—not yet."

A waiter filled our water glasses. I was glad for the diversion.

Our conversation ended anyway when Tony Currie stood. "While luncheon is being served, I'll make the introductions. As you know, I represent Pyramid Development LLP, which has been awarded the privilege of preserving this wonderful piece of history and bringing it seamlessly into the modern world." He paused, allowing what must have been a favorite sales point to take effect. "Seated on my right is Martyn Lee-Jones, newly appointed general manager of Cliff House."

Lee-Jones got halfway to his feet, holding his napkin. He had a handsome face with a chiseled chin and a high forehead, crowned with a mane of dark hair going silver at the temples—the kind of face that looks well on a corporate brochure.

Currie continued. "Martyn will be responsible for the overall running of Cliff House, including Cliff's Edge, our fine-dining restaurant, which is providing our lunch today. His father, Philip Lee-Jones, was Netherfield's director of finance at the time of its transfer to the National Health."

"When do you expect residents to begin moving in?" I asked.

"Three of the proposed forty-seven residences in the main structure have already been sold," Currie said. "Move-ins should begin next spring. If all goes well, we'll be adding a number of larger, detached homes on the grounds."

"Do you commute from London?" I asked.

"Fortunately, no. I'm currently occupying one of the flats. I keep in touch with my office via phone and computer."

"Lucky you," I said. "The setting is spectacular."

"Seated on your right," Curry said, "is Ms. Nicola Netherfield, our in-house design consultant and member of the Society of British and International Design. And, yes"—he made a moue of satisfaction as if nailing a punch line—"her great-great-grandfather was Horace Netherfield, who built this magnificent structure. Her father, Dr. Cosmo Netherfield, was medical director under the private scheme. Nicola ensures the interior design is consistent with our overall vision of effortless, contemporary elegance. She will also work with our new residents, helping them make design decisions and coordinating certain issues such as approved window coverings and outdoor furniture."

Ivor mumbled something that sounded like *impressive.*

The Cliff House project *was* impressive—and incredibly expensive. Maintaining a great house like Finchley Hall was costly enough. Turning a Victorian hospital into townhouses and flats had to cost a fortune.

I was mentally multiplying forty-seven residences by an estimated two million pounds each when Currie said, "Unable to be with us today is Niall Walker, son of Charles Walker, chairman of Netherfield's board of trustees in 1961. He had a family event this weekend. Sends his regrets. At the end of the table, however, we have Dr. Oswin Underwood, Netherfield's archivist and official historian. His father, Dr. David Underwood, was Netherfield's chief psychiatrist from 1950 until its closure in 1967."

"Netherfield has been my life's work." Underwood's voice sounded like it wasn't used very often. He was at least a decade older than the other board members, with a pale, narrow face made even longer by a white Van Dyke beard, giving him the look of someone plucked from a prior century.

"Cliff House sounds like a family affair," I said.

"Which gives the board a personal interest in the success of the project." Currie smiled. "As for myself, I've always had a passion for preserving England's architectural treasures."

"We simply couldn't allow this magnificent building to be lost," Nicola said. "Oswin can tell you."

Dr. Underwood peered at us through his wire-rimmed eyeglasses, frowning slightly as if he wasn't entirely sure who we were and why we were all there.

Waiters appeared with plates of food on a rolling cart.

Remembering names has never been my gift. While I still had them in my mind, I went through the names of the board members one by one.

Tony Currie, chairman of the board and managing director of Pyramid Development. I made a mental note to pull up the company website online. Currie struck me as competent and slick. His gray suit said *I'm in charge* in a classic BBC accent, although I'd detected a slight undercurrent of London Estuary in his speech.

Martyn Lee-Jones, newly appointed managing director of Cliff House. He looked like an aristocrat—or someone playing one on the stage. Handsome, arrogant—a bit of a playboy? I'd caught him looking at me a couple of times with unbusinesslike interest. Including an employee on the board of directors struck me as unusual. Of course, he did have that family connection.

Nicola Netherfield, design consultant and Netherfield royalty. In place of a wedding band, she wore a topaz ring, the center stone surrounded by diamonds. Her elegant suit probably had a designer label. Maybe she'd inherited her great-great-grandfather's fortune.

Niall Walker, the missing board member. His father had been one of the Netherfield trustees. Speculation about him would have to wait.

Last, *Dr. Oswin Underwood*, Netherfield's archivist and historian, son of a former psychiatrist. He looked as dry and dusty as old books. Why was he on the board? Aren't board members usually people with business expertise or influence?

Currie, Lee-Jones, Netherfield, Walker, Underwood. If someone gave me a pop quiz, I was ready.

* * *

A white-sleeved arm slid a plate in front of me. "Chilled crab salad on ruby lettuce, madam," said a voice in my ear. "Served with whole grain crumpets and a sweet custard of apples and blackberries."

"The food looks amazing," I said to Nicola.

"A sampling of what Cliff House will offer our residents and their guests," she said. "Organic, obviously. Locally sourced and seasonal."

When the last plate was delivered, I took a bite. *Wow.* If they were trying to make a good impression, it was working.

Conversation during lunch was awkward as the Cliff House board members seemed determined to find common points of interest between us. The closest we came was when Martyn Lee-Jones discovered that Ivor's maiden aunt, long deceased, had once lived in the same Surrey village as Lee-Jones's cousin's husband's family—but not in the same decade. Work that one out.

Ten minutes later, Ivor's eyelids were drooping. I woke him by telling everyone he'd once saved a Yorkshire terrier from the jaws of a Ganges River crocodile. Which was true. While Ivor was describing his technique—"Always go for the eyes"—Nicola Netherfield and I got a bit more personal.

"No, I've never married," she said in answer to a question I hadn't asked. "My choice, of course. I've had loads of opportunities. How about you?"

"I'm a widow," I said. "Recently engaged to a detective inspector in the Suffolk Constabulary."

That stopped her. She recovered quickly. "How interesting. Where will you live?"

She would have to ask that. "We haven't decided."

She slipped me her business card. "Well, if you should need design help, give me a call."

As the waiters were clearing our plates, Currie said, "Before we make a move, I've asked Dr. Underwood to give you a brief history of Netherfield Sanatorium."

Ivor and I exchanged a look. *The things we do to make a living.*

Dr. Underwood extracted a sheaf of papers from inside his jacket and smoothed them out. Lifting his bearded chin, he launched into what sounded like a canned speech. "The inspiration for Netherfield Sanatorium was born in the late eighteen sixties by Horace Netherfield, a self-styled doctor of homeopathy who manufactured nerve pills reputed to cure a panoply of disorders, including dyspepsia, sleeplessness, headaches, social anxiety, restlessness, weak hearts, congested livers, and female neuroses. With the help of clever advertising, he amassed a fortune. In 1868, tragedy struck when one of his patients, a man suffering from melancholia, took his own life. The widow charged Netherfield with gross negligence. He won the lawsuit, but the experience changed him. From that time, all his packaging included a disclaimer. Around the same time, he developed an interest in the treatment of what was then called *lunacy*. Of course, in the nineteenth century—"

I was trying to pay attention. I really was. My eyes drifted to Martyn Lee-Jones across the table. He lifted his wine glass and gave me an almost imperceptible wink.

"—when Netherfield became impressed with a novel French theory about the treatment of madness—'cure by distraction.' The idea was to dissipate abnormal or harmful thoughts by transferring the patient's attention to something pleasant or benign.

"At that time, those suffering mental health disorders among the upper classes were treated privately at home. Among the poor, *care* was often a euphemism for locking the patient away, out of sight. If a family member became dangerous or unmanageable, he was sent to one of the public madhouses, where patients were routinely drugged and shackled.

"In contrast, Netherfield and a handful of similar institutions organized along the lines of the French theory were designed for fee-paying patients among the middle classes who suffered from what was termed *a temporary imbalance of the mind*. Since the patients were expected to recover, the goal was not to warehouse them but to provide heathy mental occupation, physical recreation, and a restful, aesthetically pleasing environment—creating ideal conditions for a return to sanity."

Martyn Lee-Jones was still watching me. Was he one of those men who imagine themselves to be irresistible?

"Netherfield," said Dr. Underwood, "resolved to spend a substantial portion of his wealth on the establishment of a sanatorium for the mentally ill. A spacious site was chosen here on the Suffolk coast. He hired a London architect to draw up plans, and the project was completed in less than three years. In 1888 Netherfield Sanatorium was officially opened by Princess Louise, later the Princess Royal, with 67 patients and 59 resident staff. Soon the hospital reached its capacity of 430 patients, cared for by a team of doctors, day nurses, night nurses, personal attendants, and domestic workers numbering 327.

"The building and grounds of Netherfield were intentionally grand, like a fine hotel or country estate. Amenities included a swimming pool, a billiards room, tennis courts, a cricket pitch, theater, hairdressing salon, and even separate Turkish baths for men and women. Patient facilities were state of the art—private suites with modern toilets, baths with hot and cold running water, fireplaces, windows overlooking the grounds, and in the larger suites, space for live-in domestics. Public rooms were elegant. Caged songbirds graced the hallways. Patients were allowed to keep domestic pets. They were encouraged to work in the estate gardens or to pursue their own hobbies. Most were allowed to walk to the village and to receive visitors."

Statistics followed—staff/patient ratios and average costs by year, cure rates.

Oh man. I love history, but this was too much, even for me.

Ivor sat with his hands folded across his stomach. He was falling asleep again. I nudged his foot under the table.

"In 1948," Underwood said, "the National Health Service was introduced in Great Britain. Fewer people were willing to pay for private care. Gradually, as patient counts declined, Netherfield began to struggle. By 1961 the board of trustees felt they could no longer operate as a fee-paying system and made plans to transfer the sanatorium to the National Health. Negotiations took more than a year, but the scheme became final in January of 1962. Private suites were combined into dormitories—more beds, more patients. However, the building and grounds proved increasingly costly to maintain; and in 1967 all patients were transferred to St. Catherine's Hospital in Ipswich, where additional services, such as job training, were offered. St. Catherine's was itself closed in 2012 and patients transferred to Care in the Community, a deinstitutionalization program under which physically and mentally disabled people are treated and cared for at home rather than in hospital.

"After 1967, Netherfield was used as a lying-in hospital and then, briefly, a language school. The great building stood empty for nearly twenty years until, six years ago, several of us approached Pyramid Development with a plan to transform the estate into a gated residential community."

Several of us? Was Dr. Underwood including himself?

"Very informative," Ivor said before Underwood could get in another word. "Were you planning to allow us a glimpse of the . . . *erm*, items you wish to sell?"

I looked at Ivor across the table. *Cure by distraction?*

Chapter Three

❧

The items intended for sale had been gathered into one of the ground-floor rooms whose original purpose became obvious when we saw *Patients' Library* printed in gold lettering on the door. The books and the bookshelves had been replaced by a large-screen TV, a jumble of folding chairs, and a Plexiglas lectern.

Tony Currie held the door for me. "We use the room for presentations to potential residents. In future, the space will be an open-plan office complex."

Tall windows, the lower portions mullioned and the upper arches sectioned by quatrefoils, looked out over the front lawns. Near the lectern, a cork board displayed architectural drawings and an artist's rendering of the completed project. It looked ambitious to me. How many wealthy people would choose to live in an out-of-the-way seaside village in Suffolk?

Objects from Netherfield's history lined the room's perimeter, larger items on the floor, smaller ones on folding tables. The number and variety of objects was impressive—oak and walnut furniture, bronze and marble statuary, small alabaster sculptures, chimney pieces and fire grates, decorative art glass. What caught my eye were a collection of ornate wire-and-wood bird cages. Some were shaped like domes; others resembled Victorian conservatories or small Gothic cathedrals. They were charming and should bring a good price.

Where was the Van Eyck?

I scanned the room, bracing myself for the inevitable rush of heat, the sudden pounding of my heart, the rush of blood to my face, the thirst. This is what happens to me in the presence of fine antiques of great age. It has since childhood. Don't ask me to explain, because I can't. Nor can I explain the impressions I sometimes get—of a word or a phrase or even a sense, real or imagined, of the emotional atmosphere in which the object once existed.

The summer I was six my parents took me to a showing of the "Treasures of Tutankhamun" at the Metropolitan Museum in New York City. Strangely, it wasn't the objects of gold that remain in my memory but a small wooden chair.

"It's made of ebony," my mother told me.

"Why is it so small?"

She'd smiled. "Because it was made for the king when he was a little boy—younger than you, I imagine."

We were standing there, looking at the chair, when I asked, "Why did they kill him?"

She'd looked at me, startled. "What makes you think someone killed him?"

I couldn't answer her. *I know, I know*—the current theories favor some congenital disease or an unfortunate tumble from his chariot. Maybe that's true. All I know is I had an overwhelming impression of treachery and fear. I can't explain it. That's why I've never told anyone. Not my parents, not my husband, Bill. Certainly not Tom. How could I? First I'd have to explain it to myself, and that was something I'd never been able to do.

"Where's the Van Eyck?" Ivor whispered.

I shrugged. Was this the old bait-and-switch? Had the board piqued our interest by dangling a medieval masterpiece in front of us, only to renege once we were there? It had happened before.

Ivor bent to examine a small bronze of David with the head of Goliath. "What do you think?"

"Very nice. Is it signed?" As Ivor pulled out his magnifier, I felt my cheeks flush—not the full-blown experience this time but a kind of pleasurable buzz. I knew that feeling, too—the subtle but heady enjoyment of exquisite design, fine craftsmanship, and the smell of old dust. These items were lovely, mostly Victorian, in wonderful condition, but nothing here could be considered a treasure.

I tucked my hair behind my ears.

"What do you think of this?" Nicola appeared beside me. She was examining an inlaid mahogany longcase clock.

"It's beautiful," I said. "Early nineteenth century."

"And these?" This time she wanted my opinion on a pair of parcel-gilt tea canisters.

"If they're as old as I think they are, they should do very well at auction."

"I thought so too," she said, cocking her head to one side. "Good size. Very graphic."

"Where's the Van Eyck? I expected to see it today."

"Oh, you will. Tony's a bit of a showman. You know what they say—'sparkle and shine.'" Nicola cheeks turned pink. "Don't listen to me. I always say too much. Tony's grand." She wandered off, still pink.

Tony was speaking to Ivor. "In addition to what you see here, we have a number of small items—little boxes, very fine, a bequest. They're in a safe offsite. We'll have them delivered to you separately for appraisal."

"Excellent."

"Now for the real treasure." Currie strode to the door and flung it open. Two young men in green jumpsuits wheeled in a tripod holding something covered by a black cloth.

"Ladies and gentlemen, may I present *Christ Healing the Demoniac* by Jan van Eyck." Currie whipped off the cloth to reveal an oil painting in a fine gold frame.

I took in a breath. The image was powerful, emotional—the vibrant, luminous pigments typical of Van Eyck, the incredible detail and use of space, drawing the viewer's eye toward the central figures. The scene was the countryside, more Europe than Holy Land. A crowd had gathered around the figure of Jesus, extending his hand toward a naked man writhing on the ground. The emotions on the man's face—shame, agony, despair—were transformed by a tiny speck of light in his right eye. *Hope.*

Ivor was speechless, and he's rarely short on words.

I felt the same way. This was a Van Eyck, a real Jan van Eyck, painted sometime in the fifteenth century. I braced myself for the inevitable reactions that usually make people ask me if I need to lie down and take an aspirin.

I waited.

Nothing.

I felt confused, disoriented. My eyes were telling me one thing, my gut another.

"Magnificent," Ivor was saying. "Larger than I expected. The subject matter is unusual as well. I'd say this was a private commission."

"It's incredibly beautiful," I said, and it was. The colors had depth—intense lapis blue, rich carmine red, velvety umber, copper green. I peered closer, taking in the nearly imperceptible strokes that dragged the borders of Jesus's seamless linen tunic into the darker background, intentionally softening the edges of his garment.

"You can almost feel the texture of the cloth, can't you?" Ivor pulled his small magnifying glass out of his breast pocket again and examined the brushstrokes. "Hmm, yes."

I tried again, moving closer to the painting, this time examining the craquelure, the distinctive pattern of tiny cracks that develop during the drying of the paint and the aging process. Everything looked right. Exactly right. I took a breath and let my eyes linger on that luminous blue.

Again, nothing.

Except . . . a niggling at the back of my brain. A shadowy, cynical sneer.

And something else.

Treachery. Danger.

Like Tutankhamun's little chair. Now I was really *was* confused. I stood there, trying to make sense of what I was feeling.

Ivor was examining the back of the painting. "Wood panels. Oak, I think."

"Ivor, can we talk—alone?" I whispered.

He gave me a puzzled look but turned to Currie. "Do you mind if my colleague and I have a quiet word? Shouldn't take long."

"Yes, of course. Take your time." Currie shepherded the other board members out of the room.

When the door closed, Ivor said, "What is it, Kate? Is there a problem?"

"I can't explain it," I said. "It's a feeling. Something's wrong with the Van Eyck."

"What is it? Technique? Composition?"

All I could do was shake my head.

Ivor looked at me for a long moment. "What I see looks right, but attribution rests on the appraiser's instinct, her eye, her gut feeling. Are you telling me your gut tells you something's wrong?"

"I suppose that's it—a gut feeling. There's nothing specific I can point to. Honestly. It's just a feeling—or rather, a lack of feeling." That was as far as I was willing to go.

"You do realize—" He made a small quizzical motion with his head. "Without the painting, there's not a lot going on here. And you must know if we cast doubt on the painting's value, they may decide to offer the auction to someone else."

"I know." I also knew this auction would create international interest, enhancing the reputation of The Curiosity Cabinet—not to speak of the commission. Ivor's bank account was currently on life support. Could I swallow my instincts for Ivor's sake?

No, I couldn't. My integrity was at stake.

"I'm sorry," I said.

Ivor studied me for a moment. "All right. Time to face the board members."

* * *

Four faces stared at us, demanding an explanation.

I watched Ivor.

"As I'm sure you are aware," he said mildly, "the Van Eyck is certain to generate lively interest in the international art world. Only twenty paintings are currently attributed to the artist, a handful more contested. This is not one of them, which will necessarily raise questions."

Lee-Jones started to object, but Ivor held up his hand. "I anticipate a brilliant auction. However, without the painting, the other items, charming as they are, will fly under the radar, so to speak."

"What do you mean 'without the painting'?" Lee-Jones's lips pressed together, His jaw tightened.

Nicola Netherfield crossed her arms.

Underwood looked confused.

"I think you'd better explain," Currie said.

I was starting to sweat.

Ivor gathered himself up to his full height—not quite five feet four, mind you. "What we have here is a very fine oil painting on wood of a biblical scene in a gilded frame, not the original frame but quite early. In determining the value of a painting, an appraiser must consider five major elements. The first is *provenance*, meaning the chain of ownership. You have assured me you can produce documents tracing the Van Eyck back to its purchase by Horace Netherfield in France in the mid-nineteenth century. Excellent. I understand that document also states the painting had been previously owned by a single family since the early sixteenth century." He gave them his nothing-to-worry-about-I'm-a-professional smile. "The second element is *attribution*, which is by nature subjective."

Lee-Jones cut in. "Are you saying there's a problem? We've had others view the painting, and no one has implied—"

"Please allow me to finish," Ivor said. "The third element is *technique*. Does the painting give evidence of the artist's craft and style—the brushstrokes, his handling of color, and all the other tiny characteristics that set him apart? That will require a more thorough examination, of course, but I can say there is no obvious cause for concern."

"Then what's your point?" Nicola asked.

Ivor ignored her. "Fourth, we consider the *signature*—or in some cases, the lack of one. With Van Eyck, the question of signatures is complex, and I haven't time at the moment to explain. I can say, however, the lack of a signature creates no particular problem."

The board members were looking impatient. Martyn Lee-Jones rolled his eyes.

Ivor carried on. "The fifth and final element in determining the value of a painting is *scientific analysis*. After consultation, Mrs. Hamilton and I recommend subjecting the painting to a full range of tests—infrared photography, X-radiology, spectrography, pigment analysis."

There was a combined intake of breath as all four board members prepared to protest.

Currie got there first. "Surely that's unnecessary. Except for a short period in the nineteen sixties when the painting was cleaned, the Van Eyck has been on public display for one hundred and thirty years. What could scientific analysis tell us that we don't already know?"

Now for the tricky bit.

Ivor steepled his hands, pointing at Currie with his fingertips. "That is precisely the point. What do you hope to receive for the Van Eyck?"

"That's for you to tell us, surely," said Martyn Lee-Jones testily.

Nicola's chin went up. "We thought between thirty and forty million pounds."

"Not a bad estimate," Ivor said smoothly. "However, if you follow the auctions, you will know that a percentage of very fine paintings remain unsold because bids don't reach the reserve, the price below which the owner of the painting isn't willing to sell."

"What does this have to do with the Van Eyck?" Dr. Underwood asked.

"Everything," Ivor said. "There are no guarantees in the world of fine art. Wonderful paintings fail to sell, not because people aren't interested in owning them, but because parting with that kind of money takes courage and confidence. Forgeries are not uncommon. Experts have been fooled. My point is this: scientific analysis can uncover fakes, but it can also remove all shadow of doubt." He stopped to let that sink in.

Was it my imagination, or had they all turned a few shades paler? Maybe more was riding on the sale of the Van Eyck than Ivor and I had realized.

"And this means what exactly?" Lee-Jones rolled his hand. "Spell it out for us."

"This means," Ivor said, "that scientific analysis can provide potential buyers with the confidence they need to, ah, cough up the cash, so to speak."

The silence was as thick as week-old gesso.

"How long would scientific analysis take?" Currie asked. "We hoped to have everything sold by the end of October."

"I'd say no more than two or three weeks," Ivor said. "I know a facility in Cambridge—Apollo Research and Analysis. Top of their field. There may be a wait list. I recommend contacting them as soon as possible."

"The cost?" Currie asked.

"Twelve to fifteen thousand pounds." Ivor didn't blink. "Possibly a bit more."

Martyn Lee-Jones scowled. "Colossal waste of money."

"This is a decision for the full board," Currie said. "Niall isn't with us today."

"Don't wait too long," Ivor said. "If you want the sale completed by the end of October, the decision must be taken rather quickly."

Currie handed Ivor a thick black binder. "We've prepared an inventory. Make an appointment with Miss Armstrong in reception. She'll set up times for you to examine the pieces at your leisure. If you have questions, I'll pass them along to the board."

"Thank you." Ivor tucked the black binder under his arm. "If you wish to go ahead with the analysis, I'll arrange for Apollo to collect the painting."

I caught Nicola glaring at me. I was the one who'd poisoned the well, and she knew it.

After giving our details to Miss Armstrong, Ivor and I strode out into the sea-scented air. Above us, a black-headed gull spread its wings and called *ke-ke-ke*.

"I'm sorry, Ivor. I know this jeopardizes the auction."

He ignored that. "Did you catch what Martyn Lee-Jones said? *We've had others view the painting.* You asked me why the board contacted me rather than one of the internationally known auction houses in London. It's possible there's something wrong with the painting, something they hoped we wouldn't catch."

I didn't like the implication, but it was plausible. The board may have chosen Ivor because they assumed he could be easily fooled. Ivor wasn't easily fooled. He was as savvy a dealer as I'd ever known. Yet he'd trusted me enough to jeopardize the entire project, and all I had to go on was that cynical sneer and a vague impression of treachery and danger.

Who was in danger? Pyramid Development? The Cliff House board? Or us?

Chapter Four

∾

That evening Tom and I wedged ourselves into our favorite corner table at the Three Magpies in Long Barston. Lighted candles flickered on the dark wood tables, highlighting the angles of Tom's face.

He reached for a slice of the Magpies' famous sourdough.

The first time I'd met him, I'd thought he looked like a monk. Now he was the least monk-like person I knew. Intense, yes. Serious? Often, and appropriately so. But never ascetic or detached.

People aren't always as they appear.

And the Van Eyck? It was a stunning piece of art. Ivor had seen nothing to arouse his suspicions. Neither had I, to be honest. So what was my problem? I didn't have one—or one I could explain. Ivor said attribution was a matter of instinct, a visceral feeling honed by experience. My experience wasn't as vast as Ivor's, but I'd been appraising antiques and works of art for years. I *had* developed an eye. But in the world of fine art, an eye had to be backed up with evidence. Reasons. Explanations. Facts.

I had none of these. Nothing I'd seen had raised red flags, and yet—

"How was your day at Cliff House?" Tom broke into my thoughts.

"Truthfully? A bit strange. Undercurrents on the board. They were eager to impress us with the Van Eyck. We've recommended scientific analysis."

"You mean the painting might not be what it seems?"

I wasn't prepared to go that far. "Scientific analysis can confirm that a painting is authentic. That's what we're after. Since *Christ Healing the Demoniac* isn't one of the paintings officially attributed to Van Eyck, scientific proof of age, materials, and technique is essential. A newly discovered Van Eyck will rock the art world. There will be questions. We need to be able to answer them."

I took a sip of wine. We'd ordered a bottle of Sancerre to share, and Angus, our waiter, had promised to give us time to enjoy it.

Jayne Collier was bustling in and out of the kitchen. She and her husband, Gavin, owned the pub, which, thanks to their excellent cuisine and Lady Barbara's patronage, had become *the* place to eat in Long Barston—and with its lovely guest rooms on the upper floors, *the* place to stay as well.

I caught her eye. She gave me a thumbs-up. Jayne liked Tom a lot.

"Have you identified the man in the graveyard?" I asked Tom.

"Took a while. Since we didn't find a car, we figured he must have been staying overnight in the village. Turns out he'd booked a room here at the Magpies for two nights. Checked in late afternoon, stowed everything in his room, had an early dinner, and went out."

"Did he say where he was going?"

"Not specifically, Jayne said, but when he wasn't back by ten, she began to worry."

"Who was he?"

"His name was William Parker. Retired CID from Peterborough in Cambridgeshire."

"How did you figure that out?"

"He had an ID card from NARPO in his wallet—an association of retired police officers. The police in Peterborough have informed his relatives—a son and daughter-in-law."

"Do they know why he was in Long Barston?"

"I haven't heard."

"Any word on how he died?" I dipped a piece of sourdough into a small pot of herbed olive oil.

"That's not as clear-cut as we'd like. Severe allergic reaction is the likely cause."

Angus chose that moment to take our orders. We decided on roasted chicken, the nightly special.

"Good choice," Angus said. He went to tell the kitchen. Then he returned with a chilled bottle of water and left us to our conversation.

"You said Mr. Parker died of an allergic reaction," I said. "I hope it wasn't to anything he ate here. The Colliers would feel terrible, and it wouldn't do their reputation any good."

"Nothing to do with food. The technical term is *anaphylaxis*. There was a tiny puncture wound on his neck, surrounded by an area of inflammation. Initially the coroner thought it was an injection site."

"He didn't look like a drug addict."

"He wasn't. And he didn't inject himself."

"He was murdered?"

"By a bee. We found a medical emergency ID card in his wallet. Turns out he was allergic to bee venom."

"How awful."

"Yeah. Nausea, vomiting. Throat swells, cutting off oxygen."

"The poor man," I said.

"Indeed." Tom topped up my wine. "Let's talk about something more pleasant. Like us."

"What about us?"

"Since we've given up on the topic of where we'll live—"

"We haven't given it up," I protested. "We've just postponed the decision."

"We will have to decide, you know. No avoiding it."

"We're not avoiding it. We're temporarily setting it aside while we make other decisions."

"All right, then. Let's make some other decisions—about the wedding, for example. When and where? Have you given it any thought?"

"Of course I have."

"Conclusions?"

"It's not my decision alone, Tom. What do *you* want?"

He laughed. "My darling Kate, I don't care where we get married—in a church or a registry office; in Ohio or Long Barston or the top of the Eiffel Tower, if you fancy that. All I want is to marry you, and the sooner the better. So when and where shall it be?"

A tiny, joyful explosion went off in my heart. I opened my mouth to say something when his mobile pinged.

Tom glanced at the screen. "Sorry—it's Cliffe. He wouldn't call if it wasn't important."

Tom slid out of his seat and strode toward the door.

Giving me time to consider my answer.

The traditional answer, the expected answer, would be to have the wedding in Jackson Falls, Ohio. My mother would be matron of honor. My best friend Charlotte would be a bridesmaid. All my friends would be there.

The friends you haven't spoken to in nearly six months? My conscience can be snarky.

My children posed a problem. Christine was already back at Oxford. Michaelmas term at Magdalen College wouldn't begin until mid-October, but she'd snagged an assistantship with her tutor, checking and rechecking footnotes for his forthcoming book on Edward of Woodstock, the Black Prince. As for my son, Eric, who knew where he would be—working on his doctoral thesis at Ohio State or off on another research trip somewhere?

On the other hand, if the wedding were held in Suffolk, I'd have to consider my mother's new husband, James Lund. Had he recovered enough from his recent heart attack to travel internationally? Only a month ago they'd gotten married in a lovely restored barn in the Norwegian-heritage community of Stoughton, Wisconsin. I'd been matron of honor. Off they'd gone on their honeymoon, and I'd started dreaming of England again.

That's what I wanted to tell Tom.

My children had been born in Jackson Falls. I had a thriving antiques business there and a growing reputation as an appraiser. I owned a three-story Victorian in the town's historic district. I had friends—good friends. All this was true. But ever since Tom and I nearly collided on that snowy road in the Hebrides, my heart had felt increasingly at home with him.

Returning to Ohio for my mother's wedding, I'd rejoiced in the faces and places I'd missed in the two months I'd been away. But no sooner had I settled in than I began to long for Tom—and for England. So, yes, the traditional solution would be to marry in the church on Jackson's Falls' main square. I'd tried to picture it—I really had.

But in those quiet moments when I imagined myself walking down the aisle, the picture in my head was always Long Barston's small fourteenth-century jewel, St. Æthelric's.

"Sorry," Tom slid in beside me. "The police in Peterborough have interviewed Mr. Parker's son and daughter-in-law. They don't know why he was in Long Barston, and they never heard him mention anyone called Vivian. The son says his father's allergy was long-standing and well known. He always carried an epinephrine autoinjector."

"An EpiPen. So why didn't he use it?"

"Good question. We didn't find one in the graveyard or his hotel room."

"That's ironic, Tom—the one time he needed it, he didn't have it."

"We'll interview the son ourselves in a day or so," Tom said. "Which reminds me—I'm going to be away for several nights, starting tomorrow."

"Special assignment?"

"Sorry—can't talk about this one."

I felt my heart twist. "Dangerous?"

"Consequential. I should be back Thursday or Friday. Unfortunately, I'll have to make an early start in the morning. How about dinner at my house Friday night? I'll cook."

I must have looked alarmed because he added, "Don't worry. Mother won't be there. She's off to London with a friend. They go every year—see a few plays, try out the latest restaurants, shop till they drop."

This was sounding better and better. "Then I'll come." I traced his lip with my forefinger.

He gave me a sly smile. "Back to this wedding of ours. When and where?"

"How about November? We met at that time of year, remember?"

"But that's almost three months away."

"There's a lot to do—a dress, flowers, reception, invitations. Just because we've both been married before doesn't mean we can't have a proper wedding. Besides, November will be here before you know it."

"All right, *early* November. I'll check on flights to Cleveland."

"No, Tom." I took his hand. "I want to get married here, at St. Æthelric's."

"You do? Truly?" He reached for me.

Unfortunately, Angus chose that moment to deliver our food. "Cheers."

*　*　*

Around nine we pulled up to Rose Cottage in Tom's new black Land Rover Discovery. His old silver Volvo had suffered minor damage and major blood stains in our escape from disaster last May at Hapthorn Lodge.

The days were shortening. The sky was nearly dark. Through the lighted window I saw Vivian at the kitchen table, leafing through a magazine.

"Do you have time to come in and say hello?" I asked.

"She'll try to feed me," Tom said.

"She can't force you to eat," I pointed out logically. "And she will appreciate hearing the news about William Parker if it's not confidential."

"All right. But just for a few minutes. And no food."

As we entered through the small entryway into the kitchen, the aroma of apples and cinnamon greeted us.

"What a nice surprise," Vivian said, feigning astonishment. The fact that she was wearing her tweed skirt and twinset instead of her robe and slippers told me she'd been waiting up for us. She closed her magazine. "Come, sit. I made a nice apple crumble this afternoon. Double cream, extra thick."

Tom and I looked at each other. *Resistance is futile.*

"Sounds delicious," Tom said. "Small portion for me."

"And me," I added.

Vivian got up and pulled a heavy pan out of the Aga's warming oven.

"We had a lovely dinner," I said. "A lot to eat."

Ignoring me, Vivian spooned generous helpings of warm apple crumble onto three vintage ironstone plates. She topped each with a huge dollop of cream and carried the plates to the table.

Tom took a bite and closed his eyes. "Vivian, this is marvelous."

He was right. The apples had that sweet-tart flavor I love, topped with a crunchy layer of oatmeal, butter, brown sugar, cinnamon, and (I detected) a hint of clove.

"Early apples from Lady Barbara's garden," Vivian said. "One of the heritage varieties."

"Heavenly," I murmured between bites.

"Have you identified our man?" Vivian asked Tom. "Did you find his car?"

He'd just taken the last bite of his crumble so I answered, "No car, but they know who he is. It took a while because he'd booked into the Magpies and left his identification in the room."

Tom wiped his mouth on his napkin. "His name was William Parker. The police in Peterborough have located his son. They're going to—"

Tom's sentence trailed off. Vivian's face had gone white. She clutched the edge of the table.

"What's wrong?" I asked her. "Are you ill?"

She ignored me. Her eyes were on Tom. "Did you say William Parker from Peterborough? *Will Parker?* In his seventies?"

"Vivian," Tom said, "are you saying you knew him?"

"A very, *very* long time ago." Her eyes filled with tears. "I was in love with him."

* * *

Later, Vivian and I sat by the fire in her small, comfortable sitting room. She'd changed into her gray wool robe and slippers. Fergus the pug was curled up at her feet, his head on his paws, snoring softly.

"The summer of 1963?" I said. "You must have been—"

"Seventeen." She stared into the flames.

That meant Vivian was—I did the math—seventy-four or seventy-five. I'd assumed she was almost eighty—a fact I would never utter to a living soul.

"Will was eighteen. Oh my, he was a handsome lad." She stared off into the past. "Tall, broad-shouldered, blond hair falling over his forehead. He looked like an American pop star."

"You say you were at a holiday camp with your parents?"

"Hopley's—on the coast. 'Hopley's for Happy Hols.'" She gave a little hoot. "We spent four summers there, my parents and I. That was our last. It's not what people want today, but you have to understand, Kate. The war was behind us. Harold Wilson would soon be prime minister. He told us we'd never had it so good. Fewer than half of British families owned cars then, and there was no such thing as cheap flights to Spain. The camps were affordable, and they offered everything in one go—private chalets, meals, entertainment, organized activities, childminding. Big cheesy Hollywood-style variety shows every night. Cocktail dancing for the adults. Even most working-class families could afford it. The equivalent of today's all-inclusive cruise, I suppose." She wiggled her toes at the fire. "Besides Will, there were two boys from London in our crowd that summer. Jack—stocky, pugnacious. He reminded me of the ill-tempered bull terrier my uncle once owned.

The other boy—Frankie. Thin, small-boned." She furrowed her brow. "And Mary Something. She was from Norwich."

"Did you keep in touch?"

Vivian shook her head. "My father died that next winter, and my mother didn't have the heart to go as a single."

"Did you ever hear from Will?"

"Oh, no. I never imagined he'd remember me. Boys don't, do they? But girls—oh my. Those first romances, the innocent ones that are mostly in our imaginations, they never leave us. Life was different then. The Beatles were singing about holding hands. My parents' main complaint was I played my record player too loud. For years I dreamed about Will—actually dreamed. We'd be back at Hopley's—or I'd meet him on the street somewhere, and the old feelings would rekindle." She looked at me, her face serious. "I've thought about him so often, wondered what he'd done with his life." She took a shaky breath. Her eyes glistened. "And now he's dead, right on my doorstep. Why was he here, Kate? Why had he written my name? I have to know."

"Maybe he said something to Jayne at the Three Magpies."

"I should have thought of that." Vivian jumped to her feet, causing Fergus to yelp. "I'll call her now."

"Vivian, it's nearly ten thirty. She'll be in bed. We can stop in for lunch tomorrow after church and ask her in person."

"You're right. Probably best."

I had no idea what Jayne might say, but I did hope Vivian wouldn't be disappointed.

Some dreams are better left alone.

Chapter Five

Sunday, August 23

The bells of St. Æthelric's pealed as worshippers streamed out of the cool stone nave into the bright morning sunshine. An overnight shower had pearled the grass and weighed down the mophead hydrangeas blooming along the east side of the village green.

Vivian and I headed for the Three Magpies, hoping to catch Jayne Collier before the Sunday rush. By silent agreement we skirted the graveyard path, which was shorter but held memories that were all too fresh in our minds. Instead, we took the paved walk through the pollarded yews, past the Rectory gardens, and along a row of semidetached cottages lining the west side of the triangular green.

The sky was clear, that shade of blue that promises a fine day, but I could tell Vivian was troubled. A man was dead, a man who'd probably been on his way to see her after more than fifty years. Never one to let sleeping dogs lie, she was determined to get to the bottom of it.

I'll admit to being curious as well. I've never liked mysteries.

The Three Magpies opened at eleven for their traditional Sunday roast. We were among the first to arrive.

We chose a table in the bar, near the front windows. Outside, the planters overflowed with rosy dahlias and frothy clouds of love-in-a-mist.

A waitress I'd never seen before handed us menus. "Today's roast is bone-in prime rib," she said. "Specials on the chalkboard. The soup is chicken and white bean."

"Thanks," I said, taking the menu. "Is Jayne here? We'd like to speak with her if she's free."

The waitress smiled. "I'll check."

Moments later, Jane Collier appeared, untying her white apron and pulling the loop over her head. She flipped the bar flap and joined us at our table. "Always a pleasure to see friends."

"Do you have a few minutes?" I asked.

She glanced at her small gold wristwatch. "Fifteen at the most. We'll be getting busy soon, and Gav will need me in the kitchen." She gathered up our closed menus. "Have you decided? If you don't want the roast, the butternut squash ravioli is excellent. Or the summer salad with asparagus, white beans, and roasted artichoke." She signaled the waitress. "Bring us a bottle of that new Jean Claude rosé. On me. And I'll have a sparkling water as well."

Vivian and I ordered the summer salad with a cup of the soup.

"Business must be good," I said. "You've hired additional wait staff."

"We're not complaining." She must have noticed Vivian's face because her smile faded. "Everyone's so upset about that poor man. Shocking—especially for you, finding his body and all."

"I knew him years ago," Vivian said.

"You *knew* him? Was it you he'd come to see, then? That's even worse."

"It looks like it," I said. "We don't yet know why."

"What was he like?" Vivian's eyes misted over again.

"A lovely older gentleman. I never dreamed—" Jayne stopped when the waitress brought her mineral water. She took a long sip and began again. "He'd booked online. Arrived late afternoon on the bus from Bury. I showed him to his room—one of small doubles near the back. He was fit for his age."

"Tom said he was ex-CID from Peterborough," I said.

"Yes, I can see that. I thought at the time he must have held some role of authority in his day. You can always tell."

"Did he say why he'd come to Long Barston?" Vivian asked.

"Not specifically. I did ask if he had relatives in the area. He said no. He'd come to find someone."

Vivian's hand went to her throat.

The waitress delivered a trio of slim wine glasses and an exquisite wine bottle with a textured-glass shoulder and a pretty Art Nouveau label.

Jayne filled our glasses with the pale pink liquid; then gave herself about an ounce. "Tell me what you think. The salesman described it as elegant with aromas of currants and oranges. I can never tell. Either I like it or I don't. It's meant to be a transitional wine. Perfect for summer into autumn."

We each took a taste.

"Lovely," said Vivian. "Not too sweet."

I agreed. Steering Jayne back on track, I asked, "Did Mr. Parker say anything else?"

Jayne picked up her glass and swirled it. "He seemed a nice man. Looked you straight in the eye when he spoke." She furrowed her brow. "He did say one thing that was odd. We were serving dinner. I was in the kitchen with Gav when the new waitress, Jenny, came to tell me he'd sent his compliments. I went out to say hello and to ask if he'd enjoyed his walk. He'd taken a stroll around the church after checking in—to stretch his legs before dinner. But when I asked him, he said, 'I thought I saw someone I knew. Someone who shouldn't be here.'"

"What time was that?" I asked, making a mental note to tell Tom.

"Let's see. He'd booked his table for seven, and he left for his walk around six, so sometime during that hour."

I glanced at Vivian. It couldn't have been her. Between six and eight o'clock we were having dinner at Finchley Hall.

"Was he upset or pleased?" I asked.

"Confused, I think."

I took another sip of the cool pink wine. Parker could have been mistaken about recognizing someone near the church. People look alike.

But what if he wasn't?

* * *

After lunch, Vivian and I made the fifteen-minute trek through Finchley Park to Finchley Hall. By car, the trip actually took longer because the roads, laid out in the fifteenth century, skirted the perimeter of the vast original estate grounds. The purpose, no doubt, had been to funnel visitors toward the stately home via the long, impressive, tree-lined drive. We approached the house from the back, through the restored Elizabethan garden.

We'd been summoned by Lady Barbara, whose upcoming move into private apartments in the east wing was scheduled to take place after the Christmas holidays when the National Trust would take possession of Finchley Hall. She had decisions to make. While all rooms in her new suite needed plasterwork, updated electrics, and new decoration, a few rooms—a kitchen and laundry facilities, for example—would have to be created from scratch. Her immediate task was to sign off on the arrangement of rooms.

She met us at the door. "Come in, come in." The large entrance hall was draped with canvas sheeting. Conservators from the National Trust were in the process of restoring the antique oak paneling, repairing cracks and splits and correcting some minor bowing.

"Advance warning," Lady Barbara said. "The Trust will be doing some work in Finchley Park the first week in September. The path near the koi pond will be closed. You'll have to use the Chinese bridge."

"Really? Is it safe?" I asked. No one actually used the eighteenth-century bridge anymore.

"Perfectly safe, they tell me, as long as you watch your step and hold onto the railing. I'll let you know before it happens."

"They've identified our man," Vivian said.

"Oh, I am glad." Lady Barbara took Vivian's arm. "I want to hear everything, but let's talk about it over tea. Right now I want you to have a look at the rooms I've chosen. I'm sure you're good at picturing things, Kate. Most of my furniture will be too large, but I have no wish to acquire anything *new*." The emphasis she put on the word *new* told me this was not a compliment. I understood. My mother's attitude toward furniture manufactured after around 1910 was something like a master sommelier's attitude toward wine-in-a-box.

We followed Lady Barbara up the main staircase and made our way through several corridors, up a half staircase and down again. Like most historic houses, Finchley Hall had been added onto, rearranged, and remodeled by almost every new generation.

"This is it," Lady Barbara said as we passed through a door into the east wing. "My suite will include the small drawing room with the Portland stone fireplace, my private sitting room, the morning room, and the small oak-paneled library." She stopped. "The first door on your left will be my new bedroom," she said. "I'm afraid you'll have to use your imagination."

We stepped into a large room with windows overlooking the Elizabethan garden and the park beyond. The view was amazing, but the room itself, except for a charming oak mantelpiece incorporating the figure of a finch, the family symbol, was dark and cheerless. The wood floor was laid with a frayed beige rug, and the walls were covered with acres of heavy, brown Victorian wallpaper glued like linoleum to the four walls.

Lady Barbara must have read my mind—or perhaps my face. "Don't look at the decoration, Kate. All that will go. Just picture the bones, the proportions."

By that standard, the room was lovely—high-ceilinged, with graceful neoclassical plasterwork. I was beginning to see the possibilities.

We followed Lady Barbara into a sort of anteroom and then another, smaller bedroom.

"This will be a dressing room with fitted closets and a modern bath. Very convenient."

"I hope Francie Jewell is planning to stay on."

"I'm pleased to say she is. She'll have her own small apartment just across the hall, with a bedroom, sitting room, and bath. Now that her husband's gone—and good riddance, I say"—Lady Barbara made a moue of distaste—"she feels quite at home here."

"I hope they don't expect her to use the big kitchen," Vivian said. "It takes a full day to get there from here."

Lady Barbara laughed. "The Trust will install a compact modern kitchen and laundry facilities in one of the rooms along the hall."

"Will the original kitchen on the ground floor be open to the public?" I asked.

"Not exactly the original. The theme will be the war years and the time of deprivation afterward. All the public rooms will be returned to their appearance at the end of the last war. Fortunately, we have photographs. We were requisitioned as a rehabilitation center in 1941."

"Will the Trust help financially with your private rooms?"

"They'll pay for the plumbing, electrics, and plasterwork repair. The decorating will be up to me, and frankly I don't know where to start. I've never made decisions like that. I've just lived with the decisions made by past generations."

Like all great houses in England, Finchley Hall was an amalgam of styles, from the early Elizabethan core to the parquet floors and plain paneling of the Edwardian dining room.

"I've been contacted by *British Interiors* magazine," Lady Barbara said, her face pink with pleasure. "They want to do a before-and-after piece on Finchley Hall, featuring my wing."

"You might need professional help," I said, fishing in my handbag for the card Nicola Netherfield gave me. "This woman is on the Cliff House board. She's good, although her fees may be high."

"We'll see." Lady Barbara tucked the card in her pocket. "The Trust is providing a design consultant, but I'm not sure how much actual help he'll be. Anyway, come along now. Francie will be bringing tea, and I want to hear all about our man in the graveyard."

We gathered around the fireplace in Lady Barbara's sitting room. The vintage wallpaper, a design of urns and flowers, was badly faded and peeling off the walls.

"Do you think I could find this same design?" Lady Barbara asked. "I've always been fond of it. I do need to feel at home, you know."

"You might find something similar, but it will take some looking."

Francie placed the tea tray on a low table, and Vivian poured out.

"All right. Let's hear it," Lady Barbara said. "Who was our man, and how did he die?"

"His name was Will Parker," I said. "He was an ex-detective sergeant from Peterborough. Late seventies, a widower with one son. He died of a bee sting."

"Oh my hat." Lady Barbara tsked.

We filled in the details we knew, which weren't many.

Vivian set down her cup. "The thing is, Barb, I knew him— years ago, when I was a girl."

"I see. So that's why he'd jotted down your details. He'd come to look you up."

"I suppose so. But why? I have to know." Vivian gave a little sob, turning it into a cough.

"You must visit his son in Peterborough," Lady Barbara said. "He'll have answers."

Vivian sniffed. "I couldn't do that."

Lady Barbara shot her a pointed look. "You'll never know if you don't ask. This Will Parker wanted to say something to you. Aren't you curious?"

"Of course I am," Vivian snapped. "But I'd be a stranger, barging in on a family tragedy. I couldn't."

"Yes, you could." Using a pair of silver tongs, Lady Barbara dropped a scone on Vivian's plate. "Call first, of course. He'll be eager to speak with his father's old friend."

"Do you really think so?" Vivian looked at me. "Would Tom give us his details?"

"Probably not. But he might contact the family and find out if they're willing to meet you."

"If they agree, would you go with me?"

"Of course, if I can."

"And you, Barb?"

"No," Lady Barbara said. "I have too much on my plate at the moment. You two go. You can tell me all about it when you get back. There's a mystery there, and I want to know what it is."

So did I. Why *had* Will Parker wanted to see Vivian after fifty-eight years? Who was it he saw near the church—the person who shouldn't have been there? And the biggest question of all: If the man knew he had a life-threatening bee-sting allergy, why wasn't he carrying his EpiPen?

Chapter Six

~

Monday, August 24

I arrived at The Cabinet of Curiosities the next morning at eight thirty. Ivor was already at work, cataloguing a group of fourteen eighteenth-century snuff boxes we'd received on Saturday by special courier from Cliff House. They were a bequest, gifted to Netherfield Sanatorium in the 1960s under the will of a grateful— and hopefully cured—patient.

Ivor had the small boxes lined up on the counter. "Which is your favorite?" He handed me a pair of white cotton gloves.

I studied them as I pulled on the gloves, feeling my heart kick up a notch. "They're all wonderful, but if I have to choose, I'd say this one." I picked up an unusual box in the shape of a dog's head, formed from amethyst quartz.

"What can you tell me about it?"

Quiz time again. If there was anything Ivor loved more than putting me to the test, it was discovering a lapse in my knowledge. Which he could then remedy.

"Well, it's definitely not the most expensive," I said, turning the amethyst head in my hand to study it. "I like it. It looks German to me. Probably from Dresden. Lower Saxony is famous for amethyst quartz." I opened the box. "The clasp at the dog's neck is marked eighteen-carat gold. The eyes aren't diamonds, although they may have been at one time. Late eighteenth or early nineteenth century?"

"Well done. And which box will bring the highest sale price, hmm?" He gave me his pure-as-the-driven-snow look, which meant he was up to something.

My eyes fell on a gold box set with diamonds and rubies. On the lid was an enamel portrait of a military man with the silly forward-swept hairdo popular in the Regency period.

Nope—that would be too easy. "All right, I don't know. I'd say this one because of the gold and precious stones, but I'm probably wrong."

"Not a bad guess, but you are wrong. Feast your eyes on this." He picked up an interesting gold and enamel box, an elongated oval, divided into three compartments. The box wasn't as flashy as the jeweled one, but as soon as I saw it properly, I knew he was right. My mouth went dry and my cheeks started to flush.

"The box is made of tricolor gold, finely enameled, and framed with natural pearls. Do you recognize the decoration on the lid of the central compartment, hmm?"

"Cupid and Psyche, I think." The star-crossed lovers were caught in an amorous embrace.

"Now look at this." He opened the left-hand compartment and up popped a tiny mechanical model of the couple who, in an impressive display of balance, stood on a seesaw, flanked by a cherub playing a harp.

"Wow. I've never seen anything like it."

"Nor have I." He opened the compartment on the right, which concealed a watch with jeweled hands and numbers. "Once wound, the watch runs for thirty hours and drives the mechanical lovers by flipping this small lever. The fortunate owner could meditate on the triumph of true love while sniffing tobacco and telling time to a choice of two soundtracks."

"Incredible. How much will you appraise it for?" I asked.

"I'll have to do more research, but right now I'd guess somewhere in the neighborhood of sixty thousand pounds."

"That's some bequest. Could be a million here, all told."

Ivor shut down his computer and closed the lid. "Any news on the dead man?" He began wrapping the snuff boxes in cotton and packing them in a sturdy wooden box.

"They've identified him," I said, removing my gloves and dropping them on the counter. "His name is Will Parker. He was ex-CID from Peterborough. One of Vivian's old boyfriends."

"Wrinklies reunion?"

"Don't you dare say that to Vivian. She's broken up over it. The coroner claims he died from an anaphylactic reaction to a bee sting, but the funny thing is—and this comes from his son—he was well aware of the seriousness of his condition and always carried an epinephrine injector. So why didn't he have it with him?"

"Forgot to pack it?"

"Maybe. Anyway, Lady Barbara thinks Vivian should meet the family."

"His wife might not be thrilled."

"He's a widower. I'm going to ask Tom to contact the son and find out if they're willing to see us—if I can have a day off to drive her to Peterborough."

"You don't have to ask, Kate. By the way, where is our dashing detective inspector?"

"On some terribly important secret mission somewhere." I smiled. "I'm sure he'll call me tonight if he can."

Ivor fit the cover on the box of snuffs. Without looking up, he said, "Kate, what *was* your problem with the painting? The brush-strokes? Something in the pigments?"

"I'm sorry, Ivor. It's nothing I can put into words." *Well, that's true.* "It's a feeling. I could be mistaken."

"If you're right, they won't thank us."

"I know."

"Which reminds me—Tony Currie phoned." Ivor slid the wooden box under the counter. "The board is willing to go ahead with the analysis of the painting. I've suggested cleaning as well."

"That was quick."

"Apparently, Currie prevailed against intense opposition. The other board members were incensed at what they called a monumental waste of time and money. Currie argued that my explanation of the benefits of scientific analysis made sense and would probably result in a higher sale price. They relented when he threatened to pull Pyramid out of the project, although they can't have taken the threat seriously. Pyramid has too much invested. At any rate, the Van Eyck will be collected this week."

A pit opened in my stomach. Ivor had put himself in a precarious situation because of me. If analysis revealed nothing alarming, he'd be a hero. But there were so many things that could go wrong—what if *Christ Healing the Demoniac* had been left unfinished at the time of Van Eyck's death, and was completed by one of his students? That would lower the value considerably. What if the painting had been damaged at some point in its history and cut down from a larger size? What if restoration had been attempted, using substandard materials? I hadn't seen evidence of any of this. And yet—

At least we'd know the truth.

Ivor peeled off his white cotton gloves. "I told Apollo Research the board insisted on having the painting back in time for an October sale. Currie was quite insistent on the point."

"I noticed that."

Ivor looked up. "I think they're in financial trouble."

* * *

I left the shop at five thirty. The day had turned busy when two coach tours of seniors from London pulled into the village for lunch and shopping. Lots of questions. No sales.

When I got back to Rose Cottage, a large pot of something savory was simmering on the Aga. I realized I hadn't eaten lunch.

"Hello—anyone home?"

A friendly woof came from the living room. I found Vivian on the sofa with a pile of photograph albums. Fergus, curled up in his basket, raised his head and wagged his corkscrew tail.

"I wasn't sure I still had this." Vivian was holding an album bound in faded navy fabric. "Photographs from that last summer at Hopley's. Come look."

I sat beside her, and she spread the album on our laps.

"Oh, Vivian—look at you." She and another girl, smaller, mouse-like, pedaled a side-by-side bicycle in front of a croquet lawn. Vivian's light brown hair was pulled into a ponytail. Her brows were drawn together, and her mouth was set in a determined line. "Who's the other girl?"

"Mary, the one I told you about."

"You don't look happy."

Vivian huffed. "Mary only pretended to pedal." She peered at the photo. "She was a strange little thing—secretive, sly. We'd never have been friends at home."

"Why?"

"She was a loner. We'd all be doing cartwheels and handstands on the beach, and she'd be searching for pretty rocks and shells. You're too young to remember those mood rings—they supposedly changed colors according to your mood. They were just cheap things, but I'd bought one with my own money just before we left for Hopley's. One day I couldn't find it, and then I saw Mary with it on her finger. She insisted she had one identical to mine, and I couldn't prove otherwise." Vivian frowned. "Wonder whatever became of her?"

I turned the album pages, seeing more photos of Vivian—swimming in an open-air pool, playing miniature golf. In several, Mary lurked in the background, always looking away from the camera.

"What's she holding?" I asked, pointing at something wrapped in blue paper.

"Cadbury's Dairy Milk chocolate. They sold the bars at the ice cream kiosk. She was addicted."

Vivian turned the page. "There we are—the five of us. Look—I've written the names." Her fingers brushed the white-ink letters on the black page: *Jack, Frankie, Will, Me, Mary.*

The black-and-white photograph showed five teens, arm in arm, in front of an ice cream kiosk. Jack and Frankie looked exactly as Vivian had described them. Jack struck a serious pose while making bunny ears over Frankie's head. And Will Parker—*oh yes*. He had been a handsome lad, all right. Tall and rangy; smooth, lightly bronzed skin; a blond curl draped across one eye. Vivian stood next to him, her shoulder touching his chest. Mary had another of the Cadbury bars in her hand.

"Mary looks younger than the rest of you."

"She was fifteen," Vivian said. "Jack and Frankie were sixteen."

Below that were some beach shots. Will doing a handstand on a flat rock. Vivian stretched out on a blanket and leaning back on her elbows. Mary tucking up her skirt as she waded in the ocean.

I laughed. "Is that your father?" The photo showed an ordinary looking man dressed in a grass skirt with a coconut bra.

"Oh my, yes." Vivian covered her mouth. "Fancy dress night. He doesn't look like a banker, does he? I think mother went as a hat-check girl that year. They'd prepare for weeks in advance, assembling the costumes, planning it all out. Our week at Hopley's was the highlight of the summer for my parents. People tended to go the same week every year, so they'd meet up with people they knew. A bit of glam—at least that's what we thought at the time. My parents danced every night under a spinning mirror ball. The cocktails came with little umbrellas—the height of sophistication."

My stomach growled.

Vivian looked up. "I'm sorry, Kate, going on and on. You must be starving."

"Something's cooking. Smells wonderful."

"Beef and barley stew. I made brown bread earlier. We can have it with that Wensleydale cheddar I got last week. How about a game of whist after?"

"Oh, I'm sorry." I put my hand on her arm. "I can't tonight—computer work. If Tom calls, I'll ask him about contacting Will Parker's family."

"Imagine, meeting Will's family after all these years." Vivian sucked in a breath and blew it out. "And then I remember he's dead."

* * *

After dinner, I climbed the stairs to my room under the thatch.

The computer work I'd mentioned to Vivian involved searching online for whatever I could find about Pyramid Corporation and the Cliff House board of directors. People take it for granted that clients check up on antiques dealers and auction houses—and they should—but we investigate our clients as well. Our professional reputations are at stake, after all.

Delving into confidential financial reports would require access I didn't have. Still, very little happens these days that goes unnoticed on the web. There would be something.

Bypassing Tony Currie for the moment—I'd get to him when researching Pyramid Corporation—I began by plugging in the names of the other board members, expecting to find the shiny online profiles people pay to maintain.

When I typed in "Dr. Underwood," the first thing that popped up was a Wikipedia article on the history of the Euthanasia Movement in Britain—confusing until I realized the Underwood mentioned as an early proponent wasn't Dr. Oswin Underwood but his father, Dr. David Underwood, the psychiatrist. When I added "Oswin," all I found was an advertisement from the Miracle Library, inviting guests to a lecture series on local history, every Friday at seven PM. Underwood was described as an expert on the history of Victorian lunatic asylums and the author of a brochure about Netherfield Sanatorium, written for the tourist board.

Nicola Netherfield turned out to be a well-known interior designer. There'd been a spread on her in one of the British architectural magazines when she designed a London flat for Tony Currie and his wife. That was interesting. The photos showed a sleek contemporary living area, glassed in on two sides, overlooking the London skyline. I was impressed with the design. Not so impressed with Currie's wife, twenty years his junior—tall, blonde, and dressed in an off-shoulder peasant dress with bare feet.

At first, all I found on Martyn Lee-Jones was an announcement to the effect that he'd recently been appointed general manager of Cliff House, and that I knew already. However, more searching and a little patience turned up the puzzling information that he'd previously served as the CFO of a large and prosperous import firm based in Kent. Had he been fired? Why else would he give up an executive position to become what was essentially a manager? Attempts to learn anything about his private life failed.

I was getting bored when I typed in the name of the one board member I hadn't met—Niall Walker. He turned out to be a solicitor in Cambridge, the senior member of Walker & Palkot, a firm founded in the 1950s by his father. According to an article in *The Telegraph*, the firm had once been sued by the niece of an elderly widow who claimed the senior Walker had pressured her aunt into appointing him executor of her estate, which included—*golly!*—a valuable collection of eighteenth-century snuff boxes. The aunt had left them in her will to Netherfield Sanatorium in gratitude for her time there as a young woman.

Something about that didn't sit right with me. Or the niece, apparently. Unfortunately for her, the firm won the suit by providing ample evidence, both in writing and on film, that their client had made the decision freely, with no undue influence. I would mention it to Ivor, but I couldn't see how we could become entangled in a court case that had been decided in 1961.

I was about to delve into Pyramid Corporation when Tom called.

"Hello, darling." I could almost see him, his eyes crinkling, that half smile with the power to turn me into a teenager. "I've missed you."

"You've only been gone two days."

"Going off me, now we're engaged?"

I laughed. "I've missed you, too. Are you finished there—wherever you are?"

"Not quite."

"When are you coming home?"

"Friday. Unfortunately, Mother will be home after all, so dinner for two at home is out. How about the Trout?"

"Perfect. Has the trip been successful?"

"Oh, yes."

"You're going to miss field work when you're sitting in that big detective chief inspector's desk."

"If I am sitting there, you mean. I haven't been formally offered the job."

"We'll talk about it on Friday," I said, feeling a tug somewhere beneath my breastbone. If we moved to Ohio, what would Tom do? He'd mentioned a former colleague who'd opened a private investigations agency in Toronto and was hoping to expand into the U.S. I supposed Tom could become some sort of security expert for firms doing business in the UK.

"Hey—before I forget," I said. "Will Parker told Jayne at the Magpies that he saw someone in the village he thought he knew—someone who shouldn't be there. It might have been his killer."

"Interesting." I heard a male voice in the background. "I'll have to ring off in a minute," Tom said. "Call you tomorrow."

"Before you go—a request. Vivian would like to meet William Parker's family. Could you get word to them—ask if they're willing?"

A moment's silence told me he was weighing his response. "I'll run it past Eacles. If he agrees, I'll ask Sergeant Cliffe to make the contact. He'll let you know."

"Thank you. Vivian will be grateful. So will I."

We spoke for a few more minutes—a private conversation—and ended the call.

Smiling, I turned off my phone and plugged it in.

In less than a year, Tom had become an essential part of my happiness. In spite of my initial resistance, I'd fallen hopelessly in love.

Resistance? Who are you kidding? inquired my inner voice.

I did resist, I countered virtuously. *For several days.*

Feeling like I'd lost the battle but won the Irish Sweepstakes, I returned to my research.

Getting behind the public face of Pyramid Corporation wasn't easy. According to their website, the company, founded in 1998 by two chartered surveyors, was recognized as a leader in historic renovation and luxury housebuilding in the residential areas of London and the adjoining counties. I scrolled through a list of their developments, finding the Cliff House project near the end.

One of our newest sites is the previously abandoned Netherfield Sanatorium on the Suffolk coast near Miracle-on-Sea. Pyramid visited the site three years ago and immediately recognized the potential of the Grade I listed building. Suitably inspired, Pyramid joined a group of local investors, and negotiations proceeded through the complex planning stages whilst addressing conservation issues with English Heritage and the Victorian Society. When completed, the development will include 47 flats and townhouses in the main structure with a proposed 22 bespoke dwellings on the forty-acre grounds.

Local investors? That was interesting.

I scrolled through images—the artist's rendering I'd seen in the sale room; an aerial view of the site; a formal portrait of the Pyramid board standing in front of the arched entrance (Tony Currie front and center); and several shots of the entrance hall with its cool, contemporary elegance.

Scrolling through line after line in the search results for Pyramid brought more of the same—impressive construction and restoration projects, delighted purchasers, accolades from local authorities. I was about to call it a night when a headline caught my attention:

Pyramid Development LLP seeks to offset recent losses.

Yes, I clicked on it. The article had appeared two weeks earlier in the *Financial Times*:

Pyramid Development LLP, one of England's premier housing developers, said on Friday it was working diligently to restructure its debt and avoid bankruptcy protection. Pyramid's move to raise fresh capital comes after a report earlier this month that the company had just six months of cash reserves. Tony Currie, Managing Director, said revenue for the third quarter is expected to be £39 million, well below market expectations. "This is a temporary shortfall," Currie said. "We have every confidence in the future."

Well, well. If the Van Eyck was all it claimed to be, the sale would put a nice big dent in that shortfall.

Chapter Seven

⁓

Thursday, August 27

Three days later Vivian and I packed a picnic lunch and headed out in my Mini Cooper for a journey that would take us north of Cambridge, through the ancient town of St. Naots, and eventually to Peterborough, the city where Will Parker, ex-CID, had lived and worked. Depending on traffic, we'd arrive around one thirty, giving us time to get our bearings before our two o'clock meeting with Hugh Parker and his wife Stephanie.

Ivor and I had spent Tuesday at Cliff House, working our way through the inventory of sale items, cataloguing them and setting estimated values. The Van Eyck painting was ready for pickup the next day by Apollo Research and Analysis.

That evening, Sergeant Cliffe had phoned to let me know the Parkers had agreed to meet and asked us to arrive any time after two o'clock.

Vivian had immediately gotten busy enlarging and framing an old Brownie camera snapshot of Will at Hopley's. I bought a sympathy card, which we'd both signed.

The day was sunny but cool. We stopped and ate our sandwiches near St. Naots, site of a ninth-century priory destroyed by the Danes in 1010. I remembered reading about the ground radar study in 2006 that had uncovered the priory's foundations, lost for centuries beneath a Waitrose parking lot. Goes to show—what you see on the surface is never the full story.

Autumn was settling early into Cambridgeshire. Before us stretched a patchwork quilt of fields. In some, the barley had already been cut and bound in golden stooks to dry. Wood pigeons circled above, gathering seeds for their larders. In the hedgerows, hedgehogs were fattening up on creepy crawlies in preparation for their winter hibernation.

We entered the A1 north of St. Naots, exiting twenty minutes later at Yaxley and following the GPS to a new housing estate south of Peterborough. The Parkers lived in a two-story semidetached brick house on Marine Drive. The estate was fairly new, with several homes still under construction.

Hugh and Stephanie were waiting for us, an attractive couple in their early fifties.

"Welcome. We're so glad you've come." Stephanie had chin-length brown hair and warm olive-green eyes.

Her husband stood behind her, a tall man with fair hair turning white at the temples. "Please, come inside. We really are grateful you've traveled all this way."

I expected Vivian to take the lead, but she was staring mutely at Hugh Parker.

"We're so sorry for your loss," I said quickly. "It must have been a terrible shock."

Vivian made a sound of agreement, but I could tell she was struggling not to cry.

We followed the Parkers into a spacious living room furnished with a matching leather sofa and loveseat. A large abstract painting hung over a built-in gas fireplace. A number of floral arrangements sat around the room—from the funeral, I guessed.

Vivian and I sat on the sofa. Hugh and Stephanie sat next to each other on the loveseat.

"We appreciate your willingness to meet with us so soon after your father's death, Mr. and Mrs. Parker," I said.

"Hugh and Stephanie, please," he said.

"And I'm Kate." When Vivian still said nothing, I added, "Vivian met your father at Hopley's when they were teenagers."

Vivian pinned her upper lip with a knuckle.

"Are you all right?" Hugh Parker asked her. "Can we get you something?"

"No, thank you. It's just you look so much like your father."

"People always say that," Stephanie agreed.

"Hearing from us must have been a surprise," I said.

"We didn't know what to think when DS Cliffe phoned us." Stephanie's brow creased. "To hear that someone who knew Will more than fifty years ago just happened to be there when he died—well, it's just such a coincidence, isn't it?"

"Dad always said there's no such thing as coincidence." Hugh reached for his wife's hand and looked at us. "He was a policeman—CID. I think you know that."

"I could have predicted it," Vivian said. "Truly. Even back then he was playing detective."

"His father was a detective constable. Dad was a detective sergeant," Hugh said. "Retired at seventy. He'd been rather at loose ends since. Never one to put his feet up."

Vivian pulled the photo from her handbag and handed it to Hugh along with the card.

"Thank you." He gave her a twisted smile and gave the card to his wife.

"I took the photo myself," Vivian said. "I'm sorry the quality's not better."

"Well, it's lovely, isn't it?" Stephanie leaned over to view the photo. "We don't have any of Dad at this particular age." She looked up. "My goodness. He was a handsome lad." She got to her feet and placed the photo on the mantel beside one of a white-haired man holding up a plaque.

"Is that a recent photo of your father?" I asked.

"Taken the day he retired." Stephanie brought it over and handed it to Vivian.

I heard a small intake of breath.

The photo showed a handsome older man—the man I'd seen in the graveyard—standing in the middle of a group of officers. A sign on the wall behind them said *Goodbye Tension—Hello Pension*.

"That was a sad day for him," Hugh said. "Without a case to work on, he was lost."

"It's a lovely card," Stephanie said, tucking it back in the envelope. "I'll just put the kettle on."

"I believe your mother is deceased as well," I said when she'd gone.

"She died soon after Dad retired," Hugh said. "We offered to have him live with us, but he wouldn't hear of it. Said he was better off on his own. We saw him mostly at the weekend. He'd come over for Sunday dinner and then stay for a few hours to watch something on BBC Four. Dad loved documentaries, all sorts."

"Did he live nearby?"

"Fifteen minutes. When he retired, my parents sold their home and moved into a flat within walking distance of the shops. Easier for Mum to run, they said. She'd been poorly for a few years. Arthritis—and bone cancer, as we learned later."

"Did your father tell you why he traveled to Long Barston?" Vivian asked.

"To find you, I should think. The police showed us the note. It was his handwriting, all right."

"Did he happen to mention why he wanted to find Vivian?" I asked.

"You must understand," Hugh said. "Dad was independent. All he said was it had to do with an old investigation. A cold case, I assumed. I wondered why he was getting involved. I wish now I'd asked more questions."

Stephanie entered the room, carrying a tray with a teapot, cups, and a plate of small fluted tea cakes. "Baked fresh this morning," she said. "My daughter-in-law's recipe."

"How many children do you have?" I asked as Stephanie poured.

"Two sons." Hugh spooned sugar into his cup and stirred.

"That's our oldest on the left." Stephanie pointed out two framed photographs on the side table. "He works for British Air in Montreal. His wife is Canadian. We see them and our two granddaughters once a year when they fly over for their summer hols—not nearly enough. Our younger son lives in London. He's a constable with the Met—about to take his sergeant's exam."

"I'm sorry it was you who found my father's body." Hugh held his teacup but hadn't yet taken a sip.

"I just wish we'd found him sooner," I said. "The coroner said he died from a reaction to a bee sting."

"And that puzzles us," Stephanie said. "Dad knew he was allergic to bees—had been for years. He always carried one of those injector things—just in case. At first we assumed he must have been trying to inject himself and couldn't manage it, but the police said they didn't find an injector at the scene or in his room at the pub."

"Could he have forgotten to pack it?" I asked.

"We checked his flat first thing," Hugh said. "It wasn't there. Then we wondered if he'd been due for a replacement and had forgotten to pick it up. He got a new one every year like clockwork. But when we contacted the chemist, we were told it wasn't time."

"A bit late for questions." Stephanie spread her hands. "Still, it does bother us."

"More to the point, it would have bothered Dad," Hugh said. "He didn't like unanswered questions. That's why he was such a good copper." He placed his teacup on the coffee table and addressed Vivian. "I understand you met at Hopley's Holiday Camp. I don't remember Dad mentioning Hopley's."

Vivian's eyes flicked. "No reason he should. There were five of us around the same age that week, so we spent time together. Two other boys from London and a girl from Norwich."

"What was Dad like then?" Hugh asked.

Vivian's face softened. "Oh, he was a lovely boy—tall and blond, like you." She flushed. "I had a crush on him, in case you haven't guessed. Of course, I'm sure he didn't remember me."

"I'm sure he *did* remember you," Stephanie said kindly. "We always remember our first love, don't we?"

"Actually, that's partly why we've come," I said.

Vivian's cup rattled in the saucer. "It's just, if your father traveled all the way to Long Barston to find me, I can't help wondering why."

"I wish I could tell you." Hugh shrugged. "All we know is the trip had to do with the past—well, it would if he'd gone to look you up, wouldn't it? Other than that, we have no idea."

"There was that package," Stephanie said. "Remember? The trip thing came up after that."

Hugh looked at his wife. "That's right. I'd forgotten." He turned back to us. "Dad received a package in the mail sometime before his trip. He seemed disturbed by it—well, not disturbed so much as puzzled. It was after that he told us he was going to Long Barston. At the time, I didn't connect the two events."

"Who was the package from?" I asked.

"He never said. And he never told us what was in it. He only said he'd received a package, and it reminded him of an unsolved mystery—his exact words."

"Did you mention the package to the police?" I asked.

"Why would I?" Hugh shrugged. "Dad died from a bee sting—what he always feared. What I want to know is why he didn't have his EpiPen with him. He carried it for more than thirty years."

"We drove him to the station that morning." Stephanie wiped away a tear. "He seemed a bit distracted—like he used to get when he was working a case. That was the last time we saw him." She took her husband's hand. "We're going to miss him terribly."

"If you find anything to explain the trip, will you let us know?" I handed her my card. "That's my mobile number at the bottom. Call anytime."

* * *

The Suffolk nights were growing cold. That evening at Rose Cottage I made a fire in the hearth. After supper, Vivian and I carried small glasses of port into the sitting room. Fergus, as usual, curled up in his basket.

Vivian had been unusually subdued on the ride home from Peterborough. I understood. Finding Will Parker's body in the church graveyard had ended a fantasy she'd clung to for nearly sixty years.

I watched her now, lost in the past with her memories. Vivian was a deeply private person. In all the months I'd known her, she'd never once mentioned a lover. If she wanted to talk about Will, she would.

The crackling fire and the port did their magic.

"It's funny how a single week in your life can stay with you." Vivian propped her feet on the ottoman and gazed into the flames. "I'm embarrassed to admit how often I've thought of Will these past years."

"Don't be." I lay back and put my feet on the ottoman beside hers.

"It was all so innocent, Kate. Holding hands at Bonfire Night. Kisses behind the ice cream kiosk. I feel silly dwelling on it."

I turned my head to examine her profile, backlit by the flames. Will Parker had been her first boyfriend, with all the emotions and fierce drama that entailed.

Vivian dabbed at her eyes with a hanky. "In my heart, there was always the possibility we'd meet again somewhere. I don't mean start up a romance—I realized he must have gotten married, had a family. But I always imagined I'd see him again. Just once."

"Did it help meeting his son?"

"A little. But now I'll never know why he came to Long Barston."

"His son said it had to do with a cold case."

"In Long Barston? *Ha!* Until you arrived, we hadn't had a serious crime in thirty years."

I laughed. "You're saying I brought crime to rural Suffolk?"

"Of course not. It's just—"

My cell phone rang. I pulled it out, thinking it might be Tom.

It was Stephanie Parker. "I hope we're not intruding, but you did say to call if we found anything. After you left this afternoon, Hugh drove over to his father's flat. We were curious about the package he'd received. I'm going to put him on now."

"I'll put you on speaker," I said. "That way Vivian and I can both hear."

"I might be making more of this than I should." Hugh's voice came through the line. "But you got me thinking about that package. I found it in his closet. A small box. No return address."

"What was inside?"

"A gun. No, *no*—not a real one," he said, hearing me gasp. "One of those cigarette lighter things."

Vivian yelped and grabbed my arm. "Was it small, curved, dark with a brass barrel and fittings?"

"I heard that," Hugh said. "Yes, exactly. Like a toy derringer, but heavy and well made."

"I know that gun." Vivian's voice rose alarmingly. "He found it that summer at Hopley's."

I stared at Vivian. "Who sent it?" I asked Hugh.

"No name. It may have been a joke, except I know my father didn't think it was funny. He was concerned, perplexed. I've been thinking, trying to remember if he said anything else."

Vivian leaned forward, covering her face with her hands.

I took the phone off speaker and put it to my ear so I could hear better. "When did the package arrive?"

"It was postmarked August sixteenth in London—Lower Regent Street. That means he would have received it on the eighteenth, I guess. He called me Friday morning, the twenty-first, to say he'd be out of town for two nights."

"Let me talk to him." Vivian snatched the phone. "You're sure he didn't mention me—or anyone else? Jack? Frankie? A house with a funny name?" She listened for a moment. "Will you call back if you do remember? Anything at all, truly. All right. I understand. Thank you." She clicked off and handed me the phone.

"Vivian, what's this all about? What house?"

Fergus had lumbered over to her. He pushed himself up on his hind legs and licked her hand.

The phone rang again. This time it was Tom.

"Is Vivian with you?" He sounded tense.

"Yes. We just heard from the Parkers. A few days before their father left for Long Barston, he received an anonymous package in the mail. It contained a cigarette lighter in the shape of a derringer. Vivian remembers it from that summer at Hopley's."

"And she thinks it's connected with his death?"

"How could it be? The coroner said he died of natural causes."

"Not any more. We just got the test results. Will Parker died from an anaphylactic reaction to bee venom, all right, but no bees were involved."

"*What?*" I listened as Tom explained.

When we'd disconnected, Vivian nudged me. "What did he say?"

"He said the venom that killed Will Parker came from both honeybees and yellow hornets—a combination, like the venom doctors use to reduce the severity of a reaction."

"What does that mean?"

"It means that unless a bee and a hornet ganged up to sting him simultaneously in the exact same spot, Will Parker was murdered."

Vivian shot me a guilty look.

"What is it?"

"There was more to that week at Hopley's than a teenage crush, Kate. I haven't told you everything."

Chapter Eight

Vivian and I sat on the double bed in her chintz-papered bedroom. She'd changed into her gray robe and slippers. I'd put on a pair of navy sweats and a long-sleeved white T-shirt. Fergus eyed me resentfully from the rug. I was on his side of the bed.

"He was *murdered*?" Vivian's face was pinched and white. "How can that be?"

"All I know is it's been confirmed. The bee venom used to kill Will Parker is readily available and injectable."

Ribbons of steam rose from our mugs of strong tea, laced with lemon, honey, and a shot of whiskey—Vivian's all-purpose cure for headache, sore throat, chill, shock, fright, boredom, disappointment, rainy days, and missing out on Tesco's weekly half-price promotions.

"Who would have done such a thing?" Vivian took a sip. Then another. "And how could they know he'd react that violently?"

"His allergy wasn't a secret." I settled myself more comfortable against the pillows. "I think you'd better tell me about Hopley's."

"I don't know where to start."

"At the beginning." I took a sip and felt the warm liquid slide down my throat.

Vivian crossed her ankles. "I picked him out right away. Cutest boy in camp. The first night there was a pizza party for the teens. Will and I hooked up with Jack, Frankie, and Mary—more by default than anything. The others teens were all younger. The second night Mary and I went looking for the boys and found them near the ice cream kiosk. Will told us he'd discovered an abandoned house. He said something terrible had happened there. They were planning to investigate. He asked if Mary and I wanted to go along."

"How did Will know the house was abandoned?"

"He'd already been inside. He said no one had lived there for a long time."

"So you and Mary went."

"Of course—well, Mary didn't want to go at first, but she didn't want to be left out either, so we all went. The house wasn't far from the camp."

"What sort of house?"

"A very odd one. Ultramodern, white, plain as a barn. Flat roof, curved glass windows, a sort of tower with glass blocks. And little round windows high up that looked like portholes on a ship. I can't remember the name of the house—there was a sign—but we learned later it came from a tree growing in the front garden— some species I'd never seen before. Spiky leaves, hairy cones."

"You mean a monkey puzzle tree?"

"*That's it*—Monkey Puzzle House. The property was surrounded by a dense hedge that concealed a barred metal fence. Will had found a way in where someone had pried the bars apart. On one side of the house there was a doctor's surgery, closed up tight. We got in through a door at the back where the bolt had pulled away from the strike plate. My first impression was the family had simply walked out one day and never returned. There were dishes on the drainer, an ironing board and iron set up. A dog's bowl with something furry and horrible. But then—" Her voice faltered.

"But then?"

"We saw the drawing room." She folded her hands, rubbing one thumb along the other. "Will was right. Something terrible had happened there. Furniture was overturned. Drapes had been pulled off the rings. A glass ashtray lay smashed on the floor. The worst was the blood near the fireplace, all dried up and black but unmistakable. And bloody handprints and footprints as if someone had fallen in it and struggled to get away. And there was something else, too. Vomit, maybe." She shuddered.

"Someone had been murdered?"

"That's what Will thought."

"Why didn't you notify the police?"

"Kate, we were teenagers. Mostly we didn't want anyone to know we'd been there. Will made us swear we'd never tell anyone, ever." She gave a mirthless laugh. "I'm breaking my promise."

"And you thought you could figure out what had happened?"

"Will did. The other boys thought it was a bit of a laugh, but he was serious. Now I understand why. He'd grown up with crime and investigations."

"It sounds gruesome."

"It was at first, but Will made it into a kind of game, a challenge. He said whatever happened in the house had happened years before. It was a crime scene. All the clues were there. We just had to find them and figure it out."

"And you went along with it?"

"I just wanted to be with Will. And it *was* thrilling in a way. He made it seem like an adventure, a mystery to be solved. The drawing room was the only room with actual evidence of violence. Everywhere else, it was just weird. In the library, we found a book lying open, like someone had gotten up to do something and planned to come right back. The kitchen looked as if someone had finished cleaning up from dinner but hadn't had time to put the dishes away. In the largest bedroom, upstairs, we found a wallet, car keys, and eyeglasses on the bedside table. Who leaves those behind? And there was a suitcase on the floor, filled with men's clothes. In another bedroom, a young girl's clothes had been tossed on the bed as if she had just changed. In another, a bouquet of dead roses sat in a glass vase. Towels hung on a rack in the bathroom. The whole thing was creepy, like one of those old horror films where the slasher jumps out of a closet."

"Weren't you afraid someone would find you in the house and charge you with trespassing?"

"Not after that first time. We were young—invincible, you know. And it was obvious the house had been abandoned for a long time, just as Will said. We found a calendar in the kitchen from May 1961. The last date crossed out was May 19th. Will said that was a clue. Whatever happened had happened on that day or the next."

"Let me get this straight. You were there in July of 1963, but whatever happened to the family had happened in 1961, two years earlier."

"That's right. I didn't think about it at the time, but someone must have been maintaining the exterior. The taxes must have been paid. But we felt sure we were the only ones who'd been inside since it happened—whatever it was." She took a drink of her whiskey-laced tea.

"What about the cigarette lighter gun?"

"I'm getting to that. We went back every night that week. We'd meet right after the evening meal and head for the house, making sure we were back in camp before they locked the gates at nine. It was getting dark by then, anyway, and there was no electricity in the house. We began splitting up, going through each of the rooms. making a list of clues. Then we'd sit in the library—that was the room least affected—and propose scenarios, what each of us thought had happened to the family. But we had to defend our theory with evidence. Will kept track of everything in a notebook. It was exciting, like we were actually doing something important and people would find out later that we'd cracked the case. Like Cluedo."

"Cluedo?"

"You know—*Miss Scarlet in the drawing room with a candlestick.*"

"Oh—you mean *Clue.*"

"In England it's called Cluedo. It was really popular just then, so we patterned our investigations—that's what Will called them—after the game. We each chose a weapon to be our game piece. Will's was that cigarette lighter shaped like a gun, which the boys thought was cool. My game piece was a rope—really a twisted silk curtain cord we found hanging on a hook by the window." She furrowed her brow. "I'm trying to remember what the others chose. One of the boys, Jack I think, had a dagger. Someone had a spanner. It must have been Frankie because Mary had a chrome candlestick shaped like a torch. We'd do our investigating separately. Then we'd sit in a circle in the library, and when it was our turn to propose a theory, we'd place our weapon in the center. Will would write down what we said and the evidence for it. Then the others would say why that could or couldn't have happened, and he'd write that down, too. He said we were narrowing the possibilities, and that in the end, we'd come up with a scenario that fit all the evidence."

"What clues did you find?"

"We started by figuring out who the family was. That was easy. There were letters and bills. A driving license in the wallet. I don't remember the names anymore, but the father was a doctor. We already knew that because of the surgery, but Will found medical records in his study. We found the wife's handbag—that's strange, isn't it? Women don't go anywhere without their handbag."

I had to agree.

"They had four children, three daughters and a son. Oh, wait—I do remember one name. The youngest daughter was called Dulcie, short for Dulcett. I remember thinking it was so much prettier than Vivian. We knew she was younger than the others because there were dolls and stuffed animals in her room. Anyway, we started building a profile of the family, to see if there were clues there as to what had happened."

"And what did you find?"

"Nothing that gave us any real answers. Just curious things, like the fact that the mattress on the bed in the parents' bedroom was missing. Jack said it was because they were murdered in their sleep, and someone took the mattress away because it was soaked with blood. And then there was the blood near the fireplace. Will said they must have been trying to phone for help because that's where the telephone was." She wrinkled her nose. "We had all sorts of theories. The family was killed by burglars, by drug addicts caught raiding the surgery, by an escaped mental patient. The scenarios got more ridiculous as we went along." She huffed. "A bizarre blood-cult ceremony. Charades gone awry. Alien abduction—that one was Jack's suggestion. Will said Jack wasn't taking it seriously."

"Why didn't you just ask someone?"

Vivian made a face. "I told you. Will made us swear and hope to die we'd never tell anyone, ever. If we asked someone what happened, we'd have to explain why we wanted to know, and that would give our investigation away. And then, I suppose, because we wouldn't have had a mystery to solve. Will was obsessed, but by the end of the week, the rest of us were frankly getting a bit bored with it all. Then the week was up. We all went home."

"Haven't you been curious all these years about what really happened in the house?"

"I wasn't all that curious then. I mean I was, but the big draw for me was Will. I just wanted to be with him, Kate. I was besotted. He was all business. He really thought we could figure it out and enlighten the world or something. When I heard he was CID, my first thought was, 'Of course, what else?'"

"So you went every night and played the game?"

"It was exciting, doing something our parents wouldn't approve of. Every night Will would write down what we'd found, and he'd rank the theories according to the evidence. He made us swear, too, that we wouldn't take anything out of the house. Some of the evidence he collected in a metal box he'd found. He said we had to leave everything there for future investigators. He talked about that a lot, that we were doing the spade work. We'd lay it all out for someone to find later."

"What was your conclusion?"

"I don't think there was one. At the end of the week, Will organized everything—all the clues, all our investigations, our game pieces, and the evidence we'd collected, and he put everything in that metal box. He wrote out a sort of document of our findings, pages and pages, and he made us all sign it. We were the Five Sleuths." She laughed. "Then the week was over, and I never saw any of them again."

"And now, fifty-some years later, someone sent Will the game piece he'd used—the gun—and Will told his son something had resurfaced about an old case. Then he was murdered."

"By the person who sent the gun, do you think?"

"I don't know, but they must be connected. The person who sent the package might be one of the four other Sleuths—well, three others since we know it wasn't you. Who else could it be?"

"You're saying either Jack, Frankie, or Mary returned to the house, located the box with the game pieces, and sent the gun to Will? Why?"

"Well, *someone* found the metal box. Where did Will hide it?"

"He wouldn't tell us. Said it was better we didn't know."

"Will Parker's game piece arrived in the mail and just days later he traveled to Long Barston to see you." I glanced at Vivian to see her reaction.

"Did he think *I'd* sent the package?"

"Maybe. Or maybe he wanted to know if you'd received a package too. And let's not forget what he told Jayne Collier—'I think I saw someone I know—someone who shouldn't be here.' That couldn't have been you because we were having dinner at Finchley Hall. Have you ever seen any of the others in Long Barston?"

"You must be joking. After nearly sixty years? I wouldn't recognize them if I had—or them me. We're all in our seventies." She downed the rest of her tea and set the cup on the bedside table. "I would like to know what happened to that family."

"I would too. It may be the key to Will Parker's murder." I slid off the bed, causing Fergus to woof hopefully. "Let's see if we can find out."

* * *

"Okay—where was this holiday camp?" I settled back on Vivian's bed with my laptop and logged onto her Wi-Fi.

"Miracle-on-Sea."

"*What?*" I stared at her. "That's where Ivor and I went last week—to that Victorian mental hospital. Why didn't you say something?"

"You never told me where you were going, did you? But now you mention it, I remember the sanatorium. You could see it from camp—the towers, anyway. What was it called?"

"Netherfield."

"I remember."

I typed "Miracle-on-Sea" into the search bar and added "Monkey Puzzle House."

A series of articles popped up. And images.

"Is this the house?" I turned the computer screen toward Vivian.

She sucked in a breath. "Yes. I told you it was strange."

The house with its plain white surfaces and aerodynamic design looked like a steamship in drydock. I scanned the first article. "Seems the exterior of the house was used in some films and TV series. Listen to this:

Monkey Puzzle House on the Suffolk coast has been selected as an exterior for the film version of the classic British mystery An English Murder *by Cyril Hare, slated for release later this year. The house, built in 1932 and unoccupied since the early 1960s, is a stunning example of the Streamline Moderne or Modernist architectural style, representing the final phase of Art Deco when Britain faced a worldwide depression and architects embraced a new aesthetic focused on functional efficiency and industrial design.*

The film's director, Paul Gorey, said, 'The moment we saw the house, we knew we had to use it. We spent a packet on exterior renovation but feel certain the expense will be worth it.'

"When was the article written?" Vivian asked.
"April of 2002." I continued reading.

'Due to a legal battle over ownership rights, the home of the late Dr. Simon Beaufoy—

"Beaufoy—that was the name of the family," Vivian said. "Go on."

—has been sealed up for more than forty years. 'We were denied access to the interior', Gorey said, 'so we can only speculate about what one might find within.' Monkey Puzzle House is no stranger to the visual arts. The house was featured in a 1992 documentary about the architecture of the early twentieth century. The exterior has also been used as a location for several television dramas, including the 1997 miniseries based on Agatha Christie's The Little Grey Cells of Hercule Poirot *and the more recent* Dr. Thorndyke, Detective *series by Austin Freeman.*

"Nothing about the family and why they abandoned the house?"
"I'm looking." I scrolled through the search results. "Oh—here's an article from the same newspaper, and it's more recent—last year."

The historic Beaufoy house near Miracle-on-Sea is on the market after the executrix of the estate, Justine Beaufoy, died at the age of 79. After decades in legal limbo, the Monkey Puzzle House near Miracle-on-Sea is finally for sale. The house was abandoned after the tragic poisoning deaths in 1961 of Dr. Simon Beaufoy and his wife, Mrs. Nancy Beaufoy.

I looked at Vivian. "Poisoning deaths? You said there was blood."

"There was blood. You don't forget a thing like that."

"But it says 'deaths,' not 'murders,'" I said. "That implies accidental poisoning."

Vivian huffed. "You wouldn't have convinced Will of that. Besides, how do you accidentally poison yourself?"

"Lots of ways, I should think. Let me finish reading."

Since the deaths of the Beaufoys, the estate was administered by their eldest daughter, Justine—

Vivian was making little noises of agreement.

—who, with the support of her younger sister, Millicent, blocked the attempts of their brother to force a sale. Grayson Beaufoy, second oldest of the siblings, died in 2010 at the age of 66 in a boating accident off the Suffolk coast. After Justine's recent death, the surviving sisters, Millicent, 72, and Dulcett, 68, contacted a local estate agent.

Although the house is in a derelict state, the architecture and period furnishings reveal what the once-grand home must have looked like in its heyday. Inside, prospective buyers will find six bedrooms, three bathrooms, and six living spaces. The property includes an attached doctor's surgery as well as a garage and utility space. Also included in the sale is a 1959 Bentley Saloon. Surrounding the home are four acres of gardens and trees.

Fordyce Estate Agents are handling the sale. Up until March 25, prospective buyers are invited to place their best and final offers for a chance to renovate this historic property.

"I want to see the house again," Vivian said.

"I'd like to see it, too, but I'm more interested in finding out what happened to the Beaufoys."

I was about to Google the name *Beaufoy* when my cell phone rang.

I glanced at the caller ID. "It's the Parkers again."

"I suppose you've heard," Stephanie said. "Will was murdered. Hugh is in shock."

"I'm so sorry." I scrambled to think of something to say that didn't sound lame. "You were right to be skeptical about the EpiPen."

"Thank you, but I didn't call for sympathy. Something else has turned up. We'll notify the police tomorrow, but in the meantime, we thought you should know. When Hugh was at the flat today, he found his father's laptop and decided to bring it home. We had quite a time figuring out the password—it turned out to be the date he entered the police force as a constable. Two eleven sixty-four. I'll let Hugh tell you what else he found."

"It's Will's computer," I whispered to Vivian and turned the phone on speaker again.

"We haven't gotten very far," said Hugh Parker, "but I checked Dad's search history and found several lines of research we thought you'd want to know about. At the top of list was Monkey Puzzle House. Ring any bells?"

"Like Big Ben," I said.

"And four names. He'd made a list—Jack Cavanagh, Vivian Bunn, Frank Keane, and Mary—no last name, just some question marks. It doesn't appear he found anything for Frank Keane, but he did find a Jack Cavanagh who once owned an industrial cleaning service near Stanstead airport."

"That proves it," Vivian said. "Will Parker was investigating the deaths at Monkey Puzzle House."

"Was there an address or contact information for Jack Cavanagh?" I asked.

"Sorry, no. I'll keep looking."

"And you still haven't found the EpiPen?"

"Not a trace. We think the killer must have taken it." His voice cracked.

"I'm going to put Vivian on. She can tell you about Monkey Puzzle House."

I clicked off speaker, handed Vivian the phone, and she began to tell her story.

As she did, I thought about the three remaining sleuths—Jack, Frankie, and Mary. Surely they couldn't be murderers. Not at their age.

But one of them could very well be the next victim.

Chapter Nine

❧

Friday, August 29

Tom arrived home late the next morning and phoned to say he'd pick me at seven for dinner.

The day seemed never-ending. No customers at the shop. Not even browsers. Ivor busied himself checking the online auctions. I perched behind the counter and thought about Will Parker. I'd felt unsettled ever since the conversation with his son and daughter-in-law the night before. Stephanie had proposed a theory that someone her father-in-law put behind bars might have sought revenge. That was possible. But I couldn't ignore the connections to Monkey Puzzle House—the anonymous package with the game piece, Will's cryptic suggestion that the package was connected with a cold case, the names of the Five Sleuths on his computer, his trip to Long Barston to find Vivian.

Had Will Parker believed Vivian sent the package or had he come to warn her? In my mind, everything hinged on the identity of the person Will Parker saw the night he was murdered—the one he thought he recognized.

Long Barston is a relatively small village. Someone else might have noticed a stranger in town that night. Two strangers, actually. I pulled out my phone and tapped a message to the Parkers:

This is Kate. Would you text me an image of the photograph taken the day Will retired? Someone here might have seen a stranger that night. I'd like to ask around.

I had other questions too. How easy would it have been to inject Will Parker with bee venom? Who knew the severity of his allergy? Most important, was Vivian in danger?

Maybe the police had learned something.

If they had, how much could Tom tell me?

*　*　*

The Trout, a tiny fourteenth-century pub outside Tom's village of Saxby St. Clare, was one of our favorites. Authentic, unspoiled, intimate, no pretensions. Just a short menu of delicious entrees, lovingly prepared by the publican's wife—and privacy. We loved the Three Magpies in Long Barston, but there was no chance whatsoever of spending time there without the whole village knowing what we had to eat and drink, what we talked about, and how many times we went to the loo. Here at the Trout we were practically anonymous.

"Scene of the crime," Tom said as a young woman showed us to our favorite table for two, tucked into a small bay window.

"Proposing to me was a crime?" I pretended offense, remembering the night three months earlier when Tom had gone down on his knee in that very pub.

"Guilty as charged."

I grinned at him. "How was the trip—successful?"

"Very. I'll tell you all about it, but first I want to hear about the Parkers in Peterborough. They've been informed about the murder."

"Yes, I know. They called last night. I asked them to send me this." I pulled up the photo of Will Parker on my phone. "How much do the police know?"

"About Will Parker's death?"

"About the summer at Hopley's, about Monkey Puzzle House and Cluedo."

"The child's game?" He looked at me sideways. "You'd better tell me."

"Here's the short version. In July of 1963, Vivian's family spent a week at Hopley's Holiday Camp. You know that much. Here's what you don't know: Vivian, Will Parker, and three other teens stumbled onto a crime scene—or at least that's what they believed." I explained about the deaths of the Beaufoys in 1961 and about the house, which the oldest daughter refused to sell.

My story was interrupted by the waiter, who brought menus, handwritten on small parchment sheets.

When he'd gone, I finished the story, ending with the blood in the drawing room and the game of Cluedo with the five game pieces.

"Fifty-eight years later, someone sent Will Parker the game piece he'd used that week—a cigarette lighter in the shape of a small derringer. Will was convinced the Beaufoys had been murdered. The night before they were to leave Hopley's, Will put the gun, the dagger, the candlestick, the spanner, and the rope in a large metal box he'd found and hid it somewhere in the house along with a list of motives and some pieces of evidence he considered important. He made each of them sign their names—they called themselves the Five Sleuths—for the benefit of what he called *future investigators*."

"Hmm." Tom's eyebrows drew together.

"Something's on your mind," I said.

"According to my source in Peterborough, DS Parker earned quite a reputation for himself over the years. They called him the Pit Bull because once he got his teeth into a case, he wouldn't let go. After a few years of retirement, I can imagine how receiving that game piece in the mail would have fueled his old instincts."

"What bothers me," I said, "is how the killer knew about Will Parker's allergy to bee venom. That suggests someone who knew him personally, someone who knew he'd have an EpiPen with him and made sure he couldn't use it. But I can't figure out what any of this has to do with Monkey Puzzle House."

"We don't know Will Parker's death was connected with Monkey Puzzle House, Kate. I have great respect for your intuition, as you are well aware; but in this case, you may be on the wrong track."

"What do you mean?"

"Assuming one thing is the cause of something else. Like saying 'Your parents nicknamed you *Lambie*; therefore they must be sheep farmers.'"

"Go on."

"It's more likely Will Parker was murdered by someone with a grudge against him. A criminal, for example, who'd felt unjustly convicted. Even a relative who blamed him for not making his wife get treatment for her cancer earlier. Just because the two things—the arrival of the package and the murder—happened in sequence doesn't mean they're related."

He had a point. "But how does the missing EpiPen fit in? He always carried it."

A waiter delivered a bottle of sparkling water and a plate of the Trout's artichoke and spinach dip with ciabatta toast. Tom dipped a finger of toast in the cheesy dip. "Maybe he left the EpiPen on the bus. Things like that do happen."

"Exactly on the one day in forty years when he would actually need it? Come on, Tom—that's too much of a coincidence."

"Even Hercule Poirot was prepared to accept one coincidence in a case. By the way, what *did* happen to the owners of the house? I'm sure you looked it up."

"The house was owned by Dr. Simon Beaufoy, his wife, and four children. The parents were poisoned—accidentally, the article implied. Somehow the children survived, and they kept the house, empty but exactly as it was on the night of their parents' deaths. About a year ago the oldest daughter died—she was the executor—and the house was put up for sale. Someone, at some time, must have found Will Parker's metal box, read the evidence the teens compiled, and saw the five names. I don't know what to make of that, but whatever that person's motive for sending the package, Will Parker took it seriously enough to look up the other Sleuths—the names he remembered, anyway—and he traveled all the way to Long Barston to talk with Vivian. Someone made sure he never got that opportunity."

"You're taking a lot for granted," Tom said. "All we really know is that Will Parker was injected with the kind of bee venom used medically in the UK."

"How easy would that have been?"

"Quite easy, but it would have had to be planned out in advance. It's possible he did it himself."

"Committed suicide? No, Tom. That doesn't wash. He'd been doing research. You said it yourself—he was the Pit Bull."

"All right, I agree. Eacles has his heart set on a criminal Parker put behind bars. He even has a candidate—a burglar Parker nicked just before his retirement. Insisted Parker planted evidence. He was released two months ago."

"Stephanie Parker mentioned something like that. But how did this criminal find the game piece?"

"That's the catch. Do the Parkers believe Will's death was connected with Monkey Puzzle House?"

"Not yet. But they know he wanted to find Vivian. Obviously, someone didn't want him to talk with her."

"What are you saying?"

"I'm saying there's a connection. And don't say 'Here we go again.' There are too many unanswered questions."

"I won't—there are unanswered questions. But I'm paid to investigate crimes, Kate, not coincidences. We start with what actually happened. Murder by bee venom. Unusual, I admit. Then we trace it back in time, looking for motive and opportunity. But not six decades back in time. If I tell DCI Eacles I'm investigating a potential crime that occurred in—when was it?"

"In 1961. But I'm not asking you to investigate. Just listen."

"You mean 'listen—and then do a little research in the police databases,' right?" He signaled for the waiter.

"Would you?"

"Kate, you know I'd do anything for you. Well, outside of something illegal or immoral. You are my best friend, my love, my reason for living. Have I ever told you that?"

"Not in those precise terms." I was melting. Any moment I'd slide into a puddle of goo on the floor.

"Well, you are. So how can I help?"

"Is there any way you can find out what really happened to the Beaufoy family in 1961? I didn't come up with anything online except the bare bones. The Beaufoys were poisoned, and the article made it sound like a tragic accident. But what if it wasn't? He was a doctor, after all. Why didn't he recognize the symptoms and call for help? And why was there blood near the fireplace? What if someone knows it was murder and wanted to make sure Will Parker never talked with Vivian?"

"Kate, we're talking fifty-eight years—sixty if you go back to the actual event. That's longer than either of us have been alive. Even if the deaths in 1961 were suspicious, what happened to rake it up again so long after the fact?"

I was about to say I couldn't imagine when I had one of those unexpected mental leaps. "If you mean what changed, I can answer that. The house was put on the market. People had access to Monkey Puzzle House for the first time since 1961. I think the killer found the metal box and realized those long-ago children were onto him—or her."

"All right, look." Tom shook his head. "I do have a few favors to call in. I'll see what I can find. But don't expect anything startling. People are accidentally poisoned all the time—by food, household cleaning agents, pesticides, their own medications. Thankfully, most cases have nothing to do with murder."

The waiter chose that moment to arrive. "Have we decided?"

We both ordered the house specialty, grilled filet of Scottish salmon.

As Tom scanned the wine list, I reflected on the joys of life. You reach a fork in the road that requires a choice, a new path. My mother had chosen the path that led to Dr. James Lund. Now they were off on an extended honeymoon. They might never celebrate their tenth wedding anniversary, but they were seizing the joy while they could. *One crowded hour of glorious life.* No regrets. No looking back. As usual, Linnea Larson—now Linnea Lund—had paved the way for me. Life had brought me to this incredible place, sitting in one of Suffolk's most historic pubs with the most charming, handsome—

"What's going on with the Van Eyck painting?" Tom said, landing me with a thump back in the present.

"Nothing yet. The testing lab picked it up this morning, but that reminds me. The holiday camp where Vivian met Will Parker is located within a mile or so of the old Netherfield Sanatorium—now Cliff House. Another coincidence?"

"I think I mentioned a holiday camp there."

"You did, but I didn't know it was Vivian's holiday camp. That makes two coincidences, one more than allowed."

He gave me a wry smile. "Now who's the Pit Bull? I told you—I will try to find out what happened to the Beaufoys. Just don't blame me if there's nothing to learn."

Our dinners came—wildly delicious as usual—and we changed the topic to our upcoming wedding.

"Since we've settled on St. Æthelric's," Tom said, "I had a word with the rector yesterday. He suggested the first Saturday in November. We can have the reception in the church hall if you like."

"You're kidding, right? Lady Barbara would never forgive us. She'll insist on having the reception at Finchley Hall. And—I should have told you earlier—she intends to give us an engagement party. A small affair with close friends. She suggested next Friday, the fourth. Will that work with your schedule?"

"I'm sure it will." He laid down his knife and fork. "So we're agreed on the first Saturday in November for our wedding? I want to pin this down. Make sure I get plenty of time off for a honeymoon." He put his arm around me. "Somewhere private and romantic."

"Yes—all right." I smiled at him, feeling a little giddy. "I'll get the word out. My family will want to book flights."

"Now we're on a roll, let's push on to the honeymoon. Beach? Mountains? African safari? Cruise to the North Pole? Whatever makes you happy. I don't care in the least."

"Let's not rush that decision," I said. "Let's wait until the perfect idea occurs to us."

"All right." He poured me a glass of pinot noir. "We're really knocking the decisions out now. Where shall we call home?" He shot me a sidelong glance.

Oh dear—the decision I'd been avoiding. Believe me, it wasn't because I had any reservations about spending the rest of my life with Tom. But the question of where we would live as a married couple brought up two thorny issues. First was the possibility of Tom giving up his promotion to DCI and moving to a small town in Ohio where he knew no one and had no connections. No matter how hard I'd tried to picture it, I couldn't. The second issue was even thornier—Tom's house in Saxby St. Clare. Could I live in England? Absolutely. I'd come to love this small corner of Suffolk and the people now very dear to my heart. My mother wasn't alone anymore. My children were about as likely to remain in Jackson Falls as I was to take up train-hopping as a hobby. And there were such things as airplanes.

The problem was Tom's mother. I knew for a fact she couldn't afford to buy a place of her own, and Tom would never ask her to leave. Did that mean if I agreed to settle in Suffolk, I'd be sharing a house with Liz Mallory? That wasn't just a bridge too far—that was the bridge over the River Kwai. Explosions to follow.

When I didn't respond, Tom said, "I've already told you—I'm willing to move to the States. More than willing. Just tell me what you want."

A small, dark cloud took up position over our heads.

Chapter Ten

After clearing our dinner plates, the waiter delivered small bowls of Pavlova, the baked meringue dessert, with fresh raspberries. My absolute favorite.

"The problem is, Tom, I don't know what I want. I don't know what *you* want. More to the point, I don't know what will make us happy."

"We've already made the important decision—we want to spend the rest of our lives together. Where on the planet that takes us is secondary." He took my hand. "How about narrowing things down? Which countries are out of the running?"

"My Spanish is appalling. How about yours?"

"Mine, too, and we're probably too old to learn Russian or Chinese or Finnish, so we'll have to rule those countries out."

"Probably best." I took the first bite of the Pavlova. *Oh my.*

"We're making progress," Tom said. "Nowhere in Asia or South America, then. Or France."

"Why not? Your French is quite good."

"It's France." He took a bite. "How's your German?"

"Excellent, as long as I converse with children under the age of three. Now, I *can* recite a poem in Norwegian, but that's probably not enough, is it?"

"Probably not."

"I suppose the North and South Poles are out?"

"Let's say nowhere within five thousand miles of the polar ice caps. Too cold."

"Not too close to the equator, either. I don't like to sweat."

"Australia? New Zealand?"

"Poisonous snakes. Poisonous spiders."

By the time the waiter arrived, we were laughing like a couple of teenagers.

"Coffee and cognac by the fire?"

I gathered up my handbag. Tom slid his phone into the pocket of his jacket.

A few small logs were burning in the grate. We put our feet up on the low bench. Tom put his arm around me, and I leaned against him on the ancient leather sofa.

Coffee and drinks arrived on a tray with four squares of gourmet chocolate.

"This really is the scene of the crime," Tom said. "This is where I proposed—right here."

"And where I said yes."

He smiled at me. "So I can't think of a more perfect place to give you this." He reached inside his jacket and pulled out a small, black box.

I felt a lump forming in my throat.

He lifted the lid, and there, nestled inside, was a ring. A diamond ring, a square Asscher cut on filigreed platinum.

When I could speak, I said, "Tom, it's beautiful. It's antique. Art Deco."

"Do you like it?" he asked, looking suddenly unsure. "I know it's old-fashioned. We can have it reset if you like."

"No, please. It's perfect."

"My great-great-grandfather Hartley purchased the center diamond in South Africa in the 1880s. His son, my great-grandfather, had it set in 1921 for his bride. Later, my grandfather gave it to my grandmother. I remember her wearing it. Uncle Nigel always planned to give it to his own bride. Unfortunately, he never succeeded in narrowing the field. Now it's mine to give to the most beautiful, fascinating, intelligent, and charming woman I've ever known."

I blinked away tears. "I thought your cousin was Nigel's heir."

"He is—as far as the house and the estate are concerned. Fouroaks is an old estate, entailed on the eldest male heir. But Nigel has a sizable fortune of his own, Kate. Turns out he was rather good at investments. He's free to leave his personal property to whomever he chooses. That's where I've been—to Fouroaks. Nigel summoned me. He's in the process of making a new will. The ring is mine—and now it's yours, darling Kate. It's a family heirloom with great sentimental value for me, but that means nothing if you don't like it. Truly, Kate. If you don't, you must say so."

"May I try it on?"

He pulled the ring out of the box and slipped it on my finger.

"I love it." I sniffed and wiped my eyes. "It's beautiful. It's stunning. It's—*big*." I broke off, wondering if a thief might consider it worthwhile to chop off my finger.

"Too big? I know you're not one for ostentation."

"No." I had to smile. "It's not too big. It's perfect." I kissed him. Then I kissed him again.

"Does it fit?" Tom asked.

"Almost. This feels like a seven. I wear a six."

"I know a jeweler in Bury. I'll have it resized—if you're sure. You are sure, Kate, aren't you? You're not just saying you like it to please me."

"Tom," I held up my left hand, watching the stones sparkle in the firelight. "You told me once love isn't measured in diamonds. I agree—it isn't. But to wear a ring that means something to you, not something you picked out in a jewelry store but a ring that comes from your heart, that makes it very precious to me, no matter what it's worth."

Now he was the one having trouble speaking. He cleared his throat. "That's good, then."

"Let's not tell anyone about the ring until I can actually wear it, all right?"

"Of course—whatever you want. We can unveil the ring at Lady Barbara's party."

"Yes, let's do that." As soon as I said it, an unpleasant thought reared its unpleasant head. "If it's a family ring, why didn't your mother get it?"

"Long story, Kate. Uncle Nigel didn't approve of my father—on solid grounds, as it turned out. He was never faithful. He had designs on the inheritance he assumed my mother would get. It all came out later. As head of the family, the ring belonged to Nigel, but when mother announced she was engaged, he offered the ring to her, along with several other pieces of their mother's jewelry. She said no, Kate. In fact, she refused to take anything from him—even a wedding gift. She was that bitter—and that determined to prove my father wasn't after her money. Nigel's never mentioned it, but I think her refusal hurt him deeply. She still resents the fact that he was right. Over the years, Nigel's done all he could for her—and for me. He's been the father I never had."

"What about your daughter, Olivia? Shouldn't the ring go to her?"

Tom almost choked on his coffee. "*Olivia?* Not in this lifetime. Olivia calls engagement rings 'symbols of bondage.' The only jewelry she wears is made of stainless steel and pierces various parts of her body." He shot me an ironic smile. "I did ask. She said—her exact words—'I'd sooner wear a chastity belt.'"

"Maybe she'll change her mind."

"That isn't going to happen. Besides, Olivia has her own trust fund from her great-grandfather Hartley. She can buy as many rings as she likes."

I remembered Tom saying Nigel lived in a castle in Devon, but I'd assumed it was an exaggeration. Now I was beginning to wonder.

"Nigel is going to adore you, Kate, as I do."

After all Tom had said about Uncle Nigel, I was pretty sure I was going to adore him, too. "And you're positive your mother won't mind about the ring?"

"Why would she?"

I could think of several reasons. In Scotland, Tom told me his mother didn't like Americans. He'd also told me I'd win her over.

Tom picked up my hand and kissed it. "Mother will be delighted. You'll see."

Maybe. When the ravens abandon the Tower of London.

Chapter Eleven

~

Saturday, August 29

Since tourist season was winding down, Saturday hours at The Curiosity Cabinet had switched to afternoons only, one to four. I met Ivor there just after twelve thirty. We unpacked several boxes that had arrived the previous day and then began to prepare a gray marble head of the Roman goddess Minerva for shipment to Germany. The head, second century A.D., had recently sold to an antiquities dealer in Berlin. Packing was complicated, requiring an entire roll of cotton batting, what seemed like an acre of bubble wrap, several gallons of packing peanuts, and three sturdy boxes, the final one a wooden crate.

"You're quiet this morning," Ivor said, sealing up the second box with tape. "Something bothering you?"

"Of course not."

Where to start? I still had serious misgivings about Liz Mallory's reaction to my engagement ring, but out of loyalty to Tom, I wouldn't share them with Ivor. Besides, we'd decided to keep the ring a secret until Lady Barbara's party.

"There's news about the man who died in the graveyard," I said, deciding to work up to the information I'd learned about the financial woes of Pyramid Development. "He was murdered—injected with bee venom, which caused a severe allergic reaction, leading to death."

"Really? That's terrible."

"Will Parker was ex-CID. He'd come to see Vivian." I gave him the bare bones about Vivian's week at Hopley's and the Five Sleuths. "About two weeks ago, Will Parker received an anonymous package containing his game piece—a cigarette lighter in the shape of a derringer pistol. He told his son he'd received new information about a cold case."

Ivor wound a strip of clear tape over a layer of bubble wrap, securing it in place. "You're implying the deaths then and the murder of Will Parker now are related. Kate, do you realize how old that first killer would be today? Assuming he wasn't a child in 1961, he'd be in his late seventies or eighties. Or dead." He lowered the second box into the final peanut-filled crate for shipment. "Even if a killer exists, why would he assume the Five Sleuths, now pensioners themselves, could identify him?" He lowered his brows. "*Can* Vivian identify him?"

"No. But I don't like unanswered questions. And Vivian's determined to find out why Will Parker came all that way to see her. I don't blame her."

"I don't either," Ivor said. "A little digging into the past never hurts."

"Unless you dig up a murderer."

"Well, if there's anything I can do to help, let me know."

"Thanks, Ivor." I tapped a few keys on the computer keyboard and the printer spit out a mailing label. "Speaking of the past, I did some research into the history of the Cliff House board. Guess what I found?"

"The project is in financial trouble. They haven't sold enough units to recoup the initial outlay of cash. They're in debt to several subcontractors."

"How do you know that?"

"I *can* use a computer, Kate. I also know about the lawsuit involving the snuff boxes and Niall Walker's law firm."

"What do you think—was the old lady coerced?"

"No way of knowing. Maybe she truly had fond memories of Netherfield. The way Dr. Underwood described it, the sanatorium sounded like a holiday at a five-star resort."

"Did you know Nicola Netherfield designed Tony Currie's London flat? That's probably how they met. And Martyn Lee-Jones gave up a well-paying executive position with a successful import firm in Kent to become manager of a residential community on the Suffolk coast. Why would he do that?"

"Good question. Did you learn anything useful about Dr. Underwood?"

"Just that he's an expert on Victorian mental hospitals and wrote a pamphlet on Netherfield. Oh, and his father was an advocate for euthanasia. But why is Underwood on the board? Did he invest money in the project? The Pyramid website mentioned a group of investors."

"Nothing to do with us, Kate." Ivor fixed the mailing label on the crate. "Our concern is the auction. Apollo Research promised to have preliminary results on the Van Eyck by Monday."

A pang of guilt seized me. "I hope the painting is genuine. Have you seen the original sale documents?"

"Everything appears to be in order. Horace Netherfield bought the painting on a trip abroad with his wife in 1877. He was taken by the image and decided on the spot to make it the centerpiece of his proposed sanitorium."

The bell jangled and a young man entered the shop. "Browsing," he mumbled.

"Help yourself." Ivor waved a hand in the direction of the display cabinets. "The cabinets are numbered. If you have questions, you have only to ask."

"Thanks." The young man bent to examine a nearby cabinet of ancient Norse jewelry and other small metal objects from the pre-Norman period.

"Do we know the name of the family who owned the painting before Netherfield bought it?" I lowered my voice.

"No—and there's no reference to *Christ Healing the Demoniac* in the literature."

"Doesn't that worry you?"

"Not really. If a painting has been out of circulation for nearly six centuries, it's possible—" Ivor stopped speaking as we realized the customer was doing all his browsing in our immediate vicinity.

"Are you looking for something in particular?" Ivor asked him.

The young man looked up. "A gift for my grandmother."

"We have objects in all price ranges," I said. "What does she like?"

"She likes paintings. In fact, she might want to sell one or two, now that she's moving into a care home."

Ivor looked at me. We were thinking the same thing.

"Why don't you bring your grandmother in?" Ivor said. "We'd be happy to discuss it with her."

"I will. Thanks." The young man ducked out the door.

"Ivor—was he listening to our conversation?"

"Or waiting for us to walk away from the counter. Remember that face."

"Should I say something to Tom?"

"What would you say? He hasn't done anything illegal yet."

"True." I thought about my conversation with Tom at the Trout. Suspicions aren't enough to launch a police investigation. They needed evidence of a crime.

"What are you doing Tuesday?" Ivor asked.

"Nothing particular—why?"

"I'd like you to deliver the snuff boxes to Cliff House. I'll feel better when they're out of the shop."

"Sure. Anything else I can do while I'm there?"

"Purchase one of their flats?"

"I'll check my piggy bank. Which reminds me—did you know Hopley's, the holiday camp where Vivian met Will Parker, was in Miracle-on-Sea?"

"Was it indeed?" Ivor looked up. "I'm surprised no one claimed an escaped metal patient from Netherfield killed the Beaufoys."

"That was one of the theories, as a matter of fact, but the newspaper article implied the poisoning was accidental."

"A common euphemism."

"What do you mean?"

"I mean it may have been murder-suicide, hushed up for the sake of the family."

"You mean Dr. Beaufoy murdered his wife and then took his own life?"

"Or the other way around."

It was an excellent point. I remembered Will Parker's conviction that something terrible had happened in that house. Murder-suicide was about as terrible as it gets. Ivor implied the true nature of the crime might have been concealed for the sake of the children. I should have considered them—four children who escaped poisoning that night. There would be files, records from an inquest. The two oldest—Justine and Grayson—were dead, but how about the two younger girls? Surely they'd know what really happened to their parents and why the house had been abandoned all those years. They might even know who found Will Parker's metal box. Someone would be able to tell us where they lived.

* * *

We closed the shop at four, and I was back at Rose Cottage by four thirty. Vivian had left a note on the kitchen table. She and Fergus were helping Lady Barbara sort through wallpaper catalogs. I'd find cheddar scones in the Aga's warming oven.

I put the kettle on, made myself a mug of Yorkshire Gold, buttered a scone, and carried everything up to my room under the thatch.

I was sorry Vivian wasn't home. On the way back from The Curiosity Cabinet it occurred to me she might like to tag along on Tuesday when I delivered the snuff boxes to Cliff House. Since we'd be near Miracle-on-Sea, we could visit what was left of Hopley's Holiday Camp and probably find Monkey Puzzle House as well. I was as curious as she was to see the place.

In the meantime, I'd try to learn as much as I could about Jack Cavanagh. If Will Parker found him, I could, too. I pulled out my computer and typed in *Jack Cavanagh London*.

The search results numbered in the thousands. I'd have to narrow it down, but how? Vivian said Jack Cavanagh had lived somewhere in or near London in 1963, but who was to say he still did?

The only other information I had was his age. He'd been sixteen in 1963, which meant if he was still alive, he'd be seventy-four. Two years younger than Will Parker. I could always pay one of those people-finder services, but last May when I'd done a background check on the rector, Edmund Foxe, I'd gotten the information I needed through Yahoo UK. It could work again.

On the Yahoo site, I typed in *Jack Cavanagh age 74*. This time the results numbered in the hundreds rather than the thousands. Then I remembered one more piece of information. Hugh Parker said Jack Cavanagh once owned an industrial cleaning service near Stanstead. I added that to the search bar and pushed *enter*.

One entry popped up. An obituary. Recent.

Suddenly on 16th August, Jack Cavanagh, aged 74 years. Former co-owner of Bright Star Cleaning Services. Survived by wife Helen; daughters Susan and Cheryl. Funeral service to be held at Marchmont Crematorium on Wednesday, 19th August, at 10:30 a.m. No flowers. Donations to Cardiac Research UK. All enquiries to Just Cremations, West Ealing.

I read it again. Jack Cavanagh was dead. Another coincidence? *Donations to Cardiac Research UK.* A seventy-four-year-old man dying of heart failure isn't headline news. And yet what were the chances of Jack Cavanagh and Will Parker dying within a week of each other?

The sound of a door opening below told me Vivian and Fergus had returned. I heard Vivian urging Fergus to stand still while she cleaned his paws.

"Vivian," I called down the stairs, "can you come up here for a minute? I found something on the computer."

She lumbered up the stairs.

"Look at this." I showed her Jack Cavanagh's obituary.

She pursed her lips in thought. "You know I never pry into people's personal affairs, but I think we should phone Jack Cavanagh's wife."

I was momentarily silenced, wrapping my head around *Vivian Bunn* and *never pries* in the same sentence. "What would we give as a reason for calling?"

Vivian huffed. "An old friend wishing to extend condolences."

"First of all, you're not an old friend. And second, we don't have the phone number."

She waved at the computer. "It's in there somewhere. Look in the British Telecom white pages."

I did, and sure enough, there was the number—Jack Cavanagh, Asbury Gardens, West Ealing.

"Use your mobile," Vivian said. "So she can't trace my number."

Little chance of that. Vivian's landline was still listed under the name of her old boss, Cedru Finchley-fforde. Still, it wasn't worth arguing. "Fine, but when she answers, I'm handing the phone to you, *old friend*."

I dialed, but the number went immediately to a recording.

"Out of service," I said. "She must have moved."

"Look her up."

"How am I supposed to do that?"

Vivian gave me a disapproving look.

"Oh, all right." I typed in the name, but after finding no trace of Helen Cavanagh in West Ealing or any of the surrounding areas, I gave up. "We're not going to find her."

"The funeral home will know where she lives."

"Vivian—they're not going to give that information to just anyone. Besides, they're probably closed."

"And people die during business hours, do they? Look up the number and hand me the phone." She'd set her jaw in that determined line I'd seen on the old photograph from Hopley's.

I found the website for Just Cremations, punched in the number, and handed the phone to Vivian.

"Hello, Just Cremations? Sorry—could you speak up? I'm a bit deaf." Vivian's voice had taken on an elderly quaver. "I do hate to bother you, but I've had no luck contacting the family of Jack Cavanagh. I'm an old friend, you see. I knew Helen before we were married, and I wanted to send her flowers. Is she still at Asbury Gardens, West Ealing?" Vivian listened. "Oh, I see. Silly me. I probably knew that. My memory isn't what it once was, either. She lives with whom, did you say? Yes, I'll contact her. Lovely girl. She was married to . . . Of course—*Cooper*. How could I have forgotten? Thank you. You've been very kind."

Vivian clicked off and handed me the phone. "They were separated. Helen lives in Eastwick with her daughter Cheryl." She pronounced *Cheryl* with a *ch*, like *cherry*. "Look her up. Cheryl Cooper."

"I'm sure you've broken some law, but I admit to being impressed."

Vivian gave me a self-satisfied smile.

It didn't take long to find Cheryl Cooper in Eastwick. This time, in case Vivian got my cell number posted on some international watch list, I made the call. Someone answered on the third ring.

"Four nine oh nine," came a mellifluous female voice.

"Hello." I attempted to sound cheerful and non-spammy. "Is this Helen Cavanagh?"

"Hold on a moment." I heard a few muffled words. Then another voice.

"What d'yer want?" *Surly.*

"I heard about your husband's death, and I was wondering if—"

"Warned yer to stop callin' me, didn't I," she hissed. "I'm givin' no statements. I 'ad nuffink to do wi' 'is death. 'Eart problems it were. Doctor said so."

"I think there's some misunderstanding. I'm calling because a friend of your husband's—"

"Owed yer money, did 'e? Well, it's yer problem, luv."

"No, no. Nothing like that. It's about Hopley's Holiday Camp, back in the—"

"And yer finkin' I'm takin' a 'oliday any time soon? Do me a favor." She hung up.

I blinked.

"Maybe I should have tried." Vivian plucked a piece of invisible lint off her cardigan.

"She thought I was a reporter. Then she said something about owing money. I never got a chance to explain."

"Never mind. We'll think of something." Her eyes lit up. "We could pretend to be the Irish Sweepstakes, calling to verify her husband's winning ticket."

"Don't be ridiculous."

Vivian shot me an aggrieved look. "We'll have our dinner while we think."

We headed for the kitchen, where Vivian had a filet of locally caught haddock ready for pan frying, a Caesar salad, a loaf of her amazing treacle bread, and a bottle of Chablis cooling in the fridge. I'd just spread a layer of olive oil in the pan when my cell phone rang.

I recognized the voice.

"Hello, this is Cheryl Cooper. You phoned my mother."

"Yes, yes I did." I turned off the gas. "She misunderstood my intentions."

"She's been under a lot of stress since my father's death. Are you from insurance? If there's anything we can do to speed things up . . ."

"I'm not from insurance—sorry. I was calling about something that happened a long time ago, when your father was sixteen. At Hopley's Holiday Camp."

"I know all about that. Dad talked about that summer at Hopley's a lot—some game they played. Are you calling from the States?"

"I'm American, but I'm living in Suffolk right now. Long Barston. A friend of mine was one of the group that summer."

There was a moment's silence. "Can you meet me somewhere? Something's bothering me."

"About your father's death?"

"I can't talk now. Mother'll be wanting her tea."

"Where should we meet?"

"There's a Starbucks on the M11, just after you turn off the A120. Shouldn't take you more than thirty minutes from Long Barston."

"When?"

"Tomorrow, but it has to be early. Half eight. I clock in for my shift at ten."

"I'll be there. May I bring my friend, Vivian?"

"No. Just you."

Chapter Twelve

Sunday, August 30

I found the Starbucks east of a complicated intersection involving three interconnected roundabouts, one of which I had to navigate twice.

Vivian, none too pleased at being excluded from the meeting with Jack Cavanagh's daughter, had prepared me with questions. She couldn't let go of the idea that her old boyfriend was killed because he'd come to Long Barston to see her and possibly to impart new information about the deaths at Monkey Puzzle House.

I wasn't writing that off either.

The night before, I'd considered texting Tom about Jack Cavanagh's obituary but decided to wait until after my meeting with his daughter. If his death turned out to be unsuspicious—one of those coincidences Tom and I had talked about—I could forget about conspiracy theories.

Inside Starbucks, I ordered a coffee—milk, no sugar—and found a table. Cheryl Cooper, née Cavanagh, showed up at precisely eight thirty. I had no trouble identifying her. She entered the shop, looking uncertainly from face to face. Since I was the only other female there at the moment, it didn't take her long to find me.

"Kate?" In her early fifties, Cheryl Cooper was large and squarely built. Her clothing, dark slacks and a voluminous navy sweater, had been chosen, I imagined, to conceal. Her handbag was the size of a small carry-on, slung over her shoulder and positioned over her stomach like a shield.

"I'm Cheryl, Jack's daughter. Thank you for meeting me." In person, her voice was even more pleasant that it had been on the phone. Low-pitched and resonant.

"It's nice to meet you," I said. "Can I get you something? Coffee? Tea?"

"I'll get it. Got a gift card for my birthday."

I watched as she ordered, noticing how she used her sweater and handbag as camouflage. She returned with a large paper cup topped with mounds of whipped cream.

"Looks delicious," I said.

"Double Chocolate Chip Frappuccino. My weakness."

"Where do you work?"

"Call center. This month I'm on day shift, but we take it in turns."

"Customer service?"

"Suicide hotline. You'd be surprised how many people call in—all sorts. Most aren't really contemplating suicide. They just need someone to chat to about their problems. A fair number are abused women and girls."

I took a longer look at Cheryl Cooper, seeing patient brown eyes and an expression of candor. "How did you end up in that job?"

"The usual way." She gave a small laugh. "I was a victim. First my father—" She stopped and sucked in a spoonful of the cream, shaking her head. "I don't mean sexual or physical. Verbal abuse was his thing—especially when he'd been drinking. Then there was my ex-husband. Same pattern, except he got physical. When I left him, I went into a shelter, got counseling. Then I entered a program to become a counselor. No degree, but I'm trained to listen and to encourage honesty."

"Is abuse why your parents separated?"

"Of course. Alcohol intensifies emotions. My father chose to take his anger out on the women in his life." She spooned more cream into her mouth, then took a long sip on the straw.

"How about Susan—she's the oldest, right?"

"Suze flew under the radar. Dad wasn't drinking as much in those days. Worked all hours. Susan left home at seventeen. She was ten years older, so we hardly knew each other. Later the business failed. Dad's partner cheated him. That's when the anger and the alcohol took control."

"Do you mind telling me why you wanted me to come alone?" I asked.

Cheryl gave a slight shrug of her shoulders. "We'd spoken on the phone. I felt comfortable with you. I'm not good with strangers."

I stared at her. "But you work at a call center. You must deal with strangers every day."

"On the telephone, yes. Never in person. On the phone there's anonymity—a wall of protection. No one can see you. No one can touch you. When the client gets upset or angry, it's just a voice. I can deal with that."

"How long were your parents separated?"

"Six years. After I got my own place, Mum moved in with me. I've been going down to Dad's twice a week for a couple of years—stock the pantry, make sure he's eating properly, throw some clothes in the washer."

"Heart disease?"

"Congestive heart failure complicated by hypertension and an aortic aneurysm. We knew he could go any time. He'd been strong all his life—a bully, really—and that made him seem that much more pathetic."

"It was kind of you—after what he'd done."

"Honestly, the visits weren't so much for him as for me. Facing your fears is the beginning of healing."

"Which is what you've done."

"I can help others." Cheryl wrapped her fingers around the tall paper cup. "That makes a difference."

"How did your father die?"

"Alone. In bed."

"How did you hear?"

"Phone call from the public health nurse. She stopped in twice a month to make sure he was managing his heart medication. When he didn't answer the door, she had the porter use his key. I'd been in London that week. Mandatory course in suicide prevention."

"He died of a heart attack?"

She nodded. "They said he must have mixed up his pills or something. But I'm having a hard time with that. In spite of all the alcohol he'd consumed, my father's mind was sharp. He organized his own pill minder every week. Never let me do it for him."

"Your mother mentioned something about him owing money."

"Dad did a bit of gambling down the pub. Mum's afraid someone's going to pressure her to make good on his bets." She stirred her Frappuccino, swirling the remaining cream into the liquid. Removing the straw, she tipped back the paper cup and took another long drink.

"Cheryl, why did you call me back? You didn't have to."

She looked up, froth on her upper lip. "I told you. I thought you were from insurance. Dad had a small policy from his years at the company. They've been delaying, implying he might have taken his own life."

"Is that possible?"

"Absolutely not." Cheryl squared her shoulders. "He was afraid of dying, terrified he'd die alone in his sleep. Ironic, really."

Cheryl drained the cup and glanced at her wristwatch.

She'd have to leave for work soon, and all I'd learned was that Jack Cavanagh had died of a massive heart attack at the age of seventy-four. Why had she wanted the meeting?

"Cheryl, I'm sorry for your loss, but I shouldn't take any more of your time. Frankly, I had wondered if your father's death had something to do with the summer of 1963 and an abandoned house near the holiday camp. Obviously, that's not the case."

Her answer took me by surprise.

"Are you sure? Because I'm not." Cheryl was using her thumbnail to score vertical lines along the rim of her cup. "I didn't tell you the truth just now. It wasn't insurance on my mind when I

called you. The day before my father died, something odd happened. I'd phoned him from London to check on him. He said
he'd had a phone call, someone who'd asked questions about the
old days. I could tell he was disturbed, Kate, but I don't know
why."

"Was the caller a man or a woman?"

"I didn't ask. I was late for a session and had to ring off. Next
morning, the nurse found him dead. That's the real reason I wanted
to meet today. I needed to tell someone, and since you mentioned
Hopley's—" She shrugged.

"What did this caller want to know?"

"Dad mentioned a house near Miracle-on-Sea. That's all I
know."

"Monkey Puzzle House."

She stared at me. "How do you know that?"

"My friend Vivian Bunn and your father were two of five teenagers who explored that abandoned house in 1963. One of them,
Will Parker, a retired CID officer from Peterborough, had recently
been looking into the case. Something happened that made him
suspicious." I explained to her about Cluedo and the game pieces.
"Could Will Parker have been the one who called?"

"I don't think so." She furrowed her brow. "In fact, it couldn't
have been. Dad said the caller was someone he didn't know. I think
what frightened him was the fact that this person seemed to know
things about him. Like they'd done research."

"Did the caller say what he wanted?"

"I should have asked." Cheryl's chin trembled. "There's something else. I think someone searched Dad's flat. It wasn't torn up
or anything, but I could see things were out of place. Dad was a
creature of habit. He put things back where they belonged."

Was it as simple as that? Someone talked his way into the flat,
intending to rob him, and Cheryl's father died of a heart attack in
the process? "Was anything missing?"

"I don't think so."

"Had your father received a package recently?"

It was a shot in the dark, but the look on Cheryl's face told me I'd hit the mark.

She opened her large handbag and pulled out a brass letter opener with a carved jade handle. "I found this paper knife in his desk drawer. I'd never seen it before. There was an empty box in his rubbish bin. No return address."

"Did you keep the box?"

"No."

"Do you remember where it was postmarked?"

"I'm sorry, no."

"Did your father keep a daily diary or jot down appointments somewhere?"

"You mean did he write down the name of his visitor?"

"It would help."

"I didn't see anything. The flat is cleared out now. Why don't you ask that detective? Maybe he knows something."

"I'm afraid that's not possible. Will Parker was murdered—a week ago Friday."

"*Murdered?*" Cheryl's mouth slackened.

Two of the Five Sleuths were now dead—both recently and both after receiving anonymous packages. I wouldn't suggest it to Cheryl Cooper—not until I had proof—but I couldn't rule out the possibility that her father had been murdered too. If so, the killer had made sure it looked like another natural death.

* * *

That afternoon, Tom and I had planned to take a walk along the Stour, the river that runs through Long Barston and forms most of the boundary between Suffolk and Essex.

After my meeting with Cheryl Cooper, I stopped home to change clothes, grab a quick lunch, and tell Vivian what I'd learned about Jack Cavanagh.

Vivian was waiting for me in the kitchen. She'd made a pot of tomato soup and a loaf of oat bread. "What did the daughter say?"

I began with the alleged cause of Jack Cavanagh's death—heart attack brought on by a possible mix-up in his medication. Then I added his daughter's misgivings about that conclusion, plus her story about the caller asking questions, the possible theft, and the package with the paper knife.

Vivian had been ladling soup into two large bowls. The ladle clattered against the pot. "Did you say a paper knife?"

"Brass with—"

"With an etched design and a carved jade handle."

"Another one of the game pieces?"

She nodded. "That was the dagger I told you about. Something nasty's going on, Kate." She leveled her gaze at me. "Will was right. Something terrible happened in that house. Will's death—maybe Jack's too—is connected with those poisonings. I'm sure of it."

I wasn't sure of it—not yet. But the look on Vivian's face told me we were thinking the same thing.

"Vivian—if anyone comes around asking questions about Monkey Puzzle House, do not let them in."

Chapter Thirteen

The day was perfect for a hike—sunny, cool, and dry underfoot.

From the church, Tom and I walked down the High Street, past the shops and the Suffolk Rose Tea Room to the Stour bridge. The footpath, ten feet or so below the road, was accessed by a series of zigzag steps built into the bridge abutment.

Since the damaging floods the previous May, the footpath near Long Barston had been repaired. A thin column of smoke rose from the fields in the distance—a rare sight since the UK's ban on burning stubble. The early autumn foliage was beginning to flame, which made me think of the Van Eyck—those glorious, intense hues laid on, layer by layer.

"An hour's walk should get us halfway to Little Gosling," Tom said. "There's a country pub there. Not particularly brilliant with food, but we could have a cup of tea—or a glass of wine, if you like."

"Sounds lovely."

The river flowed eastward, merging into the Stour estuary and eventually the North Sea. The Stour isn't a deep river, seldom over five feet. Here, at Long Barston, the depth was less than two feet. Clear olivine water sparkled in the sun as it washed over fallen branches and divided around rocks. I breathed in the scent of wet moss and rocks.

The path was narrow, making conversation difficult. We tramped along in companionable silence, listening to the murmur of flowing water. After ten minutes or so, we stopped to watch a heron, perched on one leg amid a stand of purple loosestrife.

"Are you going to tell me about Jack Cavanagh's daughter?" Tom asked.

"Sure, but first tell me what you learned about the Beaufoy deaths."

"You won't be pleased." Tom pulled two water bottles out of his pack and tossed me one. "The poisonings were never considered a crime—I learned that much. Actually, that's all I learned."

"Why?" I took a drink and handed the bottle back.

"Because there's almost nothing to learn. Come on, let's keep going. I'll explain." The path widened, allowing us to walk together. "I didn't expect to find anything in the police records. Most noncriminal files were purged years ago. But I had hoped to learn something from the records of the Coroner's Court in Ipswich. That's where the inquest was held."

"And?"

"The Beaufoy files are missing. Except for a summary, which lists the date of decease, twentieth of May 1961; the verdict, accidental poisoning; and the names of those who gave evidence."

"What does that mean?"

"It means someone removed the files." He pushed a branch out of the way to let me pass.

"Removed?"

"Old files—those before 2017—are stored in the archives at the Suffolk Records Office. Assuming the inquest files weren't suppressed, they were either misfiled or accidentally destroyed." He gave me a sidelong glance. "Or someone stole them."

"Who gave evidence?"

"The two oldest children—Justine and Grayson. They didn't depose the younger daughters, fifteen and eleven. Others gave testimony as well—the cook, the gardener, a doctor from Netherfield Sanatorium where Beaufoy worked."

"Hold on a minute." I stopped walking. "You're saying Doctor Beaufoy worked at Netherfield Sanatorium?"

"Beaufoy had his own practice, but he also performed admission exams at Netherfield and took care of minor physical complaints among the patients and staff. Digestive problems, broken bones, concussions. All that was recorded in the summary.

"Did they suspect the cook?"

"Her name was Alice Evans, a young woman of twenty-two. It doesn't appear she was a suspect, although without her actual testimony, I couldn't tell you why not."

"And no one at the coroner's court today knows where the documents ended up?"

"Not a clue. To be fair, it's been sixty years, Kate. No one working in the coroner's office today was even alive in 1961."

"So the records no longer exist?"

"I didn't say that. They may have been misfiled."

I made a noncommittal sound, but a case of simple misfiling sounded unlikely to me. "Who would have had access to the files?"

"Anyone deemed an interested person—law enforcement, next of kin, involved organizations."

"Like someone at Netherfield?"

"I suppose so. Disclosure would be determined by the senior coroner at the time. In the sixties, that would have been the senior partner at the law firm from which the coroner was always appointed. When a coroner retired, the post was simply handed down to the next in line."

"What was the name of the law firm in 1961?"

"I can probably find out."

The path narrowed again, and Tom strode ahead.

At least I had a name. *Alice Evans*, the family cook.

The police were investigating the murder of Will Parker, not the poisoning deaths of the Beaufoys sixty years ago, but for Vivian's peace of mind, I had to do something. And in the absence of the inquest files, the least I could do was talk with someone who actually knew what happened that night—one of the surviving Beaufoys, for example, or Alice Evans. If she'd been twenty-two in

1961, she'd be . . . eighty-two now. According to my mother's new husband, eighty is the new sixty.

I could also find out if any of the Cliff House board members remembered hearing about the Beaufoy deaths from their parents. Everyone in the area must have talked about the case for months. I might also try to locate Frank Keane and Mary—if Vivian ever remembered her last name. Maybe they'd been contacted by a stranger, too, asking about that summer. Or one of them had sent the packages.

The wind picked up, dappling the sunlight through the trees and casting shifting patterns on the footpath. I zipped up my lightweight jacket.

Tom said once that I see patterns and connections others don't. This time the connections seemed to center on Netherfield Sanatorium. Doctor Beaufoy worked there at the time of his death. Four of the Cliff House board members had relatives who worked there in 1961 as well. And then there was Monkey Puzzle House, barely two miles from Netherfield. That's where the Five Sleuths played Cluedo and Will Parker hid the metal box.

Was I imagining patterns—like those people who see a human face in an automobile grille or the image of the Virgin Mary in a grilled cheese sandwich? Para-something. *Pareidolia*—that was it. I'd read about it once. Scientists say we're primed to see faces in the natural world—and once we see them, we see them everywhere.

Had I imagined a pattern because I wanted the events of the past week to make sense? I didn't think so. Miracle-on-Sea was a small community. Someone knew what happened that May night in 1961. Someone found the metal box with the game pieces. Someone murdered Will Parker—and maybe Jack Cavanagh.

"Tom," I said, catching up to him, "if Dr. Beaufoy worked at Netherfield at the time of his death, the parents of the Cliff House board members would have known him pretty well. Some of them were doctors themselves. They worked with him. Maybe one of them removed the inquest files."

"Why? Because the information was incriminating? Are you suggesting someone on the Cliff House board murdered Will Parker to conceal a sixty-year-old murder?"

"Not really." The path circled an ancient hollow oak tree. "If the evidence pointed to a killer, that person would have been arrested and tried. My point is"—I stopped to run my hand over the gnarled old bark—"someone on the board might know the story. They might be able to fill in some of the blanks."

"Back to Jack Cavanagh's daughter." Tom said. "How did you find her?"

"Her name is Cheryl Cooper, and I found her online through her father's obituary. Jack's estranged wife lives with Cheryl in Eastwick. The couple separated six years ago."

"What did the daughter say?"

I started with the basics—Jack Cavanagh's failed business, the cheating partner, the drinking, the anger, the verbal abuse, the gambling. Then I got to the point. "He died of a heart attack while Cheryl was away at a conference in London. He'd had a bad heart for years. But—"

"I knew there'd be a *but*."

"Just listen. Sometime before his death Jack Cavanagh received an anonymous package containing the game piece he'd used all those years ago at Monkey Puzzle House. Just like Will Parker, Tom. But in Jack's case it was a brass paper knife shaped like a dagger. The day before his death, he got a phone call. He told his daughter because it upset him. He said it was someone he didn't know."

"Not Will Parker, then."

"No, but whoever it was, man or woman, asked him questions about the old days. The next morning the visiting nurse found him dead. The doctor who examined the body assumed he'd mixed up his heart medication, but here's the point—Cheryl is certain his flat had been searched. So who was it—the person who phoned or someone else?"

"A heart attack in the course of a robbery?"

"Nothing was missing."

"They're sure it wasn't suicide?"

"Cheryl is convinced it wasn't."

"She thinks her father was murdered?"

"She didn't say that, but I know she's suspicious. Especially when I told her about Will Parker's murder."

"You said someone asked her father about the old days, but how do we know which old days he meant? Maybe someone was interested in the old days when Jack Cavanagh ran his industrial cleaning business. He might have been involved in something shady."

"Oh, maybe." I groaned, startling a man fishing on the riverbank. "I can't prove it, but something's going on, and Vivian is involved. She wants to see Monkey Puzzle House again."

"And do what?"

"Just see it. Someone recently bought the house. We probably can't get inside, but I know Vivian. She won't let it go."

"I can't stop you."

"Don't say that." I took his arm and turned him toward me. "I'm not asking permission, but I would like your approval. Or at least your—"

"Surrender?"

"No—your help."

He blew out a breath. "What do you want me to do? I tried to find information on the Beaufoy family. That was a dead end."

"Agree with me that it's odd. Odd enough to look into."

"We *are* looking into it. An elderly man, an ex-policeman, was murdered on our patch. We're doing everything we can to find his killer."

"That's good, but how about Jack Cavanagh? How about Frank Keane and Mary Something?"

Tom turned to look me in the face. "You're afraid Vivian's in danger, aren't you?"

I didn't have time to answer. My cell phone rang. It was Ivor.

"Kate, I just got a phone call from Apollo. They already have preliminary results on the Van Eyck. There are concerns."

"Should we turn around?" Tom asked when I told him. "We could be back by three."

I shook my head. "The reports were preliminary. No sense panicking."

But I was panicking, a little. If the tests proved the painting was a fake, Ivor and I would have to break the new to Tony Currie and the Cliff House board.

Then I reminded myself we didn't have the final results yet. There was still a chance the bad news would turn out to be a botched cleaning job or some heavy-handed over-painting that would have to be removed. Which meant I didn't have to deal with it yet.

Besides, Tom was leaving again for a few days of meetings at Constabulary Headquarters in Martlesham Heath. I decided to forget about medieval pigments, missing files, and conspiracy theories and spend the rest of Sunday with him.

Good choice.

Chapter Fourteen

～

Monday, August 31

When I arrived at the shop, Ivor was behind the counter, using a soft horsehair brush to clean a set of Wilkie Collins first editions. Each of the books would be cleaned, interleaved with special paper to absorb odors, and stored in acid-free clamshell boxes.

"Good morning." He laid the brush on a square of white cotton fabric.

"Tell me about the test results."

"They analyzed the pigments, all of which were consistent with fifteenth-century pigments and the heat-bodied linseed oil Van Eyck was known to have used."

"That's good, right?"

"Except for one tiny problem." Ivor pulled off his white cotton gloves. "The blue."

I stared at him. "You mean it wasn't natural ultramarine?" Ultramarine is one of the oldest known pigments, used by artists for at least fifteen hundred years—a brilliant, intense blue made from lapis lazuli, rare and thus expensive. A synthetic was developed in the 1830s, identical in composition and structure but detectable under a spectroscope.

"No, it was natural ultramarine, all right. But they also found traces of something that shouldn't be there. That's all I know. They said they were going to repeat the test in case there had been contamination. The head of forensics wants to meet us at the lab next Saturday to go over the final results in person."

"That's not such bad news." I felt relieved. "A long time to wait, though."

"True." He placed the book he'd been working on in one of the clamshell boxes and slipped the soft brush into a white cotton bag. "Cliff House tomorrow, right? I told them you'd drop off the snuff boxes. You're to text Martyn Lee-Jones when you're fifteen minutes away. He'll meet you in the lobby to take possession. I emailed you his contact information this morning."

"I got it. I'll pick up the boxes on the way out of town. By the way, Vivian is going with me. We're going to have lunch in Miracle-on-Sea and do a little time travel."

"Time travel?" He waggled his eyebrows. "There's a day in 1965 I'd like to live over again."

"Why is that?" I crossed my arms and grinned at him. Ivor's exploits in the Merchant Navy were the stuff of legend.

"Long story. Let's just say it involved a public bath house in Singapore, a shipment of faulty bath salts, and an invasion of snakes."

"I can't wait." I laughed. "In the meantime, I assume I shouldn't say anything to Lee-Jones about the spectrography."

"If he asks, tell him the tests are incomplete and leave it at that."

"Fine with me."

"I do have news, though." Ivor smoothed the top of his head where his hair used to be. "I have a client in London, an investment banker. I asked him to take a look at Pyramid Development and the Cliff House project."

"Did he find anything interesting?"

"More than interesting, given the connection of the current board members to the final Netherfield board of trustees." Ivor slipped the box of books behind the counter.

"They have a personal interest in the success of the Cliff House project."

"Not only a personal interest, Kate—a financial interest as well." Ivor eased himself onto one of the stools behind the counter. "When Netherfield was placed in the care of the NHS, a contract was drawn up—unusual even then—stipulating that if the facility was ever permanently closed, ownership would revert to the board members or their survivors."

"So that's why Underwood and Lee-Jones are on the board. They're part owners."

"Not only that, Kate. According to my source, each of the board members chipped in a sum of cash for the start-up. Tony Currie insisted on it before he agreed to take on the project. I can't say I blame him. If Cliff House fails, Pyramid won't be the only loser."

"No wonder the board balked at testing the Van Eyck. They're counting on the proceeds to put Cliff House in the black."

"That's why Tony Currie pulled rank. As majority shareholder, he understood what the others didn't—that given our recommendation, the only path forward was to remove any doubt about the painting's authenticity. He's got a lot riding on the project himself."

"It's a stunning building, but do you think wealthy people are clamoring to invest millions in a home on the Suffolk coast?"

"Currie must think so. He's something of a legend in the City, Kate—real rags-to-riches story. Came from nothing. As a lad, he was in one of the East London gangs. Had a string of arrests by the time he was fifteen, on his way to hard time."

"What changed?"

"Wised up, according to my friend. Decided to put his intelligence to good purpose. He started as an apprentice to a chartered surveyor and clawed his way up the ladder—stepping on a few toes in the process. There are people who would like very much to see him fail. Under that polished exterior, he's a scrapper, a street fighter, but insecure. Out to prove something, maybe to himself."

"What about his personal life?"

"Two ex-wives. From all accounts, the current Mrs. Currie is working her way through his fortune at a clip."

I pictured the photo of the couple in their trendy flat. The designer dress. The bare feet.

"I wonder if the marriage is in trouble. Currie told me he's living at Cliff House."

"The point is, Tony Currie's been taking risks his whole life. Nerves of steel."

What Ivor didn't say was that we were taking a risk, too. If the Van Eyck turned out to be a fake, we'd be applauded in the art world for our cleverness and integrity. But we might be considered a bit *too* clever by other high-end clients, fearing revelations about their own objects.

I didn't know about Ivor's nerves, but at the moment, mine were less than steely.

"Anything else?"

"Just that in the 1960s, Dr. Underwood's father was an advocate for physician-assisted suicide."

"I read that, too. What does euthanasia have to do with anything?"

"A curious fact."

I tried to think of a connection to the deaths of the Beaufoys and couldn't.

We spent the rest of the day rearranging the display cabinets and placing the new items Ivor had recently purchased. We did have one walk-in—a Canadian tourist who purchased a bronze tenth-century Viking cross—but my mind was still on the information provided by Ivor's friend in London. Had the board members purposely withheld information about their financial connections to the Cliff House project, or had they simply considered it none of our business?

It was four fifteen when Ivor decided to close up for the day. He was noticeably limping. If Tom and I moved to the States, how would he manage?

We said goodbye. I grabbed my jacket and headed for Rose Cottage.

The hawthorn hedges in Finchley Park were thick with glossy, dark-red haws. Clusters of prickly green nut shells hung from an old sweet chestnut tree. We were having a stretch of fabulous weather, day after day of sunshine and temperatures in the mid to upper sixties. I know British people dream of hot sand and palm trees, but not me. Give me a day that requires a sweater anytime. Give me a night that calls for a log fire.

Must be the Viking genes.

My mind was on the Van Eyck painting—and the possible connection between the Netherfield board of trustees in 1961 and the deaths at Monkey Puzzle House. The problem was the time gap. Tom was right. Even if one of those original trustees had murdered the Beaufoys, I couldn't see what it had to do with events unfolding right now.

I needed someone to help me sort through the possibilities. Normally that person would be my mother. She had a way of asking the right questions, of clarifying my thoughts. But I'd promised myself not to call her on her honeymoon. I liked James Lund. I liked him a lot. He deserved to have his new wife all to himself, at least for the weeks they'd planned to be away.

At Rose Cottage, a clamor of rooks circled the thatch before coming to rest noisily in the tall trees. In the distance, the late-afternoon sun shimmered on Blackwater Lake.

Should I call Tom? He would listen, but he might despair of me.

I was about to pull out my cell phone when it rang.

"Kate, it's me." I could hardly hear Tom over the hum of background conversation. "Can't talk long. I have news about Jack Cavanagh."

* * *

I flew into the cottage, greeted Vivian with a wave, pointed at my phone, and dashed upstairs.

"I have news, too," I said, "but I'd rather hear about Jack."

"His daughter Cheryl filed an exhumation order this morning. She's demanding a second autopsy. She thinks her father was murdered."

"Really?" Our meeting at Starbucks had accomplished more than I dreamed. I just hoped I hadn't misled her.

"There's something else, Kate. Eacles will join the staff at Martlesham Heath before the end of the year—Lord help them. I've been asked officially to take his post."

"What did you say?" A pit opened up in my stomach.

"Nothing. Not until we've talked. This is a decision that affects us both."

"Will you have time to call me later?"

"No, Kate. Not on the phone. We need to discuss this in person."

"You're right. As soon as you get home, then."

"As soon as I get home." I heard him take a breath. "I don't have an agenda—you know that. I said I'll do whatever makes you happy, and I meant it. I like my job, and I think I could make a difference as detective chief inspector, but it won't work if you're not all in."

"Oh dear." I gave a little laugh. "We are a pair, aren't we? Both trying so hard to make the other happy, we never say what we really feel."

"I've told you how I feel, and you're going to have to do the same because they need an answer by the fifteenth of next month. There's another candidate for the job. A DI from Essex. I know him. Good man."

"How about your mother?" I scrunched up my face, not sure I wanted to hear the answer. If Tom moved to the States, Liz Mallory would never, ever, *ever* forgive me. And if I moved to England—*nope*, moving into Tom's house in Saxby St. Claire was off the table as far as I was concerned. I was going to have to tell him that.

"This is our decision, Kate—not hers."

I closed my eyes. "Still. You do have to consider her."

"We'll talk about it when I get home. What's your news? I've got about five minutes."

It's not news. Only vague suspicions. "It can wait," I said. "See you soon."

Chapter Fifteen

⌒

Tuesday, September 1

To say Vivian was impressed with Cliff House would be like saying Elizabeth Bennet didn't hate Pemberley. Vivian was entranced. All morning she'd been like an overstimulated child, chattering about what we might learn at Hopley's and Monkey Puzzle House. And now this—a grand, red-brick Victorian edifice, crouched like a heraldic lion on a promontory overlooking the sea.

The gates swept open. This time I hardly had to tap the brakes.

"Do you think they'd give us a tour—or at least let us see one of the finished townhouses?"

"We can ask," I said. What Cliff House needed was a few dozen like Vivian Bunn, but with much bigger bank accounts.

Once inside, we stood in the grand entrance hall, awaiting the arrival of Martyn Lee-Jones. The receptionist, Cordelia Armstrong, eyed the box I was holding and asked if I'd like to leave it on her desk. No way would I pass off the snuff boxes to anyone but a board member.

"Ms. Hamilton." He came striding through from the office wing and greeted me with a tight-lipped smile.

I handed him the box. "They're wonderful. Exceptional, actually. Ivor's estimates are inside."

"Any word on the Van Eyck?"

I knew he'd ask. "Nothing definite. We'll let you know as soon as we get the final report."

"When will that be?"

"Soon. In the meantime, let me introduce my friend Vivian. She's familiar with this part of Suffolk. Her family vacationed at Hopley's."

"Hopley's closed years ago."

"I know," Vivian said. "We're having lunch in town. I hope to see what's left of the old camp."

"And we'd like to find a house—maybe you know it. Monkey Puzzle House."

His head jerked back. I'd caught him off-guard. "Yes, of course I know it. I was raised in the area."

"Then you must remember the tragedy that took place there in the early sixties, the poisonings. The house was recently sold. Vivian and I read a newspaper account."

"You can hardly expect me to remember the deaths. I was two years old when it happened."

Interesting. He'd placed the year exactly. "I understand your father and Dr. Beaufoy worked together at Netherfield."

"In different areas of the hospital."

"How well did he know the Beaufoys?"

"I couldn't say." His eyes narrowed in suspicion. "Why do you want to know?"

"Curiosity." I let him absorb that. "So—about the snuff boxes, if you have questions, let us know."

"I *do* have questions, but not about the snuff boxes." He raised a forefinger, and for a moment I thought he was going to shake it at me. "I want to know why you pushed for a forensic examination of the Van Eyck. Your colleague, Mr. Tweedy, made it sound like the usual procedure, but I've done a little investigating, and I know very well it isn't the usual procedure."

"I don't know who you've been talking to, Mr. Lee-Jones, but in the case of a painting of the importance of a newly discovered Jan van Eyck, it certainly is standard procedure." Okay, so I was making most of this up, but it wasn't actually untrue. "You might know that in 2011 Sotheby's sold a seventeenth-century painting by Frans Hals to an American collector for just over eight million pounds. The painting was subsequently discredited. Sotheby's is still trying to collect reimbursement from the Mayfair art dealer who sold them the painting. We don't want to risk putting you in that kind of jeopardy."

He snorted. "So you're doing this for *our* sake? Or to cover your own backside?"

"Both." I kept my eyes steadily on his. Lee-Jones and I certainly weren't lovers, but I had an image of us, balanced like Cupid and Psyche on that seesaw.

Vivian, pretending not to listen, had wandered over to examine the faux Hockney.

"The Van Eyck is genuine," he said, "purchased by Horace Netherfield in 1877. It hung in the Great Hall until a month ago—right there." Lee-Jones pointed at the fireplace where Vivian was trying to disappear. "That's nearly a hundred and fifty years. We have the documents to prove it."

"Then you have nothing to worry about."

"Oh no? How do we know you're not working with this Apollo company? I know how these things go. They claim the painting isn't genuine. We sell it for a fraction of its worth. Then you buy it privately and resell it for a fortune."

"Come now, Mr. Lee-Jones. Even if that were true, which it is not, we could never get away with it. Everyone in the art world would know. *You* would know. Mr. Tweedy's reputation would be ruined."

"Just watch your step," he snarled. "Don't say I didn't warn you." Brushing past me, he turned on his heel and, cradling the box of snuffs, disappeared down the hall.

Vivian sidled up to me. "What do you say we skip that tour?"

* * *

The seaside village of Miracle-on-Sea was spread out along the Suffolk coast like—I was about to say a string of pearls, but that wouldn't be accurate. More like a string of plastic pop-beads—cheap and out of fashion.

I wasn't expecting much. I'd seen an article in *The Telegraph*, listing Miracle-on-Sea as third on a list of the top ten most deprived seaside towns in England. Decades of decline in British domestic travel and the resulting collapse of property values had reduced the once-lively middle-class playground to a tidal pool of cheap flats and boarding houses. Young people escaped as soon as they could scrape together the money for a bus ticket to London.

Vivian and I parked our car in a lot at the edge of the village and headed for the promenade, a commercial stretch dominated by charity shops, pound stores, cheap souvenir stands, and take-away stalls. The statue of a giant fish marked the beginning of the sea walk.

"I don't remember any of this," Vivian said. "There used to be a pier with carnival rides and a fun house."

"The pier collapsed in a storm in 2010," I said. "Never rebuilt." We gazed out at the rows of wooden pilings, barely visible above the waves. "Let's look for a place to eat."

About a quarter mile along the strand, we found a decent-looking restaurant, Wee Willie Winkle's, a seafood café with an outdoor seating area defined by faux box hedges and umbrella-shaded tables. The sea breeze snapped the striped awning, but the air was mild, and the sun was doing its best to dodge the wispy clouds sailing over the water.

A bored-looking waitress with a deeply lined face and improbably dark hair handed us each a plastic-covered menu. "What'll it be, luv? Tea? Coffee? Lemon squash?" She tapped my menu with her pen. "I'd go with the fish and chips or the seafood linguine if I was you. Don't bother with the grilled octopus or the salmon burger."

Taken as read. We ordered two pots of tea, and when she returned, Vivian ordered the fish and chips, and I ordered the linguine.

The food was better than I feared. Seagulls shrieked, occasionally swooping to snag a crumb of bread or an errant chip.

Even on a fine day in August, the promenade was mostly deserted. A young woman pushed a baby stroller. An amoeba-like blob of teens chattered like magpies, the three in front walking backward.

"What an unpleasant man." Vivian speared a chip. "Imagine, accusing you and Ivor of double-dealing."

"Chalk it up to fear," I said, wondering if the Van Eyck was the only thing Lee-Jones was worried about.

Vivian chewed thoughtfully. "I hope we can find Monkey Puzzle House."

"You hope? I was counting on you to navigate."

"I'm not sure I can even find Hopley's. It has to be that direction." She pointed away from the sea. "But I couldn't take you there."

The waitress stopped by to clear our plates and to see if we wanted one of Wee Willie's famous ice cream towers. We declined.

"I overheard your conversation," she said without a hint of embarrassment. "You won't be able to see Hopley's. The whole site is closed, scheduled for demolition later this month. You might have a peek through the fence."

"Can you point us in the right direction?"

"Sure. Go back the way you came. Just before the giant fish, turn right on Seaview—it's a steep walk uphill, mind. You can't miss it."

"Is there access for a car?" I wasn't sure Vivian could make it on foot, but she'd never admit it.

"Let me think." The waitress scratched her head with her pen. "It's a narrow street. No parking. I suppose you could turn around near the gates."

"We're also hoping to find Monkey Puzzle House. Do you know it?"

"Where those people died back in the sixties? There was an article in our local paper not long ago—when the place was sold, although I can't imagine what the new owners want with it. Needs tearing down if you ask me. To get there from Hopley's, you'll have to come back down to Marine Parade and then turn on Harbour Lane, two streets this side of Seaview. Up the hill about a mile, on the right."

An old man approached us along the promenade, leaning like a sailor against the wind. He touched his flat cap and gave us a gap-toothed grin.

On impulse I asked the waitress, "What do you know about the history of the town—the old Netherfield Sanatorium, for example?"

"Not a thing, luv. Moved down from Skegness last year, didn't I? Boyfriend got a job at the new power station."

"Thanks anyway."

We paid the bill and were about to leave when she said, "If it's history you're after, the person to ask is Percy Pike." She cackled. "If he don't know it, you don't need it."

"Where would we find Mr. Pike?" Vivian asked.

The waitress pointed at the old man who'd just passed us. He'd found a seat on an iron bench on the opposite side of the promenade. "He's here every afternoon but Sunday. Feeds the seagulls. Watches the tide come in." She glanced over her shoulder. "Look—I don't have any customers at the moment. I'll introduce you."

We crossed the promenade.

Percy Pike was even older than I'd first thought. He was all bones, with a long narrow nose, rheumy eyes, and a face that looked more like a skull than flesh and blood. Over a grimy white sweatshirt, he wore a formal black suit jacket with satin lapels, several sizes too large for him.

When the waitress explained we were interested in Netherfield Sanatorium, he chuckled. "Neverland, eh? Have a seat."

"Nether*field*," I said, enunciating more clearly.

"I heard ye. We called it *Neverland* back then—like the book, you know. The lost boys." This time his chuckle turned into a cough.

He moved to the end of the bench. I sat at the other end, leaving room for Vivian in the middle. She shot me a resentful look. Percy Pike wasn't smelling too fresh.

"Were you familiar with Netherfield before it was transferred to the National Health?" I asked.

"'A course. We all were. They'd let some of the patients wander into town. We got to know them—and their little quirks. One man chatted to his dead wife, as if she were right there beside him. Pleasant chap. Another refused to look you in the eye. Had a little dog on a leash. If you spoke more than three words to his master, the dog would bare his teeth and snap." Percy's face clouded. "A young woman jumped off the old pier once. Never heard why. Harmless, they were, for the most part. And they had the dosh all right. Shop owners welcomed them. We were sorry when the National Health took over. Everything changed."

"Did you know a family named Beaufoy? They lived just west of town."

He closed one red-rimmed eye against the sun. "Died, didn't they. Tragic."

"Yes, it was. What happened?"

"Couldn't say. Hushed up. Poisoned was what Mrs. Thorpe said, and she'd know."

"Who is Mrs. Thorpe?"

"Who *was* she, you mean. Cleaner. Dead now herself. She went back to tidy the place up after, but she wasn't allowed. House was shut up tight as a drum."

"What happened to the children?" Vivian asked.

"Moved to Upford, south of Ipswich, if memory serves. Eldest girl bought a cottage there."

"Justine?"

"Yes—that's it. Called her Justy. Died last year. House was finally sold."

"How about the other Beaufoy children?"

"The son, Grayson—Gray—went off to university. They sent the youngest girl to an aunt and uncle in Jersey. She were only a child 'a course, ten or eleven."

"Her name was Dulcie," Vivian said. "And the next oldest was Millicent."

"Ah, Millie." The old man's eyes twinkled. "Now she were a beauty—even at fifteen. All the boys were mad for Millie, they were. One older fella was really keen. Her father wasn't best pleased."

"Did you ever know the cook—Alice Evans?" I asked.

"'Course I did." He brightened. "Pretty little thing. Age of the eldest Beaufoy girl. A champion cook. I was sweet on her back then—not that I did anything about it. Shy lad I was. Never opened my mouth, if you can believe it."

"Is Alice Evans still alive?"

"Wouldn't know. She moved away right after it happened. If you're cook for a family what's poisoned to death, you're not going to get another place anytime soon, are you?"

"Where did she go?"

"Found a job on one of them Cunard liners, her brother told me. We were mates. She ended up in Chicago. Never heard from her again, more's the pity. Did I tell you I was sweet on her?"

"You did. Is Alice's brother still alive?"

"Alive? No, darling."

"Who purchased Monkey Puzzle House?" Vivian asked.

"Chap named Walker—solicitor. Niall Walker."

The hair on the back of my neck tingled.

The missing Cliff House board member.

*   *   *

"You say Niall Walker is on the Cliff House board?" Vivian clicked her seatbelt as we made a left turn out of the parking lot. "I suppose it's not surprising. Maybe he's a history buff. Or a fan of Art Deco."

"Could be," I agreed. Monkey Puzzle House was an architectural treasure—and the prices paid by media companies for the privilege of filming there might offset the cost of renovation. *Still.* This whole business was beginning to look like a web spun by a directionally challenged spider.

"Funny that Lee-Jones chap didn't mention it."

I'd been thinking the same thing.

We found Seaview Terrace. I turned west.

"Kate," Vivian turned toward me. "Do you think Jack Cavanagh was murdered?"

"I don't know." I hadn't told her about the exhumation yet. Why add fuel when the fire's already ablaze?

"I wish I'd paid more attention back then."

"Maybe seeing the house will jog your memory."

"We need to talk to people who were around in 1961." She gave me a severe look. "And don't say they're all dead."

"I wasn't going to."

Vivian had taken a notebook out of her handbag. "I'll make a list of people to interview." Her pencil scratched across the paper. "First Frank Keane. Then Mary if I ever remember her last name. And of course, the two surviving Beaufoy sisters in Upford. They might not want to talk about the deaths of their parents. We'll need a good excuse. Hedgehog protection—something like that."

"We could always tell the truth." I pulled left to avoid a dog trotting up the lane.

"I suppose so," Vivian said, completely missing my irony. "As a last resort."

I put the car in low gear. The waitress from Wee Willie's had been right. Seaview was a narrow street, lined on both sides with boarded-up shops. It ended at the entrance to Hopley's, now closed off with a high chain-link fence. A sign informed us that the twenty-acre site would soon be the home of a new caravan park.

Another sign said *No Admittance*, but someone besides workmen had been there. Graffiti was everywhere, the kind of stylized glyphs that signal gang activity. *Good grief.* Drugs had reached even a dying seaside village populated almost entirely by old-age pensioners.

I parked beside a commercial waste receptacle, and we got out of the car.

Inside the fence, to the right of the main drive, I could see the remains of a concrete swimming pool, partially filled with slimy green water. A sign atop a low building declared "It's Heaven at

Hopley's" in peeling paint. The windows were boarded up with plywood.

"That was the dining hall and games room," Vivian said. "It seemed so glamorous then—and luxurious. Everything free except alcohol. The drinks came with little paper umbrellas. Height of sophistication." She planted her walking stick in the scrubby grass. "You can just see the chalets—there, on the right. Each one had a loudspeaker. Every morning, seven AM, we'd hear that voice—*Good mooorning, campers. Riiise and shine.*"

I don't know what I'd been expecting. With a name like *chalet*, something alpine, maybe. The reality was a long row of identical pebble-dash boxes, inches apart, with overhanging porches and corrugated metal roofs. Most of the windows were broken. Some of the roofs had fallen in.

"It has been a *very* long time, hasn't it?" Vivian stood with one hand on her walking stick. She turned to me, her chin trembling. "Let's get out of here."

Chapter Sixteen

⁓

Like Hopley's, like most memories when we try to revisit them, Monkey Puzzle House turned out to be a disappointment. We parked in the lane behind a transport van with its rear cargo doors open. Inside we saw a jumble of coiled electrical cords, folded canvas drop cloths, and an array of workmen's tools.

The hedge Vivian had described was overgrown but still thriving. Someone had hacked through it at the front, removing the fence and creating a wide access over which chunky gravel had recently been laid.

"It's smaller than I remember," Vivian said.

We stood gazing at the plaster-like exterior. The once-pristine surface was crumbling and stained. Near a bank of curved glass blocks, a large chunk of the sand-and-cement-mix rendering had broken off, exposing yellow brick.

"Looks more like a candidate for demolition than renovation," Vivian said.

I knew better than to take her arm, but I stayed close as we picked our way across the gravel. Pounding noises came from inside the house. I was about to suggest we take a few photos and get back in the car when a young woman in khaki shorts and a navy T-shirt appeared in the open door.

"This is a construction site. I'm afraid you'll have to leave."

A young man, also wearing shorts, followed her out. Both were covered in what looked like plaster dust. "This is private property," he said. "We're not open for tourists."

I stared at him, amazed to recognize the face I'd memorized in *The Cabinet of Curiosities.* "I saw you in Ivor Tweedy's antiquities shop last Saturday."

His mouth opened. "Ah, yes. What a coincidence, eh?" He attempted a smile.

"You were looking for a present for your grandmother. Did you find one?"

The young woman turned to him, frowning. "Your grandmother?"

"I meant *your* grandmother," he said. "Doesn't she have a birthday coming up?"

"Not until November."

"Early bird and all that, eh?"

The young woman, realizing more was going on than she understood, let it drop. She smiled apologetically. "As Terry said, the house isn't open for tourists. I suppose you could take a few photos as long as you're here, but it's really not safe."

"We *are* sorry," I said in what my husband used to call my butter-wouldn't-melt voice. "I'm Kate Hamilton. This is Vivian Bunn. We saw an article on the house, and we've come all the way from Long Barston to see it."

"It is amazing." Her manner softened. "We're the Walkers. I'm Zara. This is my husband, Terry. My father-in-law owns the house."

Light dawned. "Your father-in-law is Niall Walker. We heard he'd bought the property. I know him—or know *of* him, to be accurate."

"Do you have a particular interest in the house?" Terry asked.

"The architecture, of course," I said, trying to sound knowledgeable.

"I came here when I was young," Vivian said. "We were vacationing at Hopley's Holiday Camp. I've been curious to see it again after all these years."

An older man, medium height, burly, with close-cropped gray hair, strode out of the house. He wore jeans and a light denim shirt with the sleeves rolled up. "What's going on?" The question was addressed to his son. "Who are these people?"

"You must be Niall Walker." I held out my hand. "I'm Kate Hamilton. I'm helping Ivor Tweedy with the appraisals at Cliff House. I was sorry you couldn't be there for our meeting."

"Family social event. Couldn't be helped."

"This is my friend Vivian Bunn. She visited the house a couple of years after the tragic deaths in 1961."

"Nice to meet you," Walker said, his belligerence melting away.

"The house made quite an impression," Vivian said.

"A classic example of Streamline Moderne." I squinted up at the curved windows and flat roof. "I understand the exterior has been featured in a number of films and TV shows. Are you planning to continue that?"

"We hope so," Zara slipped her hand through her husband's arm. "We might open the interior for filming as well. Right now we're trying to determine if that's possible."

"My son is a remodeling contractor," Niall Walker said. "We're keeping costs down by doing as much of the preliminary work as we can." He turned to Vivian. "You say you came here as a child?" From his tone, I wasn't sure he believed her. "Were you friends with the Beaufoys?"

"Nothing like that." Vivian shook her head. "The house was abandoned by the time I knew it. We were campers at Hopley's—July of 1963. There were five of us who knocked around together that week." She gave him a conspiratorial smile, "I'm afraid we were trespassing. I don't suppose the police would prosecute after all these years."

"Your secret is safe with us." Niall Walker grinned at her. "Would you like to see inside?"

His son looked puzzled. "Dad?"

"There's no real danger. Just watch where you step." Walker took Vivian's arm.

"I'll be fine," she said.

I wasn't so sure.

We followed the Walkers through the open door into the reception hall. Terry and Zara excused themselves, saying they had to get on with their work.

A free-standing staircase with curved metal-pipe railings occupied the round tower created by the glass-block window. I'd seen a similar staircase in TV episodes of *Hercule Poirot*. Here many of the glass blocks had cracked, allowing creepers to trail along the floor and climb the wall. Dust and debris lay thickly on every surface.

An archway led to a large living room, paneled exactly as Vivian had described, with fitted slabs of honey-colored wood—maple was my guess. Those on the outside wall were ruined as the ceiling over the curved picture window had partially fallen in. Any furniture that once occupied the room must have been carted away.

"The architect was clever," Walker said. "The wood panels aren't merely decorative. A number of them conceal hiding places." He put the heel of his hand on the edge of a panel near the fireplace. I heard a click, and the panel swung open, revealing a shallow cavity tucked between the vertical joists. He looked at Vivian. "I'll bet you found lots of hiding places here, didn't you? Children are clever like that."

"I don't remember," Vivian said. "It was a very long time ago."

He smiled at her warmly. "What *do* you remember?"

"The blood. By the fireplace."

"Ah, yes." His lips twitched with an emotion I couldn't read.

Sure enough, even after all those decades, the faint outline of a darkish stain still marred the raised brick hearth and the floorboards.

"We read about the deaths here," I said. "Why were the authorities so sure the poisonings were accidental? Wouldn't blood stains indicate violence?"

"You'd think so, wouldn't you?" Walker said. "I believe the story was the doctor and his wife were in the throes of the poison when one of them fell against the edge of the brick."

"Where did you read that?" I asked. "Is there a contemporary account somewhere?"

"My father may have mentioned it."

Perfect segue. "Yes—your father. I understand he was Netherfield's solicitor then. He would have known the family quite well. Did he say anything else about the deaths?"

"He never dwelt on it, at least not around me. It must have been a painful memory for him, and as Miss Bunn said, it was a very long time ago. Shall we walk on?"

I stayed where I was. This was my chance to find out what the board members knew about the deaths, and I wasn't going to squander it.

"Did you know any of the Beaufoy children? I heard they moved away, and of course they would have been a few years older than you—but perhaps you met them."

"I don't believe I ever did."

"Do you know what *kind* of poison killed them? Perhaps your father mentioned it."

"He didn't." Walker's eyebrows drew together. "I don't mean to be rude, Ms. Hamilton, but exactly what is your interest?"

Oh dear—I'd gone too far. I smiled and gave a little shrug. "This *is* the kind of story that interests people, isn't it? An unsolved mystery. A house with old secrets—or at least a house with unanswered questions. There wasn't much online. I thought you might be able to fill in some of the gaps."

"I wish I could help."

"You might be able to help," I said, pulling up the photo of Will Parker. "Have you ever seen this man? He was a retired policeman. The police believe he was investigating the Beaufoy deaths. He was found dead ten days ago."

Walker took my phone and studied the photo for just a shade too long. "Terry, Zara—have you noticed this man hanging around?" They appeared in the hallway. Walker showed them the photo. They shook their heads.

"We've never seen him," Walker said, returning the phone. He turned his smile on Vivian. "If you don't mind my asking, Miss Bunn, what did you teens get up to in here—bit of snogging?"

Snogging—the old-fashioned British word for making out. Not usually a game for five players.

Vivian colored slightly. "We were pretending to be private investigators, searching for clues in what we thought was a murder."

"Fascinating—watch your step there." He took her arm, guiding her around a cardboard box filled with rubbish. "And what clues did you discover?"

"It was just a game. I haven't thought about it in years."

"Our brains are amazing, you know." Walker tapped a finger against his temple. "You might have uncovered an important clue without realizing it. We find that to be true in legal work, especially when we're interviewing potential witnesses in a criminal case."

We'd arrived in the kitchen, where Terry and Zara were removing a bank of rusted metal cabinets. They stopped working and removed their goggles.

"Are you hoping to restore the cabinets?" I asked Zara.

"Terry says they're too far gone," she said.

Vivian poked me with her elbow. "There's the ironing board."

The simple wooden board had been shoved against one wall. A small, black-handled iron lay on its soleplate, the braided fabric cord draped over the dingy board cover.

"Careful where you step," Walker said. "Some of the floorboards were rotten."

Most of the original linoleum tiles had been pulled up, exposing a rough wooden subfloor with several portions cut out.

"Quite a project," I said, wondering if Walker was funding it personally, banking on potential TV and movie contracts to come.

He was chatting with Vivian.

"I do remember the library," she said in answer to a question I hadn't heard.

"Let's go there next, then," he said, "although there's not a lot to see."

He was right. The room had been taken apart, the shelving and most of the walls removed, leaving a skeleton of old beams. Here, though, the herringbone floor looked salvageable.

"So what sinister clues lurked in the library?" He adopted a conspiratorial tone.

"We found a gun—actually a cigarette lighter in the shape of a derringer."

"See? I said you'd remember something. That must have been exciting. What else?"

"Some medical papers—files, I think. That's all I can remember. Upstairs we found a wallet, a pair of eyeglasses, and a set of keys on a bedside table."

"Well, that *is* sinister." Walker laughed. "I'm afraid we can't go upstairs. The flat roof has partially collapsed. We'll have to call in the heavy equipment."

Restoring Monkey Puzzle House to its former glory was sounding more and more like one of the twelve labors of Hercules. We walked through the rest of the first-floor rooms, most of which had been cleared and stripped. Walker kept up a steady commentary, describing what the house had looked like when he first bought it. "What were *your* impressions when you saw it for the first time?" he asked Vivian.

"All I can remember is snapshots," Vivian said, "probably unreliable. Naturally you want to know as much as you can about the history of the house, but I'm not the one to ask. You might try contacting the two youngest Beaufoy daughters. We've been told they live in Upford, near Ipswich."

"Excellent idea," he said. "We'll do that. As you said, Kate, old houses have old secrets."

"Are you looking for any particular secrets?" I smiled.

"I'm not sure what you mean. Our goal is preserving history. If you remember anything interesting, Vivian, be sure and let us know."

The tour was over.

Back at the car, Vivian and I were surprised to see Zara.

She glanced over her shoulder toward the house. "You weren't fooled by that grandmother business, were you? I thought I should explain. Niall heard about your recommendation to have the Van

Eyck analyzed. He wanted to check you out. He sent Terry. That's all there was to it. As I'm sure you've guessed, my husband isn't the cleverest liar in the world."

I pulled up the photo of Will Parker. "You're sure you've never seen this man around here? He may have been asking questions."

Zara blinked at the photo. "No . . . I don't think so. In fact, I'm sure I haven't."

She wasn't the cleverest liar in the world either.

* * *

"What did you think of Niall Walker?" I asked Vivian once we were back in the car.

"Charming man."

"He was charming," I said. "He seemed especially interested in your explorations of the house. Don't you wonder why they're ripping the place apart?"

Vivian's head whipped around. "You think they're looking for something? It can't be the metal box. That's already been found."

"They're looking for something, and Walker was pumping you for information."

She looked at me in astonishment. "You think that charming man is the one who sent the game pieces and murdered Will Parker?"

"I wouldn't go that far." I was pretty sure the Walkers *had* recognized the photo of Will Parker, but I didn't want to tell Vivian until I had proof. To change the subject, I asked her to find my phone in my handbag. "Would you mind checking my messages and phone calls?"

She found my phone and clicked it on. "You've had two missed calls from Tom. Oh—and a text, just now."

"It must be important. He's in meetings all day. Read it to me."

"It says *Call me about Frank Keane.*"

I waited until I found a lay-by and pulled off the road.

Tom picked up on the third ring. "Hello, beautiful."

"Tea break?"

"How did you guess? We gather again in five minutes."

"What did you learn about Frank Keane?" I held my breath. "Is he dead?"

"He's alive, living in Stevenage. I have a friend in the Hertfordshire Constabulary."

"Pays to have friends. What did he find out?"

"You mean what did *she* find out. DI Pippa Harmon. I met her on that homeland security course in Scotland—just before you and I met in Glenroth."

"Should I be jealous?"

"She's a grandmother in her late fifties. And a damn good DI."

"What did she say?"

"Turns out Frank Keane is a retired accountant—in the early stages of dementia, but otherwise in pretty good health for his age. His wife is the caregiver."

"Tom, thank you."

"Almost forgot—how was Hopley's and Monkey Puzzle House?"

"Too long to tell in five minutes. I'll explain when I see you."

We rang off.

"Well?" Vivian folded her arms over her chest, daring me to withhold information.

"How far away is Stevenage?"

"From Long Barston?" She frowned. "Hour and a half, maybe two hours?"

"How about Upford?"

"Shorter. Forty-five minutes."

"What would you say to another road trip?"

Chapter Seventeen

～

Thursday, September 3

I opened my eyes Thursday morning to another beautiful, clear September day.

The evening before, I'd made contact with Frank Keane's wife. She'd assured me her husband would be delighted to receive visitors and suggested eleven, just after his morning nap, when he'd be most alert. I'd also found Millicent and Dulcett Beaufoy in the British Telecom white pages. They still lived in Upford, a village about eight miles south of Ipswich. That was the good news. The bad news was they never answered their telephone. I'd tried several times. No voice mail kicked in, asking us to leave a message. Once I thought I heard a tiny click, as if someone had picked up the receiver and set it down again.

The other bad news was the fact that Stevenage and Upford were in opposite directions from Long Barston. That meant that Vivian and I wouldn't have time to visit both the Keanes and the Beaufoys on the same day. On Thursday we'd head southwest to Stevenage to see the Keanes, and on Friday we'd get back in the car and drive east toward Upford.

With those decisions made, Vivian and I spent Wednesday evening planning and checking our routes, first on Vivian's old ordnance survey maps and then, because Vivian's maps were so old they didn't even show the M1 motorway, on Google Maps.

On Thursday we left Long Barston at ten AM and headed west on the A1092.

As we drove through the lush Hertfordshire countryside, Vivian read to me from a website she'd pulled up on my cell phone. Stevenage, she said, was once a tiny village, famous for its six hills, burial mounds for wealthy Roman families. Change came after the Second World War when Stevenage was chosen as the first of the so-called *new towns*, relocation sites for people displaced by the London bombings. Within a decade, the populace had swelled from 7,000 to about 60,000.

We approached, not on the M1 motorway but on the surface road, passing by Rooks Nest House, E. M. Forster's childhood home and the model for *Howards End*.

The Keanes lived in a bay-fronted, semidetached Victorian period house in the heart of the Old Town. The door was answered by a tiny birdlike woman in black leggings and a gray linen smock dotted with paint. A long white braid, also dotted with paint, hung over her left shoulder. "Excuse my appearance. I've been working."

"Mrs. Keane?" I asked.

"Yes, but call me Jean—Jean Keane." She'd opened the door to let us enter. "When I married Frank, his mother suggested I change my name to Joan or Jeanette." Her laugh was as high and clear as silver bells. "You must be Kate. And you're Vivian. I understand you knew Frank when he was a boy."

We'd stepped into a narrow hallway.

"He was Frankie when I knew him," Vivian said. "He and another lad, Jack Cavanagh, were staying at Hopley's in Suffolk. I think their parents were friends."

"The boys were cousins," Jean said. "Jack's mother and Frank's mother were sisters. The families would vacation together every year at Hopley's." She took Vivian's cane and propped it against a ceramic umbrella stand. "Come this way. Frank's in the lounge."

The house was filled with color. The walls in the lounge were painted a rich malachite green. The dining room, visible through a glossy white archway, was a deep lapis blue. It was set up as a painter's studio, with an easel near the window and pots of pigments everywhere.

"You have visitors, dear," Jean said.

A small, elderly man sat in a lounge chair by the hearth. He appeared considerably older than Vivian, although I knew he wasn't. He wore a thick cardigan sweater with a shirt and colorful striped tie. He looked up and smiled. "Visitors? Lovely. Do we know them?"

His fingers pressed on the arms of his chair.

"Please don't get up, Mr. Keane," I said. "If it's all right, we'll join you."

"Yes—just there," Jean said. "Pull the chairs a bit closer. He's hard of hearing."

"You don't know me, Mr. Keane," I said. "My name is Kate. But you might remember my friend, Vivian Bunn."

His forehead wrinkled in thought. "I don't remember anyone named Vivian." He looked at his wife. "Do we know anyone named Vivian?"

"From Hopley's, Frankie," Vivian said. "A long time ago. We explored that house, remember?"

Light dawned in the watery blue eyes. "I do remember that house. What was it called?"

"Monkey Puzzle."

"That's right." He was nodding. "And your name was . . . ?"

"Vivian. There were three boys that summer—you, Jack Cavanagh, and Will Parker—and two girls—Vivian and Mary. The Five Sleuths. I'm Vivian."

"Yes, of course—*Vivian*. I knew you a long time ago." Color had returned to his cheeks. "Jean, I knew this woman a long time ago. At Hopley's. Have I ever told you about Hopley's?"

"Many times." She laid her hand on his thin shoulder. "I'll make tea, Frank. You'd like that, wouldn't you?"

"Lovely. Or maybe our guests would care for something stronger?"

"Early for that, dear," Jean said. "We haven't had lunch yet."

"Haven't we?" He looked puzzled.

"Frankie—is it all right if I call you that?" Vivian asked. "I've been telling Kate about Hopley's—the summer of 1963. Do you remember?"

"You don't soon forget something like that, do you? That house—I don't mind telling you now I was scared silly. Jack was too, although he'd never have admitted it. It was that older boy—what was his name? The one who got us inside."

"Will Parker. Did you know he became a police officer—CID?"

"Did he? I can't say I'm surprised. Quite an adventure we had. I haven't thought about it in years. Jean, did I ever tell you about Hopley's?"

"Yes, you have. Many times."

"What a place, eh?" He looked at Vivian. "Remember the train? *Hop on the Hopley's train.* Ha!"

"And that voice on the intercom every morning—do you remember?"

"Good mooorning, campers. Riiise and shine." They said it in perfect unison.

"About that abandoned house," I said, attempting to steer the conversation back on track, "and the game you played. Cluedo."

"That's it—*Cluedo.*" He raised a shaky finger. "Jean, did I ever tell you about that summer at Hopley's?"

"Yes, you did. A great adventure." She smiled at him.

"You had a game piece, Mr. Keane," I said. "Do you remember what it was?"

"A spanner. Found it in the garage."

"Did someone post it to you recently?"

"Did someone—? I, ah . . ." His eyes clouded again. He closed his mouth and looked at his wife.

"I'll put the kettle on now, shall I?" she said. "Kate, why don't you help me while Vivian and Frank chat about the old days."

I gave Vivian a meaningful look.

She inched her chair closer to Frank's. "Do you remember the ice cream kiosk? They had a special ice cream treat—on a stick, with layers."

"The fruit pastilles—yes. Of course, I liked the chocolate cornettoes best."

"I preferred the toffee bars."

Their voices faded as I followed Jean through her studio. She'd been working on an abstract design in bright yellows and reds. The light from the east-facing window brought out a shimmer in the yellow.

"Are these watercolors?" I asked. "They're so vibrant."

"I use them full strength—much richer than the pale wash of hues you often see."

"What causes the shimmer?"

She laughed. "Pearl powder. I'd be blackballed from the local academy, but I'm doing this to please myself, so why not?"

She opened a door into the kitchen. The cabinets were white, the countertops black—painted concrete, very chic—and the walls a lively robin's egg blue.

"You mentioned the spanner," she said, filling the electric kettle. "Frank still remembers the past. It's the present that doesn't seem to get recorded in his brain." She opened a tall cupboard door and brought out a small rectangular box that had been unwrapped. "He received this a couple of weeks ago." Setting the box on the table, she unfolded the flaps. Inside was what Americans call a wrench—dark metal, about twelve inches long.

"Who sent it?" I asked.

"We don't know. Look at the postmark—Marylebone, August sixteenth. There was no return address and no note of explanation inside."

"Did Frank recognize the spanner?"

"Yes. Right away."

"Was he upset? Worried?"

"He was pleased. He thought it was his birthday." She measured out tea leaves into a perforated silver infuser. "Did Vivian receive a package?"

"No, but the other two men did— Jack Cavanagh and Will Parker. Anonymous packages with the game pieces they'd used at Monkey Puzzle House."

Her eyes opened wider. "Why would someone do that?"

"It might have been a joke. There's one person in the gang that summer we haven't been able to contact. The girl named Mary. Has Frank ever mentioned Mary?"

"I don't think so." She opened a tin and arranged a few biscuits on a plate. "We heard Jack died recently. The family hasn't been close in decades. The sisters had a falling out years ago, but Jack's oldest daughter, Susan, sends us notes every once in a while."

"His younger daughter, Cheryl, found the package, but not until after his death." I considered telling her about Will's murder and Cheryl's suspicions, but decided there was no reason to worry her until we'd gotten the results of the second autopsy on Jack Cavanagh. "Has your husband received any visitors recently, wanting to talk about Hopley's?"

Jean laughed. "Yes, he has—*you*." She poured boiling water over the tea leaves, swished it around, and capped the pot.

I laughed, too. "No one else?"

She shook her head. "I don't think so. A neighbor, Mrs. Harker, comes over several times a week to stay with Frank while I do the shopping or attend my painting class at the Arts Society. Sometimes I just take a walk. I can't leave him on his own anymore. He has a tendency to wander. I'm sure she would have said. Let's go back in, shall we?"

I handed Jean my card. "If someone does show up, will you let me know?"

* * *

On the drive back to Long Barston, Vivian was unusually quiet.

"Are you sad?" I asked, imagining it had been difficult seeing someone her own age in such a fragile condition.

"I'm thinking." She took a swig of tea from her thermos.

"About the passage of time?"

"Good Lord, no. About murder. Someone threatened Will, Jack, and Frankie. Why?"

"We don't know the game pieces were meant as a threat." I was trying not to alarm her. "Will Parker may have been murdered because of something that happened when he was on police duty. And Jack Cavanagh's death may have been accidental after all. People have been known to mix up their pills."

"And maybe St. Paul's Cathedral was built by a race of giants from another planet." She jammed the cap on the thermos with the heel of her hand.

"I wish you could remember Mary's last name. She's the only one of the five we haven't found. Maybe she sent the packages."

"Are you suggesting a timid woman in her seventies broke into Monkey Puzzle House on her own, managed to locate a metal box hidden there for almost sixty years, and then somehow discovered our current addresses and mailed the game pieces for a lark?"

"All right—it does sound far-fetched."

"You're the one who was so sure this all had to do with the poisoning deaths of Dr. Beaufoy and his wife."

Actually it was her, but I let it go. "At least Frank Keane is alive and safe. No one would harm an old man with Alzheimer's."

Vivian gave me a stern look. "I hope you're right."

Chapter Eighteen

～

Friday, September 4

Vivian and I left for Upford early the following morning. My goal was to interview the Beaufoy sisters and be back in Long Barston by early afternoon. Tom had promised to pick me up a few minutes early for our engagement party. I had a lot to tell him.

The fields swept past. The grain crops, wheat and barley, had already been harvested. In some fields, the farmers had turned their chickens loose to gobble up the fallen heads. In other fields, the autumn plowing had already been completed, leaving furrows of fine, sandy loam.

The address we'd found for the Beaufoys—Wren Cottage, 27 Bramble Walk—led us to the east side of the market town of Upford, close to the Essex border. A sinuous red-brick wall snaked along the road on our right. We were so taken by the sight, we almost missed the turning toward the village center.

Wren Cottage stood at the end of a leafy lane. It was an attractive stone bungalow, painted that shade of yellow you often see in Suffolk. A large front garden was surrounded by a picket fence, through which rocket and mint were growing. A woman knelt in one of the beds, a wide-brimmed straw hat on her head.

"Hello there," Vivian called. "Lovely garden. Glorious colors."

The woman looked up, startled. "Thank you. I live for my garden. Can I help you?"

"We're from the Society for the Preservation—"

I gave Vivian a surreptitious poke in the back. "Are either of the Beaufoy sisters at home today?"

"Why are you asking?" The woman stood with a grunt and came to meet us at the gate. She was a pleasant-looking woman in her mid to late sixties, tall and sturdy, with a broad, unlined forehead, bright blue eyes, and sandy, chin-length hair threaded with gray.

We introduced ourselves. I said, "Vivian saw your former home, Monkey Puzzle House, years ago when she vacationed at Hopley's."

"Hop on the Hopley's train, eh? Quite a place in its day." She clicked the lock on her garden shears. "I'm Dulcie Beaufoy. What would you like to know?"

"We'd like to know what happened," Vivian said.

I stifled a gasp. "She means the history of the house. It's so unusual."

The woman cocked her head, studying us. "Who sent you?"

That was a strange comment. "No one sent us. We saw the house and heard you lived in Upford. Do you have a few minutes?"

She looked at us for another long moment, deciding. "I suppose so. I have to warn you. My sister, Millie, can be unpredictable." She removed her hat and tossed the shears in the flower bed. "Come through the gate."

We followed her along a flagged walk to the front door, which stood open.

"*Millie*," she shouted. "Two women are here. They want to ask us about Monkey Puzzle House."

Inside, someone groaned.

"Is your sister all right?" I asked, horrified.

"Millie had a stroke about a year ago. The left side of her brain was affected, the speech center. As you might imagine, it's extremely frustrating for her, not being able to communicate. I'm the only one who can understand her. Come in. I'll make tea. She'll like that."

The living room was attractive, with a low, beamed ceiling and warm, honey-colored wood floors. Matching sofas covered in pink-and-brown-patterned slipcovers formed a right angle in front of a stone hearth.

Millicent Beaufoy sat in a high-backed chair near the front window. Her iron-gray hair was thin, revealing patches of scalp. One huge blue eye stared at us. The other drooped. Her pale lips moved, but nothing came out except a sort of low growl.

Whatever beauty Millie Beaufoy had once possessed was well and truly gone, leaving a twisted mouth and pale, sunken cheeks etched with deep lines. Her good eye blazed with some powerful emotion. An irrational fear shot though me, which I immediately dismissed. This unfortunate woman posed no threat to us or to anyone.

"Millie, this is . . ." Dulcie hesitated. "What did you say your names were?"

The growl subsided. Millie's head sank into her shoulders.

"I'm Kate Hamilton, Miss Beaufoy," I said, "and this is Vivian Bunn. We're from Long Barston." I looked at Dulcie. "Is it *Miss* Beaufoy or is she married?"

"Never married, either of us."

"We're here about Monkey Puzzle House, Miss Beaufoy. Such interesting architecture." I crouched near the high-backed chair, putting myself on a level with the old woman. The fingers of her left hand grasped the soft arms of the chair. Her claw-like right hand lay curled in her lap. She bared her teeth.

I looked at Dulcie. "Are you sure she doesn't mind we're here?"

"She likes company. We don't get many visitors these days. Please take the sofa—yes, right there. Millie has trouble hearing, so you'll have to speak up." Dulcie moved a wooden chair next to her sister and sat. She took Millie's paralyzed hand in hers and kissed it. "Our older sister, Justine—Justy—died about a year and a half ago. Six months later, Millie had the stroke. Even before that, she wasn't in the best of health. She's diabetic, so she needs daily injections. I have to give them now. She's totally dependent on me. I don't mind. It's my purpose in life—tending my garden and caring for my sister." She smiled at her sister and patted her hand. "She and Justy took care of me when I was a child. I was the tagalong—unplanned. My sisters practically raised me."

The groaning started again. It was almost—*hostile* was the word that came to mind.

Millie's left arm shot out, missing Dulcie's face by inches.

"Millie—it's *all right*." Dulcie grabbed her sister's arm and lowered it. "We always have tea around this time. I expect she's afraid we'll miss it, now you're here." She leaned toward her sister. "I'll put the kettle on in a minute, dear. You can have one of those jam tarts you're so fond of."

"When did you move back from Jersey?" I asked Dulcie.

"Jersey?"

"We heard you were sent to live with an aunt and uncle on the Isle of Jersey after your parents' deaths."

The groaning started again.

"I *know*, dear." Dulcie patted her sister's papery cheek. "It *was* sad. But Kate's right. I was sent away." She turned to us. "Justy didn't think she could manage with all of us. I don't hold it against her—she was only twenty when our parents died, and I was a bit of a handful."

Was Millie often violent? Dulcie seemed to be coping, but it couldn't have been easy caring for someone in that state.

"To answer your question," Dulcie said, "I came back to this house in 2002. My sisters needed me."

"What did you do in Jersey?"

"Computer work, mostly."

"How about your brother—Grayson?"

"You seem to know a lot about the family." Dulcie's eyes narrowed.

"I read an article in the newspaper," Vivian said. "About the house being sold."

"I see. Well, poor Gray died in a boating accident at sea."

"I'd like to ask about the house," Vivian said. "I saw it in 1963, two years after your parents' deaths. I've always wondered why you kept it unoccupied all those years."

"*Eee-ahh.*" Millie shook her head. She was trying to speak.

"Gray wanted to sell," Dulcie said. "Justy refused point-blank. She wouldn't let anyone near the house. The cleaner managed to salvage some of our clothes—that was it."

"I understand the house was used as a film location during those years," I said.

"If you've seen it, you know it's unique. The money was helpful. Our parents left us a trust fund, but it isn't unlimited. We've had lots of enquiries over the years—people wanting to buy the house. A few were quite insistent. Justy always turned them down."

Millie let out a screech.

"That's true," Dulcie told her. "There were break-ins as well."

"Was anything taken?"

"How would we know? Justy refused to have the incidents investigated. She never even reported them to the police."

A strange reaction. Unless Justy was hiding something.

"So after Justy died, the house went on the market," I said.

"Millie and I agreed it was time. As I said, our parents left us an income, but it can't last forever."

"Did you visit the house during those years?" It occurred to me the sisters might have found the metal box, although why they would send the game pieces to the Five Sleuths, I couldn't imagine.

"I never did. Of course, I wasn't here for most of that time."

Millie's left hand was pounding softly on the arm of the chair. I could almost feel her frustration. "Your sister is trying to say something."

"She is," Dulcie agreed. "I think she's trying to say she went to the house a couple of times with Justy. Isn't that right, dear?"

"*Aaah-enn . . .*" Millie's shoulders sagged. The effort of trying to speak was exhausting her.

"Did she ever find a metal box?" I asked.

"Ask her yourself," Dulcie said. "She understands everything."

"Millie," I leaned forward and spoke into her ear. "Did you find a metal box at Monkey Puzzle House?"

Millie looked blank. Either she hadn't understood me or she didn't know what I was talking about. There was something else I wanted to ask, but I couldn't remember what it was. "Do you have any questions, Vivian?"

I never learn.

"Yes—why didn't you and your siblings die with your parents that night?"

Oh, golly. The faces of both sisters changed.

Millie's good hand closed in a fist. The noises began again. "*Aawoo aaa.*" Saliva ran from the corner of her mouth.

"You don't have to answer that," I said quickly. "It's none of our business."

"There's a simple answer," Dulcie said. "We weren't home. The traveling fair came every year in May—horse races, games, rides, kiosks selling food on the pier and promenade. Millie should have been home that night. Isn't that right?" She took the paralyzed hand again. "She'd gotten herself grounded—a boy, naturally." She flashed us a smile. "Millie was always the pretty one. Anyway, the rest of us had gone to the fair. Millie sneaked out and went to the fair anyway. Lucky for her or she'd have died, too."

"What kind of poison killed your parents?" Vivian asked before I could stop her.

Dulcie shrugged. "No one told me anything."

Without warning, Millie's good arm shot out again. I think she'd been aiming for her sister, but she ended up delivering a glancing blow to the side of my head.

I'd had enough. "Our visit is obviously distressing your sister. You were kind to invite us in—strangers, asking questions—but we won't stay for tea. We really should be going anyway. Come on, Vivian."

As I stood, Millie grabbed my arm with her left hand. Her short nails bit into my flesh. I pulled my arm away. "I'm sorry we've upset you by talking about the past."

Millie snarled and jerked her hand away.

Dulcie walked us out to our car. "I'm sorry, Kate. Millie isn't usually violent."

"I'm sure she didn't mean to hurt me," I said. "Can you really understand what she's trying to say?"

"Truthfully?" Dulcie ran her fingers through her thick hair. "Not always. But I think it helps Millie with her frustration."

"Before we go, may I show you a photo? The man in it, Will Parker, was murdered recently. He was an ex-policeman. We think he was investigating your parents' deaths."

"Really? I wonder why." Dulcie took a long look at the photograph. "He was a handsome man. I feel sorry for his family."

"Do you remember ever seeing him?"

Her blue eyes held mine. "No—I'm sure I haven't. No one ever comes to see us."

We got in the car and drove away. What was it I'd wanted to ask?

* * *

"You don't have an unspoken thought, do you?" I glared at Vivian. "You could see how upset Millie was, and you had to go and bring up their parents' deaths? Millie probably feels guilty. If she'd been there that night, she might have been able to call for help."

"If she'd been there, she'd be dead." Vivian pulled down the visor and patted her hair.

I sighed audibly. "What do you think was going on with Millie?"

"She was frustrated."

"She was enraged. Did you see her pounding the arm of the chair? When she grabbed my arm, she dug her nails into my flesh." I held out my arm so Vivian could see the red marks.

"Why would she do that?"

"I don't know. Unless she didn't want Dulcie giving us all that information. Especially about the poisoning."

"Millie was a girl back then," Vivian said, "thwarted in love. Maybe she poisoned her parents because they'd grounded her—serve them right and all that."

"Or maybe," I said, remembering what old Percy Pike had said, "it was the older boy, the one her father didn't approve of. Maybe they were in it together."

"Wouldn't that have been the first thing the police suspected?" Vivian asked reasonably. "Anyway, where would a young boy get poison?"

"I don't know, but it sounds to me like the oldest sister, Justine, ruled the roost. If one of them was guilty, and she knew it, she probably told them to keep quiet and tell the police the same story."

"She couldn't have forced the coroner to lie."

"No, but she might have tampered with the evidence—or concealed it."

I thought again about the missing inquest files. Justine was of age. As an interested party, she'd have had access to the records. I could see her removing the files to protect her sister, but would she have done it to protect an older boy her parents disapproved of? That seemed less likely, unless they were in it together.

"I almost forgot," Vivian said. "Lady Barbara said to remind you the path through the park will be closed starting next Monday. We'll have to take the bridge."

I probably said something like "Okay, fine," but my mind was still on the sisters.

Just past Boxford, I turned right onto the A134, heading into the sun. "Vivian," I said, pulling down my visor, "even if Millicent Beaufoy murdered her parents all those years ago—accidentally or on purpose, with or without the help of her boyfriend—she's in no condition to have killed Will Parker or Jack Cavanagh today. And even if she did find the metal box in Monkey Puzzle House, she can't have wrapped up the game pieces and mailed them without help."

"So maybe she had help," Vivian said. "Remember, she didn't have the stroke until six months after Justine's death. With the older sister dead and out of the way, either of the two surviving sisters could have entered the house at any time."

"Dulcie denied it." I passed a vintage sports car, chugging along with the top down.

"You believed her?"

"Why wouldn't I? It sounds to me like Justine was afraid someone would find incriminating evidence in the house. Did the Five Sleuths find any proof of murder?"

"I wish I could remember," Vivian said, not bothering to argue the point. "You're probably right about Dulcie. She wasn't shy about giving out information. It's probably never occurred to her that Millie could be guilty of murder. Of course, she was shielded from all of it—sent away to live in Jersey."

I held the wheel with one hand, rubbing the red marks left by Millie's nails.

Two questions nagged at me.

How ever did Dulcie cope? And was she safe?

Chapter Nineteen

I stood in front of the full-length mirror in Vivian's bedroom, admiring my dress, chosen by Charlotte, my best friend and fashion guru—a garnet red, watered-silk affair with black grosgrain straps and sash. She really did have a gift for fashion.

I'd done my part—smoothing my hair into a ponytail and pulling out a few tendrils as Charlotte had taught me. I'd even applied a layer of red lipstick over my usual cherry lip gloss.

The engagement party was set for seven PM. Vivian and Fergus had gone over early to help Lady Barbara and Francie Jewell put the finishing touches on whatever they were doing. Tom and I had been instructed not to arrive even a minute early.

Tom's car pulled up to Rose Cottage at six thirty. He met me at the door.

"You look beautiful. That dress reminds me of the one you wore to the Tartan Ball in Scotland, when we first met."

"You mean the one I borrowed from a teenager with a twenty-four-inch waist? I thought I was going to pass out."

"Mmm, yes . . . I remember." He smiled absently, opening the car door for me.

"Where's Liz?" I slid into the passenger's seat of his Range Rover.

"Mother said she'd meet us at the Hall." He snapped his seatbelt. "We have a few minutes to spare. Fill me in. You and Vivian did a little time travel, if I remember."

I told him about our visit to Miracle-on-Sea. "Percy Pike, who's quite a character, told us Millie Beaufoy had an older boyfriend her parents didn't like."

"Did Percy Pike know the name of this boyfriend?"

"He didn't. Maybe the cook will remember, if we can find her." I paused, deciding how to phrase what I had to say next. "Vivian wonders if Millie and/or the boyfriend killed her parents because they were trying to break up the romance."

"What's her evidence?"

"She doesn't have any, but we both have a feeling there's something the sisters don't want us to know."

"Like what?"

I shot him a look. "Like whatever it is they don't want us to know."

He laughed. "Back up a bit. Tell me about the visit to Monkey Puzzle House."

I filled him in on the Walkers and their plans to renovate the property. "Niall asked Vivian all kinds of questions about the Five Sleuths and what they'd uncovered. I think the Walkers are looking for something in the house."

"The metal box?"

"Someone already found that, remember? Which reminds me—no, I'll tell you about that in a minute. I want to finish the Walkers."

"What are they looking for?"

"I don't know, but I showed them a photo of Will Parker. They denied ever seeing him, but I'm pretty sure the daughter-in-law, Zara, recognized him. Then you called about Frank Keane, so we went there on Thursday. And what do you think? Frank Keane received a package too. The spanner he used as his game piece. Just like Will Parker and Jack Cavanagh. He doesn't remember much, but he does remember Hopley's and Monkey Puzzle House."

"When did you visit the Beaufoy sisters?"

"Yesterday. They live in a cottage with a huge garden, which seems to be Dulcie's main interest in life. Millie had a stroke that left her paralyzed and unable to speak. She needs constant care. And she's a diabetic, which means Dulcie Beaufoy knows how to give injections."

"Let me get this straight. Vivian suspects Millie of killing her parents because she had a boyfriend her parents didn't like, and you suspect Dulcie of killing Will Parker because she knows how to give injections?"

I had to smile. "Put that way, no. The whole set-up just felt odd. I kept trying to think of something I wanted to ask them." I stopped. "Oh—I just remembered what it was. When we first got there, Dulcie asked if someone had sent us. I thought that was a strange thing to say. Why would she think someone sent us? I should have asked."

"Did you learn anything?"

"Dulcie knows her parents were poisoned. I think that's all she knows. She seems naïve, sheltered, but then she grew up on an island, away from her siblings. Millie, on the other hand, was extremely agitated. Maybe she didn't like our questions. Or maybe she was afraid Dulcie would blurt out more than she should. She nearly bashed Dulcie in the head—and she took a swing in my direction at one point." I checked my lipstick in the mirror. "I know strokes can affect different parts of the brain. Millie's stroke affected the left side of her body and her speech center, which has to be frustrating for her, but maybe it damaged some other part of her brain, and she's not capable of controlling her emotions."

"Time to go." Tom started the engine and slipped it in gear. "You know none of this is enough to reopen a sixty-year-old closed case. To do that, we need proof of wrongdoing."

"Will Parker's murder isn't enough?"

"To open an inquiry into his death, yes. To look into deaths that took place in 1961, no."

As we were pulling through the Finchley Hall gates, I said, "When will they do the second autopsy on Jack Cavanagh?"

"We haven't heard yet. But Kate—Frank Keane is alive and well. So is Vivian."

"I'd feel a lot better if we could find Mary and make sure she's okay, too."

"Let's put this behind us—just for tonight, okay? This is our engagement party."

* * *

It was precisely seven when Tom knocked on Finchley Hall's huge front door.

Francie Jewell answered. This was one of the rare occasions when she donned her proper black maid's uniform with the frilly white apron. "The guests of honor—come in, come in." She hugged me and took the black angora sweater I'd worn over the dress. "Tonight we're in the Great Hall. This may be one of our last big parties."

It was true. The National Trust had completed the work on Finchley Hall's roof. Repairs and updating on the plumbing and electrics were moving along quickly. By autumn, they'd be tackling the ground-floor rooms, those slated for public viewing, transforming Lady Barbara's elegantly dilapidated interiors into facsimiles of what they might have looked like in the years following the Second World War.

As we entered the Great Hall, a cheer went up. So much for Lady Barbara's "small affair with close friends." The large room was packed. I recognized a cross section of village life—shopkeepers, the ladies from the Suffolk Rose Tea Room, even the old gardener Arthur Gedge, looking surly as ever. Tom's colleagues from the Suffolk Constabulary were there as well—Sergeant Cliffe, Constable Anne Weldon, even Detective Chief Inspector Eacles. I recognized a couple of the checkers from Tesco, too, and the nice lady from the village co-op. They'd all come to wish us happiness. Or to drink Lady Barbara's champagne.

One of the servers handed us flutes of the bubbly.

"Thank you all for coming," Tom said, raising his glass.

"Yes—thank you," I echoed.

Friends gathered round to offer handshakes, hugs, and best wishes.

The room glittered. A banner had been strung across the huge marble fireplace—*They're Engaged!* Finger food had been set out on platters, including Vivian's famous cheddar cheese straws.

Tom and I joined Angela Vine and her fiancé, the rector, Edmund Foxe.

We hugged. "You must be busy, with your wedding just a week away."

Edmund put his arm around Angela's waist. "Our families are meeting for the first time tonight. Hattie sends her regrets. She's busy in the kitchen."

"We hear there's a surprise in the works." Angela flashed a smile.

"Tom?" I looked at him.

"The *ring*," he whispered, patting his jacket pocket.

Edmund Foxe mimed zipping his mouth. "Haven't told a soul."

He and Angela wandered off to greet some of Edmund's parishioners, and we were hailed by ex-footballer Ralston Green, a hulk of a man known locally as the Gentle Giant.

He clapped Tom on the shoulder. "So you're takin' the plunge, mon." He'd lived in the UK since he was s toddler, but Ralston could put on a convincing West Indies accent when it suited him.

"Where are Yasmin and Ertha?" I asked. Ralston's wife, Yasmin, was the local mail carrier. His mother, Ertha, a tiny woman in her nineties, had helped solve a murder last spring.

"Ertha's not feelin' too well at present," Ralston said. "Nothin' to worry 'bout." He chuckled. "Can't keep that old woman down for long, you know."

Tom asked Ralston about some new equipment the EMTs had managed to snag in spite of the recent round of budget cuts, and I took the opportunity to locate my friend Jayne Collier from the Three Magpies.

Jayne stood near the large front windows, holding a glass of champagne. I was surprised to see her husband, Gavin, talking with aging hippie Steven Peacock, proprietor of the Finchley Arms.

"Swords lowered?" I asked, nodding toward the two men.

"Something like that." She gave me a wry smile. "Ever since Gavin helped them when their cellars flooded last May, Stephen's actually been civil. Wish I could say the same for Briony."

I was about to say something witty when we heard a bell ring. The room became quiet.

Lady Barbara stood in front of the enormous hearth, looking lovely but frail in a pale blue silk sheath. "Kate, Tom—please join me. This evening we're here to celebrate you and your commitment to each other."

Tom took my hand.

"Where is your mother?" I whispered as we made our way through the crowd. "It's seven thirty. Maybe she's not coming."

"She'll come."

Lady Barbara lifted her flute of champagne. "Dearest Kate and Tom, while we don't yet know the date or the place of your wedding, we do know that in the space of nine months, you have both become very dear to us. Your friends, your colleagues, the entire community wish you every happiness in your new life together. Selfishly, we hope you will remain with us for many years to come, but we know you will make the best decision for yourselves. We ask only that you don't forget us." She shook her finger at us playfully. "Now, ladies and gentlemen, raise your glasses to Kate and Tom."

"To Kate and Tom" came the echo.

Liz Mallory appeared near the archway to the entrance hall. She wore a little black dress, elegant with her slim figure and silver hair.

"She's here," I whispered.

Tom reached into his pocket, pulled out a small leather box, and opened it. The Art Deco ring dazzled in its platinum setting. He slipped the ring on the fourth finger of my left hand. "Kate, may this ring remind you always of my love, my trust, and my unwavering loyalty."

A sigh rippled through the crowd. People lined up to admire the ring and wish us well.

"My word. Ever so lovely."

"Thrilled for you, my dears."

"You make a good pair, the two of you."

"We do hope you'll settle nearby, Kate. Don't forget about us."

Liz Mallory stood before us.

"You made it," Tom said. "We were beginning to worry."

I held out my hand to show her the ring. "Liz, it's the most beautiful ring I've ever seen. I'm so honored to wear it." The words died in my throat.

Her mouth was set in a hard white line. "How *could* you do this?" she hissed at Tom.

"What are you talking about?" I felt his body tense.

"That ring belongs to Olivia." The words came through clenched teeth. "You had no right to give it to *her*. No right at all."

She turned on her spiky black heels and left.

*   *   *

Somehow I made it through the final forty-five minutes of the party. What saved me was the old gardener, Arthur Gedge, who by a random turn of events had been the only one standing near enough at that moment to hear Liz Mallory.

"Miserable old cow," he'd said under his breath.

I could have kissed him.

Blinking to hold back tears, I'd set my teeth and smiled as people kept coming, offering their congratulations and best wishes.

You can do this, said my inner voice—supportive for once.

By nine, the last of the guests had said their goodbyes. Vivian insisted she was staying to help clean up. Francie Jewell would walk her home.

Tom and I escaped to his car.

At last we were alone.

"Kate, darling, I'm so sorry." His voice was thick. I'd never seen him cry.

"The last thing I want is to come between you and—" I stopped, unable to go further.

"Between me and my mother?" Tom huffed.

"No, darling. Between you and your daughter."

"You haven't. You won't." He turned to face me. "Olivia isn't like that. She's kind, she's—" He lowered his chin. "I talked to her, Kate, before any of this. She's happy for us. She's happy you'll be wearing the ring." He pressed his fingers to his forehead. "I'll never forgive her."

I tried to slip the ring off my finger. "Maybe we should take a step back."

"Our engagement?" The look on his face nearly broke my heart.

"No, silly—the ring. It doesn't matter. *You* matter."

He grabbed my hand, stopping me. "Leave that ring where it is. She's not winning this one. Not this time."

"Winning?"

Tom was silent for a moment. Then he slumped in his seat. "When Sarah died, my mother moved in with us—with Olivia and me. It was the only solution. My job doesn't run to regular hours. Olivia was only twelve, a vulnerable age. She needed someone to look after her. She needed a woman."

"I know that, Tom. It was a good decision."

"Good for Olivia, maybe. But little by little, my mother began taking over—deciding things, establishing rules and routines as if it were her house. As if Olivia were her child. At first I was grateful—I'm ashamed to admit it, but I had no emotional energy left to do anything except work and make sure Olivia was all right."

"I understand that."

"But gradually, our lives fell into a pattern—a pattern I never fully recognized until tonight. She's been arranging my life—or trying to—for twelve years. Tonight it stops." He pulled his Range Rover around in the Hall's courtyard and headed for the long, tree-lined drive and the gates. "Look—no decisions tonight, all right? I'll take you home. I'll be staying in Bury for the time being. There's a flat I can use. If I see her, I might say things I'll regret."

"What things?"

"Like telling her we're moving to Ohio—permanently." His eyes were dark with emotion. "That's what I want, Kate. A new start. Tonight has made my decision."

I put my hand on his, feeling the warmth of his skin.

"No decisions tonight, remember?"

Chapter Twenty

Rose Cottage was dark. Tom stayed to make sure I got the door unlocked and the lights turned on. In the kitchen, he took me in his arms.

"You're right. The decision is ours, not mine. Are you free in the morning?"

"Afraid not. Ivor and I have an appointment at Apollo Research in Cambridge."

"Too bad. I'm in meetings all afternoon."

"I could meet you for dinner at the Trout."

"Good plan. But don't meet me. I'll pick you up here at six thirty."

He was leaving when I asked, "When will you talk to your mother?"

"I don't know. Soon." He kissed me.

The door closed, leaving me alone—well, almost alone. Fergus lay in his basket by the fire. He gave a questioning woof—*Where's Mummy?*—and trundled into the kitchen, where his leash hung on an iron hook.

"Come here, you," I said, bending down to attach the leash to his collar. "Mummy will be home soon."

He cocked his head. His corkscrew tail twitched.

Outside, wispy purple clouds stretched across the coral pink horizon. A few stars already winked in the fresh-ink sky. St. Æthelric's square tower, a solid black silhouette, rose above the tree tops.

You had no right to give it to her. Liz's words were stuck in my brain.

I'd never had an enemy before—someone who actually wished me harm. Tom and I had enough complications in our relationship. We didn't need this. We didn't deserve it.

The more I thought about Liz's behavior at the party, the angrier I got. And the angrier I got, the more I wanted to talk with my mother.

"All done, Fergus?" The solid little pug led the way back inside. Once I'd hung up his leash, doled out the treat he deserved for being a good boy, and refilled his water bowl, I headed upstairs to my room.

I kicked off my heels and lay on the bed, my head on the big square Euro-pillow and my cell phone in my hand.

I'd promised not to call my mother on her honeymoon—my idea, to be fair, not hers.

How long does a honeymoon last, officially speaking? They'd been gone two months. In a week or so, they'd return to Oak Hills, the senior living community where they met, and get busy shoehorning the furniture from two separate apartments into their new three-bedroom.

We had communicated during this time. I'd sent regular texts, updating her on life in Long Barston. She'd answered back—interested, chatty. But you can't have a real conversation by text, can you? You can't pour your heart out.

I looked at the phone. Bit the edge of my lower lip. And dialed.

She answered on the third ring. "Linnea Lund speaking." *Smooth as silk with her new name.*

"Hi, Mom. I'm sorry to call."

"I'm glad you did. I know you're busy, but it's been a long time since we've really talked."

"How are you? How's James?"

"We're both fine. Having a wonderful time. We'll be back at Oak Hills Sunday night. On Monday our friends are throwing us a party."

I could hear her smiling. "That's wonderful, Mom. I'm happy for you."

"I know you are, darling. How was *your* party? Tonight, I think."

"Yeah—it was tonight."

"Kate, what's wrong?" I'd never been able to fool her.

"Liz Mallory."

She made a small irritated sound. "What's she done now?"

That was all it took to bring tears. I grabbed a Kleenex and told her.

"I'd never take something that belonged to Olivia."

"Of course you wouldn't. *That woman.*" It wasn't easy to push Linnea Lund to anger.

"Tom's staying at an apartment in Bury tonight—maybe until the wedding. Liz is going to blame me."

"Probably."

"What do I do?"

"My darling girl, you do nothing."

"Should I give the ring back?"

"*What?*"

"Give the ring back."

"Are you out of your mind?"

"But—"

"If you give the ring back, she'll have won, Kate. Is that what you want?"

"Of course not. All I want is to enjoy this time with Tom—making plans for the future, looking forward to our life together. I want to live my life without her in it."

"That's not going to happen. Liz is Tom's mother. Olivia's grandmother." The line went silent for a moment. "What you really want, darling, is for her to love you."

Was it that simple?

When I said nothing, she continued. "Have you heard the old saying, 'Beware the naked man who offers you a shirt'?"

"What's that supposed to mean?"

"It means you can't accept something from someone who's in no position to give it."

"So what do I do?"

"You do whatever you and Tom decide together. You *will* have a mother-in-law, you know—the real thing, not the picture you've painted in your head."

"Speaking of paintings, Ivor and I find out tomorrow if the Van Eyck is the real thing."

"I was wondering about that. What's your gut feeling?"

Her question took me by surprise. "Truthfully? I think there's something wrong with it. It's brilliant. Stunning, in fact. But the definitive answer will come from Apollo Research."

"Perhaps you already have it."

That wasn't what I wanted to hear. "Give James my love."

"And Tom mine. I'm so glad you found each other. Don't let Liz spoil your happiness."

Downstairs, Fergus barked joyfully. Vivian was home.

"Kate—where are you?" I heard her calling from downstairs. "*Kate.*"

I jumped out of bed and dashed into the hall in time to see her trundling up the stairs.

"What is it?"

She patted her chest, sucking in air. "After you and Tom left, Barb and I were chatting about your ring." She swallowed and took a breath. "All of a sudden I *knew.*"

"Knew what?"

"The name I've been trying to remember—it's Mary *Diamond.*"

*　*　*

"Vivian, we can't telephone now—it's after ten o'clock."

I'd carried my laptop down to the sitting room where Vivian and I sat side by side on the sofa. Thanks to the ever-useful British Telecom directory online—why don't we have something like that in the States?—we'd found two Mary Diamonds in Norwich. Vivian wanted to call them both immediately.

"She may have gotten married," I said reasonably. "Her name might not be Diamond."

"But maybe it is. We'll never know if we don't call."

"Why don't we look up the two addresses first? Maybe that will tell us something."

I got busy with Google Street View. The first address turned out to be a small semidetached house in a working-class neighborhood. I couldn't be sure when the photo had been taken, but children's toys were visible in the front garden—a bike, a small trampoline, a folded-up stroller. "This doesn't look like an elder—an *older* person lives there."

"Maybe she lives with her son or daughter."

"But then she likely wouldn't be called Mary Diamond, would she?"

"Okay, fine. What's the second address?"

The second address turned out to be a residential care home—Sunny Shores Care Home, located near one of the green zones along the Yar River. That was possible. Mary Diamond had been fifteen in 1963. Which meant she'd be seventy-three now—not old by modern standards. Of course, she could be in poor health. Or then again, she could be married, and this would prove to be another person entirely.

"There's the phone number." Vivian pointed at the large numerals under the words *Call to Schedule Your Visit.*

"I told you—it's too late."

"Someone will answer. They're bound to have people on duty 'round the clock. Besides, that's a main number. It's not going to ring in her bedroom, is it?"

"What good will it do if we can't talk to her?"

"We can find out if she's *able* to talk to us. We can ask if she's in good health—that kind of thing."

"Oh, all right." I handed her the phone.

Vivian dialed. Someone must have picked up almost immediately because she said, "Oh, my, I expected to leave a message." That quavery voice again. "I'm an old, old friend of Mary Diamond, and

I was wondering if my daughter could drive me over sometime this weekend to visit." She gave me a guilty look. "Mary won't remember me, but I—" She stopped talking. "*What* did you say? When? I see. Well, yes, I suppose I could. Thank you."

She hung up and looked at me.

"Well, *Mom*?" I said.

"Mary died two weeks ago. They want me to collect her things."

I buried my head in my hands. "Give me the phone. I have to text Tom."

Chapter Twenty-One

~

Saturday, September 5

Cambridge isn't "the city of dreaming spires"—that's Oxford—but it might be. The spires are there. So are one-way streets, pedestrian zones, and traffic-control bollards. Ivor and I made our way at a snail's pace into the center of town. We were lucky to find a parking garage on Chesterton Lane, only a block or so from our destination.

Apollo Research and Analysis occupied two terraced Georgian townhouses in a mostly residential area northwest of the university proper. We rang the bell and were admitted by a young man who introduced himself as Gregor, a third-year student from Slovenia, studying art history at Fitzwilliam College. He made a phone call, and within minutes a tall man with ox-yoke shoulders appeared. He wore a pristine white lab coat and a pair of safety goggles atop his partially bald head.

"Welcome. I'm Dr. Philip Zechner. If you come this way, we'll get started." He had a slight Germanic accent.

"Thank you for meeting us on Saturday," Ivor said as we made our way through a warren of offices. A blue light glimmered over a door with a sign reading *Do Not Enter. Radio Spectrometry in Progress.*

"We try to work with our clients' schedules as much as possible."

Zechner ushered us into a small conference room where a flat monitor and what looked like a doctor's X-ray reader hung on the wall. A laptop and a green file folder sat on a faux-wood table.

"If you don't mind," Zechner said, pulling off the safety goggles and stashing them in the pocket of his lab coat, "before we get to any questions you might have, I'd like to present our findings. Since this will be a high-level report, I'll use nontechnical language. Our printed report contains all the details. We've prepared copies for you and for each of the Cliff House board members. Along with our bill, of course."

We agreed.

He opened the file, extracted some papers, and began.

"Our standard policy is to use less expensive, noninvasive methods first, resorting to more sophisticated testing—and cost to our clients—only if necessary. If it looks like a duck and quacks like a duck, no need for DNA testing, eh?" He chuckled at what was probably a standard joke.

"We began with the frame," he said. "This one is early eighteenth century, gilt oak with mitered corners, in the continental style typical of the period. If the painting was indeed made in the fifteenth century, the original frame was replaced at some point. Regrettable but not surprising."

I could see Ivor's left knee starting to bounce. *Just tell us if it's a forgery.* But Zechner wasn't about to be rushed.

"Next we considered the support medium—in this case, Baltic oak panels typical of early Netherlandish painting. Using dendrochronology, the scientific dating of tree rings, we were able to determine that both the upper and lower planks were felled sometime during the final quarter of the fourteenth century C.E. This is the earliest possible date, mind you. Allowing for an uncertain number of years for seasoning, we are prepared to say our findings are consistent with an early to mid-fifteenth-century date."

I wanted to ask how in the world they were able to establish the date so precisely, but decided not to rock the boat. I'd read the report.

"Finally, we examined the painting itself," Zechner said.

Ivor shifted in his chair.

"I'm sure you know that Van Eyck signed and dated several of his paintings on the frame, along with his motto, *Als ich kan*, translated roughly 'As well as I can.' Since the only known example of a signature on the painting itself is the famous Arnolfini portrait, we didn't consider the lack of a signature here to be significant.

"We also considered the technique, the fine brushstrokes, the layering of pigments to create depth, the reflective nature of light and shadow, the mastery of tiny details such as individual strands of hair on Christ's head and the two- or three-day's beard growth on the demoniac. All consistent with Van Eyck. But the surface of a painting is only the beginning."

Zechner clicked some keys on his laptop and an image popped up on the monitor—a shadowy drawing of a man in flowing robes kneeling (in prayer?) beside a large cave.

"The image you see was produced by a technique called infrared reflectography, which reveals what lies beneath the surface of a painting—underdrawings, for example, or *pedimenti*, the revisions an artist might make during the process of creation. Here we discovered an underlying painting of an unidentified man, probably a saint. The panel was recycled. Once again, not uncommon. Oak panels weren't cheap, and if a painting didn't achieve what the artist was aiming for—or if the painting was done by an apprentice—the panels were simply painted over."

Zechner punched a few more keys, and the image became a complex network of fine lines. "This is where things can get interesting, because infrared reflectography also reveals the depth and pattern of the craquelure—the distinctive pattern of cracks that appear over time in the skin of a painting. This is often the smoking gun, because craquelure is almost impossible to reproduce, generally resulting in cracks that are too regular. There are techniques, however, using formaldehyde and a special baking process that have been known to achieve rather remarkable results, especially when a new painting is layered over an old one in which the craquelure is already well developed. Complicating this further is the fact that craquelure on Baltic oak tends to be fairly regular anyway. Nevertheless, the fact that the panels were recycled opens the possibility that the underpainting of the praying saint was already centuries old when *Christ Healing the Demoniac* was begun." I felt rather than saw Ivor stir. "Exactly how old is difficult to determine as craquelure depends partly on age and partly on variables in the drying process. Our report goes into greater depth, but the bottom line is this: our tests were inconclusive."

"And the pigments?" Ivor did that hand-rolling, hurry-up thing.

If Zechner noticed, he didn't show it. "Early pigments were tempered with egg yolk, which dries quickly. That meant only small amounts of paint could be mixed at one time. Van Eyck was one of the artists who pioneered the use of heat-bodied linseed oil as a binder, which extended the drying time of the paint, allowing the artist to build up translucent layers and to mix larger quantities of paint, ensuring color consistency. Our analysis showed that all pigments and binders in the painting are identical in composition to the mineral and plant-based pigments used by Van Eyck in the fifteenth century."

"So you're telling us your pigment tests were also inconclusive?" Ivor's knee was bouncing again. "You don't know if the painting is genuine or a forgery."

"I didn't say that." Zechner's eyes took on an unacademic gleam. "Our last resort would have been mass spectrometry, searching for tiny amounts of the radioactive isotopes unleashed across the globe after 1945. Nowhere to hide from that. But first, we decided to scan several microscopic grains of paint. The samples, each smaller than the width of a human hair, were extracted with a fine scalpel and examined under a stereo-zoom microscope, which produces a three-dimensional image. If anything is embedded in the paint—dust, insect parts, pollen, dandruff, cat hairs—it will emerge. A skilled forger may use the panels, pigments, and binders of the past. It's the present he can't control. Something from the modern world is bound to attach itself in some form to the painting. That's when I notified you of an anomaly, something that shouldn't be there. We repeated the test to ensure there'd been no cross-contamination—and we found the same thing. Embedded in a speckle of blue paint was a tiny fiber." He changed the image on the screen again. This time we saw what looked like a rod with irregular striations, extending diagonally from the bottom left corner of the screen to the upper right. "We isolated the fiber and subjected it to infrared spectroscopy."

"What is it?" Ivor's voice had risen a notch.

"Polyacrylonitrile. Acrylic fiber." Zechner folded his arms over his chest, grinning. "I picture the forger in his studio somewhere—Italy, perhaps—wearing an Orlon jumper."

"Not Italy." Ivor shook his head. "There's only one man who could have pulled off such a masterpiece, and he lived in a small village in the French Alps."

* * *

"You're kidding." Tom held his menu toward the light of the candle burning on our corner table at the Trout. "As simple as a stray fiber?"

"If only our presentation to the Cliff House board could be as simple. They're not going to be happy." I handed my menu to Tom. "Actually, that's an understatement. They're going to flip out."

"I'm sure Ivor can handle it."

"You're probably right." I made a face. "He claims he once held off a gang of pirates with an old lady's walking frame when the crew of the pleasure boat they were on jumped overboard."

"Where was this?"

"Off the coast of Suriname. Anyway, Ivor says the only person who could have reproduced something as magnificent as *Christ Healing the Demoniac* was a French artist—Gerard Bibeau. He's known to have forged dozens of Old Dutch Masters, including Frans Hals, Jan Steen, and Pieter Breughel."

"When was he caught?"

"He wasn't. He died of natural causes in the nineteen sixties—a heart attack in his studio. That's how they knew. On the day he died, he was putting the finishing touches on a fake Vermeer."

"But you said the painting in question was purchased by Horace Netherfield in—when was it?"

"In 1877. I know. It doesn't add up." I gazed into the candle flame. "I'm sorry, Tom. I'm rambling on about work, and you're living in a police-provided bed-sit."

"My decision. I don't think I can have a conversation with my mother right now without losing my temper. What she did was unforgiveable."

"Have you told her you've moved out permanently?"

"Not yet."

"Won't she be worried?"

"That's the least of my concerns."

Our conversation was interrupted by the pub owner, who took our order—the evening's special, his wife's famous coq au vin.

"What is your main concern right now?" I asked.

"You, Kate. *You* are my main concern. You are my future. What I need is a complete new start with you. I'm ready to contact my friend in Toronto—the one with the private investigations firm—and tell him it's a go. I can live anywhere. Why not Jackson Falls, Ohio? You can keep your business going. Eric and Christine still need a home base between terms. Your mother isn't far away. I know I'm going to love her."

"And she's going to love you, too. But there's a problem."

"Which is?"

"*Your* mother."

"I know, believe me."

"What I mean is your relationship with her. She's your mother—Olivia's grandmother." I was sounding like *my* mother. Not a bad thing, come to think of it. "The longer you leave things unresolved, the harder it will be to make things right."

"I'm not sure I want to make things right."

"Yes, you do." I put my hand on his. "When you were a child, she was all you had."

"I had Uncle Nigel."

"In the summers, yes. But it was your mother who cared for you. She had to be both mother and father. You told me she worked all hours, providing for you."

"Only because pride kept her from taking an allowance from Nigel."

"You're not making this easy, Tom. What I'm trying to say is that right now, you are all *she* has."

"She has Olivia."

"And you're going to make Olivia choose between her father and her grandmother?"

Tom said nothing.

"Where else could your mother go?"

"Are you saying we should all live together in Saxby St. Clare—Happy Families?"

"Good Lord, no. I'm no martyr. I'm saying we should get our own place, somewhere close to your work. We can pool our resources. I'll sell my house in Jackson Falls. I've already contacted a realtor. I should have sold it years ago."

"No, Kate. If you sell your house, that money stays with you. For your kids."

"We can talk about that later. I propose we live in England for a year. See how it goes. You take the promotion. Maybe we lease a flat in Bury for the time being."

"What about your antiques business?"

"My friend Charlotte has hinted more than once that she'd like to buy me out. She's done wonders with the shop. That would mean more cash to invest in a property one day—if we decide to do that."

"I can't ask you to sell your shop. You love the antiques business."

"I enjoy the antiques business. I love you."

Our dinners arrived, tender pieces of golden brown chicken simmering with onions and mushrooms in a rich, garlicky red wine sauce. At the Trout it came with caramelized, rosemary-dusted root vegetables and a loaf of homemade sourdough bread. The proprietor set down our plates and dashed off, returning with a bottle of Burgundy wine.

"From the wife and myself. To celebrate your engagement." He grinned. "Couldn't help noticing the ring."

"Thank you." Tom stood and they shook hands. "Tell your wife how much we enjoy her cooking."

"Make her day." He trotted off to greet another couple at the door.

"So what about my idea?" I asked, taking my first bite of the chicken.

"We don't have to decide tonight."

"Now who's postponing decisions?" I wiped a speck of sauce from the corner of his mouth. I wouldn't press him. "Did you get my text last night?"

"About Mary Diamond? Yes."

"Were you able to learn anything about her death?"

"The police in Norwich were called to the scene. Standard procedure—unexplained death in a care home. They were told Miss Diamond was a recovering alcoholic. Years of drinking had done irreversible damage to her heart and liver. She'd been sober since arriving at the home, but she somehow managed to get hold of a bottle of whiskey. Polished it off, lay down on her bed, and died."

"How did she get the bottle?"

"That's the part they can't explain. They don't keep alcohol on the premises. The staff claims to know nothing about it."

"Strange."

"Yes. The police are checking it out."

"The lady at the care home—the administrator—told Vivian that Mary Diamond was a ward of the court. No will. No assets. They want Vivian to pick up her things. Do you have a problem with that?"

"No. I'll let Norwich know." He speared an olive. "Just be careful."

"I always am."

We'd finished the wine and most of the chicken when my cell phone, which I'd put on mute, vibrated.

"Sorry," I said, pulling the phone out of my handbag I looked at the screen. "It's Frank Keane's wife. I'd better take the call."

I answered as I headed outside. "Jean, hello. Is everything all right?"

"Oh, Kate." She sounded frantic. "Frank has gone missing. The police are searching. If he's wandered off, he won't have gotten far, but he'll be so confused and frightened."

"What do you mean *if*?"

I heard a sob. "My neighbor came over to stay with him while I went to the shops. She says he had a visitor. Since he was with Frank, she decided to run home and check on her daughter, who was meant to be studying for exams. She was only gone ten minutes. When she returned, the house was empty. She assumed the visitor left the door unlocked and Frank wandered away, but we just don't know."

"Did she get a description?"

"Man. Average height. She didn't pay much attention."

"She must have noticed something that could help. Clothes, an accent."

"She's pretty shaken up right now. Blaming herself. The police are interviewing her. If she remembers anything, I'll let you know."

"I'm so sorry, Jean. Call the minute you hear something."

I returned to the table.

Tom looked up. "What's happened?"

"Frank Keane is missing. The police in Stevenage are searching for him."

He put down his knife and fork.

"There were five of them that summer, Tom. Three are dead. One is missing. That leaves Vivian. I'd like to go home."

* * *

Rose Cottage was lit up like a used car lot in Cleveland. I hadn't been home since early that morning when I'd left to pick up Ivor for our meeting in Cambridge.

Vivian met us at the door. She handed me a small box wrapped in brown paper.

Inside was a mass of tissue. "What's this?" I asked.

"Look inside."

I placed the box on the kitchen table. Inside, nestled in the tissue, was a faded and badly frayed cord, the color of old gold.

A burst of comprehension rocked me. "It's the rope from Cluedo. Your game piece."

"Stop," Tom said. "Don't touch the box again. I'll be back."

In minutes, he returned from his car with a pair of the latex gloves he carried with him everywhere. He examined the cord and the tissue. "Nothing else inside." He spread out the brown paper to check the postmark. "No return address. Mailed in London— Gray's Inn. Postmarked August sixteenth." He looked at Vivian, who'd slumped into a kitchen chair. "When did you say this arrived?"

"The parcel delivery van came around four thirty. It came in this." She handed Tom a plastic mailing bag with the Royal Mail logo and a printed label: *We apologize for the unavoidable delay in delivering your package.*

"I just spoke with Jean Keane," I said. "Frank is missing."

Vivian covered her mouth.

"Under the circumstances, you probably shouldn't stay here," Tom said.

"I'll call Lady Barbara," Vivian said. "One of her forty-seven bedrooms should be available."

Chapter Twenty-Two

Vivian and I packed the essentials we would need for several days. Tom stowed them in the back of his Range Rover, along with Fergus's bed and supply of food, treats, and toys.

Lady Barbara and Francie Jewell met us in the Finchley Hall courtyard.

"My dears, I'm so sorry." Lady Barbara held out both her hands. "You were right to come to me. This house has protected its inhabitants from all manner of threats for centuries."

We followed her up the main staircase. Tom carried our bags. I carried Fergus's gear.

"I've given you the Green Bedroom," Lady Barbara said. "As long as you don't mind the squeaky bed. And if you don't mind sleeping on the trundle, Kate. I'm told it's quite comfortable."

I laughed. "I'll be fine."

"Queen Victoria slept in the Green Bedroom twice, and Edward the Seventh once. He came to stay for the shooting season in 1935—along with a certain Mr. and *Mrs.* Simpson." She arched an eyebrow.

She was trying to put us at ease, and it was working. At the first landing, we turned right into a long hallway lined with portraits.

"More Finchleys?" I asked Lady Barbara.

"One does tend to accumulate relatives over the course of six hundred years." Lady Barbara opened one of the heavy carved oak doors. "Here we are."

Tom, Vivian, and I followed her inside.

The Green Bedroom was, in fact, green. The walls were hung with a heavy wool-flock paper in a faux damask design, dark juniper on sage. The bed and matching bergère chairs were covered in a similar silk damask, worn and faded but still lovely.

"Put the bags on the blanket chest, Tom," Lady Barbara said. "Francie, take away the bed covering if you please and bring two of the satin duvets. Kate, you'll have to make up the trundle. Linens are in the bottom drawer—there." She indicated a fine oak chest of drawers.

I felt like I'd been invited to stay the night at Downton Abbey.

"Come along, Tom," Lady Barbara said. "We'll leave Kate and Vivian in Francie's capable hands." She turned toward the door, allowing her fingertips to brush the top of a chair, the edge of the armoire, and finally the doorframe. It was subtly done. If I hadn't known her eyesight was failing, I wouldn't have noticed. "Get settled, you two. When you're ready, meet us in the sitting room. I want to hear *every*thing."

Francie Jewell rolled the old silk bed cover expertly over the long bolster pillow. "Water closet and sinks through that door." She pointed with her free hand. "Bath is the next door on your left. Let the tap spill for at least ten minutes. It's quite a run from the boiler. I'll bring up towels." She hoisted the bolster over her shoulder and disappeared.

Fergus eyed his basket near the white marble fireplace.

Francie returned with the duvets. "I'll take Fergus for a walk and then put the kettle on."

Francie Jewell certainly lived up to her name. Lady Barbara was lucky to have her. I hoped she would remain at Finchley Hall for a very long time.

Once Vivian and I had unpacked our clothes and lined up our toiletries on the oversized porcelain sinks, we joined Tom and Lady Barbara in her private sitting room.

Francie had laid a fire in the hearth, and she'd set out tea things along with a plate of cheese and grapes.

"We'll have a light supper at eight o'clock," Lady Barbara said. "You're welcome to stay, Tom."

"That's kind, but I'm expected at headquarters first thing in the morning. We're checking possible sightings of a stranger in the village just before Will Parker was murdered."

"Is Vivian in danger, do you think?" Lady Barbara's pale blue eyes were clouded with concern.

"We're taking no chances."

"It's the same pattern," I said. "A package arrives containing one of the game pieces. Someone telephones or pays a personal visit. And then—"

"The Grim Reaper." Vivian finished my sentence. She reached down to pat Fergus's head. He'd curled up at her feet, still panting from the exertion of climbing the staircase.

"That's not going to happen again," Tom said. "With your permission, Vivian, I'll arrange to have CCTV cameras installed at Rose Cottage in the morning. If someone comes looking for you, we'll get an image."

Vivian shook her head. "What is the world coming to?"

What the world was coming to, I couldn't have said. But if something—or someone—was coming for Vivian, they'd have Tom to contend with.

*　*　*

Tom and I left Vivian and Lady Barbara in the sitting room and wandered downstairs to the library. We needed to talk—alone.

The library, one of the formal rooms on Finchley Hall's ground floor, was a huge, oak-paneled vault with walls of leather-bound volumes and, in a domed glass case, the Finchley Cross, a stunning gold and garnet Anglo-Saxon pectoral brooch, dug up along with the rest of the Finchley Hoard in 1818. After the tragic events the previous May, Lady Barbara had donated the Hoard to the Museum of Suffolk History in Bury St. Edmunds, but she'd kept the cross. It had been part of her childhood.

The library would be on public display when Finchley Hall opened for visitors. Even though the theme was the lean years after the Second World War, the conservators had decided to leave the library in all its high-Victorian splendor—including the trophy heads on the walls and the glass cases with small stuffed animals in pathetic, anthropomorphic poses. *Ugh.* So intense was the Victorian craze for taxidermy, it had been considered chic to pin a dead animal on your hat and call it *haute couture.*

Tom and I sat on a buttoned leather sofa in front of the cold fireplace. The light from an amber mica lampshade cast a glow but no warmth in the cavernous room.

"Did you ever locate that criminal Will Parker put behind bars?"

"It wasn't him. He's been in hospital for a month. Ruptured appendix."

I pulled my quilted jacket around me and tucked up my feet. "I can't stand the thought of Frank Keane out there alone in the dark. It's supposed to get down to the low fifties tonight. He must have been a lovely man, Tom. I always think you can tell what people are really like when they get old. The filters go. Everything distills down to the essentials."

"I checked with the police in Stevenage an hour ago. Every available cop is out searching. They'll find him."

"Will they? Jack Cavanagh died unexpectedly on August sixteenth. Two days later Mary Diamond was found dead. Three days after that, Will Parker was murdered. Now Frank Keane is missing—he may be dead too. I think the same person is behind all of it."

"Yes, I daresay." Tom looked dejected. "We won't have the results of Jack Cavanagh's autopsy for another few days at least, but I wouldn't bet ten shillings against the findings."

"Serial killers kill for the sake of it, don't they? This person is eliminating a small group of elderly people for a reason. We have to figure out what that reason is."

"He's clever, I'll give him that. Will Parker had a severe allergy to bee venom. Jack Cavanagh had a serious heart condition. Mary Diamond was an alcoholic in poor health. They all died of natural causes. End of story—until you noticed the connection between them."

"Thanks to Vivian. And now Frank Keane, an elderly man with Alzheimer's, wanders off. Oh, Tom. I hope they find him alive."

Tom stroked my hair. "The minute I hear something, I'll text you."

"I'm freezing."

He put his arm around me. "Come on. I'll warm you up. "I nestled into his solid warmth. If there was a killer, I couldn't help wondering what he was planning for Vivian.

"The time gap still bothers me," Tom said. "If someone murdered the Beaufoys in 1961, why would the killer suddenly worry he'll be caught?"

"New evidence must have come to light. Something Vivian and the others found but didn't know was important."

"But what did they find? Evidence pointing to a killer who may be dead himself? That's what stops me in my tracks, Kate. I just don't see it."

"Remember what Sherlock Holmes said? 'When you've eliminated the impossible, whatever is left—however improbable—must be the truth.'"

"So what's the improbable truth in this case?"

"That's what we need to find out. We know this much—the evidence the Five Sleuths collected in 1963 was placed in a metal box that lay hidden for years. Someone recently found it. It's the only explanation. They must have read through the evidence and realized the clues pointed to the killer. For some reason we've yet to discover, that person feels compelled to eliminate the people who know the truth."

"I can almost believe that, Kate. Except the Five Sleuths never knew the truth, did they?"

"Vivian doesn't, but that doesn't mean Will Parker didn't guess the identity of the killer. Maybe he'd never gotten that crime scene out of his mind. Hugh and Stephanie said something about new evidence. Maybe the new evidence helped him figure it out, and he contacted the killer."

"A killer who's most likely in his eighties or nineties and in a care home? Come on, Kate."

"Okay, I agree. But how about the killer's son or daughter?"

"Grandchild, more like. What motive would a grandchild have to murder five elderly people? Family shame? That's not enough."

He was right. It wasn't enough. "So who did kill the Beaufoys?"

"No one, according to the coroner's verdict. Their deaths were ruled accidental."

"Do you believe that? Blood was spilled at that house, Tom. The inquest files are missing. Someone has gone to a lot of trouble to suppress the truth."

"All right, then. Who do you say committed the murders?"

"One of the inmates at Netherfield with a grudge? A family member of one of the patients? Millicent Beaufoy, alone or in cahoots with her older boyfriend?"

"*Cahoots?* Do Americans really use that word? I heard it on TV as a boy—those old American westerns." He laughed. "Do you know I really thought everyone in the States rode a horse and spoke with a Texas accent?"

"Back to suspects." I sat up. "How about someone Dr. Beaufoy worked with at Netherfield?"

"I still don't see the connection with the deaths now."

"I don't either, but whatever is going on, this case has roots in the past. Think about this—except for Tony Currie, every one of the Cliff House board members had a relative on the Netherfield board at the time Dr. Beaufoy was killed. I showed Niall Walker the photo of Will Parker. He denied ever seeing him, but I think he was lying. I think Will Parker was asking questions."

"And that's the reason he was killed? Most of the current board members weren't alive in 1961."

"Dr. Underwood would have been in his late teens. If he had a crush on Millicent Beaufoy, that could be our connection between the deaths then and the deaths now. And that gives him a motive to kill anyone who might know the truth."

"Do you believe that?"

I smiled ruefully. "Actually, I can't see him working up that much passion for anything except history."

"I still think the motive for the killings today has to be more than covering up a sixty-year-old crime. Whoever found the metal box could have simply destroyed the evidence. Without evidence there's no case. No, Kate. The motive has to be something that affects people's lives now. Remember your mother's question last May—what changed?"

"The house was sold."

"There has to be more. Something we're not seeing."

"It would help if Vivian could remember what was in that box."

"Maybe she will." Tom stood and pulled me to my feet. "I really must be going. Put on your shoes and zip up your jacket. You can walk me to the car."

Outside in the courtyard, the fragrance of late roses mingled with the herby scent of boxwood. Tom pointed at the clear inky sky. "Look—the North Star. See? Right there. And a hint of the Milky Way."

We gazed up in silence for a moment.

"Tomorrow's the day Vivian and I are driving to Norwich," I said. "The care home wants her to dispose of Mary Diamond's things."

"And you're hoping to find out if she was murdered."

"At least I might find out if someone sent her one of the game pieces."

"You're the one who should be setting up that private detective agency. I could work for you. *Tommy and Tuppence*."

"Sorry—if you work for me, it would have to be *Tuppence and Tommy*."

"I don't mind."

"You never answered my earlier question. When are you going to speak to your mother?"

"Soon." He took my hand.

"She needs to know how things stand, and she needs to hear it from you."

"I know." He bowed his head. "I love her, but I'm not going to let her engineer my life."

"You need to tell her that. Well, maybe not in those words. You will have to face her."

He ran his thumb over the engagement ring. "As long as you wear this ring, Kate, I can face anything."

"The ring will look even better with a wedding band next to it. Are you're planning to wear a ring? I've never asked."

"Of course. Through my nose if you'd like."

I laughed. "Are you implying I lead you around by the nose?"

"You don't. But if you ever wanted to—"

I elbowed him in the side. "I have no desire to lead you anywhere, Tom Mallory."

"You'll follow, then?"

"How about side by side?"

Chapter
Twenty-Three

~

Sunday, September 6

The next morning, while Vivian was getting ready for our trip to Sunny Shores Care Home, I wandered down to the breakfast room and found an urn of coffee, a tiered plate of toast and muffins, a bowl of hard-boiled eggs, and Nicola Netherfield.

"What are you doing here?" I immediately put up my hand in apology. "Oh, I'm sorry. That sounded rude. I'm just surprised."

"You shouldn't be." She laughed. "You're the one who gave Lady Barbara my card. I'm only too happy to help." Several large wallpaper books and heavy rings of fabric samples lay spread out on the floor and the sofa.

The door opened. Lady Barbara entered, carrying an embroidered Chinese silk jacket. "This is the color I was talking about. Oh—Kate. Thank you for recommending Nicola. She's already been a great help."

I was wondering how much Lady Barbara would have to pay for this help when Nicola said, "There's nothing much going on at Cliff House these days, as I'm sure you've noticed, Kate. I told Lady Barbara I'm waiving my usual fee. All she'll have to pay for is the cost of whatever paint and fabrics she chooses."

"That's very generous." Could it be true, or was there a catch?

"The truth is," Nicola said, "this project will mean publicity for me. A magazine spread, news coverage. Priceless." She stuffed one of the fabric rings in a heavy canvas carryall and picked up two of the wallpaper books. "Actually, I was just leaving."

"Let me help," I said. "What else goes?"

"Those two rings on the sofa. I'm leaving the others for Lady Barbara to consider." She turned to her client. "I know exactly the color you're after. I'll be in touch."

I picked up the two heavy fabric rings and followed Nicola downstairs and out to her car.

She loaded everything in the back of a sleek white Lexus SUV. "I appreciate the help. And thanks again for the recommendation."

"It must be hard, dividing your time between Cliff House and London," I said.

"I have the use of a flat at Cliff House, but I do get down to London frequently. Actually, I was in London the entire week before our initial meeting. New client. I had to take the early morning train back on Friday."

"Tony Currie must commute to London as well."

"He does. As a matter of fact, we were on the same train that day. He gave me a lift from the station."

"Do you have another minute or two? I'd like to ask you about Netherfield."

"Sure, but I don't know what I can tell you." The breeze loosened the tendrils of her hair. "Dr. Underwood is the expert."

"Vivian and I visited Monkey Puzzle House last Tuesday." I mentally crossed my fingers, praying she wouldn't ask why I was bringing it up.

"Yes, I heard. You met Niall and his son."

"What's your opinion on the feasibility of saving the house?"

"Fifty-fifty. Niall's pretty determined. He usually gets what he wants."

"About Netherfield. Your father must have known the Beaufoys quite well."

"Of course. He was medical director, an administrative job mostly, but he and Dr. Beaufoy were great friends. All the doctors were close. They shared the Netherfield vision. Martyn's father, too—Philip Lee-Jones. He was the financial man, but they were all friends. He's still alive, you know—ninety-two."

"How about Niall Walker's father?"

"He was Netherfield's solicitor—led them through the divestment process when the National Health took over. They all knew him, of course, but he wasn't part of the inner circle."

"And Dr. Underwood's father—Dr. David Underwood?"

"Oh, that," she said as if I knew. "Yes, very sad."

"Tell me about it." I smiled sympathetically, inviting her to confide in me.

"You didn't know? He shot himself."

"He did?"

"He'd been charged with assisting the death of one of the patients at Netherfield. A man who'd struggled with depression for years. This was just before the National Health took over. The family sued him for malpractice. Lost his license, his career, his reputation, his house—everything. Apparently, he couldn't live with the shame."

"When did you say this was?"

"The hearing? Nineteen sixty-two. Oswin was in his second year of medical school. My father and the others stepped in to make sure he could continue."

"Dr. Underwood is a *medical* doctor, not an academic?"

"He had a small practice in Miracle. Retired now. His real love is history." She tucked the stray strands of hair behind her ear. "Look—don't mention this to him, will you? Oswin's a sweet man—a little dithery at times but harmless. He's quite sensitive on the subject."

"But the other doctors were all good friends?"

"Well, there was some kind of a falling out between Martyn's father and Dr. Beaufoy at one point, but I couldn't tell you what it was about."

"Serious?"

"Yes—for a while, according to my father. I think it had to do with a disagreement over treatment or something. They must have made it up because Philip Lee-Jones was a tremendous help with the Beaufoy children after the tragedy. Don't mention that either, if you don't mind." She rolled her eyes. "I always say too much and end up regretting it."

"How do you know all this if you weren't born yet?"

"Father was a bit of a talker too. Family trait, I guess." She laughed, then turned solemn. "My parents never thought they'd be able to have children, and then I came along—born when they were in their late forties. My father liked telling stories about Netherfield. It is our heritage, after all."

"Do you mind looking at a photograph?" I pulled Will Parker's photo up on my phone and showed it to her. "He was investigating the deaths of the Beaufoys."

Nicola studied the photo. "I think I saw him at Cliff House. It would have been—oh, several weeks ago. Why would he be investigating those deaths now?"

"That's what we're trying to figure out. Someone murdered him."

She took in a breath. "That's the body you discovered in the graveyard, isn't it?" I saw a spark of fear in her eyes. "How terrible. Poor man."

"The police think his death may be connected with Netherfield."

"I can't imagine why it should be." She opened the car door. "I'd best be on my way. Tony is expecting me before lunchtime."

I watched her drive off, wondering if they were a couple.

And why Nicola Netherfield was afraid.

* * *

The Sunny Shores Care Home was nowhere near the shore. It was near a river, though—the Wensum, which coils through Norwich like the Thames coils through London. We found the residential care facility in a quiet area north of the river. After parking in the visitors' lot, we walked around to the entrance. The smell of urine, disinfectant, and overcooked food met us at the door.

At the reception desk, we signed in with our names and the time and asked for Mrs. Brightwell, the director. She was finishing a care conference with one of the families, we were told, so we settled into a pair of uncomfortable chairs in the lobby.

Vivian looked exhausted. The drive from Long Barston had taken an hour and a half—including a stop for coffee at the Wild Bean café in the BP station just off the Thetford bypass. Vivian hadn't suggested packing a hamper, which worried me as she packs hampers for trips to Poundland in Bury. She probably hadn't slept well. I hadn't either. A snippet of a dream—a nightmare, actually—circled through my brain. I was driving a car—from the back seat, which was inconvenient. A sharp bend in the road appeared. I couldn't turn fast enough, and off I went, sailing through the air, knowing this was it. *My death.*

I'd woken up, out of breath and tingling with dread.

Was that how Will Parker had felt, knowing his body was shutting down? Was that what Jack Cavanagh had felt with the first searing chest pain? And Mary Diamond? Maybe her death was easy, just giving in to the alcohol and oblivion.

Frank Keane came to mind. I'd texted Tom first thing that morning. The police in Stevenage still hadn't located him.

"Thank you for waiting." Mrs. Brightwell, a middle-aged woman of comfortable girth, wore a navy-striped power suit and low block-heeled pumps. "It was good of you to come. We always wait at least two weeks before disposing of possessions, in case a friend or relative turns up. Miss Diamond didn't own much, poor thing, but we hate to turn everything over to the charity shop if there's someone who cares."

Vivian shot me a guilty look. We couldn't truthfully claim to have cared about Mary Diamond. But I supposed Mrs. Brightwell hadn't cared much either.

"How did Mary end up at Sunny Shores?" I asked.

"She was well known to the authorities. Alcoholism, shoplifting, vagrancy."

"Was she homeless?"

"She had a council flat, but she spent most of her time on the street. The alcohol had taken a toll. The council stepped in, made her a ward. They're the ones who decided she needed looking after. When the social worker dropped her off, all she had was a few items of clothing—we burned them, they were that horrible—and a paper sack filled with her collection."

"Her collection of what?" Vivian asked.

"Nothing in particular, but it was important to Mary. She used to push her things around in one of those wheeled carts."

"It sounds like she had mental health issues," Vivian said.

"Social deficits, I'd say. She was perfectly rational."

We followed Mrs. Brightwell up a flight of stairs and past what looked like a nurses' station. A young woman, dark-skinned with a short Afro, watched us from the corner of her eye. She wore a dark blue collared tunic over white slacks.

"Aides wear dark blue," Mrs. Brightwell informed us. "Nurses wear light blue."

Mary Diamond's room was located about three-quarters of the way down the hallway. The narrow single bed had been stripped. A sealed cardboard carton rested on a brown vinyl lounger. A striped tote bag, sealed with paper tape, sat beside it on the floor.

"Don't open her things here, if you don't mind," Mrs. Brightwell said. "If there are items you wish to donate or discard, do so locally. We have to be careful about the deceased's property. Two people complete the inventory—there's a copy in the box. We seal everything. The council is very keen on that sort of thing. One complaint, and they're on us like a flash."

I couldn't blame Mrs. Brightwell for her concern. Yet she seemed less bothered about the death of one of her patients than she was about potential legal liabilities. Maybe she had reason to be.

"What was Mary like?" Vivian asked.

"Would you be offended if I said strange? Recently she wasn't getting around too well. Before that we had a terrible time with her. She'd wander into other residents' rooms and take things. Like a magpie, she was. We had to search her room periodically. Obviously, it didn't make her popular with the other residents."

"When exactly did Miss Diamond die?" I asked.

"It happened on Tuesday, the eighteenth. More than two weeks ago now. We knew her health wasn't good, but still it came as a shock. I'm afraid she's already been cremated. We didn't know who to contact, you see. She had no next of kin."

"Did Mary say anything before she passed away?" Vivian asked.

"She died in the early morning hours. Shelley was on duty—one of our regular aides. She didn't mention anything—and I would remember. The family always asks."

"Is Shelley here today by any chance?"

"I believe she is. Would you like to speak with her? She's not what I'd call a chatty girl, but I'm sure she'll tell you what you want to know." Mrs. Brightwell left the room, returning with a painfully thin young woman with spotty skin and way too much eye makeup. She wore one of the dark blue tunics.

"Shelley, these women are friends of Miss Diamond. They'd like a word." She smiled at us. "I'll leave you to chat. Lots to get on with. Thank you again for coming, and if there's anything you need—" She left the sentence hanging.

Shelley chewed on her lower lip. "What do you want to know?"

Vivian shifted into her *I'm-just-an-old-dear* persona—hunched back, quavery voice. "Mary was such a lovely person when I knew her." She wiped away a fake tear. "I know she had her problems, but I was wondering if she left any message behind. Last words. Something to hold onto."

"She died very peacefully, ma'am. Quiet-like. No words."

"Did she have any visitors near the end? I'd hate to think she was alone. I don't drive, you see. But if I thought I was the *only* person who—" Vivian broke off and pulled a handkerchief from her handbag.

"No visitors that I know of, ma'am. Sorry."

"That is distressing. And you were with her when it . . . *happened*?" Vivian whispered the last word.

"Yes, of course." The answer came a little too quickly. "We're required to check the patients in this wing every half hour at night.

As I said, she died peacefully, ma'am. I'm afraid that's all I can tell you."

"And you're sure no one came to see her in the last few days? Left something, perhaps—a package?"

Was it my imagination, or did Shelley look frightened?

"You'd have to ask Mrs. Brightwell about that." Shelley glanced at the door. "I really should get back."

"Of course," Vivian said. "Thank you for your time."

"One more question," I said, stopping her. "You have no idea where Miss Diamond got the whiskey?"

"None at all. We don't serve alcohol here. Company policy."

"So you didn't know she'd drunk an entire bottle?"

"No idea, ma'am."

"But you said you check on the patients every half hour. Wouldn't you have smelled the alcohol?"

Shelley blinked. "Well, I didn't—you know, smell her breath."

"What alerted you to the fact she was dying?"

"I, erm . . ." The girl had paled. "I heard her snoring—funny-like, you know. So I checked and found her unconscious."

"Did you call for help?"

"Oh, I did. Right away. But she was gone before help arrived." She checked the watch pinned to her tunic. "I really must go." She trotted out of the room.

Vivian straightened her back. "That girl is hiding something."

We heard a small cough. Standing in the doorway was a tiny, wizened woman in a quilted pink robe. Her claw-like fingers clutched the handles of a Zimmer frame—a walker.

"You should have come earlier," she said in a high-pitched voice.

"Should we?" I asked, giving Vivian the *let-me-handle-this* look. "Why is that?"

"You might have said hello to her son."

"Mary Diamond's son? I didn't know she had one."

"Didn't she?" The woman's forehead wrinkled.

"Why don't you come in?" I said. "We'd like to hear about Mary. Was she a friend?" I moved the cardboard carton to the floor. "You can sit here." The woman looked awfully frail.

She shuffled in and sat down. "I haven't seen you before."

"I'm Kate. This is Vivian." We sat facing her on the blue-striped mattress. "What's your name?"

"Helen. At least that's what they tell me."

Was that a joke? I didn't dare laugh. "Now what's this about Mary's son? Did he come often?"

"I don't think so." Helen cocked her head. "At least he saw her before she died. More than I'll get."

"Your son doesn't visit?"

"I don't think I ever had children. That's probably why they don't visit."

I was getting the picture. Nevertheless, something useful might have stuck in her memory. "About Mary Diamond's visitor. Do you remember the day he came?"

"Is today Wednesday?"

"No, it's Sunday."

"Too bad."

I was about to ask why it was too bad when Helen miraculously returned to the topic. "Such a nice man, Mary's son. Brought whiskey truffles. Gave me three. We're not allowed alcohol here." She cackled. "No one said anything about chocolates."

"Can you describe Mary's son?"

"Two arms. Two legs. A man." She cackled again.

Vivian poked me in the side and whispered, "Ask about his hair color."

But when I turned back to Helen, her eyes were closed. A tiny whistling sound kept time to the slight rising and falling of her chest.

"Do you think she's all right?" I asked.

"She's breathing. Let's go. We can stop at the nurses' station on the way out and tell them she's here." Vivian picked up the tote bag and staggered.

"Let me get that," I said.

She shot me a look that could have stripped the silver off a Sheffield plate teapot. "I'm not too old to carry a tote bag."

I picked up the box.

Back in the lobby, the receptionist pushed the guest book toward us. "Don't forget to sign out with the time. Clock's on the wall."

I signed my name, entered the time, and gave the book to Vivian. "Would you know if Miss Diamond received any packages recently?"

"I'll check the list." The receptionist slid her chair back and grabbed a ring binder from the shelf behind her. She thumbed through a few pages. "Mary did receive a package. Saturday the fifteenth." She smiled. "Was it from you?"

"No." I shook my head. "Do you know what the package contained?"

"No, dear. Sorry. I'm sure they packed it up for you—unless it was edible, of course."

"Did anyone visit Mary in the last week or so before she died— a man, perhaps?"

"Mary never had visitors." The corners of the receptionist's mouth turned down. "Well, except those people from St. Audrey's. They visit our residents twice a month—especially those with no family. They bring homemade baked goods for those who can chew. We provide tea."

"St. Audrey's Church?"

"C of E. Three blocks south of here."

"When was the last time St. Audrey's visited Mary?"

"Let me check." She consulted another binder on her desk. "Oh my—the last visit was Tuesday, the night before she was found dead."

"Are you allowed to tell us the name of the visitor?" Vivian asked. "We'd like to thank whoever it was for their kindness."

"I don't see why not, but you'll have to check with St. Audrey's. The name says only *James W.*" She tsked. "The person on duty that evening *really* should have gotten the full name."

I gave the book a sidelong glance. I'm pretty good at reading upside down. 'James W' had arrived at 7:54 PM and left at 8:43 PM. That meant he was with Mary for almost an hour. "Does St. Audrey's usually visit that late?"

"They don't as a rule, now you mention it. We had a temp on duty that week. She wouldn't have known."

"Thank you." I smiled.

"Very kind," Vivian said. "Oh—I almost forgot. Is there somewhere nearby to get lunch? Nothing fancy."

"The Pheasant does a nice soup of the day. Salads as well. It's only a block from here, toward the church. Turn right. You can't miss it."

As we exited Sunny Shores, I noticed an old silver hatchback with a dented rear quarter parked across the street. The driver raised a newspaper in front of his—or her—face before I could get a proper look.

Were we being watched?

Chapter
Twenty-Four

After stowing the box and tote bag in the trunk of my car, Vivian and I headed for the Pheasant, which turned out *not* to be the quaint pub I'd pictured but a local coffee shop serving breakfast, lunch, and afternoon tea. We put in our orders at the counter and snagged a table in the sunny window. I scanned the street but didn't see the silver hatchback.

"You can always tell when someone is lying," Vivian said, settling herself into the ladder-back chair. "Something about the eyes. I don't believe that aide, Shelley, was with Mary when she died at all. I think the girl found her dead in the morning and fabricated the story rather than get sacked."

"You could be right."

A waitress brought two bowls of carrot and coriander soup with a pot of Earl Grey and a small loaf of brown bread to share.

Outside the window, standing at a bus stop, was the young black aide from Sunny Shores. She seemed to be watching us. I smiled and gestured for her to come inside.

She made her way to our table, looking flustered. "I'm sorry to intrude, but I noticed you through the window."

"You're off work," I said. "Why don't you join us?"

"Would you like something to drink?" Vivian asked. "A bowl of soup, perhaps?"

"Sorry, I only have a few minutes. I'm on my way to class." She took the third chair at our table and unwound the scarf around her neck. "Nurse's training. I'm in an apprenticeship program."

"I'm Kate," I said. "This is Vivian."

"I'm Bilan," she said, putting the emphasis on the first syllable. "You were friends of Miss Diamond. I thought you should know."

"Know what?" Vivian asked.

"The aide you spoke with—Shelley." Her lip curled. "She told you she was with Miss Diamond when she died, that death was peaceful, that she did all she could but it was no use."

"Close enough," Vivian said.

"That's what they always say. It's not the truth." Bilan's dark eyes blazed. "Shelley's boyfriend comes 'round nights, when she's meant to be on duty. She leaves the patients on their own, sometimes for hours. I know. I've seen it."

"Have you told Mrs. Brightwell?"

Bilan gave a bitter laugh. "I know better than that. I'd be labeled a troublemaker." Her chin quivered. "In three months I'll be fully qualified. That means I can leave Sunny Shores with a good reference. Get a proper job at a hospital." She shook her head. "I'm sorry if it sounds uncaring. My parents are proud of what I've accomplished. I won't disgrace them by being dismissed."

"Yes, I see," Vivian said.

"Still, I thought you should know." Bilan broke off. "I am sorry about your friend. What they told you about the alcohol is true. No one knows when or where she got the bottle."

"What was Mary like?" I asked.

"Eccentric. She never interacted with any of the other patients—well, except for Helen. Helen's a bit eccentric herself."

"We were told Miss Diamond received a package shortly before she died. Do you know what was in it?"

Bilan's brows drew together. "Actually, I think I do. I was on duty the day before Miss Diamond died—my shift ended at seven. I went 'round to pick up her tea tray, and there was this metal candlestick on her bedside table. Pretty, like a flame. I said, 'My, that's lovely.' And she said, 'It was a gift. For my collection.'"

Vivian and I exchanged glances. *Her game piece.*

"Did she say who'd sent it?" I asked.

"No. I did wonder, because as far as we knew, she had no family or close friends."

"But you actually saw her and spoke to her the evening before she died. Did you smell alcohol?"

"Definitely not at seven." Bilan shook her head. "I would have said something."

A red bus pulled up outside. "That's mine." Bilan grabbed her scarf and dashed out the door, leaping onto the platform just before the bus pulled away.

"See? What did I tell you?" Vivian took a bite of her bread. "It sounds to me like James W was the last person to see Mary Diamond alive."

*   *   *

As we left the Pheasant, Vivian wobbled.

"Why don't you wait here?" I suggested. "I'll get the car and pick you up."

"Certainly not." She picked up her pace. "I'm in the peak of health. Fit as a racehorse, the doctor says."

"Have you told him about your—" I hesitated. This was the tricky bit. How to bring up the subject of Vivian's unsteadiness without making her feel I was concerned. "About any health concerns you might have?"

"I don't have health concerns."

"Shall we walk to St. Audrey's, then?" I thought I'd call her bluff.

I should have known.

"We could walk—yes. We certainly could. But you probably need to get back to work. Why don't we save time by telephoning?"

That's what I did. We sat in my car. I looked up the phone number and dialed.

"Good afternoon. St. Audrey's Church. Hillary Parsons speaking. May I help?"

"I hope so. We've just come from Sunny Shores. Our friend, Mary Diamond, passed away recently, and we understand someone from the church visited her on that last day. We'd like to thank him."

"Lovely. I'll pass you on to our assistant vicar, Harry Anderson. He supervises the Visitation Committee."

A series of clicks led to a male voice. "Harry Anderson speaking."

"My name is Kate Hamilton. My friend and I have just come from Sunny Shores Care Home. Mary Diamond died there recently."

"Yes, we heard. You have our condolences, although we weren't aware she had any connections still living."

"My friend knew her many years ago. They hadn't been in touch."

"She's been on our visitation list since shortly after she arrived at Sunny Shores. In fact, we've petitioned the court to allow us to bury her ashes."

"We were told a member of your church visited her recently. We'd like to thank him."

"Him?"

"The person who visited—James W."

"When was this visit?"

"Tuesday the eighteenth of August."

"What time of day?"

"Just after seven forty-five PM."

"I see. And this person signed in as James W?"

"Yes. Is there a problem?"

"I'd say so. First, we never make visits on Tuesdays. Wednesday is our visitation day. Second, we always arrive early afternoon. Never in the evenings. Third, all our committee members are women. And fourth, ours is a small congregation. I've never heard of anyone named James W."

I thanked him and clicked off.

"There is no James W," I told Vivian. "They've never heard of him at St. Audrey's."

"I *knew* it. He's the killer. He must have given her the alcohol, knowing what it would do."

"This is a police matter," I said, pulling up Tom's cell number. "Maybe the receptionist on duty that evening can describe him. Tom will know what to do."

He answered on the second ring. "DI Mallory."

"Tom, I've got—"

"I can't talk now, Kate. Cliffe and I are headed for Stevenage. Frank's alive—barely. The police are checking CCTV in the area. I'll call when I have more news."

The sound of a horn honking told me he was already on his way to the car.

"It can wait. Let me know about Frank."

"Look—before I hang up, the firm from which the chief coroner was appointed in 1961 was Pelkot & Walker, Niall Walker's firm. His father wasn't only the chairman of the Netherfield board of trustees. He was also the chief coroner. He was the one who declared the deaths of Dr. and Mrs. Beaufoy an accidental poisoning."

"Golly."

"There's a team working on Parker's computer now. Some of his files were encrypted." A car door shut, canceling most of the street noise. I heard the engine start up. "Gotta go."

I slipped the phone in my bag. "Frank Keane's been found alive."

"Thank heaven."

I pulled out into traffic, glancing in my rearview mirror as I did.

An old silver hatchback pulled out behind us.

"Someone's following us," I said. "Hang on. I'm going to try to find out who it is." Vivian turned around in her seat. "That's the car I saw last week in Long Barston. It was driving slowly, and I assumed the driver was checking post numbers or something. But then I realized the driver was watching me."

"Why didn't you say something?" Switching lanes, I pulled in front of a white Ford Focus, blocking the hatchback. Then I made a swift right-hand turn.

Without time to change lanes, the hatchback was forced to continue on.

"Who is it?" Vivian asked.

"I don't know. Hold on." Turning the car around as quickly as I could, we reentered the main road. "Let me know if you spot him."

"There he is," she screeched. "Three or four cars ahead of us."

I sped up, passing several cars to catch him. The driver must have seen me because he sped up too. Now he was the one being pursued. *Serves him right, the creep.*

"Man or woman?" I asked Vivian.

"Can't tell from here. It's just the driver, though. One head."

I followed the hatchback out of Norwich and onto the A11.

"Watch out," Vivian said. "Speed cameras everywhere."

"Good. If he gets a ticket, the police will have his photograph."

A puff of smoke from the hatchback's exhaust told me the driver was pushing the old car to its limit. I pressed down on the accelerator, shortening the space between us. "Get his license number. There's a notebook and pen in my handbag."

Vivian scrabbled on the floor. "How long are you going to follow him?"

"As long as it takes. Until he runs out of gas."

"Or you do."

We approached a multilane roundabout. The silver hatchback shot into the circular traffic, leaving me at a complete halt. Cars whizzed by. By the time I was able to move into the circle, the hatchback was gone.

"Did you get the plate number?" I asked.

"Most of it," Vivian said.

"*Most* of it?"

"I need new glasses. The first part was *AX63*. Then *M* something."

"Take my phone and text it to Tom. And tell him about the incident in Long Barston."

Chapter
Twenty-Five

❧

"Just like *Top Gear*." Vivian gave me a satisfied smile. "I think we deserve a nice tea when we get back. Francie made cranberry scones."

"Do you mind if we stop at The Curiosity Cabinet first?" I asked. "We're meeting with the Cliff House board tomorrow. and I'd like to know if Ivor has a plan."

"Fine with me."

My heart was urging me to drive immediately to Stevenage. If Frank survived, and if he remembered anything about his visitor, the police might have their first solid clue in Will Parker's death. But Stevenage was several hours away on two-lane roads, and I knew Vivian needed to get back and rest.

I decided to be practical. Tom said he would phone if there was any news.

My thoughts circled back to the Five Sleuths. My mother always talked about the three legs of a stool in research. Two connected facts are a coincidence. Three are a pattern.

Well, I had a lot more than three connected facts—the mysterious deaths of the Beaufoys in 1961, the missing inquest files, the evidence compiled by the Five Sleuths in 1963, and the fact that someone obviously found that evidence and was eliminating them one by one (okay, I was making assumptions, but that's what it looked like). Then there was Nicola Netherfield's story about the feud between Philip Lee-Jones and Dr. Beaufoy and her reaction to the photo of Will Parker. And just today—Mary Diamond's mysterious visitor, James W, and the old silver hatchback following us.

The problem wasn't a shortage of clues, but how they were connected.

There was one more fact as well, perhaps the most important—the fake Van Eyck. According to Dr. Underwood, Horace Netherfield bought the original in 1877. If Ivor was right about the French forger, Gerard Bibeau, the copy must have been completed around the time the Beaufoys died—or were murdered. Was the forgery of the painting a separate crime, or were they somehow related? I'm pretty good at connecting dots, but if there was a pattern emerging, I couldn't see it.

As we drove into Long Barston, a group of noisy schoolchildren spilled out onto the street, lurching me back to the present.

I pulled my car around to the rear of Ivor's shop. We entered through the stockroom. No alarm beeped, which meant Ivor was there.

"It's me," I called out. "And Vivian."

We found Ivor at the counter, wearing a pair of cotton gloves. "Didn't think I'd see you today. Oh, hello, Vivian."

"What have you got there?" she asked, eyeing a collection of small framed portraits.

"Miniatures. Mostly eighteenth century. Some on ivory. Nice frames. I'm trying to place as many of the subjects as I can. Only a few are identified on the back."

Vivian bent over to examine the portraits laid out on a black felt cloth. "Well, that one's Elizabeth the First."

"You're right. She handed out miniatures like old John D. Rockefeller handed out dimes. This one is an eighteenth-century copy, though. Watercolor on ivory."

"What's this?" Vivian asked. "Part of a larger portrait?"

I looked at the tiny framed image—a single eye. Female, I thought, with delicate lashes and a slight upturn at the corner.

"You might assume it's been cut down from a larger portrait, but no." The gleam in Ivor's eye told me he'd been hoping one of us would ask. "This is what's called a *Lover's Eye*—a fad in the decades around the turn of the nineteenth century. Lovers would exchange portraits of their eyes, painted on bits of ivory no bigger than a fingernail, like this one. Both men and women wore them, with the identity of the subject a mystery. All part of the fun."

"I'm not sure I'd like the feeling of being watched," Vivian said. "Reminds me of that silver car."

I told Ivor about the driver of the hatchback. "Vivian got a partial license plate. It may be enough."

With Vivian examining the small treasures, Ivor pulled me aside. "About tomorrow—you might want to wear your running shoes."

"I'm sorry, Ivor. It's my fault."

"Losing the auction is better than selling a fake Van Eyck."

"Has your financier friend from London learned anything more about Pyramid or the Cliff House board?"

"As a matter of fact he has. The consortium—Pyramid as an entity, Tony Currie as an individual, and the four board members—guaranteed a loan. Considering the less than optimal location of the project, the lender insisted on their personal liability."

"Why would Tony Currie take a risk like that?"

"Maybe he really believes in the project. Maybe he fell in love with the building."

"It is stunning—those gorgeous traceried windows overlooking the sea."

"They built that place to last a thousand years."

"Ivor," I said, wanting to get back to the painting. "What do you think happened to the original Van Eyck? It must be hanging in a private collection somewhere."

"You worked that out, did you?" He cocked his head. "The painting Netherfield purchased in the eighteen seventies had to have been an original Van Eyck. Not that forgery is a modern practice—far from it. But the techniques used in the painting we saw were based on technology unknown until the twentieth century. So, yes, the original Van Eyck will probably remain out of sight forever. For some collectors, the goal isn't the display of wealth; it's an obsession with beauty—and possession."

"But according to everyone, the painting never left Netherfield."

"Except for cleaning, remember? That happened in the nineteen sixties."

"That's right. How long would cleaning take—long enough to copy the painting?"

"Not a chance. The painting would have been gone much longer—four to six months, anyway."

"There must be records somewhere."

"Perhaps, but it's not up to us to work that out. Our job was to determine if the painting is a genuine Van Eyck. We've proven it isn't. If the board members want to pursue the methods and means, that's up to them. Unless . . ." He let the sentence trail off.

"Unless what?"

"Unless the forgery is connected with the murders." He looked at me sideways. "That's what you think, isn't it?"

"Don't you?"

"Why would a painting forged sixty years ago cause someone to murder people now?"

"You sound like Tom." I shrugged. "All I know is Dr. Beaufoy worked at Netherfield when he died. It seems the painting was copied around the same time. Maybe he made the switch and pocketed the cash."

"You mean Beaufoy and his wife were murdered for revenge?"

"I don't know. It's a loose end. I don't like loose ends."

Ivor regarded me with interest. "There's more, isn't there?"

I told him what Nicola Netherfield said about the old Netherfield board of trustees. "She insisted they were all great buddies—except one of them was murdered, another committed suicide, and a third had a previous, serious disagreement with Dr. Beaufoy over the treatment of a patient. It would help if Vivian could remember what was in that metal box."

"Has she tried to go back to that week in 1963?"

"What do you mean 'go back'?"

"Travel back in time—mentally, I mean." He tapped his head. "Everything we've ever learned, everything we've heard and observed is in there somewhere. We just have to know how to access it."

Niall Walker had said almost the same thing. "Are you talking about hypnosis?"

"A technique I learned in northern Mongolia."

"What were you doing in northern Mongolia?"

"Defending myself against a charge of reindeer rustling—I was innocent, in case you're wondering. The point is, I may be able to take Vivian back. If she's willing."

Reindeer rustling? I decided not to ask.

Chapter
Twenty-Six

I was shocked Vivian agreed so easily. She didn't say yes at first. I think her exact words were "on a scale of one to ten, no." But she softened when Ivor explained the point of the technique, which wasn't to cure a bad habit or make her do something silly like standing on one foot and singing "God Save the Queen," but to help her to access that corner of her memory where the final night at Hopley's holiday camp was lurking. When Ivor told her he'd undergone it himself, she agreed. In fact, she seemed excited by the prospect.

We closed the shop early and headed for Rose Cottage, stopping at Finchley Hall to collect Fergus. Vivian said she could relax better in her own home, and with Ivor and me there, she'd be perfectly safe. I texted Tom to ask about Frank Keane and to say we were going to spend an hour or so at Rose Cottage. He texted back—*No news yet. I'll get word to the constable on duty.*

Once inside, the first thing Ivor did was light three candles and place them in a triangle around Vivian on the sofa. Then he pulled the curtains shut and turned out all the lights. "The first step is minimizing external stimuli."

"What do the candles do?" Vivian asked. "Concentrate energy? Create a protective shield?"

"They allow us to see. Now put your feet up—that's right, head on the pillow—close your eyes and relax."

Fergus watched the proceedings with mild curiosity.

Ivor began. "Vivian, are you comfortable?"

She nodded.

"All right. Put all thoughts out of your mind." He made a soft humming sound in the back of his throat.

This was getting weird.

"Picture yourself in a bubble, Vivian—a bubble lifting you up, up, away from everything and everyone." He hummed some more. "You're alone now, above time and space, perfectly comfortable and relaxed. Now I want you to picture Monkey Puzzle House as it was in 1963. You're descending now—down, down, entering into that world, just as it was then. You're standing outside the house. What's the first thing you see?"

"The tree, the one with the funny cones."

"Go closer. Focus on a single cone and stay there. Now what do you see?"

For a moment, I thought Vivian had dozed off. Then she said, "The cone sits at the end of a branch. It's covered with these . . . spikey things. Green tipped with gold."

"Are they sharp?"

"I don't know."

"Try touching one."

"Oh, they're soft. I remember."

"Keep your eyes on the cone. What kind of shoes are you wearing?"

"What?"

"Shoes. On your feet."

"Brown leather."

"Look at the cone again. Now look at the house. We're going inside."

"If you say so."

"Where shall we go, Vivian? Which room?"

"The library."

"Why?"

"That's where we play the game."

"Good choice. Tell me about the library."

"It smells like . . . my father's briefcase."

"Do you like it in the library?"

"Not really. But Will is here."

"Where are your parents right now?"

"At the dance with their friends."

I couldn't imagine what Ivor was doing. Just when Vivian was concentrating on something important, he'd bring up something irrelevant.

"Where are you?" he asked.

"I told you. In the library."

"But where in the library?"

"Sitting on the floor."

"Who's there with you?"

"Will. Jack and Frankie. Mary."

"Is there anything on the floor?"

"A rug."

"Anything else?"

"No."

"All right." Ivor's voice was soporific. "Let's go forward in time now to the very last night, Saturday. In the morning, you're leaving Hopley's. This is the final night of the game. What's on the floor?"

"The metal box."

Yes. This was the important part.

"Who's in charge of the box?" Ivor asked.

"Will, of course."

"What does he plan to do with it?"

"Put the evidence inside and hide it."

"Where will he hide it?"

Excellent question.

"He won't tell us. He says it's safer for us not to know."

"Safer? In what way?"

"I don't know."

"How big is the box?"

"About the size of my mother's bread box—or a little larger."

"What's inside?"

"Lots of stuff. The five game pieces. The paper Will wrote out—our theories about what happened in the house. The evidence we collected."

"Why did Will include the evidence?"

"For future investigators. That's what he wrote at the end of his report. 'We humbly submit a complete account of our investigations, along with the contents of this box.'"

"Is your name on the paper?"

"Of course. He made us all sign."

"Do you remember any of the theories?"

"I didn't read the paper. I think he put down the main ideas, like the escaped mental patient."

"Fine. Now look very carefully at what's inside the box. Can you do that, Vivian?"

"Yes, I can."

"What do you see besides the game pieces?"

Vivian's brow furrowed. "Medical papers."

"Charts and graphs?"

"No, correspondence. Letters. At the top they say Netherfield Sanatorium."

"Good. Can you read what's written on the papers?"

"No."

"All right. What else? Take your time."

"A man's wallet. A pair of eyeglasses. A set of keys."

"And?"

"A ticket stub—like for a train or a bus. A packet of matches from a hotel."

"What's the name of the hotel?"

"Sydney Villas, Dover."

"Excellent. What else do you see?"

"Some soil and fibers in a tin can. A few pebbles. A small silver key, separate from the ones on the ring."

"Soil and fibers? What kind of fibers, Vivian?"

"Little roots or something. Will told us not to touch them."

"Tell me about the pebbles. Can you describe them?"

"Like from a rock garden—or a fish tank. Oh—and there's a leather pouch."

She hadn't mentioned the leather pouch before. "Have her describe it," I whispered.

"Can you describe the pouch?"

"It's like the one my brother keeps his marbles in. Soft leather with a red drawstring."

"Why did Will include those particular things?"

"I don't know. He didn't tell us everything."

"Tell me about the silver key. What does it unlock?"

"I don't know. Not a door. Something smaller."

"Like a suitcase or a lockbox?"

"Maybe."

"What else do you see?"

"A bottle of paregoric. A photograph—no, two photographs. A letter to Dr. Beaufoy, typed on onionskin."

"Can you see the photographs? What do they show?"

"People. Men. I don't recognize them."

"Who was the letter from?"

"I don't know. It's in French."

My breath caught. *Gerard Bibeau?*

"Is that everything? Focus on the contents of the box."

The pace of Vivian's breathing had picked up.

"You see something else, don't you? Tell me what it is."

A tiny squeak. "A towel, stained with blood."

He let that sit for a moment. "Is that everything?"

"I think so."

"Let's go back outside—outside Monkey Puzzle House. Are you ready?"

"Yes." Her eyes remained shut.

"Take a breath. That's right. Now another." A second or two later, he added, "Relax. When you feel ready, open your eyes."

Vivian lay there, silent and still, for so long I was becoming alarmed. "Vivian?"

Her eyes opened. She sat up. "I need a whiskey. A large one. Now, please."

* * *

I lay on the trundle bed in Finchley Hall's Green Bedroom. Vivian was asleep, snoring softly. Fergus lay curled up next to her, his large head and short, square muzzle nestled into the pillow. The list of items she'd remembered circled through my brain. The soil and the fibers, the book of matches, the letter in French.

The clock on the mantel ticked away. Nine thirty.

Quietly, so as not to wake Vivian, I got up, pulled my sweat-shirt over my pajamas, and tiptoed into the adjoining bathroom. I closed the door, hearing it click, and flipped on the lights.

Lowering the toilet lid, I sat and dialed Tom's number.

"Kate?"

"Were you sleeping?"

"No. Going over phone logs from Jack Cavanagh's mobile."

"Find anything interesting?"

"Nothing. He only used the phone to call his daughter."

"Heard anything more about Mary Diamond?"

"She wasn't murdered, Kate."

"Wasn't she? Let me tell you what Vivian and I learned yester-day. You can decide. Mary died of alcohol poisoning, except Sunny Shores is teetotal. Someone slipped her a bottle of whiskey, knowing she couldn't resist. Not only that, Tom. A week before she died, she received a package—a chrome candlestick, her game piece at Mon-key Puzzle House. All the packages were mailed from London." Tom started to say something but I forged ahead. "There's more. The day she died, Mary received a visitor, someone who signed in as 'James W' from the visitation committee at St. Audrey's Church. He was with her for about forty-five minutes, from just before eight PM until almost nine. There is no one at St. Audrey's by that name."

"Did anyone get a description of this mystery man?"

"The receptionist on duty that night was a temp. They're trying to contact her."

"I'll alert the police in Norwich. We're following up on the silver hatchback, by the way, but honestly, there's not enough to go on. We've put out a description of the car to all police units. If the guy shows up, we'll get him."

"I hope you're not sleepy because I've got even more. Remember the day Vivian I went to Monkey Puzzle House? I told you I thought Zara Walker recognized the photo of Will Parker."

"Even though she denied it."

"Well, this morning I showed the photo to Nicola Netherfield, and she said she was pretty sure she'd seen him at Cliff House. She also told me the staff at Netherfield were tight—Dr. Beaufoy, Dr. Underwood, her father, Dr. Cosmo Netherfield, and Philip Lee-Jones, the medical director. Until there was some kind of feud between Lee-Jones and Dr. Beaufoy."

"What about?"

"She doesn't know, but Philip Lee-Jones is still alive. If he murdered the Beaufoys, his son, Martyn, has a motive for killing Will Parker now."

"I'll see if I can interview him. Did she say anything else?"

"She said Dr. David Underwood, Oswin's father, killed himself after he was sued for malpractice. The other trustees stepped in to make sure Oswin could finish medical school."

"You have been busy."

"I'm not finished. Tonight Ivor helped Vivian remember what was in that metal box. Don't ask me how. I'll explain later. The point is I wrote it all down." As I read the list, I pictured Tom's face, listening, analyzing.

"What stands out to you?" I asked.

"The soil and fibers, obviously. Did Vivian know where they came from or why they were included?"

"She didn't. Will Parker made all the decisions."

"The book of matches from the hotel in Dover is interesting— that and the ticket stub."

"But those items might have been lying around for months."

"Dover was the main ferry terminal to France."

"Oh—I'd forgotten about that. Ivor thinks the forger of the Van Eyck had to be that Frenchman I told you about. Gerard Bibeau. How about that letter in French?"

"From Bibeau?"

"Who knows? The thing is, Tom, I'm really beginning to think there's a connection between the forged painting and the deaths of the Beaufoys."

"What connection?"

"I don't know. Beaufoy stole the painting and pocketed the cash? That would make someone mad. Or someone else arranged the forgery, and Beaufoy threatened to tell. Or—that's all I can think of at the moment."

"Well, good luck tomorrow."

"We need more than luck, Tom. We need a miracle."

Chapter Twenty-Seven

~

Monday, September 6

Ivor and I left Long Barston in a drizzling rain. Temperatures hovered in the mid-fifties. The rain ceased halfway to Miracle-on-Sea, but as we approached the coast, the wind picked up, buffeting my small car and threatening to sweep it off the road.

We'd postponed the weekly appraisal day at The Curiosity Cabinet. I'd hung a sign in the window informing those interested that it would be held on Tuesday instead. I hoped no one would be upset.

Ivor was uncharacteristically quiet.

I gave him a quick glance. "I'm sorry things have turned out this way. If the painting had been genuine, the auction would have attracted international attention. As is—"

I let the sentence drop. Ivor didn't need telling the board of directors would probably show us the door and give us the boot on the way out. They'd counted on the millions of pounds the painting would bring. Maybe the whole Cliff House project rested on it.

Well, they weren't the only ones to lose. Ivor's financial condition hadn't improved over the summer. If anything, it had gotten worse. The clients who'd taken back their consignments in the wake of the theft and murder last May hadn't returned, and new clients were as scarce as Greek statues with noses. The real culprit, though, was Ivor's marked preference for buying over selling.

I'm an antiques dealer. I know you have to spend money to make money, but I also know you can't spend what you don't have.

Miracle-on-Sea stretched before us, a reminder of once-bright hopes.

The sea roiled. Angry waves pummeled the rocks and shingle.

As we approached Cliff House, low-flying clouds gave the edifice a Gothic gloom. Dr. Underwood's glowing descriptions notwithstanding, admittance to Netherfield Sanatorium hadn't been anything like spending a holiday at a posh resort. For those poor souls who passed through its gates, Netherfield had been a prison—a five-star prison, perhaps, but a prison nonetheless. I'd been taken in by the picture he'd painted.

The visitors' parking area was empty. We took the first spot and buttoned our jackets against the strong sea breeze.

Even Miss Armstrong, the receptionist, was chilly. She greeted us with a smile that looked as genuine as a newly discovered Shakespeare play. "Mr. Currie will be with you shortly." No offer of coffee or tea this time.

We took seats near the fireplace, where the logs had burned down to embers.

"Everything will be fine." Ivor said. "We may be the bearers of bad tidings, but they don't shoot messengers anymore, do they?"

"Not recently."

Ivor had his briefcase with him—packets for each board member plus the bill from Apollo Research. First we'd dash their hopes, then we'd throw a pie in their faces.

Tony Currie's swagger wasn't as convincing as it had been when we first met him. "Well, here we are, then," he said without preamble. "We're meeting in the old library. This way, please."

The board members were seated around a large round table. They glared at us.

"Don't keep us waiting," Martyn Lee-Jones said. "What's the verdict?"

Ivor pulled the packets out of his briefcase. I passed them out.

"The painting is *not* a Van Eyck." Ivor ignored the swift inhalation of breath and continued before anyone had a chance to speak. "It was painted sometime in the mid-twentieth century by an exceptionally skilled forger who used every technique known at the time. What he could not have foreseen was modern spectrography."

"That's impossible," Nicola Netherfield said. "That painting has hung in the reception hall for more than a hundred and twenty years."

"Therefore," Niall Walker spoke with feigned patience, "you must realize it cannot have been painted mid-twentieth century." He folded his arms across his chest.

"He's right." Lee-Jones turned to the others. "I told you they were trying to cheat us."

"The tests must be wrong." Dr. Underwood's beard wobbled. "We'll have them repeated—this time by someone *we* choose."

"As is your right," Ivor said calmly. "Apollo will happily share its findings with anyone you choose—including the image of an acrylic fiber embedded in a paint sample."

That stopped them.

"What does that mean?" Under her carefully applied makeup, Nicola's face had gone pale.

"It means," Ivor said, "that unless someone has discovered the secret of time travel, a modern fiber was present when the paint was applied to the panels."

"That's all you have?" Lee-Jones began. "How do we know—"

"Sit down, Martyn." Currie cut across him. "We can't ignore facts just because we don't like them. If serious doubt has been cast on the painting, we can no longer call it a Van Eyck."

"We understand your disappointment," Ivor said. "We're disappointed as well. Apollo has prepared a detailed report. Read it at your leisure and take whatever decision you feel is in your best interests. If you have further questions, Dr. Zechner has included his email at the bottom of each page."

"This can't be right." Nicola Netherfield shook her head slowly. "My great-grandfather purchased the painting in 1877. It hasn't left this building since."

"Well, it has—briefly," Currie said. "Didn't one of you tell me the painting was taken down and cleaned?"

"Yes, of course—that's it," Dr. Underwood said. "The fiber must have been deposited then."

"I'm afraid not." Ivor shook his head. "Read the report."

"Do you know when and where the painting was cleaned?" I asked. "You must have records."

"Do we have the old Netherfield records?" Currie asked Dr. Underwood.

"They're in the archives," Dr. Underwood said.

"I advise you to have someone check," Ivor said. "It could be important. In the meantime, I suggest you consider your next move."

"What next move?" Currie asked.

"Is there a next move?" Nicola spread her hands.

"Certainly," Ivor said. "You own a very fine painting—sadly not by Jan van Eyck, but it was painted by a master artist. Based on my research, I believe that man was Gerard Bibeau, a French artist from a small village in the French Alps. He studied at the famous École des Beaux-Arts in Paris but became resentful when his talent wasn't recognized by the international art critics. He'd copied a Vermeer for the practice, and when a local art gallery assumed it was an original, he realized he could make more money by forging the Old Masters than he could painting originals—and get his revenge at the same time. He was active for a relatively short period, from the mid-nineteen fifties until his death in early 1963. He copied many artists and styles but specialized in Netherlandish artists—including Van Eyck. Twenty-three paintings are known to have been completed by Bibeau. Twice that many may hang undetected in museums and private collections. At the time of his death, two paintings were left unfinished, the fake Vermeer and the *Portrait of Solon* by Joos van Gent, which still has experts wondering how he hoped to switch it for the real painting in the Louvre. Since Bibeau was skillful enough to fool the experts, it's impossible to say without evidence that he was responsible for your painting. However, I feel comfortable labeling it as an extremely fine copy of Jan van Eyck's *Christ Healing the Demoniac*, attributed to the French artist Gerard Bibeau. It isn't illegal to copy a painting or to own one. It is illegal to sell that copy as the real thing. The real thing exists somewhere. One day the owner may come forward. For now, if we can prove the painting was done by Bibeau, it has value. Not as much as a Van Eyck, but certainly worth putting up for auction."

"How much are we talking?" Lee-Jones asked. The atmosphere in the room had changed. They were listening.

"Perhaps as much as a million or more. It all depends on publicity and marketing."

Wow. I was seeing a whole new side of Ivor Tweedy. This man was a genius.

"How do you suggest we handle publicity?" Currie asked.

"Issue a press release now, something that plays up the mystery of the painting and the lengths to which the Cliff House board went to learn the truth. 'Newly discovered art forgery stuns with its beauty'—something like that. Go on television. Get one of the London magazines to do a piece. I'm sure Pyramid has plenty of contacts in the media. Lemons to lemonade."

"Yes, of course. We could contact—"

"I know a woman at—"

"How about *Architectural Digest*? We could combine the painting with the history of—"

They were talking over each other in their excitement. In fact, when Ivor presented the bill from Apollo, they hardly blinked.

Ivor sat back in his chair. *Smug* was the word that came to mind. He deserved it.

Thanks to Ivor, we'd gotten our miracle after all.

Chapter Twenty-Eight

Martyn Lee-Jones walked us to the exit. "I must say—that was totally unexpected."

Was it really? They were shocked, all right, but was it because the painting was a fake or because we'd managed to prove it?

"You do realize," I said, throwing caution to the wind, "that if the original Van Eyck was copied by Bibeau, it happened before his death in early 1963. And that suggests it happened before or around the time of Netherfield's transfer to the National Health. And that means someone at Netherfield organized it."

"Impossible."

"I've been told your father was close friends with the Netherfield doctors. Are you sure he knew nothing about the forgery?"

"Don't you dare bring my father into this." Lee-Jones's voice had taken on a dangerous edge. "He's an honorable man. He would never have agreed to such a scheme."

"I wasn't accusing him, but he's the only one of the trustees still alive. It's possible he remembers something. Of course, he is in his nineties. People do forget."

"He doesn't get around much these days, but there's nothing wrong with his memory."

"If we can pin down the provenance, it would help the sale."

"I'll ask, but it will do no good."

Ivor was pretending to examine one of his fingernails.

I was channeling Vivian. "I understand there was a feud between your father and Dr. Beaufoy. Do you know what it was about?"

"A *feud*?" Lee-Jones stiffened. "I have no idea what you're talking about. They were friends—very good friends. Why, after the Beaufoys died, my father and the other doctors took the Beaufoy children under their wing."

"That was a difficult time for Netherfield."

"Yes. It was. My father was lucky. When the National Health took over, he was hired as an administrator. Not everyone was so fortunate."

"Like who?"

"It would have been a blow for Walker & Palkot, wouldn't it? Netherfield was their largest client. And of course, Dr. David Underwood—Oswin's father."

"What happened to him?" *As if I didn't know.*

"He left the profession. Took his own life. I don't think it had anything to do with Netherfield per se, but the family lost everything. Oswin's always been bitter about that."

"Before we go, I wonder if you'd look at a photograph." I pulled it up on my phone. "This is the man whose body was found in Long Barston the night before our first meeting. His name was Will Parker. He was murdered. The police think he was investigating the deaths of the Beaufoys."

Lee-Jones stared at the photo, his lips a pale line. "I don't recognize him."

"That's odd, because I've been told he was here at Cliff House, asking questions."

"He didn't ask me. That's all I can tell you."

"Do you live in Miracle-on-Sea, Mr. Lee-Jones?"

"My family lives in Ipswich."

"So you drove in from Ipswich for our meeting on the twenty-second?"

He flinched, jerking his head back. "Are you implying I had something to do with that man's death? I shouldn't bother answering, but I will. I was home the entire night before the meeting. If the police care to confirm it with my wife, they're welcome."

Lee-Jones stomped off, and Ivor and I headed for the car.

"You will sail close to the wind, won't you, my girl?" Ivor climbed into the passenger's seat of my Mini and clicked the seatbelt. "Tom wouldn't approve."

"How else can I get information?" I snapped. "I'm sorry, Ivor. You're right. But at least I'm narrowing things down. The night Will Parker was murdered, Nicola Netherfield says she and Tony Currie were in London—not together, but I wonder. Martyn Lee-Jones claims he was home in Ipswich. Those alibis can be checked." I started the engine and pulled away.

Ivor gave a half-hearted shrug. "I'm not going to say 'leave it to the professionals' because I know you won't. Just watch your back. Will Parker was investigating the Beaufoy deaths, and look what happened to him."

On that ominous note, we dropped the subject and did a little strategizing.

We needed to make sure the publicity following the announcement of a newly discovered Van Eyck forgery would enhance Ivor's reputation, not damage it. What we needed were a few facts about the history of the painting since 1877—how the forger was contacted, when and how the original painting was delivered to a village in the region of Mont Blanc, how much the forger was paid, and how much the seller received from whoever had purchased the original. I hoped the Netherfield records—if they existed—would give us those answers.

Something niggled at the back of my mind. Had one or all of the trustees in 1961 known about the switch? Were they victims or co-conspirators?

"Ivor," I said. "Do you think the current board members knew about the forgery?"

His eyebrows went up. "You're a sharp one, you are."

"Maybe they were fooled. The painting was stunning."

"It fooled me—at first glance."

"They seemed willing to let us see the Netherfield records—at least Tony Currie was. If there is incriminating evidence, they've probably already removed it."

"You think so, hm?" Ivor gave me his angelic look. "If they did remove evidence, I'll bet my last pre-Ptolemaic coin they put it back."

"There were no coins in Egypt before the Ptolemies."

He grinned at me.

"Okay—why would they put incriminating evidence back?"

"Because nothing can change Apollo's report, Kate. They can't pretend it doesn't exist. Currie was savvy enough to recognize that. But they do have a fine copy with an intriguing history. You're the one who said it—their best bet now is to document the forgery if they can. And then feign shock."

"Even if it throws their parents under the bus?"

"Blood may be thicker than water, my girl, but you can't buy anything with it."

* * *

I dropped Ivor at The Curiosity Cabinet before stopping at Finchley Hall to inform Vivian and Lady Barbara that I wouldn't be home until six or seven. Then I headed for the hospital in Stevenage. I was afraid Vivian might insist on going with me, but she and Lady Barbara were knee-deep in the fabric and wallpaper samples Nicola Netherfield had left.

The drive took an hour and a half in light traffic. The hospital, a modern glass and steel building, was part of a larger NHS complex on the northwest edge of Stevenage.

Frank Keane, I was told, had been transferred from A&E to a room on the fourth floor.

There, in a visitors' area, I found Jean Keane and a younger woman, who was crying.

"Jean, I hope I'm not intruding. Tom told me what happened. I'm so sorry."

"It's my fault." The younger woman looked up, her eyes red-rimmed. She looked incredibly young, with a baby face and fine, light brown hair held back with a pink dotted headband.

"Nonsense." Jean took her friend's hand. "Kate, this is my neighbor, Pearl. Pearl, this is Kate. She's the one who brought Frank's old friend from Hopley's."

"That's just it." Pearl Harker pressed her hands against her cheeks. "You said Frank got such a boost, seeing his old friend. 'And here's another old friend,' I thought. And I—" She broke off, weeping into a handkerchief.

"You couldn't have known," Jean said. "If anyone's at fault, it's me. Kate warned me, and I should have said something to you." She put her arm around Pearl's shoulders. "I was only going to be gone for an hour or so, Kate. Pearl came over to sit with Frank, and when the man showed up at the door, she popped home to check on her daughter."

"When I got back, the door was off the latch, and Frank was nowhere to be seen." Fresh tears sprang into her eyes.

"Can you describe the man?"

"I've been trying to think." She shook her head. "He wasn't young, I know that. Medium height. He wore a hat—one of those brimmed caps, pulled down over his face. He was all wrapped up—coat collar up, scarf around his face. It was a chilly night."

"And the porch light was burned out," Jean said.

"Do you remember an accent, a smell, facial hair?"

"I know it sounds stupid, but I wasn't paying attention. I heard a knock on the door. The man was standing there. He said he was an old friend of Frank's. He just walked past me and said, 'Hello, Frank.' Frank brightened up right away. He said, 'How lovely to see you. Jean, put the kettle on,' and I said 'I'll be back in a mo'.'"

"Frank knew him?"

"Not necessarily," Jean said. "He's learned to cover his memory loss by going along with things. He'd have wanted to appear as if he remembered."

"Did you see a car?" I asked Pearl.

"Yes, actually. I told the police I passed it on my way across the street. Some kind of SUV or hatchback. Light-colored paint. Nothing that would stand out."

I wasn't liking the sound of this. "The make?"

"I don't know cars."

"You didn't happen to notice the number plate."

"No. Sorry." The corners of Pearl's mouth went down.

"Has Frank said anything since they brought him in?" I asked Jean.

"Not yet. He sleeps most of the time, which I suppose is good. The doctors' main concern is the hypothermia—and, of course, shock. They found him curled up under some shrubbery near the park entrance. He'd been out there on his own all night." Her voice broke. "He couldn't even tell them his name."

"Do they have any leads?"

"They're checking CCTV for a light-colored car in the area. It's not much to go on."

"I'm going to leave now, Jean, but please let me know if anything changes. Or if Frank says anything. Pearl, it was nice meeting you."

"Likewise. I wish I could tell you more."

I did too. As I left, it struck me again that if these deaths did turn out to be murder, whoever was targeting the Five Sleuths had taken advantage of each victim's existing medical condition—an allergy to bee venom, a weak heart, alcoholism, now dementia.

How did he know?

Chapter
Twenty-Nine

I got back to Finchley Hall in time to join Lady Barbara and Vivian for a casual supper in the private sitting room. The windows were cracked open, letting in the fresh September air. A fire crackled in the hearth.

Francie Jewell's kitchen wizardry had turned a humble cottage pie into a savory beef stew baked in pastry so light and flaky it would have impressed the judges at *The Great British Bake-Off*.

Once I'd been debriefed by Vivian (the agents at MI5 should be so thorough), and once she and Lady Barbara had exchanged their opinions on the appropriate penalty for a murderer who preys upon vulnerable old people (Vivian was in favor of reinstating the death penalty), I settled back to listen to the two women discuss the relative merits of wallpaper as opposed to paint.

My thoughts circled back to what weakness the killer might exploit in Vivian's case. She was fit as a fiddle (her words), except for an occasional unsteadiness, which she refused point-blank to admit. I pictured her lying at the bottom of a staircase or falling onto the tracks at a London tube station.

Her legs just gave out. Accidental death. Couldn't be helped.

I banished the frightening images by thinking about my wedding. My dress, chosen by my best friend, Charlotte, had been ordered and was on its way to England. I'd loved the photos. Charlotte had described it as "classic" in a color she called *pearl white*, which she said was definitely my color. She also said a second-time bride of middle years could absolutely wear a traditional wedding dress. Still, I imagined myself walking down the aisle with everyone all smiles, thinking *Who's she trying to fool?*

Lady Barbara and Vivian were still chattering. I was getting sleepy. In fact, my eyes were about to close when we heard a knock at the door.

It was Francie Jewell. "Inspector Mallory, ma'am. Shall I show him up?"

"Yes, of course," Lady Barbara said. "He may have news."

Tom's arrival surprised me since I knew he was on duty. He entered the room in a rush. "Vivian, Lady Barbara. I'm sorry to disrupt your evening, but I need to speak with Kate."

"Of course," Lady Barbara said, taking Vivian's arm. "We'll leave you alone."

Vivian started to protest, but Lady Barbara steered her firmly toward the door. "We'll be down the hall if you need us."

Tom drew me into his arms. "I can't stay. I'm on my way to Sudbury—there's been a shooting in a drugs lab north of town. But I wanted you to know two things. First, we found the inquest files on Will Parker's laptop." I think my mouth must have dropped open because he said, "You heard right. They're encrypted. The cyber team is trying to hack in."

"Will Parker stole the inquest files and scanned them into his computer? Where are the originals?"

"Your guess is as good as mine. No sign of them."

"What's the second thing?"

"The Beaufoys' cook, Alice Evans, died several years ago. DS Cliffe located her son. His name is Kyle Weber. He's a teacher, living in one of the Chicago suburbs. He says his mother talked openly about the deaths. He's willing to talk with you, Kate. Here's his number." He handed me one of his cards with a U.S. phone number printed in black ink. "His school lets out at three thirty Chicago time, which means he should be home"—he checked his watch—"now."

"Tom, thank you." I kissed him. "If I learn anything important, I'll text you." I kissed him again. "Oh, be careful tonight."

Then he kissed *me*, and he was gone.

* * *

Kyle Weber answered on the second ring. "Hello?"

"Kyle? This is Kate Hamilton. Inspector Mallory said it was all right if I phoned."

"Sure. No problem." In the background, a siren sounded—the American kind. On TV apparently, as it was followed by a prolonged burst of gunfire.

"You're American," he said.

"I grew up in your part of the world. Wisconsin."

If he wondered what I was doing in Suffolk, he didn't ask.

I tried to ignore the racket—more gunfire, screaming. "I think the police told you the records from the inquest are missing."

"The inspector said elderly people have been murdered."

"We think it may be connected to the deaths of Dr. and Mrs. Beaufoy in 1961, when your mother worked for them as cook."

"She had nothing to do with that. She died with nothing on her conscience."

"I understand that, and I'm sorry for your loss." *Tread carefully.* "I'm wondering if you can tell me what you know about that night. This isn't about your mother, Kyle, but in the absence of the inquest files, I was hoping she could answer some of our questions."

He must have switched off the TV because the background noise stopped abruptly. "She spoke about that night a lot. It was a traumatic event in her life, a turning point. She never got over it. But if it hadn't happened, she'd never have emigrated to Chicago. She wouldn't have met my father. I wouldn't be here."

"What did she tell you?"

"She said the worst thing was the suspicion. She had nothing to do with the hemlock. She wasn't even there that night."

"Wait a minute. You're saying the Beaufoys ingested hemlock?" I immediately thought of the soil and fibers.

"You didn't know? They'd been mixed in with a dish of candied parsnips."

"With the files missing, the only people who would know that were those present at the inquest. Even the surviving children don't know." *Or won't admit it.*

"The court cleared her of blame—absolutely—but she said people looked at her differently. She couldn't stay there."

"Could you start at the beginning? How did your mother happen to work for the Beaufoys?"

"Mother was Welsh. Her father had been killed in the Blaenhirwaun Colliery explosion south of Swansea. To keep the family together, her mother took in laundry and did some baking for the local shops. When Mom was sixteen, she went to live with an aunt in Miracle-on-Sea. Her aunt had married a Suffolk man during the war. They ran a boarding house. Mom helped with the cooking. Dr. Beaufoy heard about her and hired her. Mom said Mrs. Beaufoy wasn't much for the kitchen. Focused on her charities. So Mom would show up around ten in the morning, prepare lunch for the children, do a bit of clean-up or whatever Mrs. Beaufoy needed that day. Then she'd cook the evening meal and leave after the dishes were washed and put away. Later they offered her a room in the house so she wouldn't have to ride her bicycle in bad weather."

"What about the night of the deaths?"

"Mrs. Beaufoy had given her the evening off. The fair had come to town, and mother had been asked out by one of the local boys. She made lunch as usual and left around three. Mrs. Beaufoy was happy to let her go. Her husband had just returned from a business trip, and since the Beaufoy children would be at the fair as well, she was looking forward to an evening alone with him."

"But one of the children *was* home that night."

"That's right, but it was a last-minute thing. A punishment for something—I don't remember what."

Dulcie had said an unsuitable boy. "Why didn't she die, too?" I asked, wondering if his account would agree with Dulcie's.

"She was angry. Refused to eat with her parents. In fact, she sneaked out of the house and went to the fair after all."

"Did your mother mention a boy—someone her parents didn't approve of?"

"I don't remember that."

"What did she tell you about the poison hemlock?"

"She said the gardener had been turfing out some wild hemlock plants growing along the back of the property. He'd laid the brush on a tarpaulin, warned the family not to touch the plants or burn the rubble. He was planning to return, take everything to the landfill. Spray the area with herbicide."

"How did the hemlock get into their food?"

"That was the big question. No one ever knew. Mrs. Beaufoy told my mother she wanted to have a nice dinner ready when her husband got home. His favorite dish was candied parsnips. She said there was something she needed to discuss with him, and she wanted him in a good mood. Somehow, hemlock roots got mixed in with the wild parsnips she'd harvested. They do look alike."

Soil and fibers. Like little roots. Was it murder-suicide after all? Surely with all the drugs in the surgery, Mrs. Beaufoy could have come up with an easier way to kill her husband and herself. That raised a question. Why had Will Parker collected the soil and fibers? Did he know they were poisonous? And why the pebbles—scooped up with the soil?

"So the police knew the poison was in the candied parsnips."

"Had the dish tested. Mom said the sweetness would have partly masked the bitter taste. By the time the Beaufoys realized something was wrong, it was too late. Mrs. Beaufoy had begun cleaning up the dinner dishes when the first symptoms began. They'd probably gone to bed, sick as dogs. Vomited everywhere. Mom thought they'd gotten up to call for help when the other symptoms kicked in—cramps, hallucinations, confusion. They'd been dead for a couple of hours when the kids got home."

"What a terrible shock." I thought of little Dulcie. "When did your mother learn of the deaths?"

"Almost immediately. She was still at the fair when the cops picked her up and took her to the police station. She was the prime suspect. Questioned her for hours. First they accused her of killing the Beaufoys because they'd caught her stealing from them, which wasn't true. Then they said she'd fallen in love with Dr. Beaufoy and killed them when he rejected her. She protested, of course, but they didn't believe her until the oldest Beaufoy girl—can't remember her name—corroborated her story."

"None of it was true."

"Of course not. Mom was as honest as the day is long. She owed her life to that daughter."

If Justine Beaufoy had protected Millie from a charge of murder, at least she hadn't done so at the expense of a young Welsh girl. "Did your mom ever say anything about the daughter who was grounded that night?"

"Oh—did she ever. 'A right handful,' she called her—unruly, vindictive. One moment she'd be out of control. Then in the blink of an eye, she'd be docile, repentant. You couldn't trust her. Never knew what was going on in her brain. Mom said she was a pretty child—too pretty. Mom felt sorry for the doctor and his wife. They were at the end of their rope over that girl."

I remembered Millie's left hook—and the red nail marks on my arm. Even nearing eighty, she was strong. Had Justine protected her all those years, kept her from harming herself or others? And then Justine died, leaving the role of caregiver to Dulcie.

"So your mother left Suffolk."

"At the time, Cunard was trying to compete with the airlines as a transatlantic option. They were hiring more ship staff. Mom was in the right place at the right time. But after a couple of years, she decided to take her chances in the States. Ended up in Chicago, lucky for me."

We chatted for a few more minutes, but there was nothing more he could tell me. I thanked him and disconnected.

I tapped out a text to Tom: *Just got off phone with cook's son. I think Will P collected the soil and fiber samples because he knew or suspected it was the source of the poison. Was Parker familiar with hemlock? Ask his son.*

The response came in seconds: *We will.*

I hit reply: *Justine B stuck up for Alice when she was suspected. Was she also covering for Millie? But M couldn't have killed Will and the others. Not possible with her stroke—unless she had an accomplice. We need those inquest files.* I was so focused on the case I almost forget to ask about the shooting. I tapped out *Did you make an arrest?*

Yes.

Good. Love you. Sleep well.

Love you, my darling. Talk tomorrow night at the Trout.

Chapter Thirty

❦

Tuesday morning at The Curiosity Cabinet was given to appraisals, a weekly event that was becoming increasingly popular in the area—and beyond. We'd gotten some valuable consignments as a result. Mostly, though, people brought family mementos, worth more in their imaginations than in reality. One lady brought her father's extensive stamp collection—twenty books filled with stamps that had been canceled and steamed off envelopes. Another brought a Vampire-Hunter's Kit, complete with a pearl-handled derringer, a bottle of holy water, garlic, a wooden cross, and silver bullets (which turned out to be pewter). She'd been planning to buy a condo in Spain with the proceeds. We had to tell her it was a fake and showed her scores of similar kits, selling on eBay for an average of a hundred pounds. She left in tears.

Appraisals are always tricky. If you quote top retail prices to please a client, they expect you to back it up with cash. I've always told the truth—not that truth makes you popular. Some are offended. Others crushed. A few, a very few, are delighted.

This time there was no delight. Just the usual lot of run-of-the-mill old things. As if time alone could confer value. If that were true, rocks would be priceless.

We ended the appraisals at two, and Ivor told me to go home— or rather to Finchley Hall, which *was* my home until the police found the guy in the silver hatchback.

I set out through Finchley Park. As I passed Rose Cottage, I noticed a panda car parked in the drive. Two uniformed policemen seemed to be examining something in the gravel.

"Is there a problem?" I asked, squinting into the sun. "I'm Kate Hamilton. I live with Miss Bunn."

"Are you, indeed?" The older policeman, balding, fiftyish, grinned at me. "Lucky chap, the guv."

The younger policeman nudged the gravel with the toe of his boot. "Tire tracks. CCTV caught a silver hatchback turning around here. We picked it up again at the church. It parked for ten minutes, then drove off."

"Sounds like the same car that followed us in Norwich," I said. "Does Miss Bunn know?"

"DS Cliffe informed her. Not much to go on with, miss. Lots of silver cars on the road."

"Did you get the plate number?"

"Unfortunately not. Wrong angle."

"Thank you for your vigilance," I said, and strode off toward Finchley Hall. As the path was now off limits—the whole area between the koi pond and the lake was under construction—I crossed the Chinese bridge. It creaked ominously. The old boards were uneven and slick with countless layers of shiny red paint. It really wasn't safe.

I found Vivian and Lady Barbara having afternoon tea.

"Just in time," Lady Barbara said. "Francie's made a lovely lemon seed cake."

"Just a sliver for me, but I'd love a cup of tea."

I pulled up a chair and Vivian poured. "I suppose you heard about the car at Rose Cottage," she said. "They've sent a couple of constables."

"I just spoke with them. They weren't able to get a plate number, but it has to be the same car."

"If he's trying to frighten me, it isn't working." Vivian raised her chin.

"Another old boyfriend?" Lady Barbara said.

They laughed, which I thought was highly inappropriate. "You should be taking this seriously. Vivian could be in danger."

"Tom will find him," Vivian said. "In the meantime, we've been choosing wallpaper."

"You can help," Lady Barbara said. "This is the one Nicola says will work best. What do you think?"

A wallpaper book was propped open to a design that looked remarkably like the faded urns and flowers currently on the walls. I smiled inwardly. Even professional decorators know that pleasing the client is the name of the game.

"It's a reproduction of a nineteen thirties design," Lady Barbara said. "It comes in three colorways, but I'm partial to this one." The new wallpaper was a rosy salmon on cream, nearly identical to the current shade.

"It's perfect."

My tea had cooled slightly. I took a long drink. "I'm meeting Tom at the Trout at seven. I'd like to phone my mother before it gets too late."

"Give her our love," Lady Barbara said. "We're looking forward to meeting her."

I headed for the door but turned back as a thought occurred to me. "Vivian, are you sure there's nothing else you remember about the silver hatchback that first day in Long Barston?"

"Nothing except the damage. By the time I realized they were watching me, they'd gone."

"You said 'they.' Does that mean more than one person?"

"I used the pronoun rhetorically. I couldn't tell who was in the car."

"Well, don't go anywhere alone until they figure out who it is. You shouldn't walk in the park either, even with Lady Barbara. The Chinese bridge isn't safe. If you need something at the cottage or in the village, I'll get it for you—or at least drive you."

"Yes, mother."

I left them, both laughing.

* * *

The trundle bed rolled out easily. I kicked off my shoes and lay atop the pale green satin duvet, settling back against the pillow to dial my phone.

"Linnea Lund speaking."

"Hi, Mom. How was the welcome home party?"

"Oh, loads of fun—wasn't it, James?" I heard a male voice in the background. "Our friends decorated the commons with balloons and banners. Oak Hills provided desserts and coffee. I'd say almost a hundred and fifty people were there—any excuse to party."

I heard laughter in the background and wondered if life seemed funnier the older you got.

"How's the new apartment?"

"We love it. So much more room—of course, there's two of us now. The guest room doubles as my library and computer space. James has his own office. He consults with his old practice at the hospital from time to time. We'd planned everything before we left—the layout, which furniture we intended to take. Oak Hills moved everything. James's daughter came down while we were away and organized the kitchen. There's almost nothing left to do."

There's two of us now. I marveled at my mother's ability to accept change and adapt to new circumstances. She'd been a widow for almost thirty years. Now she was a bride again, learning the ways of a new husband, learning how their relationship would work. None of that comes with the wedding vows. It has to be learned and negotiated, bit by bit, over time. Could I be as flexible? As close as Tom and I were, we'd never shared a tube of toothpaste or worked out who cooked and who cleaned up the dishes.

I filled her in on what had happened since we'd talked—and there was a lot to tell. The visit to Monkey Puzzle House and the Beaufoy sisters. Mary Diamond and the mysterious *James W* who had visited her the night before she died. Apollo's report on the fake Van Eyck. The inquest files found on Will Parker's laptop and Vivian's memory of the evidence put together by Will Parker. Finally, the son of the Beaufoys' cook, who told me about the poison hemlock. I decided *not* to mention the silver hatchback.

"The problem is the time gap," I told her.

"Yes—something obviously was a catalyst. What was it?"

"Well, I suppose it must have been Justine Beaufoy's death and the sale of the house. Someone found the metal box."

"But we don't know *when* the box was found, do we?"

"No, except the house was shut up for all those years. The only people who had access were the Beaufoy children."

"Or someone they trusted."

Or whoever broke into the house. "That's what puzzled me about the Walkers. I'd swear they were looking for something, but how would they even know about the metal box? Besides, it had already been found. The only logical motive for killing people now would be to prevent them from identifying a murderer."

"Forgive me, darling, but I'm not completely buying that. If one of the Five Sleuths wanted to identify a murderer, they would have done it years ago. I think it's more likely the murders were triggered by a something now—a new threat, a sudden need, an unexpected opportunity."

"You mean roots in the past, but a present threat."

"Or a present opportunity. If something or someone triggered the murders, my bet is on Will Parker."

"I agree. We know he scanned the inquest files into his computer. According to his son, he was bored in retirement and talked about a cold case he was working on. Nicola Netherfield said she saw him at Cliff House, although the others deny seeing him."

"Something prompted Will Parker to investigate a very old case. Find out what that something was and the case will unravel."

"What do I do in the meantime?"

"Go over everything you think you know, Kate—piece by piece. Question every assumption. 'Is it true? How do I know it's true? Can I prove it?' Remember that mourning locket containing the braided strands of President Lincoln's hair?"

"How could I forget? The woman who sold it to you was a Lincoln descendant."

"Not directly. Through his mother, Nancy Hanks."

"She could prove her connection to Lincoln, anyway. And the locket was definitely Civil War era. The woman had photos of her grandmother and great-grandmother wearing the locket. The hair color matched the last known photo of Lincoln."

"We asked every question we could think of—except the one that mattered. Was the hair human?"

"That's right." I laughed. "The hair came from a nanny goat."

"It may have been Lincoln's goat. He kept all kinds of animals—even at the White House. Someone, generations earlier, told a lie. And that lie was repeated in good faith."

"At least it made an interesting story."

"Truth is always more interesting than fiction. It's usually more complex as well. *No, no—just half a cup or I won't sleep.* Sorry, darling. That was James."

At least they'd decided who'd make the after-dinner coffee.

"Why don't you list the facts you think you know."

"You mean now?"

"Why not?"

I grabbed my notebook. "Well, three of the Five Sleuths were killed in ways that appeared natural. *I know.* I'm making assumptions about Jack Cavanagh and Mary Diamond, but I believe they were murdered. The fourth, Frank Keane, was dumped in a city park and would have died if the police hadn't found him when they did."

"Fine, but back up, Kate. Roots always go deeper than we think. Start at the beginning—with the deaths in 1961. What do you know about those first deaths?"

"I know Dr. Beaufoy and his wife died of a fatal poisoning in May of 1961. That's been verified twice—from the summary of the inquest and from Kyle Weber, the cook's son in Chicago."

"Excellent. But how did it happen?"

"According to Kyle's mother, Mrs. Beaufoy accidentally mixed poison hemlock roots in with the wild parsnips she'd dug up for dinner."

"That's an assumption. She might have done it on purpose. Or someone else might have done it, but we'll go with that for now. Stay with the timeline—what happened that night and in what order?"

"Dr. Beaufoy had been away on a business trip. Mrs. Beaufoy gave the cook the evening off. She wanted to make a special dinner—her husband's favorites—because they were going to have the evening to themselves. The children were going to a fair on the Miracle pier, and they needed to talk."

"Which night? Do you know there was a fair on the pier?"

"I can check."

"That's what I mean. Don't take someone's word for something you can check yourself. People lie. People are mistaken. They repeat what they've been told. What else can you say?"

"At the last minute, Millie Beaufoy was grounded because of a boy she wasn't supposed to be seeing. She was kept home as a punishment. She was angry and refused to eat with her parents. Instead, she slipped out of the house and went to the fair anyway. That saved her life."

"Lots of assumptions, Kate. How do you know all that?"

"The old man Vivian and I met on the Miracle pier said an older boy was crazy about Millie. The rest of it came from Dulcie and Kyle Weber."

"See what you can verify. What next?"

"The children came home and found their parents dead."

"Presumably that will be confirmed by the inquest files when they're unlocked."

"After that, Dulcie was sent to live with an aunt and uncle on the Isle of Jersey."

"Why?"

"I don't know. Maybe Justine didn't feel capable of raising her. Or she wanted Dulcie to grow up somewhere without horrific memories. Maybe the aunt asked for her. At any rate, she returned to Suffolk in 2002 because Justine was getting older, and her sisters needed help."

"How do you know all this is true?"

"Dulcie told us."

"Something else to verify. Why did Monkey Puzzle House remain unoccupied and unsold all those years?"

"Justine was the executor of her parents' estate. She refused to sell—I don't know why, but it was confirmed by a newspaper article I read. I imagine none of the children wanted to live in the house anymore."

"Question everything, Kate. Who were the aunt and uncle in Jersey? Why was the house kept like that? I'm not saying these things aren't true, but somewhere in this story there's a key. Find the key. Then turn it and see what you find."

I thought about the small silver key in the metal box. "Should I go on?"

"No need. It's the process I want you to understand. Apply the same logic to each fact. Find the flaw."

"But what if I'm not asking the right questions?"

"You can't always know the right questions to ask, but if you keep asking, keep verifying, something will eventually turn up and change the narrative. Until you know what's false, you can't know what's true."

By the time we disconnected, I was practically vibrating. I love puzzles. I love research. What could I find out myself with only my computer and a little patience? I had two hours to kill before leaving for the Trout and decided to make good use of them.

Someone told a lie, and it was repeated in good faith.

Chapter Thirty-One

I scrapped the list I'd started and began a new one.

1. *Was the poisoning of the Beaufoys really accidental? (check inquest files)*
2. *Name of Millie's older boyfriend?*
3. *Did the children discover their parents' bodies? Who did they notify? (inquest files)*
4. *Why was Dulcie sent to Jersey—and why did she return in 2002?*
5. *Was there anything suspicious about Grayson's death?*

I paused to think, to go deeper.

6. *Where had Dr. Beaufoy traveled and what was he doing there? (Dover to France?)*
7. *What does any of this have to do with the fake Van Eyck?*
8. *Are the Cliff House board members involved?*

With no time to do more than make a start, I decided to tackle Grayson first. Somewhere online there would be information.

First I typed in *UK Obituaries*, with no results except lots of invitations to sign up for free trials to genealogy sites. Next I tried searching Suffolk newspaper obituaries. One database was free— the *East Anglian Daily Times*.

I typed in *Grayson Beaufoy* and set the date parameters for 2009 to 2011. This is what I found:

BEAUFOY Grayson John. Died in a boating accident July 2, 2010, aged 66. Dear brother of Justine, Millicent, Dulcett, of Upford. Dear nephew to Patricia Beaufoy Vautier of Jersey. Funeral service at Upford Church on Wednesday, July 10, at 2.30 p.m. No flowers. Donations in memory of Grayson should be directed to Clare College, Cambridge, or East Suffolk Sailing Club c/o O. A. Button & Sons Ltd., 24 Lavery Street, Ipswich IP39 QJ.

Dulcie's story was true. Grayson Beaufoy died in a boating accident in 2010. No hint of foul play. But more important than that, I had a name—Patricia Vautier. This had to be the aunt who had taken Dulcie in after her parents' deaths.

I checked my watch. Enough time for one more quick search. I typed in *Philip Lee-Jones Netherfield Sanatorium*.

This time I hit the jackpot.

The headline read "Tragic Death on Miracle Pier." The date: May 31, 1960.

Last Friday, May 27, Mrs. Marilyn Lee-Jones, 28, a patient at Netherfield Sanatorium, jumped from the pier at Miracle-on-Sea. Her body was found the following day, washed up on the beach near the estuary. An inquest returned a verdict of "Suicide whilst the balance of the mind was disturbed."

"She climbed over the barrier," said an onlooker who wishes to remain anonymous. "By the time we got to her, it was too late." The victim's husband, Philip Lee-Jones, said that since the birth of their first child the previous year, his wife had been given to fits of depression.

I ran my thumb along my chin. This was most likely the suicide Percy Pike had mentioned. And the son had to be Martyn Lee-Jones.

A source at Netherfield said Mrs. Lee-Jones had appeared to be improving. The decision to allow her outside the gates was taken after careful consideration by her doctors.

Could this have been the source of the feud between Lee-Jones and Dr. Beaufoy? If Beaufoy was the doctor who'd signed off on her freedom, Lee-Jones might very well have held him responsible for her death. A motive for murder? Finally I was getting somewhere.

I was also going to be late. Really late.

I shut down my computer, threw on a pair of black jeans, heels, and the red cashmere sweater Tom liked, and flew out to my car.

* * *

I made it to the Trout only ten minutes late for our seven PM booking—which might actually qualify as a minor miracle.

Tom was waiting at the bar. "Darling. I was beginning to worry." He kissed me.

"Sorry—I got caught up in some online research and lost track of time."

"And made most of it up on the way, no doubt. I remember that lead foot of yours from the Isle of Glenroth."

"I didn't want to miss even five minutes with you."

"I'll accept that." He put his arm around me. "Love that sweater."

"I know. That's why I wore it."

"They're busy tonight. Do you mind waiting for a table?"

"Not at all." I was almost literally bursting with the news about Martyn Lee-Jones, but I curbed my impulse to blurt it out. The small pub was crowded. Someone was sure to overhear.

"Glass of wine?"

"Better make it mineral water. That way I can have a glass of wine with dinner. Just one, though. I'm driving."

"My thoughts as well." He lifted his own glass of mineral water and signaled the bartender.

"I met two of your constables today at Rose Cottage."

"I heard all about it. I believe *robbing the cradle* was the phrase."

The bartender set a frosty glass with a wedge of lime in front of me. I took a sip. "That's ridiculous. We're almost exactly the same age."

"You've taken better care of yourself."

"I'll have to do something about that when we're married."

"*When we're married*—I like the sound of that."

"Your table's ready, sir." Carrying our glasses, we followed the same young woman we'd seen before to our favorite spot, a small table tucked into the bay window near the hearth. She handed us each a menu.

"I've got news," I said, sounding a little breathless.

"So do I, but let's order first. Then you can tell me."

We ordered a starter to share—Queen Anne's tart, made with artichokes, olives, and tarragon vinaigrette in flaky pastry. For the main course we both ordered the daily special—always a great idea at the Trout—halibut on a bed of linguine with prawns, chilis, and lemon.

"It's Martyn Lee-Jones," I said when the waiter had gone. "Ivor and I did some research into the board members earlier, but I just learned his mother was a patient at Netherfield Sanatorium in 1960, a year after Martyn was born. Sounds like postpartum depression, severe enough for her husband to admit her. Her doctors thought she was improving, so they allowed her to walk into the village. She killed herself by jumping off the old pier. Vivian and I first heard about it from that old man—Percy Pike—although he didn't know the name of the victim. He's the one who told us about Millicent Beaufoy's older boyfriend, remember? What if Martyn's father blamed Dr. Beaufoy for misdiagnosing his wife's condition? They both worked at Netherfield. Philip Lee-Jones was financial director."

"You mean Philip killed the Beaufoys in revenge, and then his son, Martyn, killed Will Parker and the others to cover it up?"

"It's possible, although Martyn claims he was at home in Ipswich the night of the murder."

Tom narrowed his eyes. "And just how did you come by that information?"

"I asked him."

Tom shook his head. "Is Philip Lee-Jones still alive?"

"Ninety-two. Sharp as a tack, apparently."

The waiter delivered our starter, sectioned neatly in half.

"I almost forgot," I said, slicing off a forkful. "What's your news?"

"The cyber team found a file on Will Parker's computer that wasn't encrypted. They flagged it because he'd named it 'Christmas Card List,' a ruse people often use to hide important information. Dead giveaway."

"I'll have to remember that. What was in the file?"

"It was a list. Four items. *Miracle, Intense blue, Cullinan, St. Genevieve.*

"*Miracle* must mean Miracle-on-Sea. When was the file written—before or after Will received the game piece in the mail?"

"The last time he looked at the file was the day he left for Long Barston, but that doesn't mean he wrote it then. What do the other items on the list suggest to you?"

I took a sip of mineral water, giving me time to think. "*Intense blue* could refer to ultramarine—powdered lapis lazuli. Van Eyck famously used it. So did the forger. *Cullinan* rings a bell, but I can't place it. Sounds Scottish."

"It's the name of that new Rolls Royce all-terrain SUV—the Cullinan. Costs something like three hundred thousand pounds." Tom took a large bite of the tart. "Why would Will Parker be interested in that?"

"Saw someone driving one? Planned to buy one?"

"Not unless he was coming into some serious money."

"That's a thought."

"How about St. Genevieve? Isn't she the patron saint of Paris?"

"I'll Google her." I pulled out my phone.

An image appeared. "You're right. It says here St. Genevieve was a French nun who saved Paris from Attila the Hun." I kept scrolling.

"*Hmm*, it's also a city in Missouri, a municipality in Quebec, and—*Tom*, look at this." I handed him my phone. "St. Genevieve is a village in the French Alps. Remember? Ivor told me about a painter, an art forger, Gerard Bibeau, who lived in a village in the French Alps." I grabbed his arm. "This is more proof that Will Parker was investigating the Monkey Puzzle murders when he was killed."

"You've leapt over a few hurdles in the logic chain, but I'm inclined to agree."

"What if Will Parker learned about the fake Van Eyck and decided to investigate?"

"They did call him the Pit Bull."

"He told his family he was working on an old case. My mother says if we find out what triggered his interest, we'll have our answers. We need those inquest files. And the Netherfield records. I'll call Tony Currie tomorrow—ask him for access."

"In the meantime—" Tom stopped talking while our waiter cleared away the starter and served our main courses. "In the meantime, I want to see your famous list of questions. You always have one."

"I didn't this time—not until late this afternoon, anyway. I called my mother. She told me to question everything. That's what I've been doing." I got out my list and read him the questions.

"Any answers?"

"The first question—were the poisonings really accidental?—we won't be able to answer until the inquest files are unlocked. About Dulcie, I managed to find the name of her aunt on Jersey. Patricia Vautier. I plan to track her down tomorrow."

"What we need is a list of suspects. Motive, means, opportunity." I sat back and looked at him.

"Why are you smiling?" he asked, taking a bite of his fish.

"*What we need*—You're making us sound like a PI team again."

"I told you it's a good idea. We could both join that private investigations firm in Canada."

"We could." I laughed. "But right now let's figure out who killed the Beaufoys in 1961."

"Who's on the list of suspects?"

"Family first, I suppose. The children. Any one of them could have done it, or they could have done it together, like *Murder on the Orient Express*. Except Dulcie, of course. She was only eleven in 1961. Justine would have kept her out of it."

"Motive?"

"Maybe the parents were abusing them. That suggests one of the older children—Justine or Grayson, and they're both dead. Millie had a motive if her parents were separating her from that older boyfriend. According to the cook's son, she was a handful. Unruly. Vindictive."

"But no longer physically capable of murder, Kate. Other suspects?"

"The board members. We know Pyramid Development needs cash, and I don't see Cliff House swarming with potential buyers, but how would killing old people help their finances?"

"That's still the hard stop for me, Kate. Who benefits from Will Parker's death?"

"Don't forget Jack Cavanagh, Mary Diamond, and Frank Keane."

"We haven't proven they were murdered—or targeted in Keane's case. My point is people kill each other for a reason, for some gain."

"Money isn't the only motive. That's where Martyn Lee-Jones comes in. If his mother hadn't died, she might have been successfully treated for depression. She died because one of the Netherfield doctors misdiagnosed the seriousness of her condition. If Philip Lee-Jones murdered the Beaufoys in revenge, Martin might kill to protect him."

"Which implies Will Parker contacted Lee-Jones and frightened him."

"The problem is opportunity," I said. "Remember, Martyn Lee-Jones claims he was home the night of Will Parker's murder. He says his wife can confirm it."

"How about the father—Philip Lee-Jones?"

"He may be sharp, but he's ninety-two. Martyn says he doesn't get around much anymore. And while we're talking alibis, Nicola Netherfield told me she was in London the night of the murder. So was Tony Currie. Of course, they might be lying. You could check their stories."

"I'll do that—how about Niall Walker?"

"This is where things get interesting. Remember I told you about the snuff boxes Cliff House intends to auction off? They're worth a lot of money—potentially as much as a million pounds. They were a bequest from a Netherfield patient whose niece challenged the will but lost in court. Legal services were provided by Walker & Palkot. What if the solicitor's firm Niall's father founded did stuff like that all the time—influenced older clients to turn over valuable assets—and Dr. Beaufoy found out about it and challenged them. That would be a motive for murder."

"I'll check to see if any other wills involving Walker & Palkot have been contested. How about that historian chap, Oswin Underwood?"

"We talked about that. He could have been Millie Beaufoy's older boyfriend."

"*Could* have been. There's no proof he was."

"The families knew each other, Tom. Both fathers worked at Netherfield. They must have met."

"Possible. He was eighteen or nineteen in 1961. Too old to be dating a fifteen-year-old girl."

I sighed. "Except he didn't have an opportunity either. Will Parker was killed on Friday the twenty-first of August. Underwood gives lectures at the library every Friday evening at seven."

"So Netherfield, Currie, Lee-Jones, and Underwood all have alibis for Will Parker's murder."

"Which may or may not hold up under scrutiny," I said.

"True, but that leaves the Walkers and your theory about the bequest. Is there anything concrete that ties them to the killings—then or now?"

"I don't know." I was repeating those words a lot lately. "But I'm beginning to wonder if there's a connection to the fake Van Eyck."

Tom speared a prawn. I could practically see his brain ticking over.

"Here's my problem," he said carefully. "You're talking about someone killing Will Parker and possibly the others to cover up the murders of the Beaufoys. And then you're talking about someone killing them to cover up the forgery of the Van Eyck. Which is it? Even if everything you say is true—and you know I'm inclined to believe you—what ties them together?"

He was right. The murders in 1961 and the Van Eyck forgery were like points on a plane. Something else was needed to close the circle.

"We keep looking, I guess."

I'd been so focused on the list of suspects I'd hardly tasted my food—and that really was a crime. I speared a bite-sized piece of the halibut and swirled it in the spicy lemon sauce. "What can you do about any of this, Tom? Interview the board members?"

"On what grounds? Nothing connects any of them to the Five Sleuths."

"And yet something prompted Will Parker to ask questions."

He looked gloomy. "It's what you don't know that comes back to haunt you."

Chapter
Thirty-Two

I made it back to Long Barston in just over twenty-five minutes, obeying the speed limit with the diligence of a sixteen-year-old taking his driver's test.

Since Tom was living in Bury now, it wasn't practical for him to pick me up and take me home every time we met at the Trout. Depending on traffic, the trip would add an hour and a half to his day. Truthfully, the police flat was a huge inconvenience, but I wasn't about to complain. Tom's current living arrangements—and our future arrangements, for that matter—were complicated enough. Our wedding was now a mere two months away, and we still hadn't decided where we'd live. Strangely, I wasn't worried about it. Even stranger, neither was Tom. My focus at the moment was protecting Vivian.

I was nearing the gates of Finchley Hall when I saw the car—a silver hatchback parked along the side of the road. Adrenaline fizzed like a sparkler in my chest. This was the same car I'd seen in Norwich, the car that had been tailing Vivian.

In my headlights, the silhouette looked like a man. I slowed down so I could take a good look as I passed. The driver must have seen me coming because his lights flicked on and the car roared out onto the road ahead of me.

I hesitated a fraction of a second. Then, stomping on the accelerator, I took off after him.

He picked up speed. So did I.

The driver turned onto one of the B roads west of Long Barston. *Yikes.* Hedgerows whizzed by on both sides of the narrow road. The good news was if we met someone coming from the opposite direction, he'd hit them first. The bad news was I'd then hit them both.

This was not a good decision, but I wasn't about to give up. Summoning my courage—or sheer stupidity—I sped up enough to see the plate number.

AX63 MNR

I repeated it several times out loud, picturing it in my head as I did.

Stepping hard on the brakes, I screeched to a halt as the silver hatchback disappeared over a blind summit in a puff of dark smoke.

Negotiating a quick six-point turn, I headed back to Long Barston.

Once in a lighted area, I pulled over and dialed Tom's phone, my heart still slamming against my rib cage.

"Kate, is everything all right?"

"The silver hatchback was parked near the Finchley Hall gates." I sounded breathless. "He turned off the main road at the B32. I got the plate number."

"Got it," Tom said as I repeated the letters and numbers twice. "Good work, Kate. We'll get him."

* * *

At Finchley Hall, everyone was in bed. No way could I sleep with adrenaline still pulsing through my system. Rather than disturb Vivian and Fergus, I crept into our room, grabbed my computer, and headed for Lady Barbara's sitting room.

I got out my list of questions.

1. *Was the poisoning of the Beaufoys really accidental? (check inquest files)*
2. *Name of Millie's older boyfriend?*

3. *Did the children discover their parents' bodies? Who did they notify? (inquest files)*
4. *Why was Dulcie sent to Jersey—and why did she return in 2002?*
5. *Was there anything suspicious about Grayson's death?*
6. *Where had Dr. Beaufoy traveled and what was he doing there? (Dover to France?)*
7. *What does any of this have to do with the fake Van Eyck?*
8. *Are the Cliff House board members involved?*

I'd already answered question five and crossed it out. Grayson Beaufoy died at sea—an accident. Questions one and three couldn't be answered without the inquest files. The only way to answer question two, about Millie's older boyfriend, would be to find someone who'd known the Beaufoys in 1961. To answer question seven about the fake Van Eyck, I'd need a lot more information than I currently had. That left two questions I might be able to answer with a little digging:

4. *Why was Dulcie sent to Jersey—and why did she return in 2002?*
6. *Where had Dr. Beaufoy traveled and what was he doing there? (Dover to France?)*

If Dr. Beaufoy had gone to France to arrange for the forgery of the Van Eyck painting, that might provide answers to the final two questions—a connection between the deaths, the painting, and the Netherfield trustees. I powered up my computer and logged onto Lady Barbara's Wi-Fi—used by Francie Jewell, I supposed. Lady Barbara didn't believe in modern technology. Her telephones were still rotary dial.

Dulcie told me she was sent to Jersey because Justine felt unable to raise her properly and because her older siblings wanted to protect her from the aftermath of their parents' deaths. That sounded plausible, but since I had the aunt's name, I might be able to verify it for myself. The chances that Patricia Beaufoy Vautier was still alive were zero. Even if she had been ten years younger than her brother, she'd be close to a hundred today. I was looking for death notices—and living relatives.

Finding her turned out to be easier than I expected. When I looked up Jersey newspapers, I learned there was only one still operating—the *Jersey Evening Post*. Clicking on the link, I found a tab for *Family Notices*, then *Deaths*. Plugging in *Patricia Vautier* and a date range of 1990 to 2012, I found her obituary, dated August 11, 2010.

> *VAUTIER, Patricia Beatrice (née Beaufoy)*
>   *Passed away peacefully in the tender care of Sur St. Clement Care Home on Monday, 9 August, 2010, aged 86. Predeceased by her husband, Phillipe, of Jersey, and her brother, Dr. Simon Beaufoy, of Suffolk. Survived by adopted grandson, Jules Mallett, of St. Helier. Memorial service, Sur St. Clement, 3 p.m. on Friday, 13 August. For details, contact Le Pavoux Funeral Services, St. Clement.*

No mention of children or nieces, but there'd been an adopted grandson. *Jules Mallett.* The online white pages helpfully provided an address in St. Helier and a phone number. While I waited for someone to pick up, I prayed Jersey was on Suffolk time. It was already past nine PM.

A male voice answered, "Hallo."

"I'm looking for Jules Mallett." I pronounced it *Ma-lay*, hoping I wasn't too far off.

"This is Jules. Who's calling, please?"

"My name is Kate Hamilton. I'm looking for information about Patricia Vautier of St. Clement. Did you know her?"

"Of course. Nana Pat. She died ten or eleven years ago."

"Yes, I know. She has two nieces in Suffolk, Millicent and Dulcett Beaufoy. I'm gathering information about the family." *Not a lie.* "Would you be willing to tell me how you knew her?"

"Of course. My family lived next door to the Vautiers when I was a child. We didn't have family on the island, and since the Vautiers never had children of their own, they adopted me as a sort of grandson. She was a lovely person."

"So you knew her for some years."

"Oh, yes. Almost forty. We moved to St. Clement when I was six, so that would have been around 1973."

"You must have known their niece, Dulcie, then."

"Who?"

"Patricia's niece, the one sent to live with her in 1961 when her parents died."

The silence on the line lasted longer than it should have. "I think there's been some misunderstanding. Who did you say you are?"

"I'm Kate Hamilton. American, as you can probably tell, but I live in Suffolk now. There've been a series of deaths here—" I scrambled to think of a way to put it without sounding like a nut. "The police think the deaths may be connected to the deaths of Patricia's brother and his wife in 1961."

"Are you a reporter?"

"No. I'm a friend of the Beaufoy sisters." *That's stretching the truth.* "Did you ever meet Dulcie Beaufoy? In 1973, she would have been in her early twenties."

"Look, I'm not comfortable with your questions." His voice was wary. "I will tell you this—I knew about the deaths of Pat's brother and his wife. But they never had a niece living with them. Not while I knew them."

"She never spoke about Dulcie Beaufoy?"

"No, she didn't. I don't mean to be rude, Ms. Hamilton, but I think we're done."

He hung up, leaving me dumbstruck. Was it possible that Patricia and Phillippe Vautier had raised their niece, Dulcie, without ever mentioning the fact to their adopted grandson, Jules?

I was thinking about the implications when I got a text from Tom.

Are you awake? Call me. We got him.

* * *

"That was quick," I said. "It's only been—what, an hour and a half?"

"It wasn't difficult," Tom said. "He was hitchhiking. His car had broken down on the side of the road, not too far from your last location. We know him—quite well, as a matter of fact. He's a petty criminal with a list of offences longer than your arm. Minor stuff. Nothing violent."

"Did he admit to stalking Vivian?"

"He said he was paid to watch her, see where she went, what she did."

"By whom?"

"He claims he doesn't know. He was contacted by text, no name."

"Did you arrest him?"

"We're holding him for twenty-four hours, but unless something more turns up, we'll have to let him go. We could charge him with harassment, but it wouldn't stand up in court. He never actually contacted Vivian or threatened her."

"And you believe his story—that he doesn't know who hired him? What was he supposed to do?"

"Just observe and report. Which he did. It's not illegal to follow someone in a public place. He claims he was acting in the role of a private investigator."

"Good grief."

"Exactly. I don't suppose Vivian is still awake."

"No. I'll tell her first thing in the morning. Do you think we can move back to Rose Cottage? Vivian is chomping at the bit."

"Let's see if we can find out anything more first."

"Tom, I learned something interesting tonight about Dulcie Beaufoy. Her aunt, Patricia Vautier, the one who raised her in

Jersey, died in 2010. A young boy was informally adopted by the Vautiers as a grandson when his family moved next door in 1973. He knew Patricia for almost forty years and never once heard her mention Dulcie."

"How old would Dulcie have been in 1973?"

"Twenty-three or twenty-four."

"She'd probably moved away by then. Didn't you say she'd been trained in computers? She probably took a job somewhere on the island."

"But wouldn't Patricia have mentioned her? Wouldn't they have had contact?"

"Maybe they had a falling out."

"Maybe. I'm planning to phone Dulcie in the morning. I want to see if she remembers where her father had traveled before his death. I might bring up the aunt in Jersey and see what she says."

"You don't really suspect the Beaufoy sisters of murdering Will Parker, do you?"

"Honestly, no. They're just two older ladies who've lived rather sad lives, but something doesn't add up, Tom. They may know something. One or both of them might be in danger. We need those inquest files."

"The cybersecurity team is close. I'll let you know as soon as they have something. Which reminds me, have you come up with any fabulous honeymoon destinations? Glamorous big cities? Tropical beaches?"

"Cybersecurity reminds you of our honeymoon?"

"Everything reminds me of our honeymoon. So which destination do you prefer?"

"Nothing in the middle of nowhere."

He laughed. "What's that supposed to mean?"

"I heard it somewhere—TV, I think. A honeymoon in the Scottish Highlands. Someone called the place 'nothing in the middle of nowhere.'"

"I think I like that. We met in the Scottish Highlands."

"We met in the middle of a murder investigation, in case you've forgotten. Not what I had in mind for our honeymoon."

"That's not likely to happen again, is it?"

"I suppose not."

We hung up, and I drifted off to sleep, dreaming about the Highlands littered with bodies.

Chapter
Thirty-Three

~

Wednesday, September 8

The Curiosity Cabinet was quiet all morning. Deadly quiet. Ivor and I did some dusting, a never-ending job in an antiques showroom, and one that can't be rushed. We finished around ten, and Ivor began packing up a large porcelain *famille-rose* vase—a lovely thing, the Nine Peaches pattern with a Qianlong reign mark in seal script on the foot-rim. The winning bid had been from a woman in Devon, a dealer with a shop in Exeter.

While Ivor finished up, I ducked into the storeroom to phone Tony Currie.

After reminding him that he'd promised to check on the location of the old Netherfield archives, I said, "I'd like to examine the records myself. The sooner we can back up Mr. Tweedy's theory about the provenance of the forgery, the sooner we can finalize the auction. Having the sale at Cliff House is brilliant, but we need an advertising plan, including a full-color brochure. The painting would make a striking cover image."

"Yes, of course. And we do want to go ahead with the auction in October or early November at the latest. The archives are stored on the lower level of Cliff House. I'll alert Cordelia—Miss Armstrong. Make an appointment with her. She'll give you all the help you need."

That was easy. I'd expected an argument. Since I was doing so well, I decided to push my luck. "My friend, Miss Bunn, has asked me to look into the death of an old friend—Will Parker."

"The body you found the night before our initial meeting."

"Yes. She knew him when they were teenagers. He was ex-CID. The police think he was investigating the deaths of Dr. and Mrs. Beaufoy in 1961."

"You mean the deaths at Monkey Puzzle House. You probably know Niall Walker bought the place. He'd like to use it as a film location."

"I'm surprised you weren't interested. Houses like that are rare."

"That's not really Pyramid's line. We're residential, not commercial."

"I've heard Will Parker was seen around Miracle before he died. If I text you his photo, could you take a look and tell me if you've seen him?"

"All right, although I don't get into the village much, and I spend just about every weekend in London."

"Except the weekend we first met."

"Actually, I'd been in London since Wednesday of that week. Problems with one of our subcontractors."

"Commuting must be a challenge."

"Not really. It only takes an hour by train from London to Colchester. I keep an SUV there."

"An SUV?" I pretended a flirtatious interest. "Let me guess—a Rolls Royce."

"The Cullinan? I wish. Mine's an Audi. Although the board did discuss leasing a Cullinan and a couple of Bentleys to park in the visitors' lot. Touch of class. Why do you ask?"

"Curiosity, I suppose. I've been wondering if it's feasible for people to live at Cliff House and work in London. An hour's commute isn't bad." I hadn't answered his question, but he didn't seem to notice.

"Is there anything else?"

"Netherfield's history."

"That's Underwood's line, not mine."

"Asking him would be awkward. One of the questions involves his family. I've heard his father had some trouble around the time Netherfield was transferred to the National Health."

"I have no idea. Now I really—"

"Did you know Martyn Lee-Jones's mother was a patient at Netherfield?"

"No, I didn't."

"She committed suicide."

"Ms. Hamilton, please. I can't begin to imagine what you're trying to accomplish with all these questions. Let me assure you I have no knowledge of or interest in what may or may not have happened at Netherfield all those years ago. My interest is now."

"You will look at the photo of Will Parker?"

"If you insist—for all the good it will do."

"Just text me back—please. Yes or no."

By the time we hung up, Currie was seriously annoyed. And suspicious.

* * *

"You were brilliant, you know," I told Ivor when I got back to the shop floor. "Tony Currie is eager to promote the painting as a fabulous copy of an Old Master."

Ivor slapped the label on the box with the Qianlong vase. "Sometimes you have to make the best of what you have to work with. That's what Gerard Bibeau did, you know. He was a hugely talented artist—the kind that comes along once in a century. The problem was he lived in the wrong century. He loved classical art, representational art, the kind that produces an identifiable image as opposed to abstract or Expressionist art, in which the artist paints, not the subject itself but the impression or emotion the subject evokes. Bibeau's work was almost photographic in detail. When he started out, that's not what buyers wanted. Critics called him derivative, out of fashion. The galleries refused to hang his work. Art at that time was experimental, conceptual, minimalistic. Think Andy Warhol's portrait of Marilyn Monroe or the Campbell soup can."

"I'd rather not."

"Nor I, but that's what was selling. Bibeau was so offended he decided to use his skills in another way—a way that would expose the hypocrisy in the art world. They weren't opposed to making money off the Old Masters, but they weren't willing to promote a contemporary artist of similar brilliance. Bibeau was never after money himself. He lived his entire life in a small village in France. Never married. Lived and worked in his studio. Spent only what was necessary to keep body and soul together."

"His work is finally being recognized for its merit. Ironic—and sad."

"Sadness is often behind works of great art."

And a certain degree of cynicism. I thought about the impression I'd received upon seeing the Van Eyck copy for the first time.

That's when I remembered the word that had emerged—a whisper, a shadow.

Danger.

I checked my phone for the third time. Tony Currie must have received the photo of Will Parker by now, but he hadn't responded.

Later that morning, I spent an hour following a group of Japanese tourists around the shop, answering questions with the help of their tour guide. One of them, a young woman, purchased a Victorian silver trinket box. She was delighted with her purchase, covering her smile politely with her small hand.

Since the day was sunny, I took my lunch break on the village green, enjoying the egg and cress sandwich Francie Jewell had packed for me.

The bright midday sun turned St. Æthelric's stained glass windows into a thousand faceted jewels. In the graveyard, a figure in a wide-brimmed hat and rolled-up trousers waved to me. Hattie Nuthall, the rector's housekeeper, was weeding the graves.

Dulcie Beaufoy had worn a similar hat in her garden the day we met. Maybe Tom had been right about her aunt, Patricia Vautier. It wouldn't have been easy for a childless couple to take on a girl entering her teenage years—especially one who'd just lost both her parents. Girls aren't easy under the best of circumstances. I knew that from personal experience. I could understand Patricia Vautier being so disillusioned by the experience that she'd want to put those years behind her and shower attention on the nice little boy next door.

Still, it was odd that Mrs. Vautier hadn't even mentioned Dulcie.

I crumpled up the waxed paper bag and disposed of it in the rubbish bin near my bench.

If I wanted to learn the truth about Dulcie Beaufoy, I was going to have to ask her.

Back at the shop, I made the call to Wren Cottage.

"Hullo, Kate." Dulcie sounded cheerful. "How kind of you check on us."

I hadn't called to check on them, but that isn't something you admit, is it? " I apologize again if our presence last week disturbed your sister."

"You caught Millie at a bad moment. She's quite calm now."

"That's good to hear." I wanted to jump in and ask her where her father had been in the days before his death and why her Aunt Patricia never spoke of her, but I couldn't come up with a plausible reason for getting so personal. As it turned out, I didn't need to invent a reason.

Dulcie said, "After you and Vivian left, Millie and I talked about the day our parents died. We don't often do that."

"It must be painful for you to remember."

"It was so long ago, Kate, and I was incredibly young. It seems almost like an old movie now—not something that actually happened."

"How long had your father been away?"

"Some days, I think. Maybe a week."

"Where had he been?"

"France. In the mountains somewhere."

The French Alps. The forger, Gerard Bibeau.

"I remember because father always brought us gifts when he'd been away. That time Justy and Millie got silver charm bracelets with cowbells and crossed skis and tiny hiking boots. Millie still has hers. Gray got a pocketknife—the kind with all the accessories that fold up inside. He was so proud of that knife. Father brought me a big stuffed dog, a Saint Bernard with a keg of brandy around his neck. I wonder whatever happened to it?"

"Did he bring something for your mother?"

"A lovely bottle of wine. They were planning to open it that night. And something else. He wouldn't tell her what it was. Just that it was very, very special."

"What else do you remember about that night?" I scrunched up my face, hoping Dulcie wouldn't be offended.

"Almost nothing. The fair had been so exciting—the rides, the candy floss, the lights. I was sleepy. Gray was carrying me on his back. I remember hearing someone scream. Then Justy whisked me outside. A neighbor took me to her house. I think I stayed there several days."

"You said Millie had been grounded that night because of a boy. Do you remember his name?"

"I'm not sure I ever knew it."

The questions didn't seem to be upsetting Dulcie, so I continued. "When did you realize your parents were dead?"

"Right away. Justy told me. But it wasn't as if my parents raised me, Kate. I know it sounds strange, but my life was wrapped up with my sisters and brother. Father was always working. Mother was busy with her charity work. Justy raised me. Then I had to go away and start a new life."

"When did you know you'd be going to Jersey?"

"Jersey?"

"To your aunt and uncle."

"Almost immediately. Justy said I had no choice. It was the best thing for me."

"And was it?"

Dulcie never answered. I heard a sound in the background, a human voice in distress.

"That's Millie," she said. "I'll have to hang up in a minute."

"Yes, of course." I took a deep breath. "This is none of my business, Dulcie, but do you need help with Millie—professional help?"

"I can handle her. Justy always said it was a mistake getting the doctors involved."

A strange comment, seeing their father had been a doctor. I couldn't see the relevance. "If you need help, I'd be happy to look into what's available."

"Thank you, Kate. Maybe you and Vivian will come back to see us some time. We don't get many visitors."

"I'll tell Vivian you said so. She'll be pleased."

As the line went dead, I thought about the difference between the sisters. Millie's reaction to our questions about her parents' deaths had been intense, even violent. Dulcie's had been unemotional, matter-of-fact. Of course, she hadn't seen her parents' bodies. Justine had shielded her from everything. *Or*—I paused as a new thought emerged—had Justine prevented her from seeing something she shouldn't? Children aren't good at keeping secrets.

"Kate, are you free?" Ivor's voice drifted in from the showroom. "Someone is interested in the Louis Quatorze torchères."

I tucked my phone in my handbag and stowed it in the cupboard.

Something else was bothering me. Twice now, when I'd asked Dulcie about Jersey, she'd stumbled. Was she trying to forget an unpleasant time in her life, or . . .

Or what? I had no idea. Every time I tried to dig deeper into the past, things got more tangled.

* * *

When I returned to Finchley Hall, I found Vivian and Lady Barbara in the sitting room, having afternoon tea.

272

"Have a scone," Lady Barbara said. "I promise you won't regret it."

I usually turn down afternoon sweets, but this time Francie had made her famous blackberry lavender scones with white chocolate icing. If you're going to splurge, you may as well make the calories worthwhile.

"Tom called," Vivian said between mouthfuls. "We're allowed to go home. They've had to release the stalker, but he won't be bothering us again. They're keeping the cottage under surveillance for a few days, just in case. Tom really wanted to talk to you. Your line was engaged. He said to call him as soon as you can."

I excused myself to make the call, but all I got was Tom's voice mail. I left a message and returned to the sitting room. "Did he say why he called?"

"No, but I got the impression they're working on something important. Oh—and he said he'd send one of the constables to help us move our gear back to the cottage. We're to be ready at eight o'clock tonight."

"Francie's preparing an early supper." Lady Barbara frowned. "I shall quite miss having you here."

The atmosphere in the room had changed.

Lady Barbara cleared her throat. "You know we never interfere, dear—"

It's what people say when they really mean *I shouldn't interfere, but I'm going to anyway.* "Yes?" I said.

Two pairs of elderly eyes were trained on me.

"We've been talking," Vivian said. "About the wedding."

"And what comes after that."

"What comes after that?" *Good grief—was I about to get "the talk"?*

"For you and Tom." Lady Barbara said. "First, though, we've been wondering if you've found a dress. We'd like to offer ourselves as consultants."

"Thank you, but that's taken care of. My friend Charlotte says she's found the perfect dress. It's being sent to me. If I have to have it altered, I'd love to have you both come along. Was there something else?"

"Yes," Vivian said. "Have you decided where you and Tom will live?"

"Not yet," I said, not wanting to say too much. "Things keep getting in the way."

"Like bodies." Lady Barbara took a sip of her tea.

"As soon as we make a decision, I'll let you know."

"We hope you stay here," she said. "I don't mean on the estate, although there will be a couple of tied cottages available soon, but you and Tom need your privacy."

"The thing is, we don't want to lose you," Vivian added. I was surprised to see her eyes glisten. "That's what we've been talking about. How much we need you."

Now my eyes were glistening. "Tom has a few decisions to make."

"About his mother." Vivian made a little moue of distaste.

They couldn't know about her words at the engagement party, could they? Arthur Gedge was a lot of things, but a gossip wasn't one of them. Still, Vivian and Barbara were pretty astute. They'd have picked up on Liz Mallory's negative attitude.

"Our marriage will mean a big change for Liz—and for my family, too. We have other people to consider besides ourselves."

"If you want the advice of someone older if not wiser," Lady Barbara said, "don't waste time trying to please other people. Now that you and Tom have found each other, do exactly what makes you happy. Even if it means leaving Long Barston."

"Thank you," I said, getting up to give them both a kiss on their papery cheeks. "I'm sure it's good advice—and for the record, I don't want to lose you either."

* * *

By nine that evening Vivian and I were sitting in front of the fire at Rose Cottage. Fergus was curled up in his basket, one paw trailing out.

"Vivian," I said, pulling my legs under me on the sofa, "What did you think of Dulcie Beaufoy?"

"Funny you should ask, because I've been thinking about her all day. There was something almost childlike in her manner. I don't want to say *trusting* because it wasn't that. More like unconcerned—or unaware. Naïve. Oh, that's not really it either. I can't put it into words."

"I know what you mean. Like she's not in touch with the real world. I spoke with her today. She says Millie's fine, but something doesn't feel right to me. Do you think she's so naïve she doesn't recognize danger?"

"She's strong. I think she can handle Millie."

"She's obviously capable of running the house and garden, but she's vague about her time in Jersey. And something else. She told me today that Justine as good as raised her. If that's true, why didn't Justine feel capable of raising her after their parents' deaths?"

"Families are always more complicated than they appear."

"You're right there." I noticed the dark shadows under Vivian's eyes. "Shall I take Fergus for his walkies?"

"Oh, would you? I feel quite exhausted after our ordeal. I'd like an early night."

Staying in a grand Elizabethan mansion was an ordeal I'd happily undergo any day, but I knew Vivian was tired. She wasn't young anymore, even if her doctor had pronounced her strong as a horse. "You go up. I'll bring Fergus in a few minutes. I'm going to read Apollo's report on the fake Van Eyck again. That's sure to put me to sleep."

After trying Tom's phone two more times, I left him a text and settled in to see if there was anything in the report we could use in our publicity campaign. Fifteen minutes later, my eyes were getting heavy.

That's when my phone pinged. A text from Tom.

Can't talk now. Meet you at Rose Cottage 7 AM. We got it wrong.

Chapter Thirty-Four

Thursday, September 9

I dreamed that night about Monkey Puzzle House. About stairs that went nowhere and rooms without doors or windows. Everywhere I looked, great holes in the walls exposed the skeletons of animals sacrificed in some evil ritual that was now threatening me. Scariest of all was a painting of a long-dead Victorian with one eye that followed me wherever I went.

I woke with a start. Tendrils of fear coiled in the air—until the homely sounds of pots and pans and the reassuring aroma of strong coffee wafted up the stairs. Tom would be arriving at seven. I jumped out of bed, showered and dressed in a flash, and flew down the stairs.

"Sleeping beauty awakes." Vivian stood at the Aga, pushing sausages around a pan. "I thought we deserved the full English today."

"Tom will be here any minute," I said, checking my watch. "He texted me last night. Something's happened."

"Lovely." Vivian dropped two more sausages into the pan.

Fergus woofed as the sound of car tires on gravel announced Tom's arrival. A car door slammed.

We heard a knock and Tom strode in, looking like he'd slept in his clothes. "We unlocked Will Parker's files. I spent most of last night reading them." He bent down to kiss me.

"Tell me you have the missing inquest files."

"We do—and more. Vivian, we found his notes about you."

Vivian stared at him, an egg in each hand. "What did he think I could tell him?"

"He was going to ask you about the contents of the metal box."

"I've remembered everything." Vivian's face clouded. "At least I think so." She cracked the eggs into a frying pan and set a plate of sausages in front of him. "Coffee?"

"Yes, please." He picked up a knife and fork. "I haven't eaten since yesterday around four—and that was a microwave packet of chicken vindaloo." He cut a chunk off one of the sausages and began chewing.

"Your text said we got it wrong," I said. "What did you mean?"

"Two things, actually. First, we got the results of the autopsy on Jack Cavanagh. He died of a heart attack, Kate—actually an aortic dissection—a sudden tearing of the wall of the aorta. Death is painful but quick."

I felt like the rug had been pulled out from under me. "So it was natural causes after all."

"Yes. Sorry."

"Don't be."

"What is it, Kate? I know that look on your face. You're still not convinced."

"No—I am. But I was thinking about what his daughter, Cheryl, said. She's convinced that someone searched his house. Maybe the stress put too much strain on his heart."

"Possible, but that still leaves us with no case to investigate."

I shook my head. "I need to think about this. What's the second thing?"

Tom pulled a sheaf of papers out of his jacket with his free hand. "Printouts of the inquest. Read it for yourself."

"Out loud, if you please," Vivian said.

I started reading the first page, but Tom stopped me. "Not there. That's the boring stuff." He took another forkful of sausage as he thumbed through the pages with his other hand. "The interesting part starts on page twenty-five with the testimonies of the gardener and the cook." He tapped the page. "Right there."

I read: *Testimony of Interested Persons. The coroner calls Joseph White.*

Coroner: *Please state your full name, age, and your relationship to the deceased persons.*

Joseph White: *Yes, guv . . . I mean sir. My name is Joseph White. I'm sixty-two, sir. I've been gardener at Monkey Puzzle House for ten years. Ever since they came, the doctor and his family.*

Coroner: *What can you tell us about the poison hemlock and how it got into the dish of candied parsnips?*

Joseph White: *It weren't my fault, sir.*

Coroner: *No one has suggested it was, Mr. White. Why don't you begin by telling us how you found the poison hemlock.*

Joseph White: *Yes, sir. I noticed it growing along the back of the property. My father taught me to recognize plants. He were an under gardener at Somerleyton Hall, sir. There's a boggy area along the edge of the field. That's where I noticed it, sir. I told the doctor we should inform the farmer, but the doctor told me to get rid of it straight away on account of the children. Easier said than done, sir, I told him. Not safe to burn, and it'll come back with a vengeance if we mow. So in the end, I dug it up, sir, stalk and root. Put the debris in burlap sacks. But I didn't have enough sacks, so I had to leave some in the open.*

Coroner: *Wasn't that dangerous, handling the plants?*

Joseph White: *Oh no, sir. I knows what I'm about, sir. You have to know what yer about.*

Coroner: *Can you describe your process?*

Joseph White: *Yes, sir. First I tied the stalks together with twine. Then I dug up the roots.*

I took a drink of my coffee and scanned ahead.

"Don't stop reading." Vivian slid a plate of scrambled eggs in front of Tom.

"He goes into a lot of detail here," I said. "Basically he dug up the plants and put them in burlap sacks to dry out in the sun. He planned to take them to the landfill at the old quarry. Okay— here's a new question."

Coroner: *Did you warn the family of the danger?*

Joseph White: *Oh, yes, sir. I did. Showed the missus where the plants lay. That were on the Thursday, sir.*

Coroner: *When you say Thursday, do you mean Thursday, May 18th, two days before the deaths of Dr. and Mrs. Beaufoy?*

Joseph White: *Yes, sir. I told the missus I'd be back to take care of the rest of the brush on Sunday on account of my cousin in Woodbridge had some extra burlap sacks.*

Coroner: *So knowing the danger, does it seem likely to you that Mrs. Beaufoy could have mistaken the hemlock roots for parsnips?*

Joseph White: *No, sir. It does not, sir. Very unlikely.*

Coroner: *Is it your opinion, Mr. White, that someone purposely mixed hemlock roots in with the wild parsnips Mrs. Beaufoy dug up for their supper?*

Joseph White: *That I couldn't say, sir.*

Coroner: *Who else besides Mrs. Beaufoy knew about the poison hemlock?*

Joseph White: *The cook, sir, and the children. They all knew. I made a point of it. They were there when I told her. The missus said they weren't to go near the plants or allow the dog to go near neither.*

Coroner: *How did the children react?*

Joseph White: *I couldn't say, sir.*

Coroner: *But you believe they understood the warning?*

Joseph White: *Oh yes, sir. The missus was quite firm, especially with the little 'un.*

Coroner: *Thank you, Mr. White. You may stand down. We may call on you again.*

Joseph White: *Yes, sir. Very good, sir.*

"By the little 'un, he must have meant Dulcie," I said.
"Read on."

The coroner calls Alice Evans.

Coroner: *Please state your full name, your age, and your relationship to the deceased persons.*

Alice Evans: *My name is Alice Evans, sir. I'm twenty-one years old. I work for Dr. and Mrs. Beaufoy as cook, but sometimes I mind the children. Mrs. Beaufoy is . . . was gone a lot with her charity work for the hospital.*

Coroner: *Can you take us back to Saturday, the twentieth of May, the day of the Miracle Fair?*

Alice Evans: *Yes, sir.*

Coroner: *Do you need a moment, Miss Evans?*

Alice Evans: *No sir. I'm all right.*

Coroner: *Can you tell us what happened on the day the Beaufoys died?*

Alice Evans: *The house was in an uproar, sir. The doctor was due to arrive home that afternoon, and Mrs. Beaufoy was in a state. The dog had been found dead the previous evening, and—*

Coroner: *Do you mean Friday, the nineteenth?*

Alice Evans: *Yes, sir. That evening. He didn't come home. Master Gray went searching. He found him, dead. He'd been foaming at the mouth—poisoned. Mrs. Beaufoy thought he must have eaten some of the hemlock.*

Coroner: *You're telling us the day before Dr. and Mrs. Beaufoy were poisoned, the family dog was poisoned?*

Alice Evans: *That's right, sir. Mrs. Beaufoy was in a right state over it. The doctor loved that dog, and she would have to break the news to him. She knew it would break his heart.*

Coroner: *Do you live with the family, Miss Evans?*

Alice Evans: *I do, sir. I have a room near the kitchen.*

Coroner: *Were you there the entire day?*

Alice Evans: *Just until the afternoon. Mrs. Beaufoy had given me the evening off on account of the fair, sir, and the fact that the doctor would be returning home. She said they had an important decision to make, but he wasn't going to like it, so she was planning to cook a special dinner. All his favorites.*

Coroner: *How long had the doctor been gone?*

Alice Evans: *Almost a week, sir.*

Coroner: *Was this usual?*

Alice Evans: *No, sir. He had his practice to run and his patients at the hospital.*

Coroner: *By hospital you mean Netherfield Sanatorium?*

Alice Evans: *That's right.*

Coroner: *Did you ever hear him speak of a patient or a patient's family who were dissatisfied with his work—or someone who may have held had a grudge against him?*

Alice Evans: *No, sir. Not a word of it. He was an excellent doctor.*

Coroner: *Did the doctor or his wife have any worries at the time?*

Alice Evans: *I got the impression they did, but it wasn't my place to ask.*

Coroner: *So after lunch you left Monkey Puzzle House?*

Alice Evans: *I helped Mrs. Beaufoy with a few chores. Then I had a bath and dressed. My boyfriend arrived at three, and we went to the fair.*

Coroner: *Do you mean the Miracle Fair on the pier?*

Alice Evans: *Yes. I was very excited about it.*

Coroner: *Did Mrs. Beaufoy talk to you about preparing candied parsnips for dinner that night?*

Alice Evans: *She did, sir. It was the doctor's favorite dish.*

Coroner: *Did you help her dig up the wild parsnips?*

Alice Evans: *I did not, sir. Not that time.*

Coroner: *But you were aware that she did it?*

Alice Evans: *I was. She had dug up the parsnips that morning and put them in her trug in the shed.*

Coroner: *You saw the parsnips?*

Alice Evans: *I did, sir. They were very nice.*

Coroner: *And you didn't see anything that looked different or unusual?*

Alice Evans: *I didn't inspect them, sir. But Mrs. Beaufoy knew wild parsnips. They grew along the lane in front of the house.*

Coroner: *Not along the rear of the property?*

Alice Evans: *No, sir. Along the lane.*

Coroner: *Had Mrs. Beaufoy picked wild parsnips before?*

Alice Evans: *Oh, many times, sir. I helped her on occasion.*

Coroner: *Think carefully, Miss Evans. Does it seem likely to you that Mrs. Beaufoy would have mistaken the hemlock roots for parsnips?*

Alice Evans: *It does not, sir. She knew the danger. We all did. Joe made it clear we were not to go near the plants.*

Coroner: *By Joe, are you referring to Joseph White, the gardener?*

Alice Evans: *Yes, sir. He told us we were to keep away from that area because the plants were dangerous. Even touching them could make us sick.*

Coroner: *Let's circle back to the family dog. What sort of dog was it?*

Alice Evans: *A retriever, sir. Brown and white.*

Coroner: *What was his name?*

Alice Evans: *Ranger.*

Coroner: *Was Ranger the kind of dog to get into things?*

Alice Evans: *I wouldn't have thought so, sir. Nor did Mrs. Beaufoy. She didn't believe his death was an accident.*

Coroner: *And how do you know that? Did she say so?*

Alice Evans: *No, sir, but I could tell. She was angry.*

Coroner: *Angry at whom, Miss Evans?*

Alice Evans: *I don't like to say, sir. It's not my place.*

Coroner: *I'm afraid it is your place, Miss Evans, to answer all my questions truthfully and thoroughly, holding nothing back. Do you understand?*

Alice Evans: *Yes, sir.*

Coroner: *No reason to cry, Miss Evans. You are helping the court. We appreciate your candor. Why was Mrs. Beaufoy angry?*

Alice Evans: *She thought the dog had been poisoned on purpose.*

Coroner: *Did she say by whom?*

Alice Evans: *[unintelligible]*

Coroner: *Speak up, Miss Evans.*
Alice Evans: *By one of the children, sir.*
Coroner: *Which one of the children?*
Alice Evans: *She didn't say, sir.*
Coroner: *But you have a theory, don't you, Miss Evans?*
Alice Evans: *[nods her head] I think that's why she was pun-ished—not allowed to go to the fair. It pains me to say so, sir, but there was something wrong with that girl.*

I turned the page, but the rest of the report, ten entire pages of it, was blacked out.

"What's this?" I asked Tom.

"It's been redacted." He grabbed a slice of toasted bread.

"Is that usual?"

"Highly *un*usual except in cases of national security."

"This had something to do with national security?" I asked.

"I don't think so." Tom spread butter thickly on the toast. "I think someone was being protected."

"Would Niall's father, the chief coroner, have known about it? He knew the Beaufoy family very well."

"He would have ordered the redaction. Or approved it."

I turned the page. "It looks like three others testified after the cook, but their names have been blacked out."

"We know who they are. Only three other witnesses were named in the inquest summary—Justine Beaufoy, Grayson Beaufoy, and Dr. David Underwood."

"Oswin Underwood's father?"

"In 1961 he was Netherfield's chief psychiatrist."

"Why would a psychiatrist testify in a poisoning death?" Vivian asked.

"That's a good question, isn't it?" Tom took a bite of toast. "We assumed the verdict was accidental death because that's what the summary indicated. But the cook believed one of the children purposely killed the dog."

"And the parents, by implication. Maybe the dog was practice."

Vivian put her hands on her hips. "I told you so."

Tom finished the last bite of toast. "Whoever it was, someone made sure no one would ever know."

"We know Millie was causing her parents concern, dating the older boyfriend." Vivian carried Tom's plate to the sink and wiped her hands on a tea towel. "Isn't that what the cook's son from Chicago said?"

"Actually," I said, trying to remember, "his mother said one of the daughters was unruly and deceptive. Percy Pike was the one who told us about the older boyfriend."

"Millie was grounded the night of fair. She was angry," Vivian said. "The boyfriend was probably angry too."

I rubbed my arm, still feeling the marks of Millie's nails. "Tom, if Millie murdered her parents—and the dog—what would have happened to her?"

"Things were different then," Tom said. "I believe a child convicted of a violent crime would have been sent to an institution for young offenders. Or, if they were very young, put in the care of a responsible adult."

"Millie was fifteen—not exactly a child."

"What if that child was mentally unbalanced?" Vivian asked. "What if both the younger girls were sent away—Dulcie to Jersey and Millie to a mental hospital—Netherfield, for example? I can see Justine persuading Grayson they had to keep Millie's condition a secret. Logic wouldn't have worked with someone as young as Dulcie. Children have a habit of spilling the beans."

I'd thought the same thing. "And then in 2002, Dulcie came home because Millie was released from custody, and Justine needed help handling her. Has anyone checked Millie's whereabouts between 1961 and 2002?"

Tom put down his fork. "I'll get Cliffe on it right away."

"The first thing to do is check the Netherfield archives," I said. "If Millie was admitted to Netherfield as a patient, it would have been soon after the deaths of her parents. There will be records. I'll phone Cliff House and see if we can drive over this morning."

"I'm afraid you'll have to go yourself." Tom stood and drained his coffee cup. "Cliffe and I are interviewing Philip Lee-Jones this afternoon. He's the only person still alive who may have been present at the inquest. If he was, he might remember what someone has gone to great lengths to conceal."

"Good luck," I said. "Let me know what you find out."

"There's a problem." Vivian crossed her arms over her chest. "Millie can't have murdered Will Parker. She isn't capable. And the person who abducted Frank Keane was a man."

I exchanged glances with Tom. "Maybe someone's still protecting Millie."

Chapter
Thirty-Five

I was on my way to Cliff House within a half hour. Vivian insisted on going with me until she realized we'd have to leave Fergus alone in the car. Lady Barbara couldn't dog-sit. She was in Bury with Nicola Netherfield, picking out fixtures for her new bathroom and kitchen. Francie Jewell was doing the weekly shopping.

The Cliff House gates swept open. I parked the Mini, grabbed my briefcase and handbag, and dashed toward the entrance. A stiff breeze carried the scent of dead fish and rotting seaweed. Storm clouds were gathering. Except for my car, the visitors' parking area was deserted. Where were all those potential residents, clamoring for a chance to live in a revamped mental hospital near a dying coastal resort town? Even I could see the prospects for Cliff House were looking grim. Still, they were keeping up appearances.

Cordelia Armstrong, immaculately turned out as usual, met me in the reception area. "That was quick. Mr. Currie only phoned me an hour ago."

"No reason to delay," I said. "The sooner we verify the provenance of the painting, the better."

"The archives are housed in an underground storage room. I've never seen it myself. Dr. Underwood is the only one who spends time there."

"Does he know I'm here?"

"I haven't been able to reach him. He's lecturing at the historical society luncheon today. Mr. Lee-Jones is out as well, unlikely to return until late afternoon. Not that their approval is needed, but Mr. Currie thought it only courteous to let them know of your visit. I'll keep trying."

I followed her down a flight of stairs to the storage and mechanical area of Cliff House. No damp mildewy odor, thank goodness, but the air was stale and warm, fueling a touch of claustrophobia. The brick-floored corridor was wide, with black iron pipes running in courses along the ceiling over our heads. Yellow and blue paint peeled off the walls.

The doors to several rooms stood open. In one room, an old-fashioned dentist's chair with a swing-arm drill looked vaguely ominous. In another, an oversized bathtub, rusty and unplumbed, conjured images of what it might have been used for. I felt queasy.

Miss Armstrong stopped at a white planked door marked A-312 and used a skeleton-style key to unlock the latch bolt and then, with a separate key, the dead bolt. Why two locks for a storage room—or was this room originally used for something else?

This speculation wasn't helping my claustrophobia.

The room was small, not much larger than a generously proportioned walk-in closet, and fitted on three sides with shelving. I fought the urge to flee by focusing on the clothbound ledgers, which lay in stacks on the shelving. They reminded me of the estate books in the Finchley Hall archives, filled with the details of human lives. A wooden table and chair occupied the center of the room.

"Is there some kind of organizational plan?" I asked Miss Armstrong.

"There may be. I'm not familiar." I got the impression she was as eager as I was to escape. "I'll leave you to it, shall I?" she said. "Call the main number if you need something—a cup of tea, a bathroom break. Your phone should work down here. And do ring when you're finished so I can lock up."

"I will." I propped the door open to make the small, windowless room less stifling.

I worked systematically around the room. Stacked along the left side were the minutes of the trustees' meetings, organized by year. I opened the first volume, dated 1888. Horace Netherfield himself had been chairman of the trustees. The ledgers continued until 1962, when the hospital was transferred to the NHS. If the trustees had decided to replace the Van Eyck with a forgery, it wouldn't show up in the minutes. They weren't stupid.

Along the back wall were the financial records, also in chronological order. These ledgers, hundreds of them, were smaller in size and organized according to category—balance sheets, budgets, income and expenses—and calendar year. If I'd had more time, I would have started there. They might have contained records of Dr. Beaufoy's trip to the French Alps, possibly even payments to Gerard Bibeau. But it was the patient records I needed to check first. Which doctor had authorized Marilyn Lee-Jones's request to leave the grounds, enabling her suicide? Even more important, was Millicent Beaufoy ever a patient Netherfield? I'd start there. These records were stacked on the shelves to my right. Like all the cloth-bound ledgers, the contents were marked on the spine in white ink—intakes and releases, medical and legal documents, case studies, weekly psychiatrists' reports, treatment plans.

I took a notebook and pen out of my briefcase, pulled out the intakes and releases ledger for 1961, and spread it out on the table. First I flipped to the end to see if there was an alphabetical listing of names. There was not. I'd have to go through each individual record. I began with May 20, the day Dr. Beaufoy returned from France.

Palmer, Thomas, age forty-two
Sutcliffe, Margaret, age sixty-three
Hatton, John, age twenty-three
Mortimer, Nancy, age thirty-seven.

Each patient was given a separate page with a photograph, the essential biographical details, a summary of the committal documents, the results of a preliminary physical examination, and a brief, general description of the patient's mental condition at the time of intake.

I turned page after page, scanning the faces. The majority were men. A few looked directly into the camera. Most stared off into the distance. All appeared to be well dressed. These patients had been loved by someone—or at least valued enough to pay the not inconsiderable fees Netherfield charged. Even so, there was desperation in the blank faces and hollow eyes—confusion, misery, hopelessness.

None were children.

Had I gone charging off for nothing? Maybe Netherfield didn't admit children. Maybe I was looking in the wrong place entirely.

I was considering phoning Miss Armstrong to ask her if I could have a cup of tea when I turned a page, and there she was—smiling into the camera as if she were posing for a class photo.

I took in a quick breath.

May twenty-fourth. Dora Banks was the name given, but there was no mistaking the broad forehead and high cheekbones, the fair hair, the innocent blue eyes.

Dulcie Beaufoy had changed remarkably little in the sixty years since the photo was taken. It was the smile that unnerved me. She hadn't yet realized what was happening to her.

I snapped a photo of the page with my cell phone.

I should have known. My conversation with Jules Mallett had prepared me. The reason Patricia Vautier hadn't mentioned her niece was because Dulcie had never been in Jersey. She'd been admitted to Netherfield.

Bits and pieces of information locked into place. Dulcie must have been the child the cook had described—unruly, manipulative, a right handful. The night of the Miracle Fair, it must have been Dulcie who'd been grounded, not Millie. Why?

Of course. The death of the family dog.

Mrs. Beaufoy knew Ranger had been poisoned. Alice Evans, the cook, had implied in her testimony that the doctor's wife had known who was responsible. In a flash of comprehension, I understood. That was what she'd intended to discuss with her husband that night. They had a decision to make—what were they going to do about their youngest daughter?

Whatever they might have decided that night, they'd died before they had a chance to implement the plan. And Justine had stepped in to protect the little sister she'd considered almost her own child. Instead of facing a trial. Dulcie had been given a new identity and admitted to Netherfield Sanatorium.

Justy said I had no choice. It was the best thing for me.

Justine couldn't have done it alone. Dr. Beaufoy's colleagues at Netherfield would have had to go along with the decision. *Why?* The obvious reason would be to protect the remaining Beaufoy children. Mental illness in the nineteen sixties still carried a heavy social stigma. People would speculate about Justine, Grayson, and Millicent. How about future generations—the children they might have? Who would want to marry into such a family? No one.

The evidence against Dulcie—presumably contained in the redacted pages of the inquest files—had been enough to convince the authorities that Dulcie was a danger to herself and others. I didn't know the guidelines for *sectioning* in the UK—the term used for involuntary committal—but there would have been an assessment and a recommendation by a mental health professional.

I ran my finger down the page. At the bottom were two signatures—Dr. David Underwood, the admitting psychiatrist, and Dr. Cosmo Netherfield, Netherfield's medical director. Charles Walker, the chief coroner and Netherfield's solicitor, must have agreed to suppress the evidence given in the inquest. Dr. Beaufoy's friends had stepped in to make certain no shadow would fall on the three other Beaufoy children.

According to the report, the preliminary physical examination revealed a well-nourished child of exceptional intelligence, strength, and vigor. There was no mention of murder. The psychiatric examination listed her condition as *defiant and unmanageable*. I remembered Kyle Weber quoting his mother. *Mom felt sorry for the doctor and his wife. They were at the end of their rope over that girl.*

The killing of the beloved family dog must have been the final straw, convincing Mrs. Beaufoy that their youngest daughter had serious problems. And if Dulcie heard them discussing it—I felt sick.

I read on, finding a notation from August of 1967 that Dulcie was being transferred to St. Catherine's in Ipswich. Also noted was the fact that beginning in 1972, Justine Beaufoy had petitioned the court every year for Dulcie's release. The petition was denied—until 2002.

I sat back in my chair. Dulcie had lived in an institution for forty years. In 2002, she would have been fifty-one. No wonder she seemed naïve. Whatever her issues, she'd never been allowed to develop normally. What did they call it? *Psychosocial deprivation.* I imagined the heart-wrenching decision Justine had been forced to make—a trial for manslaughter, possibly murder, or committal to Netherfield.

In September of 2002, Dulcie was released into the care of her sisters. The decision wasn't unanimous.

Even with the confirming photograph, I was having trouble taking it in. Dulcie Beaufoy, the woman who loved her garden and cared for her ailing sister, had spent the majority of her life, not on the Isle of Jersey, but in an institution for the mentally insane.

What Vivian and I had witnessed that day at their cottage wasn't the true picture.

I was about to put the ledger back when I heard raised voices and rapid footsteps coming along the corridor. Martyn Lee-Jones burst through the door. "Who gave you permission to rummage through these files?"

"Mr. Currie gave his permission. And I'm not rummaging."

Miss Armstrong followed him into the small room. "I did try to let you know in advance, sir, but you weren't—"

Ignoring Miss Armstrong, he shook his finger at me. "You have no right to be here. These records are historically important—irreplaceable. Dr. Underwood has been granted sole literary rights by the Netherfield estate. You have no authority to access this information."

The room felt uncomfortably close.

I stood and closed the ledger I'd been working on. Reaching behind me, I returned the book to its place on the shelf. "See? Everything is exactly as it was."

Lee-Jones's fists were clenched. "You may have done irreparable damage."

"I know how to handle old documents. You act as if you have something to hide."

Did I just say that?

"How dare you suggest such a thing. I insist you leave now."

In for a penny . . . "How long have you known about Dulcie Beaufoy?"

"What?"

"How long have you known she was a patient at Netherfield? That your father and the other trustees hushed it up. Is that what Will Parker found out?"

His hands were shaking. The corners of his mouth were white with spittle. "This is an outrage."

I pulled up the photograph of Will Parker on my cell phone. "Did this man contact you about the deaths of the Beaufoys?"

Lee-Jones moved toward me, his hands opening and closing in fury. "If you don't leave instantly, I'll call the local police and have you arrested."

I know when to make an exit.

And I know when to call for help

As soon as I got outside, I pulled out my phone and dialed Tom's number.

He picked up on the second ring. "Mallory."

"We really did get it wrong," I said. "It was Dulcie who murdered her parents. She was admitted to Netherfield under an assumed name."

"I know. Philip Lee-Jones just confirmed it. He, Dr. David Underwood, and Dr. Beaufoy were friends—had been since university. David Underwood was the one who got Dulcie into Netherfield under an assumed name. Philip Lee-Jones signed the necessary documents. Charles Walker redacted the inquest files. They thought they were doing their old friend a favor. Philip also admitted knowing about the forged Van Eyck. It was their last chance to save Netherfield. Dr. Beaufoy brought the forged painting and the cash payment for the original Van Eyck back with him from France. He was murdered before he could deliver the money. They still believe the money is hidden somewhere in the house."

Well, that explains what the Walkers are searching for. "And the murder of Will Parker?"

"He denies any knowledge of that. Cliffe is still with him."

"Tom—listen. I think Millie may be in danger. What Vivian and I interpreted as outrage was a cry for help. She's completely in Dulcie's power."

He made a sound of agreement. "I was on my way to question Dulcie now, but you've given me a better idea."

"What's that?"

"How soon can you get to Upford?"

"Half hour, forty minutes."

"I'll meet you there. Dulcie knows you. Introduce me. I'll engage her in conversation. You find a way to get into the house. What's a good topic?"

It came to me in a flash. "Gardening. Dulcie's obsessed with her garden."

"I'm bringing DC Anne Weldon. Kate, listen—do not approach Dulcie until I arrive. Do you understand? Stay out of sight."

Chapter
Thirty-Six

I arrived at Wren Cottage and parked my car half a block away. Dulcie was in her garden. From behind a leafy hedge, I watched her wide-brimmed straw hat as she bent and straightened over her work. She was singing, her high, clear soprano soaring over the chattering of the birds in the trees.

Tom and DC Weldon arrived ten minutes later. Anne pulled up behind me in her Vauxhall Astra. She remained in the car while Tom and I strolled up the stone path toward the cottage. Unhurried, casual. We put on our warmest smiles.

"Hello, Dulcie." I took Tom's arm. "I've come to show off my fiancé. Tom, this is Dulcie Beaufoy. Dulcie, this is"—I mentally deleted the Detective Inspector—"Tom Mallory."

Dulcie pulled off her gardening gloves and held out her large hand. "What a nice surprise. Delighted to meet you, Tom. Kate told us about your forthcoming wedding. My very best wishes to you both."

"When Tom heard about your lovely garden, he insisted on seeing it."

"Are you a horticulturist, Tom?" Dulcie removed her straw hat and let it hang down her back. "I've never had formal training myself. Just lots of experience with soil, seeds, plants."

"No training or even much experience for me." Tom ducked his head. "Just a love of nature and beauty. Your garden is spectacular. Do you have time to show us around?"

Dulcie narrowed her eyes. "You've come all this way to see my garden?"

"Oh, no," I said quickly. "I just spent a few hours at Cliff House. I think I told you my business partner and I are handling the auction. Tom tagged along, and we decided to take a chance and see if you were in."

"We're always in." Dulcie shielded her eyes against the sun. "Millie no longer drives, of course, and I never learned, but we can walk to the shops. Frankly, I find fewer reasons to go out these days. When you've been away from home for as long as I was, you appreciate the simple pleasures. Like the garden. Where would you like to begin?"

"Anywhere." Tom gave me a meaningful glance. "What's that plant there, the one with the spotted leaves?"

"Pulmonaria. You might know it as lungwort." Dulcie launched into a mini-tutorial on the use of the plant in shady areas of the garden.

So far, so good. My goal was to get inside the house to check on Millie. "Where's your sister today?" I asked.

"I left her in her chair by the window. She loves to watch me garden. There she is now." Dulcie waved at the window.

"Shall I go inside and say hello?" I asked.

"Just wave. She'll see you."

I waved. *Okay—on to Plan B.*

Five minutes later Dulcie was describing the process of hybridizing roses. "It's all in the timing, Tom. The first bloom cycle is ideal for cross-pollination. I'm in the garden by seven that morning. I use an artist's brush to apply the pollen."

"What did you name this one?" Tom pointed out a gorgeous white rose tipped with raspberry.

"Red Ranger. After the dog we had when I was a child."

"Dulcie, I'm sorry to interrupt," I said, "but do you think I could use your bathroom? We had a really spicy curry for lunch, and my tummy's a little off."

She could hardly refuse. "Of course, Kate. Up the stairs. First door on the right. Don't disturb Millie, will you? She's probably dozed off in the chair, and you know what happened last time you were here."

"I won't." I patted my stomach to reinforce the urgency. "Thank you."

As I headed for the door, I heard Tom say, "Now that *is* fascinating. You must tell me how you protect the pollinated blooms. I'm sure you have your own technique."

I ran up the steps and pushed open the door.

As Dulcie said, Millie was sitting in the high-backed chair by the window. She wasn't dozing.

"Millie, I'm Kate. Do you remember me? No, don't move. It's better if Dulcie doesn't know we're talking. I'm supposed to be on my way to the bathroom."

How could I get closer without Dulcie seeing me? The window was about three feet from the floor. Getting down on my knees, I crawled toward Millie. "Don't be frightened. I know this looks really weird, but please, act normally."

Millie's left eye, the one she could control, was huge. Her left hand pounded the arm of the chair softly. "Aaahh waa—"

"You *want*? Is that what you said?" I sat cross-legged at her feet. "I'm listening, Millie. Try again."

Half her face scrunched up with the effort. The left side of her mouth drew together. "Fff—" She stopped and took several breaths. "Fffoh—"

"Phone? Are you trying to say *phone*?"

She nodded. Tears streamed down her cheeks.

Oh, man. Maybe she was farther gone than I realized. "Do you want to call someone? Is there a telephone in the house?"

She shook her head. "Ffoh—"

"You mean my phone?" I pulled my cell phone out of my handbag. "Do you want me to call someone for you?"

She shook her head. Her left hand shot out.

"You want my phone?"

She nodded.

"I'll place it in your lap, all right?" What she intended to do with it, I couldn't guess.

I put it in her lap. With her left forefinger, the good one, she tapped on the screen.

"What do you want? Try to tell me."

Again I saw her struggling to speak. What came out was "*Woo*—"

By this time, I was almost in tears myself. Watching her was painful. "I'm so sorry. I don't know what you want." Then I had a thought. "Can you spell it? Here—" I took the phone back and pulled up my Notes app, turning the phone sideways so the keyboard was larger. I placed it again in her lap. "I'll hold it for you. Just tap the letters with your finger. Like this." I showed her.

Millie breathed in and out through her nose. Her left hand moved toward the keyboard. Curling her thumb, she used her index finger to tap out the letters.

I watched, mesmerized, as words emerged.

help dulcie afraid

I stared at her. "You're afraid of Dulcie?"

The left side of her face crumpled.

"What's going on here?" Dulcie burst through the door, followed by Tom. "I thought you needed the toilet."

"Millie and I were having a little chat." I palmed my phone. "She's trying to tell me something. About you, I think."

Tom stood behind Dulcie. He tapped his phone.

He's signaling DC Weldon.

"Oh, dear—that again." Dulcie strode over to Millie and took her hand. "She seems to think I'm in danger. That's why I didn't want you disturbing her, Kate. You did hear me say that, didn't you? And yet here you are."

"Why would Millie think you're in danger?"

"Well, that's just it—there's no reason. We don't see anyone. We don't go anywhere. There's no time. She requires care twenty-four hours a day. I carry her upstairs to bed at night and back down in the morning. I make her meals. Feed her. Bathe her. Dress her. Wash her hair."

Millie's mouth was working. "*Ahh waa . . . oohh eeah—*"

Dulcie's face had turned pink. "It's not your fault, dear."

"Millie, I know this is hard," Tom said, "but try to tell us what's going on here. Take your time. Are you afraid? Just tell us yes or no."

Millie nodded. Tears streamed down her cheeks.

"Afraid of Dulcie? Do you believe she's going to harm you?"

Millie shook her head vigorously. "*Aff fff—*" She broke off, the effort of trying to speak was exhausting her.

"Let her spell it," I said, putting my phone in her lap again

Millie tapped, the left side of her mouth compressed in a white line.

I looked at the screen. "She's written *afraid for*. Millie, are you trying to say you're afraid *for* Dulcie?"

She nodded, clearly exhausted.

"Dulcie, why is your sister afraid for you?" I asked.

DC Weldon entered the room.

Tom said, "Miss Beaufoy, I think it's best if you come with us until we can get this sorted. This is DC Weldon. She'll go with you to the police station in Ipswich."

DC Weldon took a step forward. "Why don't you come with me, Miss Beaufoy?"

"No," Dulcie shouted. "I'm not going anywhere. Millie, don't let them take me."

"We'd just like to ask you a few questions," Tom said. "Best done at the police station. Kate will stay with Millie."

"You tricked me," Dulcie snarled, "pretending to be interested in roses."

Millie's left arm flailed. She was reaching for her sister.

"I'm not leaving this house." Dulcie grabbed Millie's hand. "I like it here. This is where I live. I won't let you take me back."

"Back where, Miss Beaufoy?" Tom asked.

"As if you don't know. Justy promised I'd never have to go back there again—ever. You're working for those men, aren't you?"

"Wait a minute," I said. "What men?"

"From Netherfield. My father's friends. They want me to go back."

"Tom," I said in a low voice. "That's the question I should have asked—remember? I told you. When Vivian and I arrived, Dulcie asked who sent us. I never followed up." Louder I said, "We need to hear this, and I think Miss Beaufoy will feel more comfortable telling us right here."

Tom nodded. "All right. Why don't we all sit down and talk?"

As we pulled up chairs, I heard him whisper, "Anne, call Social Services."

Chapter
Thirty-Seven

~

I had to hand it to Tom. I'm sure he'd never conducted a more bizarre interview in his life.

Eleven people crowded into Wren Cottage's miniscule dining room. The two Beaufoy sisters, Tom, Anne Weldon, and I sat around the oval table. Standing behind us, lining the walls, were two care workers, a counselor, and a psychologist from Social Services. Add to that two lanky police officers from Ipswich, who'd brought a laptop computer so Millie could type her responses— one letter at a time—and a portable recording machine. They attempted to make themselves invisible by hulking in the doorway.

Once the recording machine was set up, Tom explained how things would work. When Millie was asked a question, she would type her response, and I would read what she wrote. If I got it right, she'd nod. If I didn't, she'd have to start again. Honestly, I couldn't imagine how she was going to make it. Pure grit, I supposed.

After stating the preliminaries and naming those present, Tom began with Dulcie.

"Your father, Dr. Simon Beaufoy, and your mother, Mrs. Nancy Beaufoy, died on the evening of May twentieth in 1961. I know this is difficult, but can you tell us what that day was like?"

"I was in trouble," Dulcie said. "Gray found our dog, Ranger, in the shed. Mother accused me of putting hemlock in his food. She said I wouldn't be allowed to go to the fair that evening."

"Did you put hemlock in Ranger's food?"

"Yes." Dulcie studied her lap.

Someone cleared his throat.

"Why did you do that?"

"He'd bitten me. I wanted to make him sick."

"You didn't intend to kill him?"

"No. I was sorry he died."

"Did you mix hemlock roots with the parsnips your mother collected?"

"Yes."

"Did you intend to kill your parents?"

"No." She shook her head vigorously. "The gardener told me it would make us sick. He didn't say we'd die."

"But you knew Ranger had died."

"Not until later. I'd already put the hemlock roots in with the parsnips. When I found out about Ranger, I tried to take them out, but it was hard. I thought a tiny bit wouldn't hurt them."

"You wanted to make your parents sick. Why?"

"I was angry. I'd been looking forward to the fair, and then they said I couldn't go. I thought if they got sick, I could sneak out of the house."

"And that's what you did?"

"Yes. I'm sorry. I really am."

I watched her, seeing not a mature woman in her sixties but a child. I'd first heard about psychosocial deprivation when a friend adopted a seven-year-old girl who'd lived her entire life in a crib in an orphanage in Romania. Dulcie's deprivation hadn't been that severe, but her childhood had been far from normal, and that had left its mark.

"When did you learn your parents had died?" Tom asked.

"Justy told me that night. She wouldn't let me see them."

"Did you tell Justy what you'd done?"

Dulcie nodded. "Yes. I was crying."

"When did you learn you were going to Netherfield?"

"A few days later. Justy told me it was for the best."

"What did you think?"

"I thought it was fine." Here, for the first time, Dulcie seemed to struggle. "I didn't know they meant for me to live there forever. We'd visited Netherfield with father many times. I thought it was a jolly place. The people were nice. I didn't mind going for a while. I had to be punished."

"Millie, I'm going to ask you some questions now. Type out your answers. Take your time—no need for complete sentences. Kate will read for you. Let's begin with the day of the traveling fair. Your father had returned home from a business trip. Do you know where he'd been?"

The one-finger process began again, easier now that Millie had a keyboard, but still grueling.

As she typed, I read the words. "France. Village in Alps."

"Do you remember the name of the village?"

"St.—" She stopped typing and looked at me.

"Was it St. Genevieve?"

She nodded.

"What do you know about your father's trip to France?" Tom asked.

Millie shook her head. She typed "Nothing."

"Tell us about the day of the fair," Tom said.

"Ranger dead. Mother angry." As she typed, Millie's speed increased. "Later Dulcie found us at fair. We thought mother relented. Didn't know."

"What happened when you returned home?"

Millie took a deep breath. She typed "please no."

"All right," Tom said. "We'll go on. Tell us about the days afterward."

"Hard to remember. Father's friends at hospital took over."

The words emerged, one letter at a time. I waited to read them until there was a pause, not wanting to rush her or put her under pressure.

"Stayed with neighbor. Dulcie crying all the time. Sad. She didn't mean—" Millie stopped typed. When she started again, she typed "Not her fault." She fixed Tom with her good eye. A wall had gone up.

I watched Tom assessing her, looking for cracks.

Millie typed again. "Justy said N only way to save Dulcie."

I looked at her. "You mean Netherfield? The only way to save Dulcie from a trial and possible murder conviction was to commit her to Netherfield?"

Millie nodded. A tear ran down her cheek.

I found a tissue in my handbag and dabbed Millie's face. "You're doing well," I said.

Millie typed "We thought months not years."

"Were the police involved?" Tom asked.

Millie shook her head. She typed "Men arranged everything."

"If no charges were filed, why wasn't it months?" Tom asked.

Millie glanced at her sister. She typed "Teenager. Defiant. Emotional. Justy no power. Pleaded but men said best for her to stay. Only way to protect."

"I was angry." Dulcie broke in. "Other patients were allowed to walk into town, but the doctors said they didn't trust me. I'd tried to escape several times. Once I got into a fight with one of the aides. She fell and broke her arm. That proved to them I was out of control. The truth was I was desperate. I couldn't understand why Justy didn't take me home. When I moved to St. Catherine's, things got worse. I felt lost, hopeless. I started cutting. Refused to take my medicine. I didn't want to live."

"What changed?" Tom asked.

"The garden," Dulcie said simply. "St. Catherine's had a garden, tended by an old man. He let me work with him, pulling weeds at first. He taught me about flowers and plants, how to care for them. After a few years he had to retire. I convinced the doctors I could manage the garden myself. That's when I began hybridizing roses. There were books in the library. I studied them."

"You said you worked with computers."

"I did that too. All the patients were given job training—those who could learn. In case we were ever released, I suppose. First I was taught how to use a keypunch machine. Later data entry and a little programming. They actually paid me. Thirty pounds a week."

"Millie," Tom said, "how did the story of the older boyfriend start?"

Her finger went to the keyboard. "True but had stopped seeing him by then. Justy told coroner I was grounded that night. Didn't mind."

"Who was the older boy?"

The tiniest of smiles formed on the left side of Millie's mouth. She typed "Can't remember name."

"Oswin Underwood?" I asked.

"*Pfft.*" She blew a scornful puff of air through her teeth and shook her head.

"How did Justine finally get Dulcie released?" Tom asked.

"Begged. Dulcie doing better since garden. Hospital having problems. Push for release into community. Finally yes." She patted her chest near her heart.

"But now you're worried about Dulcie. Why?"

Millie looked at her sister. She typed "Too hard caring for me."

"No, it isn't." Dulcie reached for her hand. "I don't mind. Truly. For so long my life had no purpose. I had no reason to exist." She looked at the faces in the room. "You can't know what that feels like. Now I have a purpose."

"Why is Millie worried about you?" Tom asked.

"It's those men from Netherfield. They're trying to have me recommitted. I won't go back. I can't. I'd rather die."

"Why do you think they want you to go back?"

"They've been pestering us ever since we sold the house. Asking questions about the night my parents died." Dulcie's fingers were working, lacing and unlacing. She lowered her eyes. "They keep asking what Father did that night, where he went. They sent that policeman."

That got my attention. "What policeman?"

"You showed me his photograph. I lied. I'm sorry."

"Will Parker," I said. "What did he want?"

"I don't know. When he mentioned Netherfield, I refused to talk. I knew the others had sent him."

"What others?" Tom asked.

"The ones at Cliff House. The builder—Tony something. The solicitor—Niall Walker. The good-looking one, Martyn. The woman, Miss Netherfield. The old one with the funny beard. They're plotting against me, looking for a reason to send me back."

"But you sold the house to Mr. Walker," Tom said.

Dulcie huffed. "He was the only one who bid on it. The house is practically falling down."

"Why did Walker want it?"

"He said to use it as a movie location, but I know he's looking for evidence so he can send me back."

I felt Millie's hand on my arm. She typed. "Talk private."

Rather than read the words aloud, I said, "I don't know about anyone else, but I could use a cup of tea right now." I gave Tom a meaningful look.

"Good idea," he said. "Anne, maybe you could help Dulcie put the kettle on."

When they'd left the room, Tom said quietly, "All right, Millie. What's the real reason you're worried about Dulcie?"

She typed "Truth?"

"Yes," Tom said. "The truth."

Millie typed "Might do something."

"Like what?"

The letters formed into words. "Hurt herself, run away. Like a child. Terrified."

"Do you think the Cliff House board is trying to have her recommitted?"

Millie shook her head. "No. Tried to tell her. Looking for something."

"What?" I asked.

She shrugged as she typed "Money?"

"Did your parents keep money in the house?" Tom asked.

Millie shrugged again. "Don't know."

"Have they threatened you?"

"Not words. Subtle threats. Not safe. Nothing I could do." Millie's left hand shook. Her nostrils were white.

No wonder Millie had tried so hard to communicate with us on that first visit. I'd interpreted her attempts to communicate as rage. It was terror—and desperation. The board members were pressuring them for information they didn't have. Millie could see the effect it was having on Dulcie—that she might do something foolish—but in her physical condition, Millie was helpless to stop it. She needed someone to listen to her.

Millie was typing. "Looking for what Father brought home from France. Valuable. Payment for something."

And there it was—confirmation of what Philip Lee-Jones had said—the thread connecting past and present, the dot that closed the circle. Dr. Beaufoy came back from France with the copy of the Van Eyck and the payment for the original. But what was that payment—French francs? British pounds?

Tom and I left at one o'clock. Millie and Dulcie Beaufoy had been taken to a residential care home in Ipswich, where they would be given meals and temporary shelter. The care workers assured me the court would appoint a guardian to make decisions about their long-term care. The psychologist said it was still possible Millie's speech could improve with therapy. I hoped that was true. I also hoped the appointed guardian would find a way for the sisters to remain at Wren Cottage where Dulcie could tend the garden she loved so much.

No matter where the sisters ended up, I promised to visit them, and I'd keep that promise. No one should be left alone in their old age without someone who cares.

On the way to my car, Tom phoned police headquarters.

"Bring 'em in, Cliffe. The lot—Currie, Walker, Netherfield, Lee-Jones, Underwood. I want to interview them at four. Whatever it takes. Conspiracy to commit fraud if you have to. I'll be there by two."

"Will you charge Dulcie?" I asked when he'd rung off.

He looked at me. "I think she's paid for her crime, don't you?"

Chapter
Thirty-Eight

The problem with being a civilian is not being allowed to sit in on police interviews.

I waited for Tom at police headquarters on Raingate Street from three thirty to well after eight PM with only a coffee and two lemon throat lozenges to tide me over. DC Anne Weldon stuck her head in the conference room once to tell me Frank Keane was improving. If that continued, the doctors would release him into Jean's care.

Finally, Tom appeared, holding his jacket. "Let's go. I'm starving."

We walked to the Dog and Partridge, a chain pub not far from police headquarters with good food and fast service. A waitress showed us to a high-top table and handed us menus. "I'll be back to take your orders."

"How did it go?" I asked. "Did they come in willingly?"

"Eventually. We had to track down Niall Walker, and we never did find Dr. Underwood. We'll interview him later."

"Let's order." He signaled the waitress.

We chose the quickest thing on the menu—fish and chips.

Once the waitress had gone to put in our orders, Tom said, "Here's the short version, but we have to begin at the beginning— May twentieth of 1961, the evening the Beaufoys were murdered. Philip Lee-Jones got a call from the police around nine o'clock. He called the others, and they all rushed over to Monkey Puzzle House."

"By all, you mean the trustees—Philip Lee-Jones, Cosmo Netherfield, Charles Walker, and David Underwood."

He nodded. "And Oswin Underwood. He was seventeen. The older men were naturally concerned about the Beaufoy children, but they admit their first thought was for the forged painting and the cash Beaufoy had brought back with him from France. Nicola's father talked his way inside and found the painting, which he rescued, but there was no sign of the cash—payment for the original Van Eyck. Beaufoy had taken an empty briefcase with him, expecting to fill it with a combination of Swiss bank notes and gold coins. Netherfield found the briefcase in the Beaufoys' bedroom—empty. Figuring Beaufoy had stashed the currency in his safe, Netherfield searched the house. He found the safe, standing open and empty. At that point, the police escorted him out."

"That was a long time ago. Would the paper currency be legal tender today?"

"No, but the increase in value of the gold coins would far outstrip the loss."

"Go on."

"The trustees turned their attention to Dulcie—getting her admitted to Netherfield. By the time they approached Justine again, wanting to search the house, she'd taken the decision to lock it up tight. No one was permitted access, not even the trustees."

"Did she say why?"

"I suspect she was afraid evidence of Dulcie's guilt would turn up. At any rate, she never did allow them inside the house. They tried everything, including telling Justine her father had been carrying important documents, that he'd consulted an eminent psychiatrist in France about a patient, but she still refused. They even offered to buy the place. They were so desperate to find the cash they actually broke into the house twice. Fortunately for them, Justine wanted to avoid the police, so she never reported the crimes."

"Why did the forgery happen in the first place?"

"I'm sure you've guessed. By the late nineteen fifties, Netherfield was in serious financial trouble. They couldn't compete with the National Health, but the trustees didn't want to give up a lucrative private practice. In order to hang on—or postpone the inevitable—they approved the sale of the Van Eyck to a private collector in Cape Town. The sale of the Van Eyck was totally legal. The painting was authentic, and they had no intention of ever selling the copy. The forger was the man Ivor mentioned—Gerard Bibeau."

The waitress delivered our food, served on the traditional paper plates.

I sprinkled malt vinegar on everything and speared a chip. "How was Bibeau paid?"

"The trustees fronted the money to pay him. Another reason to locate the cash from the sale of the original painting."

"And then?"

"The original trustees died—all but Philip Lee-Jones, the youngest—and the search for the money ceased."

"But their children knew."

"Exactly. Fast forward to a year ago when Justine Beaufoy died and Dulcie and Millie put Monkey Puzzle House on the market. That raised the tantalizing possibility that the cash and coins could still be found in the house. Niall Walker snapped it up. The board members located the metal box almost immediately in one of the concealed spaces behind the wood panels. They read the papers Will Parker wrote and decided one of the Five Sleuths must have taken the money."

"Who sent the game pieces—and why?"

"That was Currie's idea. He had one of his security people check on the Five Sleuths. What he found convinced him they hadn't located the cash after all. Will Parker had lived his whole adult life on a policeman's salary. Jack Cavanagh lost everything when his cleaning business went under. Frank Keane had been an accountant who lived frugally. Mary Diamond was practically on the streets, and Vivian had been a secretary. None of them showed any signs of ever possessing a fortune. But Currie figured if they hadn't taken the cash, they might know where it was. The game pieces were intended to jog their memories and prepare them for questions. That's what the board members did—they telephoned. Asked questions. No violence. They all insisted on that."

"You mean they contacted Will, Jack, Frank, and Mary? Why not Vivian?"

"They claim they couldn't find her until later. There's no Vivian Bunn listed in the directory."

"What did they think when the Sleuths started turning up dead?"

"The only death they knew about was Will Parker, and they assumed it was probably connected with his career in the police."

"That's what Hugh and Stephanie thought, too. Those questions must have gotten Will Parker thinking about the old case."

"No, Kate. Will Parker had already been investigating. We know that from his files. We may never know what first got him interested, but he was the one who contacted the board members. They actually showed him the metal box, hoping he could tell them where the cash had been hidden. He said he'd never seen any cash."

"Back up a minute. How did Tony Currie and Pyramid Development get involved with the Cliff House project?"

"The board members approached Currie. They owned the Netherfield building and were keen to make some money out of it. In addition to the structure, which impressed Currie, they dangled the prospect of auctioning off the snuff boxes and the Van Eyck. They didn't tell him it was a fake, although he figured it out when they told him about the lost cash."

"Who hired the thug to follow Vivian?"

"Currie. He swears he thought the guy was a private investigator. When the board members realized neither Parker nor Cavanagh knew about the cash, and that neither Mary Diamond nor Frank Keane were able to tell them anything, Vivian was their last hope. They found her living on the Finchley estate. The thug was supposed to watch her, follow her, see if she went near Monkey Puzzle House, which—thanks to you—she did."

The pub was getting warm. When we'd finished our food, we took our drinks out to the small beer garden and found a table under a black umbrella.

"Are you going to charge them with attempted fraud?" I asked.

"No crime was committed, Kate. They never went through with the sale. In fact, they agreed to the scientific testing and accepted the results. That was mostly Currie's doing. Given our findings, he realized they weren't going to be able to pull it off."

"So who killed Will Parker and the others?"

"The others? Kate, you know that's not proven."

"Well, someone kidnapped Frank Keane. And someone gave Mary Diamond a bottle of whiskey. And someone searched Jack Cavanagh's flat, probably triggering a heart attack."

"Speculation."

"I know." I took a deep breath. "So let's focus on Will Parker. Who murdered *him*? The Beaufoy sisters couldn't have, and this lot all have alibis for the night of the twenty-first. I suppose you checked."

"Of course. Martyn Lee-Jones was home in Ipswich when Parker was killed, as he said—hosting a backyard barbecue for a dozen friends."

"Nicola Netherfield and Tony Currie were in London and can prove it. Dr. Underwood was lecturing in front of scores of library patrons. And Niall Walker was at some sort of family event."

"A wedding. Dozens of witnesses."

"I give up." I downed the last of my mineral water and stood. "I'd better get back. Vivian will want to know what happened."

Tom walked me to my car.

Pieces of the puzzle floated just beyond my grasp. *The game pieces. The metal box. A soup can filled with soil and fibers. Pebbles. A leather pouch with a red drawstring. A signed document.* Evidence in a case that had been niggling at the back of Will Parker's mind for nearly sixty years. He hadn't given up. The notes on his computer proved it—and that list. What was it he'd wanted to tell Vivian— or ask her?

The thought tiptoed in so quietly I almost missed it.

Someone told a lie. And that lie was repeated in good faith.

"Tom," I said slowly. "I think we can find out what happened to the payment Dr. Beaufoy brought back from France. We need to speak with the Parkers. Tonight."

Chapter Thirty-Nine

꩜

Tom and I arranged to meet the Parkers at seven at the Newton Arms, a pub not far from the A14 on the northern edge of Cambridge. We went in my car. Tom drove.

The sign outside the pub was a copy of Kneller's famous 1689 portrait of Sir Isaac Newton—fellow of Kings College, Cambridge—at forty-six, his long, flowing hair prematurely gray.

The pub's interior was dark, with low ceilings, wooden booths, and painted brick walls hung with Newton memorabilia.

We spotted Hugh and Stephanie in a booth, drinking what looked like lemonade. Hugh stood to shake hands with Tom. Stephanie and I did that awkward hug thing you do when you like someone but don't know them very well.

"I think you've met DI Mallory," I said.

Hugh smiled. "He was kind enough to visit after we'd gotten the news about Dad's death."

"Please, sit down." Stephanie slid in next to her husband. "We've ordered a little something."

The waiter arrived with a platter of nachos and cheese, two more glasses, and a fresh pitcher of lemonade.

"We hope it will be worth your while to have driven all this way," Hugh said. "Steph and I have been talking, and we honestly can't think of anything we haven't already mentioned."

"Before he was murdered," Tom said, "your father had been investigating the deaths of Dr. and Mrs. Beaufoy, who lived in a house near Hopley's Holiday Camp. You know that much. We now believe your father stumbled onto something else. Two years before your father and the other teens explored the abandoned house, Dr. Beaufoy had returned from a trip to the French Alps with a forged copy of a fifteenth-century painting by Jan van Eyck. The copy was made by an artist named Gerard Bibeau. Did your father ever mention a painting?"

The Parkers both shook their heads.

"It's like we said." Stephanie swirled a nacho in the cheese. "Will was a private person. He didn't share his work with us."

"He never mentioned receiving the fake gun in the mail?" I asked.

"Never," Hugh said.

"But he did tell you he'd learned something about an old investigation—a cold case. Was that before or after he received the gun in the mail?"

"According to the postmark, the gun must have arrived several days before he left for Long Barston." Hugh looked at his wife. "I don't think Dad mentioned a cold case before that. Did he, Steph?"

She pressed her lips together. "It's all a bit fuzzy now."

"We know he tried to interview the two surviving Beaufoy sisters in Upford," Tom said, "and he'd contacted several individuals connected with the renovation of a former mental hospital near Hopley's."

"We read about that mental hospital, Hugh—remember?" Stephanie said.

"Did you discuss it with your father?" I asked.

"I don't think so," Stephanie said. "Dad said he was working on some new evidence and had to be away for a few nights. That's really all we know."

"Did he say when he'd be back?"

"No," Stephanie said. "Well, he did say he'd see us on Sunday as usual. There was a documentary on the ponies of the New Forest—a rerun. He was looking forward to it."

My mother's words came to mind.

Back up, Kate. Roots always go deeper than you think.

"I know you've been through this several times," I said. "But I'd like you to go back a little further. We think your father's interest in the abandoned house was prompted by something he'd recently learned. Knowing what that something was could be the key. When was the very first time your father mentioned the old investigation?"

Hugh rubbed his temple. "It might have been after he received the game piece in the mail, but then it could have been earlier, too. I'm sorry."

"Wait a minute," Stephanie said. "I think she's right. I think your father first mentioned an old case that Sunday we watched the documentary on the Hope Diamond. Remember, Hugh?"

"I remember the documentary," he said. "The diamond was discovered centuries ago in some mine in India."

"India?"

"That's right," Stephanie said, more animated now. "But it wasn't the Hope Diamond that got his attention. It was when they mentioned some rare blue diamonds mined somewhere in South Africa."

"That's it." I grabbed Tom's arm. "I knew the name *Cullinan* was familiar. Will wasn't interested in an SUV. He meant the mine in South Africa—the Cullinan mine."

Hugh and Stephanie looked confused.

Tom pulled out his cell phone, scrolled through, and handed it to Hugh Parker. "We found this list on your father's computer."

Hugh read, "*Miracle, intense blue, Cullinan, St. Genevieve.* I don't get it."

"We think Miracle means Miracle-on-Sea," Tom said. "St. Genevieve is the village in the French Alps where the forger, Gerard Bibeau, had his studio."

"I should have known," I said. "*Intense blue* doesn't refer to ultramarine pigment. It's a designation given to natural blue diamonds with exceptional depth of color. They mine them in only a few places in the world. One is the Cullinan mine in South Africa. Stephanie, can you remember exactly what your father-in-law said?"

Her brows drew together. She bit her thumbnail. "They were showing some diamonds, rough and uncut, found recently in a mine in South Africa. They looked like blue stones. Remember, Hugh? Your father said something like, 'So that's what they were.' And then he said something about never knowing when new evidence would turn up. I must have asked him what he meant because he said, 'It's something I've been thinking about a long time. An old case.'"

"I have no memory of that," Hugh said.

"You'd probably gone to the loo."

I was almost vibrating with excitement. "The collector who purchased the original Van Eyck was from South Africa. He must have paid for the painting, not with currency and coins but with uncut blue diamonds. That's what the pebbles in the metal box were, Tom—not stones swept up with the soil and fibers but small blue diamonds."

"Would a few small uncut blue diamonds be worth an original Van Eyck?"

"Probably not. I'm guessing there were more diamonds. Larger. The question is, who took them and where are they now?"

The Parkers were staring at us, dumbfounded. Hugh said, "Dad put all that together? That's why he was killed?"

"I think so," I said. "He thought he'd uncovered evidence of a sixty-year-old murder. He didn't know he was putting his own life in danger."

Tom grabbed his jacket. "Hugh, Stephanie—you've been immensely helpful. I'll keep you informed."

"Thank you so much," I said, slinging my handbag over my shoulder. "We'll be in touch."

Tom was already halfway to the door. "Come on, Kate—quick as you can. I've got to get back to headquarters. We'll have to interview everyone again."

"Someone did murder Jack and Mary, Tom. I'm convinced of it now."

On the way out the door, he tossed me my car keys. "You drive. I'll call Cliffe."

Chapter Forty

❧

I dropped Tom off at police headquarters. "You'll be up all night again, won't you?"

"I hope not."

"Call me when you can." We kissed, and I watched him jog up the ramp and into the building.

With traffic blocked on Southgate Street, I took the detour on Westgate, past the Theatre Royal, one of the few surviving Regency theaters in Britain, and turned south on the A1302. A light rain blurred the oncoming headlights. I switched the wipers on low.

The blue diamonds cast a new light on everything. Where were they now? And who had trashed at least four lives to find them?

Means, motive, and opportunity. The three essentials in an investigation. Just like the three legs of a stool my mother used to explain her research.

A *motive* was now clear—someone had been searching for a fortune in blue diamonds, and that someone had to be connected with Cliff House. They were the only ones who knew about the metal box hidden in Monkey Puzzle House. And they were the only ones who knew the identities of the Five Sleuths.

The problem was *opportunity*. Every one of them—Currie, Netherfield, Lee-Jones, Underwood, and Walker—had an iron-clad alibi for the night of Will Parker's murder. Was there someone else out there, like one of those silly novels where the bad guy appears out of the blue in the last chapter? Who else was there? Miss Armstrong, the Cliff House receptionist? I didn't think so.

The windshield wiper thrumped.

The third leg of the stool was *means*. Who had the ability, not only to dig into the medical histories of the Five Sleuths but also to kill in a way that would mimic natural causes?

The answer slid in and touched base. Someone with medical knowledge, of course.

At the next lay-by, I pulled off the road, checked my phone browser, and dialed the number of the Miracle Library. Would someone still be there at a quarter to nine?

Someone was. "Public Library. Mrs. Bundy. How may I assist you?"

"I'm so glad you're still open. I've been attending Dr. Underwood's Friday lectures—I love history—but I had to miss the last one in August. Do you record the sessions by any chance?"

"We do record the sessions. Let me take a look here . . . Oh, I'm so sorry. There *was* no lecture on August the twenty-first. Dr. Underwood was under the weather and couldn't make it—first time in twelve years. The good news is you haven't missed a thing."

"That's great. Thank you so much."

I put the car in gear and pulled onto the highway. Means, motive, and opportunity. Only one person fit all three.

* * *

When I parked outside Rose Cottage, all the lights were off. I got out my key in case Vivian was already in bed, but I found the door unlocked. *Odd.* Vivian always locked the door when she left the house or went to bed.

The back of my neck prickled.

The door swung open. "Vivian?" Silence.

I heard a low growl and switched on the lights. Someone had chained Fergus by his leash to the table. He whimpered.

"Where's Mummy?" I asked him, unclasping the leash from his collar. Vivian never left Fergus home alone for more than fifteen minutes. And she wouldn't think of chaining him up.

There was no note on the kitchen table. She always left a note. Several of the kitchen drawers stood open.

Something was wrong. Very wrong.

"Show me where she is, Fergus," I said. "Where's Vivian?"

Instead of running to the stairs, which I expected, Fergus ran to the door and whined, staring back at me with those big, round eyes.

"Are you trying to tell me something, or do you just need to go out? Hold on—let me check the house first."

Flipping on more lights, my heart lurched. Someone had turned the sitting room upside down. Cupboards were open, their contents strewn across the floor. Cushions were off the sofa and chairs.

"Vivian," I called up the stairs. "Where are you? Are you hurt?"

I climbed the stairs, bracing myself for what I might find. *Danger.*

On the landing, I grabbed a glass vase from the hall table and tiptoed toward Vivian's bedroom. Would I find her body?

I pushed open her door and switched on the light. *No body.* I took a breath and blew it out. The bedroom was a mess. The books on her bookshelf lay scattered on the floor. Vivian's underwear had been dumped in a pile on the floor. The mattress lay half on, half off the bedframe.

This wasn't a burglary. Someone had been searching for something. Blue diamonds was my guess. *Dr. Underwood.* But where was he—and where was Vivian?

Too bad the CCTV cameras had been taken down.

I ran downstairs, hooked Fergus to his leash again, opened the door, and told him to lead the way. "Find Vivian, Fergus. Find Mummy."

The dog took off in the direction of Finchley Hall. I hoped he had a plan because I didn't.

As I ran, I dialed Tom's cell. No answer. I left a breathless message. "Vivian's missing, Tom. The house is a mess. Underwood is the killer—I'm sure of it. He has no alibi for Will Parker's murder. I'm on my way to the Hall to look for them. Come as quickly as you can."

Fergus was panting, his long pink tongue hanging out. He glanced back at me over his shoulder. *Hurry up. Mummy needs me.*

The path ended with a barricade. Oh, shoot—the construction of the new path. I swung right. The koi pond loomed out of the darkness—a half acre of deep water, spanned by that rickety eighteenth-century Chinese bridge.

I muffled a scream. There they were—on the bridge, struggling. Underwood had Vivian by the shoulders. Her hands were tied behind her back. She was squirming furiously and trying to kick at him with both knees. "Stop," I shouted in my fiercest voice. "Leave her alone."

Underwood's head swung around. He stared at me owlishly, then doubled over as Vivian's knee connected with his nether parts.

Good one, Vivian.

He slapped her across the face, hard.

Vivian made a tiny screeching sound. Her mouth was covered with a strip of silver duct tape.

Fergus snarled and snapped, pulling on the leash. I had half a mind to let him go.

"One more step, and she goes into the water." Underwood's voice was unnaturally high.

I saw in a flash how easy it would be for this to end in disaster. The railing was low. Too low. Not only had the bridge been constructed at a time when people were generally shorter than today, but there were no safety standards then to prevent people from accidentally pitching over the side.

Vivian kicked at him again. This time, without her arms to counterbalance, she stumbled, hit the railing at an angle, and fell to her knees.

Underwood hauled her back onto her feet and pinned her against the railing. "Where is it?" Underwood's white spade beard bounced in fury. "Tell me *now*."

"Where is what?" I knew what he meant, but I was stalling for time, hoping Tom would check his messages.

He let out a sharp hiss. "The leather pouch. She said it was at the Hall."

A leather pouch—yes. I remembered Vivian saying it was like the pouch her brother had for his marbles.

"Now she says she doesn't know where it is. She's lying. She's the only one left."

"Whose fault is that?"

He ignored the sarcasm. "I want that pouch. One of you tell me where it is, or she's going off the bridge."

He meant it too.

Fear made me brave—or foolhardy. "All right," I said, raising my free hand in surrender. "I know what you're looking for. I figured it out. And I think Vivian knows where the pouch is. Why don't you remove that tape so she can talk."

"Oh, she can talk. She wouldn't shut up. That's why I had to tape her."

"How much did she tell you?" I was playing this completely by ear.

"She said the pouch is at the Hall, but I think she's stalling, hoping someone will phone the police."

Not a bad plan. Until she figured out she was putting Lady Barbara in jeopardy. "Then obviously, she was lying. She probably doesn't know anything."

Vivian made a sound I interpreted as *Well, thank you very much.*

"The leather pouch is in a safe deposit box at the bank," I said, grabbing the first thought that came to me. "I can take you there, but not tonight, obviously. Let us go now. We'll all have a good night's sleep, and then tomorrow—"

"Do you take me for an idiot?" He pushed Vivian against the railing so hard I thought she was going over the low railing then and there.

"Wait. *Stop.* Tell me this—why did your father lie to the other trustees? He let them think they were looking for cash."

"He owed them nothing. *Nothing.*"

"Why didn't you tell the trustees about the blue diamonds after your father killed himself? They helped you through medical school. You betrayed them."

"I betrayed *them*?" He set his teeth. "How about their betrayal of me, *hmm*?"

"What are you talking about?"

"Those men, my father's so-called friends, testified against him in court. They threw him to the wolves, knowing it was the end of his career, that he'd lose everything."

"Physician-assisted suicide was against the law in 1962. It still is."

"Helping desperate people end their pain and misery? All my father ever wanted was to help people."

"Like you helped Will Parker, Jack Cavanagh, Mary Diamond, and Frank Keane?"

He snarled. "Where are the diamonds?"

"All right, here's the truth, but you're not going to like it. Mary Diamond took the diamonds—hey, that's funny. But I'm serious. She was a magpie, always collecting shiny, pretty things. Isn't that right, Vivian?"

Vivian nodded vigorously.

"You're wrong. I searched her room. I looked everywhere."

"Obviously not everywhere, because you didn't find the leather pouch. Sunny Shores gave all Mary's things to a charity shop in Norwich. That's where you'll find the diamonds. Unless they threw the pouch away without realizing what it contained."

"Then I have no reason to keep either of you alive, do I? You"—
he shoved a finger in my direction—"tie that dog to the bridge.
Then put your hands behind your back."

I considered my options. Having none, I did what he said.

Underwood pinned Vivian to the railing with his leg and patted around his coat until he came up with the roll of silver duct
tape. "Take one step toward me at a time, slowly. If you try anything clever, she dies."

I looked into the murky water, seeing a flash of orange scales.
Vivian couldn't swim. With her hands tied behind her back, she
wouldn't even be able to keep her head above water.

I stepped toward him slowly.

"All right, turn around." Using his teeth, he tore off a piece of
tape and wrapped it tightly around my hands. "Now stand beside
her. You have one more chance to tell me the truth."

My strategy, such as it was, hadn't worked. I needed to change
tack. Fast.

A plan flashed into my mind. A very, very simple plan.

All right, it wasn't nice, but when someone has already murdered three people, and you're next in line, I think you can make
an exception.

"I've been lying to you all along." I laughed. "You almost
bought it, didn't you? You're not as smart as you think you are. In
fact, you're pathetic. A pathetic little man with nothing better to
do in life than give lectures to old-age pensioners who slip into the
library for a nice kip."

Vivian made another screech, which I interpreted as *Are you
out of your mind?*

It occurred to me I might have gone a shade too far.

"*Shut up.*" Underwood's face contorted in fury. "My work has
never been appreciated."

"Why is that? Have you ever asked yourself that question? The
answer is simple. No one cares." I was shouting now. "You're just like
your father—a failure. The only thing you're good at is killing people."

That did it. Rage made him stupid.

He charged, his hands ready to connect with my shoulders and push me over the edge.

I waited until the last second.

Then I simply . . . stepped aside.

Underwood slammed against the bridge railing and went over. For a moment he hovered, his lower half over the bridge and his upper half suspended over the water.

Until Vivian lifted her knee and tipped him over the edge.

He howled.

We heard a simultaneous splash and a crack as some part of his body must have connected with a bridge support.

Vivian and I peered into the pond. Underwood floated on the surface.

"You've got the best chance of getting loose," I said. "Try rubbing the tape against the railing."

We heard wild splashing. Underwood was flailing, gulping air.

"This is taking too long. Let me see what I can do." I knelt behind Vivian and worked at the tape with my teeth.

It came loose.

Vivian ripped the tape off her mouth. "Ouch." She moved her lips around to make sure they were still working.

"Untie me," I said. "Now take the phone out of my back pocket and call the police. I'd better go down and save his life."

Chapter Forty-One

～

Later, Vivian and I sat in the warm kitchen at Rose Cottage, drinking her famous whiskey-laced tea. Her right cheek was red where Underwood had slapped her, and the area around her right eye was turning a nasty shade of purple. Both of her knees were scuffed.

DC Anne Weldon and two other uniformed officers had been the first to respond to Vivian's phone call. Two of them helped Vivian back to Rose Cottage while the other helped me haul Dr. Underwood out of the koi pond. He'd swallowed a lot of water—and possibly a few minnows—but he was alive.

By the time we got him to Rose Cottage, the EMTs were roaring in. Ralston Green, the Gentle Giant, checked Vivian's cuts and bruises before tending to a nasty slice on Underwood's back where he'd bounced off the bridge abutment.

Underwood sat at the kitchen table, shivering, wrapped in a red EMT blanket, and dripping water onto the floor.

From his basket near the Aga, Fergus the pug tracked Underwood's slightest move, snarling softly under his breath.

Tom burst through the door. "Kate, are you all right?"

"I'm fine. So's Vivian. A few scrapes and scratches—nothing serious."

"We should get this man to hospital," Green said.

"Is he in danger of dying in the next hour or so?"

"No."

"Then he'll give a statement first." Tom pulled out a portable recorder. He hit the button. "Oswin Underwood, I'm arresting you for the murders of Will Parker, Jack Cavanagh, and Mary Diamond—and the attempted murder of Frank Keane, Vivian Bunn, and Kate Hamilton. You do not have to say anything, but it may harm your defense if you do not mention, when questioned, something you later rely on in court. Anything you do say may be given in evidence. Do you understand?"

"I didn't murder anyone."

"Do you understand the charges and your rights?"

"Yes."

"It is your right to have a solicitor present. Do you wish to call a solicitor?"

"What's the use?" Underwood looked small and pathetic.

If I'd been a finer person, I might have pitied him.

Tom sat opposite him. "We know you weren't lecturing the night of August twenty-first. You were in Long Barston. You followed Will Parker there with the intention of killing him."

"No comment."

"What did you do with his epinephrine injector?"

"No comment."

"You murdered Jack Cavanagh and Mary Diamond, didn't you?"

"No comment."

"CCTV puts your car near the park in Stevenage the night Frank Keane was kidnapped. What do you have to say about that?"

"No comment."

"All right, tell me about the diamonds."

Underwood stared at his hands.

I noticed that Fergus had crept silently out of his bed. A civilized animal under ordinary circumstances, he was staring at Underwood with a very uncivilized look on his face.

"Who came up with the idea of selling the Van Eyck. Your father?"

To my surprise, Underwood answered. "Beaufoy. He said the painting was worth millions. The money would keep them going until they could figure out a way to meet their expenses."

"A reasonable solution. But selling a painting that was the symbol of everything Netherfield stood for would raise questions about the sanatorium's financial condition. Am I right?"

"Beaufoy suggested they have the painting copied. He said he knew someone in France who could do it. The guy was good. No one would know."

Tom nodded slowly. "And then?"

"Beaufoy made an initial trip to a village in the French Alps—ostensibly to have the painting appraised and cleaned. Four months later, he returned to collect the painting. Except what he brought back was the copy."

"Who bought the original?"

"A collector from South Africa. We never knew his name. Beaufoy made the man promise in writing never to display the painting in public. He agreed. But when it came time to make payment, the man admitted he hadn't been able to get that much cash together. He said he had something just as valuable. Blue diamonds."

"Beaufoy agreed?"

"He put in a trunk call to my father. They decided they had no choice."

"Beaufoy got back from France on May twentieth, the night he and his wife were poisoned. Obviously, that wasn't part of the plan."

"Beaufoy had the painting and the diamonds with him at the house. Before he could deliver them to Netherfield, he died."

"When did you find out?"

"I was there that night—at Monkey Puzzle House. The police called Charles Walker, the Beaufoys' solicitor. Walker called the other trustees. My father and I got over there right away. Everything was in disarray. Somehow Walker got inside and rescued the painting."

"But he couldn't find the cash payment."

"There wasn't any cash. And before Walker could search further, the police shut down the crime scene."

"Why didn't your father tell the other trustees about the diamonds?"

"He was already in trouble with the medical board. He'd pleaded with the trustees to help him. They refused."

"And you never told them about the diamonds either."

"Why should I?" His lip curled. "I didn't owe them anything. When my father was brought up before the medical board, not one of them would testify on his behalf. Instead, they testified for the prosecution. They abandoned him, knowing what it would mean. He lost everything. So did I."

"The trustees helped you through medical school."

"With loans it took me years to pay off. They were wealthy—every one of them. My father and I were left out in the cold."

"How did you explain the small blue diamonds in the metal box?"

"I didn't have to. No one knew what they were. I think Dr. Beaufoy was planning to have a ring made for his wife without telling the others. He was no saint."

"Why didn't you take them?"

"I thought about it, but the others would have known they were gone and wondered why. Anyway, they were nothing compared to the bigger diamonds. They were there somewhere. I just had to find them."

"How were you able to access the medical records of the Five Sleuths?"

"I'm a doctor. I have access to the NHS records portal."

"But those people weren't registered to your practice. Access is limited and monitored."

"In theory." Underwood snorted. "No one looks at the audits on a daily basis because of the sheer volume. Trying to find someone looking at records they don't need is like finding a needle in haystack."

"We know you injected Will Parker with bee venom. Why did he have to die?"

"He knew about Jack Cavanagh, of course." Underwood's shoulders slumped. He'd given up.

"What do you mean?"

"I wasn't satisfied that Cavanagh didn't know about the diamonds. I went to see him. I searched his flat. I could see he was having a heart attack."

"Did you call for help?"

Underwood made a mewling sound.

"Speak up, please. Did you call for help?"

"I didn't kill him. I left."

"You withheld medical aid. It's the same thing. And Will Parker figured it out. How?"

"He'd been in touch with Cavanagh. When he found out he'd died suddenly, he became suspicious. Then he learned Mary Diamond died. That really put the wind up. He contacted me, suggested we meet. I knew I had to do something, so I followed him to Long Barston."

"And you confronted him in the graveyard. Why did you kill him?"

"He said he was going to warn Vivian Bunn and then turn me in to the police. He gave me no choice."

I could see the muscles working in Tom's jaw. Vivian was softly crying.

"Why did you kill Mary Diamond?"

"I didn't kill her. I just provided the means."

Physician-assisted suicide.

"Why did she have to die? She knew nothing."

"There was a chance she might tell someone I'd been there and searched her room. Not well enough, as it turned out. Some crazy woman in a pink robe wandered in, and I had to leave."

"And Frank Keane?"

"A long shot, I admit, but someone had taken those diamonds. Besides, he didn't die."

"No thanks to you."

Underwood's teeth were starting to chatter.

Fergus had worked his way toward Underwood. His ears were flat, his hackles raised. He lifted his lip and snarled.

"Get that dog away from me." Underwood kicked him.

Fergus bit him.

Good dog.

* * *

When everyone else made their exit, Tom, Vivian, and I moved into the sitting room. We'd topped up our teacups. Tom lit a fire in the fireplace.

Vivian picked up her knitting, a project she'd been working on as long as I'd known her. I knew she was thinking about Will Parker. He'd wanted to warn her. "Do you think the blue diamonds will ever be found?" she asked.

"Who knows?" Tom said. "Right now I'm more interested in how you two managed to survive attempted murder." He folded his arms, waiting for an explanation.

"You should have seen her—Kate," Vivian said. "First she made up a story about a safe deposit box and said she'd take him there tomorrow. He didn't buy it, of course, so she backtracked and told him Mary Diamond had taken the blue diamonds and they were probably in some charity shop in Norwich. Then she told him she'd been lying all along. That really got his goat." Vivian scratched her head with a knitting needle. "Of course, I was the one who tipped him over the railing."

"Kate, what is it?" Tom said. "You look like you're a million miles away."

"It might not have been a lie. About Mary Diamond, I mean. Vivian, what happened to that box and tote bag we brought back from Sunny Shores? We never got around to looking inside."

"In the hall closet."

"Get them, Tom. I think Underwood was right. One of the Sleuths did take the blue diamonds. And my money's on Mary."

It took Tom less than a minute to haul the box and bag into the sitting room. He cut through the tape with his pocket knife.

Vivian started on the tote bag. I took the box. As we pulled out each object, we placed it on the coffee table.

Other than the Art Deco candlestick, Mary's entire collection—her pride and joy—consisted of junk. Lots of beads, strung and unstrung; mismatched earrings and other cheap pot-metal jewelry; a small, tarnished silver-plated napkin ring; several crystals; a gold-painted egg; a glass paperweight; a hunk of mica; a string of gold paper clips.

"Look—my ring." Vivian held up a tarnished ring with a cloudy blue-green stone. "I *knew* she'd taken it, the little thief. But where are the diamonds?"

My fingers met something soft.

I pulled out a small leather pouch with a red drawstring.

Vivian gasped. "That's it."

"Vivian, hand me your saucer." Untying the drawstring, I opened the pouch and tipped the contents into the small porcelain dish.

Out spilled dozens of natural stones, some smooth agates. And five rough blue diamonds.

We gazed in wonder.

"These are intense blue diamonds from the legendary Cullinan mine near Pretoria, South Africa," I said. "I'd say the stones in their uncut state weigh anywhere from ten to twenty-five carats. Cut and polished, they're worth a fortune."

I picked up the largest diamond and held it up to the light. It was the color of a deep blue fjord on a summer's day.

Tom shook his head. "These five stones cost precious human lives."

Chapter Forty-Two

∾

Saturday, September 11

Two days after Dr. Oswin Underwood was formally charged with murder, kidnapping, and assault, Angela Vine and Rector Edmund Foxe were married.

The church bells tolled as guests filed into St. Æthelric's.

As Tom and I walked through the lych-gate, I checked the invitation: "Service at ten thirty. Reception to follow at the Rectory. How long do you want to stay?"

"Long enough to toast the couple and taste the wedding cake."

Sprays of white roses adorned the church. Three adorable little bridesmaids tossed rose petals along the center aisle of the nave. Angela's sister was present after all, holding a swaddled pink bundle. Two days after the hen party, she'd given birth to a daughter.

The bells ceased. The bride and her father appeared. The organist began the "Trumpet Voluntary."

Angela looked radiant in a white lace gown. Edmund brushed away a tear.

A bishop from Chelmsford conducted the service. Thirty minutes later, the newly married couple marched out, holding hands, to the strains of Mendelssohn's "Wedding March."

The reception was held at the Rectory, where Hattie Nuthall had marshaled the culinary talents of the entire village to provide enough food to serve Hadrian's army. Tom and I stayed long enough to sample the cake, a multitiered affair made by a bakery on the High Street.

"We should go, Kate," Tom said. "I promised we'd meet someone at the Three Magpies at one o'clock."

"Who?"

"You'll see."

"Will I like it?"

He never answered me. I found out why.

Entering the Three Magpies, I spotted Tom's mother at the bar. *Oh no. What now?*

Liz Mallory tossed down the last of a white wine and stood to greet us. "Hello, Tom, Kate. Thank you for coming. I've taken a booth in the corner. Would you like lunch?"

"No, thank you," we said in perfect unison.

Once we were seated, Liz said, "I want to apologize. I know what I said about the ring was unkind."

"And untrue," Tom reminded her. "It's not your ring. It's not Olivia's ring. It's mine to give, and I chose to give it to Kate."

"I know that. I said I'm sorry." Liz twisted her napkin in her hand. "Tom, I want you to come home. Until the wedding. *Please.*"

For once in my life, I had absolutely nothing to say.

"Why?" Tom asked. "Are your friends beginning to suspect something?"

"That's cruel." She threw him an accusing look. "All I've ever wanted is your happiness. I want you to come home because I love you. Because I can't stand for there to be this breach between us."

"There will always be a breach between us until you accept Kate as the person I love, the woman I want to spend the rest of my life with."

"And I'm to be cut out of your life, is that it?"

"Only if you choose to be. In less than two months, Kate and I will be married. What part you play in our lives will be completely up to you." He looked at me. "Right?"

I nodded but remained silent. He was doing pretty well on his own. All I could do was screw it up.

"And where do you plan to live once you're married?" Liz demanded.

"When we decide, we'll let you know."

"If you stay in England, I suppose it means I'll be asked to leave my house."

"*My* house, to be accurate, but no, it does not mean that. The house in Saxby St. Clare is your home, and Olivia's, for as long as you want to live there."

"But where will you live?"

"I told you. When we decide, you'll know."

Liz turned to me. "Kate, will you forgive me for saying what I did about the ring?"

"Yes, of course."

I felt like a hypocrite. Getting the words out was hard enough. Meaning them was beyond my ability at the moment.

My mother always said, *Do the right thing, and the right feelings will follow eventually.*

That I'd have to take on faith.

After Liz left the Magpies, Tom drove me back to Rose Cottage. "I have some paperwork to finish up. I'll pick you up at five for dinner."

"What should I wear?"

"Whatever you'd like. Nothing fancy."

"Where are we going?"

He smiled that half smile that always made my heart turn over. "It's a surprise."

*　*　*

We drove about five or six miles northwest of Long Barston, toward the ancestral boundary of the Finchley estate. We passed the Rare Breeds Farm, which the National Trust was planning to preserve, mostly as a draw for children. At the junction of the B road and a smaller lane, Tom turned right.

"Almost there?"

"Not far now."

After about a hundred yards, we turned right again.

At the end of the lane stood a very pretty rose-brick Georgian house. A plaque near the entrance said "Waifs House, 1780."

"Who lives here?" I asked. "Someone you know?"

"You'll see," he said mysteriously.

Cascading wisteria festooned the walls surrounding the portico, supported by two Portland stone columns. Tom knocked on the door.

His knock was answered by a pleasant-looking older woman wearing a flowered apron. "Welcome." She smiled at us warmly. "Come in. You must be Kate," she said. "I'm Mrs. Malone."

The entrance hall was laid with well-worn stone pavers.

"Come this way," she said, leading us into a snug sitting room fitted with built-in cupboards and a cozy antique fireplace housing a log-burner. "Please, sit down. Make yourselves comfortable."

She disappeared and returned with a tray bearing two small glasses of sherry. I wanted to ask who she was and why we were there, but she seemed to think I knew.

"Your house has an unusual name," I said instead.

"Yes, it is unusual. At one time this house took in what were called 'waifs and strays'—young girls in need of refuge. They were trained for employment as maids."

"How long have you lived here?"

"Almost forty years. I raised my family here. Two girls and three boys. All gone now, with homes of their own. And my husband as well. He died several years ago. The house is too large for me now."

"But it's home. I know the feeling." I sipped my sherry. "Are you a friend of Tom's family?"

"I've known his Uncle Nigel for years." That was the only explanation she gave.

Goodness. Had Nigel finally decided to take the plunge into matrimony? Was I here to meet my new aunt-in-law? But if Mrs.

Malone had known the family for years, why had Tom never mentioned her? Why was I being introduced to her only now?

"Would you like to see the house, Kate?" Mrs. Malone asked when we'd replaced our sherry glasses.

"Yes, I'd love to see it."

Mrs. Malone walked us through the ground floor. In addition to the sitting room, there was a large dining room painted coral red and illuminated by a chandelier and wall sconces. A Georgian fireplace at the end of the room was edged in marble and flanked by two Gothic-style built-in cupboards.

"A perfect setting for family dinners," she said, and I got the impression she was thinking about her own family.

We followed her down a corridor and entered a large room dominated by an inglenook hearth.

"The heart of the home." Mrs. Malone smiled. "Kitchen and breakfast room overlooking the back garden. There's a boot room, laundry facilities, and a half bath through that passageway." She indicated a hall leading from the kitchen to the back of the house. "The main drawing room is above us, on the first floor—better to catch the breeze on a warm day, you know, before there was any such thing as air-conditioning. There's also a study on the first floor and the largest bedroom and bath. On the floor above that are four more bedrooms and an additional full bath. I'll take you up later, but if you don't mind, we'll have our dinner first. Everything's ready."

"Of course." Now I really was confused.

Tom was being uncharacteristically silent.

The dining room table was laid for two, not three. Was this some kind of catering scheme—Rent a Georgian House for Dinner or something? Maybe that was how Mrs. Malone made extra money.

The meal was simple but delicious. Lamb and apricot curry over rice, served with a beetroot salad. For dessert, a jam and coconut sponge with custard.

After clearing our dishes, Mrs. Malone fulfilled her promise and showed us the two upper floors. We climbed the curving staircase, the wood the color of warm treacle and polished with age.

The first floor—what we in the States call the second floor—was divided into two parts. To the right of the landing was a large bedroom, an old-fashioned bath with a huge clawfoot tub, and a small study. On the left was the drawing room Mrs. Malone had talked about, the full length of the house, with windows on three sides. I took a peek at the third floor, too. The children's bedrooms had been up there, along with a bath.

"Your house is lovely," I said as we made our way back down.

"Not mine for much longer. It's too much for me to run these days. I'm moving in late November to a lovely flat in Manchester. Near two of my children."

For the first time, I had a clue. Was Tom thinking about buying the house?

Mrs. Malone ushered us into the small ground-floor sitting room and poured us coffee.

"I'll leave you alone, shall I? Lots to do before the move."

"Tom, you brought me here to see the house, didn't you?" I said when she'd gone. "It's wonderful—more than wonderful—but I know what listed properties go for in England. Without selling both our houses, we couldn't possibly pull it off, and I know you're not going to sell yours for a long while."

Tom leaned back against the sofa cushions, stretched out his long legs, and grinned. "I wondered how long it would take you to figure it out. What makes you think the house is for sale?"

"Mrs. Malone said she was moving out."

"She's Nigel's tenant—has been for forty years. Nigel owns a number of properties in Suffolk. This is one of them. Eventually, he'd like to sell, but for now he's asked if we would consider leasing the property for a year or two. That way he'd have someone he trusts on site to make sure the house and grounds are kept up. Do you like it?"

"Of course I like it, Tom. It's a gorgeous house. But—" I couldn't finish the sentence.

"We'd pay him, of course. It would give us time to decide what we really want. It's near Long Barston. I assume you want to keep working at The Curiosity Cabinet."

"Yes, of course. Ivor needs me." I set down my coffee cup. "How long has this been in the works—and why didn't you tell me?"

"Nigel mentioned the possibility when I went to Devon a couple of weeks ago. But he didn't want to rush Mrs. Malone into a decision. I wasn't allowed to say anything until she made up her mind. Now she has. Yesterday, as a matter of fact. She wanted to meet us."

"If you're waiting for an answer—yes. I love it. The house is too big, of course, but we could close off the upper floor and—"

"Kate." He stood and held out his hand. "Come outside. There's a lovely courtyard and a lane leading to a meadow. And there's something else you need to see."

"I'm not sure I can take any more surprises."

I followed him through the kitchen and out into a peaceful country garden, surrounded by walls and a mature hedge. The leafy patio was paved with limestone.

"What's the surprise?" I asked.

"This." Tom reached inside his jacket and pulled out a sheet of paper, folded in three. He handed it to me. It was a letter—from Nash & Holmes, Private Investigations, Toronto, Canada.

Dear Tom,

I know you turned down the position I offered you in Toronto, but hear me out. In order to expand, we need reliable, trained investigators—like you.

Here's the deal: you remain in the UK—live wherever you like. Work only the cases you choose to accept. There would be a salary—nothing to write home about—but your expenses would be fully covered. We're generous, if I say so myself. The real money is made from commissions on cases solved to the client's satisfaction.

There's a job coming up in Devon. I'm sending details by courier. Check it out. See what you think. No obligation. All expenses paid.

Talk it over with Kate. She could be a help in the Devon case. Let me know as soon as you can.

Congratulations on your wedding, by the way. I can't wait to meet the lovely Kate.

All the best, Graeme Nash

"Who's Holmes?" I asked.

"Holmes? As in Sherlock?"

"No. Holmes as in Nash & Holmes."

"There isn't one. It just sounds impressive." He grinned. "So what do you think?"

"This is a big decision, Tom. It's your career, our future."

"What about the case in Devon? No obligation. All expenses paid. What do you think about that?"

I took his hand. "I think it sounds like a honeymoon."

Acknowledgments

Some stories are pure fiction. Others, like this one, are inspired by real-life events. The initial idea for *The Shadow of Memory* came from "House on Loon Lake," a podcast on NPR's *This American Life* about three boys who explored a mysterious, abandoned house one summer. The idea for the transformation of a Victorian insane asylum into an upscale gated community was taken from Bill Bryson's hilarious *The Road to Little Dribbling* as well as similar accounts of Edinburgh's Craighouse, probably the most luxurious mental hospital ever built in Great Britain.

Writing this novel during a pandemic, I had to rely more heavily than usual on my wonderful sources, especially in the UK. I'm so grateful for the help of DI Tamlyn Burgess of the Suffolk Constabulary and the Reverend Henry Heath, assistant pastor of Holy Trinity Church, Long Melford. I also wish to thank barrister Elliot Gold of Serjeants' Inn Chambers, London; Kirsty Walker of Total Recall Vintage, Liverpool; Lauren Booth, community support officer of the Suffolk Coroner Service; and cardiologist Dr. Christopher Scott of Knoxville, Tennessee.

As always, I'm thankful for the support of my agent, Paula Munier, and for the crew at Crooked Lane Books—especially my editor, Faith Black Ross.

This book would not exist without the love and encouragement of my husband, Bob.

Acknowledgments

The Shadow of Memory is dedicated to my cousin and almost-sister, Kris—fellow Anglophile, kindred spirit, and the sharer of many adventures.

Soli Deo Gloria